PRAISE FOR

JEANNE WILLIAMS'

MAGNIFICENT BESTSELLER

"Appealing, intriguing and romantic . . . guaranteed to attract historical romance readers."
The Midwest Book Review

"*The Cave Dreamers* is a celebration of women . . . a well told, superbly researched saga of a little known people. A fine novel."
Romantic Times

Other Avon Books by
Jeanne Williams

THE CAVE DREAMERS

The Heaven Sword

Jeanne Williams

AVON
PUBLISHERS OF BARD, CAMELOT, DISCUS AND FLARE BOOKS

AVON BOOKS
A division of
The Hearst Corporation
1790 Broadway
New York, New York 10019

First Avon Printing, August 1985

AVON TRADEMARK REG. U. S. PAT. OFF. AND IN OTHER COUNTRIES, MARCA REGISTRADA, HECHO EN U. S. A.

Printed in the U. S. A.

WFH 10 9 8 7 6 5 4 3 2 1

For Bob
Who saw it first

Author's Note

Many books and references helped me in the writing of this work. I am listing only the most valuable with the hope that readers who have enjoyed the story of *The Heaven Sword* may want to go more deeply into some of the places and periods. George Ewart Evans' books have much old English farm and horse lore, especially *The Horse in the Furrow* and *Horse Power and Magic*, both Faber, London, 1979. *English Villagers of the Thirteenth Century*, by George C. Homans, Norton, New York, 1975, is a fascinating account of the village year with its feast days and farming cycle. *The Anglo-Saxons*, edited by James Campbell, Cornell University Press, Ithaca, New York, 1982, is a sumptuously illustrated chronicle with many quotes from early writers.

Of the sagas, the most readable is *Njal's Saga*, translated by Magnus Magnusson and Herman Pálsson, Penguin Books, Middlesex, England, 1971. Also interesting is another translation by the same men: *Laxdaela Saga*, The Folio Society, London, 1975. Many of my quotations are found in *Old Icelandic Poetry, Eddic Lay and Skaldic Verse*, by Peter Hallberg, translated by Paul Schach and Sonja Lingrenson, University of Nebraska Press, Lincoln, Nebraska, 1975. The University of Texas Press, Austin, 1977, has published for the American-Scandinavian Foundation Snorri Sturluson's thirteenth-century *Heimskringla, History of the Kings of Norway*, translated, with notes, by Lee N. Hollander.

The best and most luminous book I know of on Scandinavian legend is H. R. Ellis Davidson's *Gods and Myths of the Viking Age*, Bell Publishing Company, New York, 1981. It was her essay, "The Sword at the Wedding," in *Patterns of Folklore*, D. S. Brewer, Ipswich, England, 1978, that inspired this novel, for it set me dreaming of a fabulous sword that would be passed through the ages, a symbol of the luck and honor of a family.

Viking, Hammer of the North, by Magnus Magnusson, Orbis, London, 1979; *The Viking World*, by James Graham-Campbell, Ticknor and Fields, New York, 1980; and *The Viking*, by Tre Tryckare, International Book Society, Time-Life Books, 1966, are all handsomely and informatively illustrated, and have excellent texts. An interested reader will also find much of value in *The Viking Achievement*, by Peter Foote and D. M. Wilson, Sidgwick and Jackson, London, 1979; *Kings and Vikings*, by P. H. Sawyer, Methuen, London and New York, 1982; *Denmark in World History*, by Viggo Starcke, University of Pennsylvania Press, Philadelphia, 1968; and Farley Mowat's intriguing *Westviking*, Minerva Press, New York, 1968.

Packed full of lore and personal experience is *Turi's Book of Lappland* by Johan Turi, translated by E. Gee Nash, Anthropological Publications, Oosterhout, The Netherlands, 1966. Joseph Campbell's *The Way of the Animal Powers*, Harper and Row, 1983, has illuminating passages on shamanism. Time-Life International's *Lapland*, Amsterdam, The Netherlands, 1976, by Walter Marsden, has marvelous photographs and useful text. *People of Eight Seasons*, by Ernst Manker and Tre Tryckare, Crescent Books, New York, 1972, has detailed illustrations and takes the reader through all the Lapp seasons with their reindeer. *The Dawn of European Civilization*, edited by David Talbot Rice, McGraw-Hill, New York, 1966, has good sections on ancient Russia and Byzantium. Cyril Mango's *Byzantium*, Scribners, New York, 1980, relates that brilliant city's history.

No one should miss Katherine Scherman's *Daughter of Fire*, Little Brown & Co., New York, 1976, which ties together modern Iceland with its human and natural history. *Icelandic Enterprise,* by Bruce Gelsinger, University of South Carolina, 1981, reveals much about the daily life and economy of Iceland in medieval times.

The Medieval Machine, by Jean Gimpel, Holt, Rinehart and Winston, New York, 1976, proves the period to have been burgeoning with inventions. Philippe Contamine's *War in the Middle Ages,* translated by Michael Jones, Blackwell, Oxford, England, 1984, studies the strategy and equipment in this changing time. *Of Swedish Ways* by Lilly Lorenzen, Barnes and Noble, New York, 1978, is a fascinating blend of history and customs presented with a loving touch. *A History of the Swedish People,* by Vihelm Moberg, translated by Paul Britten Austin, Pantheon, New York, shows the imagination and passion of the novelist who found a lot of his schoolboy heroes were not, in reality, heroic, and *The Early Vasas, A History of Sweden 1523–1611,* by Michael Roberts, Cambridge University Press, 1968, gives more on that enterprising, ruthless man who united Sweden.

Anyone who enjoys this book will want to read these novels: *Kristin Lavransdatter* by Sigrid Undset, Knopf, New York, 1963, the finest rendering of one person's whole life that I have ever read; Undset's more somber *The Master of Hestviken,* New American Library, 1978; *Sons of Darkness,* by Evangeline Walton, Hutchinson, London, 1957, a story of Vikings in England; and Edison Marshall's swashbuckling, evocative *The Viking,* Avon, New York, 1973. Selma Lagerlöf's Swedish fairy tales are enchanting and her *Story of Gösta Berling,* translated by Pauline Flach, 1922, and *The Emperor of Portugalla,* translated by Velma Howard, 1916, both from Doubleday, New York, give good views of Swedish country life in the nineteenth century.

I want to thank my husband, Robert Morse, who gave critical comment and typed the final version; my agent Claire Smith, who encouraged the idea from the start; my editor Page Cuddy, who loved it; Jan DeVries, who worked on it; and Finn Arnesen of Oslo, Norway, editor and friend, who read the manuscript.

I am grateful to Myrtle Kraft and the Cochise County Library staff for locating some of the books I used, and most especially to Dawn Myers of Tucson, who searched libraries for material on medieval Sweden and Gustav Vasa.

The first book I ever wrote was a retelling of the Volsung Saga, complete with Ragnarok. A painting of the World Tree, Ygdrasil, by my dear friend, Esmé Glenn of Abilene, Texas, has pride of place in my home. Ten years ago, Finn Arnesen and Kjell Hallbing, the noted Norwegian author, took me on a journey around Norway, filling me with awe for the country's beauty and traditions. It is good to have woven all these threads together into what I hope is a tapestry of Scandinavian life and spirit.

Book I
The Forging
an island

I

The sea kings brought the stranger to the island on a bright day in early summer when graylag geese were building their nests and the red-branched willows were leafing out along the streams. His hands were bound with walrus-hide ropes, but he strode ahead of his captors as if they were his train, appearing not to notice Signy as he stared at the *seite*, the ancient stone from heaven, a great phallus that had buried itself deep in the soil. Beside was a natural altar, a piece of the same rock. Here was the joining of sky and earth, holy to Nerthus who was man and woman both.

Signy had tended the shrine alone since her mother, the last priestess, died three years before. The chieftains each year brought gifts and provisions. She had known that sometime they would bring her a mate, unblemished and valiant, to father the next priestess and die at year's end. If he failed in his task, men would be brought till one succeeded.

Curly-bearded Gunnar Skull-Splitter, leader of the kings, had a red head that sat almost directly on his bull shoulders. He towered over what were tall men, but standing next to the prisoner he looked oafish rather than formidable, though he was armed and the other wore only a frieze cloak.

"Guard him and mind he doesn't snatch your weapons!" Gunnar warned.

Ringed by the drawn blades of eight chiefs, the man stood quietly as Gunnar untied his bonds, but when the Viking undid the bronze pin and stripped away the mantle, the stranger spread his arms in an involuntary attempt to retain the covering. In that moment, he dazzled Signy like a flaming sword, his head the golden hilt, outflung arms the cross-guard, his body a blade broad at chest and shoulders, narrowing to clean-muscled ankles.

There was no shame in his nakedness. He could be Frey or Balder, most beautiful of gods, except for the warrior spirit that shone from him, that wild mysterious power that imbued berserkers with amazing strength and reckless courage.

This struck the sea kings, even Gunnar. Their ribald laughter faltered. "Where did you find him?" Signy asked.

"Near the Sea of Azov where Odin had his pleasure-hall after he gave himself nine wounds and won the rune secret." Gunnar blew out his sun-broiled cheeks. "I could believe this one is Odin's cub. Alone, he stood against a tree and killed three of us before a thrall sneaked up behind and stunned him with a club." Gunnar's eyes ran hungrily over Signy. She was glad she wore a voluminous scarlet cloak over her dress. "Warm him well, Signy. To lie in your swan bosom for a year would be worth death, if it could be death with honor, not a slaughtered animal's."

They would kill him with horns, plow his flesh into the fields to bring rich harvests. Signy's heart contracted. For the first time, she wondered about her father, never named to her or spoken of, and felt a rush of sorrow. Had her mother loved him? Inger had never said, but when she wasted away in fever, she called on someone and died with a joyous smile.

Signy felt cold though the sun was bright. The stranger's eyes glinted blue fire like the dancing sea. Wind whipped gold hair across a hawk face, cheekbones so high that hollows beneath were pulled taut by a jaw angled like the blade of a war axe. He watched the sea birds circle between blue sky and blue waves as if his soul flew with them and was not in his body, bared to his enemies.

The thralls returned from carrying provisions to Signy's dwelling. The Danes waded into the impatiently dancing craft, pushed into deeper water, and Gunnar called the stroke for oars that spilled silver water as they lifted. He shouted back to Signy, ''If that one's as mighty in love as in battle, you may bear twins! I doubt we'll have to find you another man.'' He guffawed and the lugger skimmed away.

Filled with tumult, Signy trembled as she unclasped her mantle and raised on tiptoe to fold it about the stranger. His abstracted gaze swung from shining wings, plunged into her. She gasped and drew back.

He could throw the cloak in her face. He could beat or kill her. They were alone on the island except for sheep who furnished milk and wool and the otter, Tym, who fished for her.

''I am sorry you must die,'' she said, though he could not understand.

Suddenly, he laughed. It was not a pleasant sound. He folded the cloak about him. It hung just below his knees, though it had reached her feet.

''Are you sorry, priestess?'' The words were slow and accented but comprehensible. ''Am I the first man, then, brought to service you?''

''You speak our tongue!'' She flushed and cast down her eyes. He had understood Gunnar's rough jokes.

''I am a trader. Besides, our languages are kin. My

folk, the Vandals, left the Daneland a few generations ago to pillage Rome and find land. My grandsire's band settled along the great river that leads from the Baltic to the Sea of Azov and to Byzantium. Many times I've traded silk, spices and jewelry from China and India for amber, furs and walrus-hide ropes like those that bound me." He shrugged. "Sometimes the sea kings come to trade and other times they're set on loot—or, it would seem, a stud."

That he spoke her language made his fate seem somehow worse. "Did Gunnar know you had the tongue?"

The stranger smiled crookedly. "I had no chance to speak before I was captured. Afterward I thought I'd learn more if they thought me unable to understand." He shrugged. "I confess that I see no advantage to knowing why they brought me here and what the end will be." His voice harshened. "I haven't many choices. The only tree of a size to yield lumber for a raft is that one by your turf hut and it's not big enough, by itself, for any kind of craft. I suppose I could swim till I froze or drowned, or bide here but refuse to lie with you."

She could say nothing, nor could she look at him. His long hands closed on either side of her face, lifting it. She felt that she was the drowning one, sinking in the depths of his eyes, which were the very color of the long summer nights, enchanted glowing blue.

"Yes," he said slowly. "I could balk them. But you are very lovely. Perhaps they'll get their will. It's not often that a man gets such beauty without vexation, gifts and wooing."

Bitter laughter was still on his lips when he set them on hers. She shrank as if from ice or fire. It was her duty to receive him; Wyrd had twined the threads of their fates together. But those threads met in a tangled snarl. She could not now accept him as a mute captive brought with a single purpose. He was a man to whom her soul had leaped, one she could have loved. She could not bear to have him take her in scorn and in despair.

Tears ran down her cheeks to mingle in their kiss. She worked her arms upward and pushed against his chest, feeling the thud of his heart beneath her palm. The cloak had fallen aside.

He raised his head. "Tears?" His fingers smudged them across her face. Still holding her, he gazed till savagery left his face, leaving stony anger. He let her go so abruptly that she staggered.

"Doomed to an island with a scared girl instead of a lusty priestess who'd at least beguile the time! A rare jest!"

He swung away, pulling her blood-red mantle to him. Signy wanted to storm at him that she'd had no more choice than he in being here, had as inexorable a destiny, but after a struggle, she controlled herself. Strangely, in spite of his contempt, she drew courage to touch his arm, more from his isolation than from thinking of her duty.

"I'll do my best to try to—beguile your time."

He didn't turn. "Do you think I'm a stallion, to paw and snort and mount whatever mare I'm led to?"

She whispered, shamed, cheeks growing hot, "But— you were ready—"

"Your tears unmanned me."

She thought wildly that Gunnar might return to find her still a virgin. How could she lie in this man's arms without tears, knowing his end? And if her tears undid him— She began to laugh hysterically.

He stared at her. "Are you mad? Weak in the mind? If I'm penned with a lunatic—"

"I think I'm no crazier than most."

She started toward the hut, thick blocks of turf set on a stone foundation that formed a third of the wall. Over the uncounted years of the shrine, the trees of the island had gone to make or replace roof supports, fashion the sheep byre and supply firewood to augment the peat cut and dried from the bog. Only the guardian tree, which protected the women and which they gripped as they strove to give birth, remained to shade the dwelling and provide a sheltering presence against storms that blew in gray and howling from towering, crashing seas.

"I'll get you something to eat," she called over her shoulder and saw that he had stopped to look at the *seite,* the great pitted black wedge rearing from the greening.

"Is this your god? I knew you Danes were heathen, but I thought at least you worshipped the noble host of Valhall."

"We do, but this is the shrine of Nerthus, who is older than any of the others. Nerthus is mother-father of Frey and Freya, who bring fertility to fields and all living things."

"Mother-father?" he mocked. "A strange god, truly."

"It is fitting for the oldest one."

He shrugged. "The gods are no concern of mine, but this rock concerns me mightily. It looks to be almost pure iron."

She frowned. "Iron?"

"The strongest metal in the world. It slices bronze like cheese."

"I've never heard of it."

"The secret of working it is known in only a few places. It must be heated many times hotter than bronze and have its impurities pounded out of it while it smolders red-hot." He threw back his head, and though there were no mountains to echo his laughter, his voice seemed to resonate from the sky: "If I can practice what I've watched smiths do, your chieftains will have a surprise when they come back to kill me."

"The *seite* is holy!"

"So will be my sword. Anyway, I won't have to dull all your kitchen tools hacking at the mass. See, there at the base is a piece that's ready to separate, just waiting for me.''

"Don't!" She feared Nerthus would blast him, but the long piece came free, perhaps fractured in its journey from heaven and the fault worn deeper by ages of thaw and freeze.

It even had the rough shape of a blade. The stranger caressed it. "As it is, this, fastened to some kind of hilt, would send a few Danes to Odin's feast. But if I can practice what I've watched smiths do, I'll have a weapon to surprise those who think to slaughter me like a tame ox.''

Unless she wished to poison him in his sleep, there was nothing Signy could do. Besides, when he had freed the shard, awe filled her. She had never noticed that fissure before. Who knew, it might be Nerthus' gift.

She left him with his treasure.

It was ritual that the priestess' man be brought to her naked, but at the bottom of the rune-carved chest were tunic and trousers of softest blue wool, supple leather buskins and a dark blue cloak. These had been folded away with frankincense and sweet-smelling herbs that crumbled to tiny flakes as Signy shook them out.

They must have been her father's clothes. Holding them to her face, Signy was gripped again with sorrow for the man she'd never known, and for her mother, too. Plainer garments of frieze were also there, but it only took Signy a moment to decide to give the best ones to the stranger.

She'd ground enough barley that morning for the day's two meals. Poking up the embers in the long-fire, a pit built in the center of the house, she hastily made flat loaves and baked them on the long-handled copper pan that rested on the coals. Heaping these on a birch platter, she added cheese made of ewe's milk, flat rye loaves and smoked fish. Rummaging through the new provisions, she added a bowl of honeycomb and a handful of nuts. There was wine from Dorestad, the great trade town on the Rhine, and she poured some into a green glass beaker that was also Rhenish.

She didn't find the stranger by the *seite*. He was at the peat diggings.

"Fine feathers," he said, lifting a fair eyebrow as she set the food on a boulder and handed him the garments. He pulled on the trousers under her mantle's cover, then gave the mantle back to her as he finished dressing. "These smell of spice, not death. The captive must be stripped of them before he's offered up."

Her mother had never said, had never given details of that final rite, but if the priestess' mate came naked, it seemed he would go the same way.

Was it to be like this all the year, constant wounding with the future and his hatred? It was natural, but Signy's eyes blurred with tears. To hide them, she turned hastily away.

He spoke with an edge of anger. "You're the wrong one for this. Must I, death-doomed, guard my tongue so that I won't distress you?"

"Say what you will!"

"I would say you are the fairest maid I have ever seen with eyes the color of woods violets. I had thought you North people all blond, but your hair falls about your white throat like a wing of night. I would say—"

She threw up a warding hand. "Tell me your hate."

"I do not want to anymore."

"Why not?"

"Because you are a prisoner as surely as I am."

"I serve the god."

"Just so. If you tried to leave, what would happen?"

Startled, she faced him. "No priestess has ever left the island." She pointed to the cairns on the highest of the gentle slopes. "Born here, we are buried here. There are a score of graves. Mine will be the twenty-first."

"What if a priestess bears a son, not a daughter?"

"Boys are taken for fosterage by one of the kings."

"And the priestess tries her luck with a new slave?"

"The priestess' mate is not a slave! He—he's honored."

The stranger's smile warped downward. "Yes, so much that your kings range far afield to capture him. It would surely be less trouble to fetch you a husky thrall."

"The father of a priestess must be freeborn and have no wound or mark on him."

"So that's why they took care not to slash at me. It cost them dearly." Dismissing the matter, he sat on the edge of the boulder. "Will you eat with me?"

She had eaten that morning but broke off half a thin loaf and nibbled at it, grateful that he was behaving in a normal way though there was nothing normal about their situation. The lore handed down by her mother had not included how to share a doomed man's time. It must be that one lived each day and did not think ahead. But she had a feeling that this man could not exist like that.

Staring at the bog and drying chunks of peat, he asked, "This is what you burn?"

"Yes. It gives a slow, steady heat."

"Not enough, I fear, for working iron. That takes charcoal."

"The only tree left is the guardian."

Though he couldn't know all that it meant, he made a denying gesture. "I wouldn't take your only tree even if you offered. But the sheep byre is of logs. I would replace that with turf."

"Uncovered turf melts back into the ground."

"I'll give it a thatching of willow boughs and reeds."

"I can't prevent you."

"Do you want to?"

She met his gaze. Again it plunged to her depths. She felt as if a light glowed there, warming the secret dark where she had always been alone. Breath squeezed around her words.

"I would rather see you contented as may be."

"Thanks for that, priestess. Even if you didn't weep when I touch you, I'm not the man to sit by the long-fire while you spin."

"In winter you'll be glad enough of the long-fire."

"I should be gladder of your body."

She colored and glanced toward the *seite*. "That's why you're here."

"I don't want you as Nerthus' sacred virgin, and virgin you'll remain unless you come to me as Ivar's woman."

"Your name is Ivar?"

"I was called Ivar of the Lake."

A lake he would never see again. "I am Signy. There will be food when you are hungry." She took platter, beaker and wine and went to the house.

A covered passage provided space for storing peat and connected the dwelling with the byre, privy and store-house. Even in storms, Signy made her way to the *seite* with the daily offering of milk, but except for that it was possible to spend the winter under a roof, mostly in the one large room where she made cheese, carded, spun and wove wool and was grateful for the presence of the sheep and Tym's visits.

She had found Tym on the shore one day, near death from what looked to be jagged gashes from a hunter's three-pronged trident. She carried him to the house and dressed his wounds with herbs. He was too weak to gulp solid food, so she gave him milk and stew till he was able to push his sleek, small-eared head against her knee and petition for some of the smoked fish she was eating. He acquired such a taste for this that after he went back to the sea, he returned almost every day and began to bring her fish.

He was waiting for her now, webbed feet planted proudly near a large cod. She rubbed his head, thanked him and broke off a piece of smoked fish from the lines strung in the storehouse. He downed it with relish. When he saw no more was forthcoming, he heaved a gusty sigh and curled up in the door for a nap.

A wide turf platform ran the length of one wall. Here Signy slept on fleeces with linen and wool bedding and pillows stuffed with sweet grass and rose leaves. The platform was wide enough for two. Her blood ran slow as thick, warm honey. Unbidden, she saw that golden head beside hers. The summer linen was clean enough, but she bundled it up and went to the chest across the room to get fresh bedding.

She might have spared her trouble. He entered the house when she called him for supper that night, sat opposite her on the turf wall-bench flanked by the chest and loom, and complimented her on pea soup spiced with cumin and mustard and grilled fish in horseradish sauce. The barley cakes had to be eaten hot, for they cooled rock hard.

"We'll fare better when the garden comes up," she said.

"This was good."

"Will you have wine? There is also mead." Except for water, the usual drink was the sweet beverage she made from fermented honey.

He praised the mead. She filled his beaker twice, but he stared at the fire more than he looked at her. She smelled thyme and rose leaves in her pillows and wondered if he did.

As if reading her thought, he rose, head almost scrap-

ing the roof logs. "Do you have some old covers, priestess?"

His tone was courteous, but she felt as if he'd slapped
her. She turned her head to hide the hot shame. "Why,
yes, but—" She had to swallow before she could continue. "I can make your bed on that wall-bench. You'll
be quite safe!"

In the flickering light, his face was all angles and rud-
dily etched planes. "You wouldn't be."

Her heart pounded. She said thickly, "It is my fate."

He reached the door in two long strides. "Perhaps I
can't escape my fate, but I'll choose the way I meet it—
and the way I lie with a woman. I won't serve the Dane's
will, embracing Nerthus' handmaid."

She couldn't tell him that already her duty to Nerthus
was far from her mind when she watched his long tanned
hands and imagined how they would feel, stroking, caressing. She got out blankets and several fleeces. He took
these but refused a pillow.

"If it rains—" she began.

"When I made my couch of willow branches and
reeds, I made a raised thatch lean-to over it."

So that was why he had borrowed her little stone axe.
Such shelter might turn a summer rain, but when the
storms shrieked . . . "Sleep well," Signy murmured.

He shot her a surprised look before he chuckled.
"Why, priestess, do you know, I think I will?"

She slept lonely, though, with restless dreams, in her
fresh, rose-scented bed. Roused next morning by a
thumping sound, she stiffened with fright before she remembered that she wasn't the only human on the island.
Dressing quickly, she combed her hair with more attention than usual and bound it with an embroidered fillet
before she went to chant the dawn song by the *seite*. Then
she milked two ewes who had lost their lambs at birth and

carried a bowl of water to the stone, ground barley and
made bread. She took loaves, honey, cheese and milk out
to where the stranger was dragging the byre logs to a de-
pression he'd dug in a slope where peat chunks were already heaped.

"If I may have coals from your fire, I can start making
charcoal," he said, thanking her as he took bread and sat
on a log to breakfast.

"Why do you need charcoal?"

"It's the only way to heat the iron enough for working."

"What will you work it with if it's so hard? My only
tools are bronze and stone."

"I found a piece of the heaven stone about the right
shape for a hammer, if you'll give me strips of hide to
fasten it to a handle. I'll search for a willow that forks in a
fashion to make tongs." His blue glance was half chal-
lenge, half measuring. "The altar fills my greatest need.
It will serve as a forge."

"A forge! The altar?"

"It's the only thing on the island that won't crack under the hammering." She glanced in fear at the *seite* as if
it might hurtle down on them to crush such blasphemy.
Ivar's face was unreadable, though she caught a hint of
sympathy in his eyes. "By your leave or without it,
priestess, I shall make this sword if my luck makes
amends for this captivity. Tell Nerthus that." When she
still looked dismayed, he laughed gently. "This may be
Nerthus' will. Didn't the sword piece come easily to my
hand?"

She had to nod and felt a little comforted, though the
god's will was a mystery to her. The prayers she made at
dawning, zenith and sunset linked her to sky and earth
and sea. These she loved and reverenced. But she had
never felt the presence of the god or had a sign from him,
possessed no certainty from which to answer the stranger.

"I will bring you coals and rawhide."

"If it troubles your conscience I'll get them myself."

Her conscience bothered her much less than knowing that he must die in a year; less, even, than her dream-ridden, broken sleep of the night before.

"I'll build your fire."

He had a purpose and she envied him. While byre logs smoldered into charcoal, he made crude tools and began experimenting with earthen and rock furnaces to make one that could create the intense heat required to make the dull black of the heaven stone glow red.

Signy went about her chores, but compared to his driving aim, the routine of preparing meals, making cheese and weaving seemed repetitious and dull. It was time to relieve the sheep of their heavy winter wool, and she enjoyed singing to them as she worked carefully with her shears. She had a name for each of the black-faced animals, which were so tame that no force was needed. But most of her work was daily, recurring with the regularity of hunger or the need to rest. At the end of the year, she'd have no sword.

And no child either, it seemed. She often felt more lonely than before he had come and tried to explain this paradox to Tym, who snuffled against her knee and besought more smoked cod. Ivar ate the food she took to him mornings and sat across from her for the evening meal, but he never lingered. He answered her questions but asked none. Perhaps loneliness was to be denied the thoughts and feelings of a person who shared your place but not your life.

He first built a rock-lined pit near the top of a slope close to the *seite* and hollowed out a small tunnel to bring air to the charcoal, but though he fed the furnace for hours, the heat never rose to what was necessary. He filled in that hole and dug another pit beside the altar.

"I must make a bellows," he said. "The charcoal needs a steady blast of air."

After many trials—and it was laughable to see his baffled scowl while lashing a fleece into a long bag with rawhide thongs—he succeeded in molding a clay pipe and attaching it snugly to the double-sided fleece bag. He laboriously worked a rounded channel at the bottom of the rock under which the pipe could just fit at the outer edge, while air was forced beneath the stone into the charcoal bed that completely surrounded the heaven rock.

"How can you tell when it's ready?" Signy asked as he began to pump the bellows.

"I'm not a smith. I'll have to guess till I take it out at just the right time."

She glanced at the crude willow tongs lying by the altar. "I hope the god won't be angry."

"Why should Nerthus mind receiving three or four sacrifices instead of one?" He grinned tightly. "A god's anger matters little to a doomed man. And I'd swear to god and sea king that you've been compelled to aid me."

Intent on the smoldering charcoal, he didn't look at her, notice that she'd put on an amber necklace inherited from time immemorial, and caught back her hair with a bronze ornament. She felt like kicking the bellows from his hand but went to the hut, took off her jewelry and went to work in the garden.

When she first heard the ring of the hammer, she tensed and awaited a thunderbolt or earthquake. There were a few more strokes, then silence. Signy hurried to peer around the wall.

Ivar was bedding the long fragment back in the furnace, but the set of his shoulders was determined, not disconsolate.

The store of charcoal dwindled. The hammer resounded and then was mute. He redesigned the bellows several times, made the furnace deeper, then shallower. When Signy saw the piece of heaven rock, it looked no different than ever except that its pits had vanished.

"The charcoal's nearly gone," Ivar said one night, scarcely touching the herring or wild greens. His hands and arms had numerous small burn scars, which he refused to let Signy treat. "I may have to sharpen the point as best I can."

She'd been jealous of his dream and the way it shut her out, but she suddenly, fiercely, hated defeat for him. "Could I help? Work the bellows or feed charcoal to the furnace?"

His eyes widened before he frowned. "You'd do that?"

The pulse in her throat throbbed wildly. She was drowning in that blue gaze and had to turn away. "I would help you."

"I thank you, priestess, but that must not be. Your god can't blame you for what I do without your leave but might strike you if you aided me."

As if her concern lightened his mood, he laughed, throwing back his head, and the long-fire turned his throat rose-gold beneath the shadow of his chin. The god could never have had a comelier sacrifice, but she rebelled at the thought of that strength and beauty ended. "The charcoal will be used up tomorrow," he said. "If I can't shape the heaven blade by then, I'll use it as it was given me from the stone. It will drink blood, even so, before mine spills."

He went out to his shelter, but as Signy tidied the hearth she yearned for him to have his wonder weapon, a wonder forged from his captivity. The guardian tree wasn't hers to give; she would sooner lop off her own arms than sever its limbs. But the roof logs . . .

And so it was when late next morning she saw him toss aside the hammer and lean against the *seite,* she hurried to him. He was heaving from exertion and sweat ran down his face as he turned to her. Still, he managed to smile and straighten.

"It seems I must be glad for what I was given."

"Ivar, there is more wood."

His gaze swept the island, came to the guardian tree, buds turning now to tiny apples. "I cannot use your tree."

"No. But the roof has support logs."

He stared at her. "And what will you do when gales swoop in from winter seas?"

"There are willows stout enough to make a laced ceiling. Over that, reeds and a cover of thin grassy sod that will knit together."

"A storm might sweep it away."

"Storms may sweep away anything." As the storm within her had destroyed her lifelong training and duty to Nerthus, leaving this fated man.

Their eyes met. She trembled but let him read her heart. His face lit like sunrise after a troubled night.

"Signy."

He called her name for the first time and took her in his arms. They sank down by the altar. His hands and mouth and loving forged her from maid into his woman. As pain tinged her delight, she gasped but opened wider to let her flesh temper him, became his eager sheath till he hilted deep a last time, sending her into a timeless ocean where she floated in all the love that had ever been or was, or ever would be.

Often after that, she stroked his golden head while sun shone on their bodies and earth made their flowery couch. "To think we wasted weeks!" he growled one day when, happily spent, she lay with her head on his shoulder. "I wanted you from the moment I saw you, thought to have my fill of you to sweeten doom. But then

I found I needed more, much more, than the body you had to yield.''

She laughed shakily, tracing his dark gold eyebrows. ''If you hadn't been so wrapped up in your forging, you'd have seen early that I could hold back nothing.''

''That's right,'' he murmured. ''You hold back nothing. Not even in the pain of your lost maidenhead did you. Is that why I never have enough? Because you give me all?''

''I love to feel you in me,'' she whispered. ''You make me whole. Without you, I'm only half.''

''Without you, I'm an aimless thrusting, wasted in the winds.'' He entered her slowly. If the god had taken her, she could not have felt more blessed in her body, or more holy.

While the roof logs charred, they bent willow boughs into tough frames, and though there was no wind, a great branch of the guardian tree crashed to the ground one night, giving them a center pole as if in kindly gift. Lashed to it, the willows were thatched with overlapping rows of reeds, and these with turf just thick enough to hold roots that would intertwine with each other and the supports. Now there was no question of his sleeping beneath her roof, though they loved best to have each other between wide sky and tender earth.

Perhaps the logs made better charcoal. Or he had learned the knack of using the bellows, or the god was content now that man and woman melded. However it was, on his third try, Ivar shaped his blade, reheating it when it cooled, till it was double-edged and pointed, impurities pounded out, tempered in waters from the ocean.

A Heaven Sword. And as, at his triumphant cry, she ran to the altar-forge and saw the glittering facets of the blade—for, of course, such crude tools couldn't smooth the surface completely—she felt a warm light in her womb and believed she was with child.

All through that winter, they joyed in each other. She carded and wove and spun for him and the child while he carved a sword hilt from a beached walrus' tusk, working it with dragons. He also made ivory counters with which they could play a game where kings' forces battled each other on the back of her biggest wood platter which he marked into squares. Tym brought them fish, and when it stormed he stayed inside with them.

Winter nights were long but never too long as they lay together. She had always hailed the lengthening days heralding summer but now she dreaded them.

"I wish winter would last forever," she told him one day when they went to break the ice on the frozen stream and fetch water.

He put his arms around her and kissed her in that gleaming frosty air. "We've had forever."

She knew that he was right and yet her heart wailed.

Ice melted. She was heavy with child. He fastened the narrowing top of the blade into the hilt, fixing it with glue made from the hoofs of a dead sheep, binding the grip with leather beneath the curved pommel.

"Not elegant like Gunnar's jewel-encrusted bronze," Ivar said, hefting it. "But Heaven's Gift will teach the sea kings that handsome is as handsome does."

"You've given the sword a name?"

"It surely names itself." He handed it to her. "All I can leave our child is a proud death and this sword. And my luck."

"Luck?" She wondered if he mocked her.

He sank on one knee and buried his face against her body. "I call it luck to have had you. I call it luck to wield a sword from heaven.

"But if we have a daughter—"

"Then she will keep it until there is a son or hero that she loves."

She dropped her spindle and caught him fiercely to her. "I cannot bear it! They'll have to kill me, too!"

"No, sweeting. You must live to hand along the sword."

He loved her then, passion tempered by heed for her, but she cared nothing for luck or honor or heaven gifts if he was taken from her.

Willows greened and flowerlets peeked from melting snow. Birds called amorously and began to built their nests. Lambs began to drop, and though heavy and awkward herself, Signy helped the ewes who had difficulties, feeling cautiously till she could straighten a tiny bent foreleg or turn the lamb to enter the world.

Ivar seemed at peace now that he could face the sea kings with a sword. Signy was not. Sometimes she almost hated the baby because it would keep her from joining Ivar. In other moments, she thought that keeping Ivar, a part of him, alive, was worth the grief and loneliness. She prayed the baby would come before the Danes, that her love could help her in her labor and have at least a short time to know his child.

She woke one dawning to cruel thumbs digging at her belly, but the pain ebbed and it was some while before another gripped her. She didn't want to tell Ivar till she was sure. The pains were still far spaced at nooning when the sea kings came.

Ivar took Signy in his arms, kissed away her tears and found her mouth with his. They yearned together, caressing each dear feature, hungering to lock the feel of the other into themselves.

Holding up her face, sending his spirit into hers with

those eyes that held both sky and sun, he made her a vow. "I will love you wherever my soul goes. You must cherish our babe for both of us and pass my honor on with the sword."

He went to meet the chieftains.

A great rending tore her entrails. She tried to follow, past reason with love and dread, but a giant fist crushed her womb and forced her down by the guardian tree.

Streaming with sweat, she gripped the trunk, let herself scream, for no sound of hers could be heard above the shouts and clashing on the strand. She could see Ivar's bright head, the Heaven Sword thrusting and fending. He had cut down four chiefs, but five still circled him. He must have been sorely wounded, for he moved draggily.

She cried out her love as he fell, and flame-shot blackness filled her skull as her body was riven from within.

Coming to consciousness at a soft wail, she instinctively took the small red creature Gunnar placed in her arms.

"A fine daughter, priestess. I cut her life cord with her father's blade."

Signy said nothing, too spent for hate; but Gunnar, whose red hair was dyed deeper red from a wound, placed the sword beside her.

"I won't ask how he made that. It was the god's desire. We won't scatter his flesh on the fields but that of the men he killed. If it's your will, we'll raise a mound for him. He was a hero."

He was my lover, Signy thought. She gathered the child to her breast, and when the small mouth nuzzled, when Signy saw the damp curls that were fair as Ivar's, at last she could weep.

* * *

A storm-blown ship reached the island when Iva, golden and laughing, was fourteen. The strong young captain fell in love with her, and when the ship was repaired, Signy blessed them and gave her daughter the sword. Iva had grown up knowing the story of its forging and had often prattled to her father as if he could hear her inside his tomb.

When the ship was out of sight, Signy drank the remedy she was free at last to use. Her limbs grew heavy while she walked to the mound. As she sank against it, Ivar embraced and loved her and the blue skies smiled.

Book II
The Hidden Sword
England
840–845

I

Meghan had two secrets. With them she clothed herself, though her single garment was threadbare, and carried herself so that Father Aiden had rebuked her the last time she brought him the fish with which they tithed because she and Gran were poor.

"Don't hold your head so high, my daughter," the priest had belched, pushing back from a roast chicken that made her mouth water. "Bear yourself with maiden meekness, and in a few more years you may find a husband, even though you were begot by a heathen Dane like the one whose hide is nailed to the church door."

She muttered something and escaped, quivering with humiliation. Even while her grandfather lived, village children had teased her about that—taunting that it was her father's flayed skin tacked under the iron door bands. It must have been five years ago, when she was seven, that Granfer found her sobbing.

"Nay, lass," he'd said, taking her on his knee and drying her tears on his tunic. "That hide was pegged up the first time Northmen reached us, the same year they raided Lindisfarne—Father Aiden makes it seven hundred and ninety-three years after our Lord's birth—and pillaged blessed Cuthbert's church, Cuthbert who was so holy that after he'd stood all night in the sea at his prayers, otters followed him ashore to warm his feet with their breath and dry them with their fur. Alas, that heathen could ravage such a sacred place! That the monks wandered with Cuthbert's bones for seven years before they found haven—''

"You're sure, Granfer?" Meghan interrupted. "That's not my da's skin on the door?"

Granfer didn't answer for a moment. When he did, his voice was as careful as when he answered some question of the thane's. "Where your father is, I know not. Sure it is that Northman sailed off with plunder and left your mother with child."

"And my mother is with the Blessed Mother, where nothing can vex her, not even me." Meghan nodded, repeating her grandmother's answer to *that* question.

"You didn't vex her. She loved you well." The old man sighed. "She was ever tender, and a fever took her while you were still at the breast."

Stroking Meghan's hair, he gazed off at the river that led to the sea. His craggy face was brown and wrinkled like leather left out in sun and rain, but beneath shaggy gray brows, blue eyes peered at her keenly. In his prime, he'd been chosen most often as Harvest Lord, directing the work and leading with his scythe. He was still the best man with horses, though he was too old to do much but gentle the colts and tend to horses that were ailing or mares that had trouble foaling.

"I can't leave you and your gran anything but the thatch over your heads," he said at last. "But I'm going to give you a secret. " 'Twould make your living were you a lad, but who knows, it might serve even a maid sometime."

She gave a bounce of excitement. "What, Granfer?"

He chuckled, hugging her as he set her down. "You'll see. When Black Killeny foals."

"Is it something you know from your selkie blood?"

"So you've heard that story, too?" he grunted. "If my da was a selkie, how come I can't swim? Nay, child, the secret's naught to do with seal-folk."

Now she stood in a copse near the river, talking to the gleaming black stallion that she'd watched her grandfather bring on that Whitsuntide before he went to bed one night and slept his way peacefully into the next world.

The thane, Eldrid, called the stallion Lucifer. He would have had him put down since no man could ride him, except that the black sired the fleetest, most enduring foals in the shire. Meghan called him Storm. He had been her friend from the time he was born. While he still lay on the straw, Granfer had opened his mouth gently and told her, "See how his tongue's shaped around summat? Get it out before he swallows it or it dries up."

Carefully feeling along the tongue, she brought out a little fibrous oval. Granfer nodded. "That be the milt. Gives foal's tongue a curve that helps it fit around the teat."

This was the secret? Meghan stared at the damp oval mass and tried not to cry. But her disappointment vanished in delight as Black Killeny nuzzled her baby. He began to try to get himself up on his knobby-kneed legs, wavered, then stood in a surprised sort of way. His short tail was crimped and springy as Meghan's red-brown hair after it had been tightly braided, and his wobbly legs seemed visibly to gain strength as he searched at his mother's underside till he put his whole being into suckling.

"Hang on to that milt," said Granfer softly as some of the thane's grooms lounged up.

When they were home, he put the milt on a stone at the edge of the hearth fire and left it there till it was dark and hard. Then he sewed it into a small frieze bag, told her to place it under her armpit, and they went to find Black Killeny and her colt. In just a few days the little fellow had grown saucy. He skittered off in small thunder, squirrelly tail bouncing, but was back in a few minutes, approaching cautiously as Granfer stroked Black Killeny and praised her for her fine son.

Meghan stroked him now in the river pasture, this stallion who had killed one groom and scared the others till none came near him. She'd never been on his back, but she was sure he'd allow her. When the priest scolded or children mocked, she liked to dream of riding him far, far away. And with her, she'd take her other secret, the sword she'd found in a cavelike hollow under a mass of hawthorn roots in this very river meadow. She could see the trees from here, stunted and gnarled from the wind. Fearing someone else might find her treasure, she'd delved a deeper ledge for it and covered the exposed roots with soil and stones.

A horse and sword. Warrior's rights, but hers, too, from heritage and discovery. If it weren't for Gran, almost blind, able only to sit by the fire these days, Meghan would have tied her few things in a bundle around the sword, climbed onto Storm and ridden to what fortune sent her.

She liked to fancy that the sword had been her father's; but the pommel, tarnished black when she found it, polished to silver wrought with dragons that swallowed each other's tails, and the hilt, after much rubbing, gleamed gold with curious beasts and birds so intertwined it was impossible to separate them. The cross-pieces of silver were carved with tendrils. Even a child could see that it was very old and precious. Meghan had glimpsed it two years ago when gathering a blooming branch to place on her grandfather's grave on May Day, for he had loved the fragrant white flowers.

Maybe his spirit had led her to it. Or perhaps it was really her father's. Facing the river, Meghan dreamed, her hand in Storm's long mane. Her father had sailed in a dragon-prowed long ship just like that one coming into sight, sailing up the river on the same Saint David's Flood that had long ago brought the blessed saints to teach the gospel.

Just like?

Shocked from her reverie, Meghan shielded her eyes to peer at the vessels coming into view. Real ships rowed by real men, oars dipping in smooth, relentless rhythm. Painted shields hung along the sides and both ends came to sharp points, but the prow was arched like a long neck. She couldn't make out the figurehead from this distance, but dragon, serpent or eagle, it mattered not. These were Vikings. And again it mattered little whether they hailed from Norway or Daneland. They'd wreak the same havoc.

Terror dimmed Meghan's eyes, but she took a long breath and forced herself to count the shields above the dipping oars, using her fingers to keep track. She bent down all ten digits twice. She supposed the same number were on the other side and in the ship that followed. Two score men in each vessel? Eldrid had that many, if churls were called in from their small holdings. The thane's great hall, the church, workshops and a number of houses were protected by log fortifications.

The long ships glided nearer. They'd land before she could run to the village. She led Storm to a big stump and scrambled on him.

His muscles flexed as she settled. "Please," she whispered, tugging his mane and bending her weight. "Please, Storm! Run!"

He stood as if considering, then swung into an easy rocking gait that ate up the distance. As she passed fields and outlying dwellings, she shouted, "Vikings!" The stallion sped through the open gate. As they neared the hall she tugged on his neck and mane. He slowed. She slid off, rolled out of the way of his hoofs. Skinned and breathless, she pushed herself up, gasping the alarm.

Eldrid himself stepped out, a thick man with a fat red face and butter-yellow hair, his eldest son, Cynwulf, behind him. Cynwulf had an angel face but was often the one who led his mates in harassing Mad Osric, the simpleton, or her, the Viking's bastard.

"What's the screeching?" Eldrid gave her a shake, scowling down at her. "Stop gabbling. Speak so a man can hear you!"

Meghan swallowed, pointing toward the river. "Vikings, lord! Two ships! They must be moored by now!"

"If you're wrong—" But he whirled with remarkable lightness for so heavy a man. "Wind the horns! Ring the church bell. Let all men arm themselves and man the walls!"

His servant ran forward with mailcoat and helmet, sword, javelin and spear. "Could you see how many?" asked Eldrid as he armed.

"On the first ship perchance twoscore shields. I didn't stay to count the other."

Eldrid glanced toward Storm, who grazed in the churchyard. "You rode that killer? I'll hear more of that—if we live!" He hurried to the walls with his retainers and all males large enough to throw stones or wield a pike or hayfork.

Women screamed. Mothers snatched up their children and bore them inside the hall. The priest joined them, calling on everyone to pray but first barricade the doors. In the confusion, Meghan hurried past smithy, stables and houses to the back of the village, where storage sheds were built against the wall across the ditch that ran inside the palisade.

Storm followed her. Meghan didn't like to leave him

inside; there was no telling what he'd do if someone tried to ride him. But she couldn't leave Gran alone with Vikings on the prowl, even though the hut was off to itself and hidden in an old orchard. Granfer's granfer had planted the trees, and the apples were few and small now, but tartly delicious.

"I must climb over the wall and run for it," she told the horse, patting him. "Bide here till they open the gate and you can pass out. If this lot be saved, you did it, so they should be grateful."

Dragging a sawhorse close to a shed, she got on top and was able to hitch herself precariously over the pointed logs of the palisade, dangling in fright a moment before she dropped.

She lay in the grass, breath knocked out, and was just getting to her knees when a shadow flashed above her.

Storm! A wonder jump, for sure, though he had surely launched himself from the eminence above the ditch that bordered the inside of the wall.

"Hurry!" she breathed, bending into a crouching run as she took the back way home. As soon as they were beyond the fields, thick trees would make it impossible to ride—and it would be best for both of them if she never did that again—though what wild joy it had been, speeding on the wind!

At the edge of the wood, Storm halted, then neighed and tossed his head, cantering off to his meadow. Meghan made her way as fast as she could to the hut in the orchard and sighed with relief when she found nothing untoward. She'd see if Gran needed anything and then wait by the path that led out of the trees toward the village. From there, she could see how the battle went and try to stop any Northman who might venture down the narrow way. She wished she had the sword, then told herself she couldn't have swung it. She'd have to make do with Granfer's big knife.

* * *

Gran was asleep by the fire. Old as she was, her skin was still pink and scarcely wrinkled, though her hair was like snow. Once she'd been Queen of the May and, later, Lady of the Harvest, matching her stroke to the Harvest Lord's, and she lived more in those days than the present, often taking Meghan for Maire, Meghan's mother, or a sister forty years dead. It was kinder so. Most times, Gran talked companionably to her gossips long under their stones or in a state akin to hers. It was seldom she remembered that her husband was dead and that her twelve-year-old granddaughter had to scavenge their living.

Oh, if Meghan had whimpered to Father Aiden, he might have given them food in the worst part of the winter, and though Eldrid gave no thought to the family of the man who'd been his chief horseman for many years, several of those Granfer had taught brought a bit of bacon when they butchered, or now and then a hare, but they were hard put to feed their own families.

Gorm, the shepherd, bought a gift of mutton each autumn, and his kindly wife, Myra, now and then gave Meghan one of her good white cheeses. Ulfric, the steward, saw they had grain enough. For the rest, Meghan fished, as Granfer had taught her, and dried some against winter. She had a patch of peas, garlic and onions, harvested some apples, and picked wild greens and berries. She earned their barley by staying in the planted fields to scare away pillaging birds. Gran had been a notable weaver, so the chest still had lengths of stout cloth and several garments. Meghan couldn't yet wear the blue or green tunics that reached to her feet, or the blue mantle that had belonged to her mother. She wore Granfer's old tunics, girdled in at the waist.

Meghan settled Gran comfortably among the sheepskins that served as cushions and covers and hurried down the path. Stopping among the trees, she gazed at the battle in fascinated dread.

Screams and shouts carried to her ears. Some of the Vikings wore mail, but most had only domelike leather headgear. Bodies lay on the ground, dragged back from the thick of fighting, and as she watched, the invaders began to retreat, fighting as they fell back from the wall, gathering up their slain and wounded.

They hadn't expected the village to be forewarned. Rather than lose more men trying to crack a tough nut, they must have decided to steer down the coast and seek easier prey.

The gate opened. Eldrid led his force after the foe, scenting a glorious victory over the feared Northmen. Meghan thought of the ships. Unmoored, they'd float down the river to the sea, leaving their owners trapped.

Doubling through the orchard, she sped through open ground to the river, a stitch in her side, breath sobbing in her throat.

There was no guard. The long ships were fastened by braided leather ropes to stumps used by fisher boats. Tugging with all her might, skinning her hands on the hide ropes, Meghan freed the loop on the first one, casting it away, and then the second. Towering above her, the dragon heads peered down, bobbing as if to pounce, before the ships, long as the nave of the church, overlapping planks tied with roots and tarred to keep out the sea, slid reluctantly into the current.

A spear sang by her. She made for the high reeds, dropping flat as an arrow passed where she had been. Then the Vikings had more to worry about than the girl who'd loosed their vessels.

As she edged cautiously about, the Northmen, seeing they couldn't escape, fought back-to-back against Eldrid's harrying band. Not a one seemed less than six feet tall except for a half-grown boy who stood near the tallest chief and wielded a knife.

The giant beside him fell, thrust clean through with a pike. The boy's cry carried above the clashing tumult, but he raised up the fallen warrior's sword. Hefting it with both hands, he swung mightily at Eldrid.

Eldrid ducked. As impetus carried the lad off balance, the thane knocked him down with his shield, lunged over him at a brawny redhead. Vastly outnumbered, for many had fallen during the attack on the wall, the Vikings battled with the savagery that had earned them the name "wolves of the sea," but they were borne to the river strand.

Meghan hadn't wanted them to raid another village, but now she cringed against the earth, not wanting to see. There was nothing she could do about hearing. Men like her father were dying, and though his blood had brought her grief, she couldn't deny it. She had doomed these Northmen, yet she was proud of the way they fought, laughing and taunting their enemies.

At last there were no more sounds of blade on blade, but there were moans and dull thuds, boasts and excited laughter among the Saxons. Meghan got to her feet, saw a mace smash into a Viking's head and was sick. When she could, she spat out the sourness and, keeping her eyes away from the slaughter on the bank, made her way through the reeds, intending to run home as fast as she could.

She was just in time to see Cynwulf bend over the Viking lad, raising his head by long fair hair, drawing his knife.

"Stop!" She flung herself in the way, shielding the unconscious youth. "He's only a boy!"

"Ay, you'd try to save a hurd-yed like yourself!" mocked Cynwulf, trying to twist her away. Meghan held to the prisoner and called wildly, "Lord Eldrid! A boon, lord!"

He strode up with some of his exulting men, wiping blood from his mace. "Was it you set the ships adrift?"

"Yes, lord, when I saw that you pursued."

"You did well. This day would have had a different end had you not warned us. What will you? A living in my hall for you and your grandmother? Meat and grain till you marry?"

The Dane's thin body stirred, bones too big for their muscle and fleshing. He reminded Meghan of Storm as a colt. "Let this one live," she begged.

Eldrid nudged the lone survivor with his foot. "Ho, the cub that swung at me with a man's sword! Young as he is but already steeped in hurd-yed viciousness. Ask for something else."

"He could tend your sheep, lord," she pleaded. "Away from the Vikings, he'll forget their ways." Eldrid was pious and she played on that. "Surely you would please God by winning him a Christian soul."

Ulfric, the steward, who remembered Granfer and sometimes gave Meghan a treat for Gran, took the helmet off his grizzled hair and wiped blood from a gash above his eye. "The lass speaks true, Eldrid. There's no credit in slaying a harmless boy. Grant her boon. But for her, your hall would be burning now with us inside it."

Eldrid shrugged. "I'll spare him, then. He can watch the sheep." He signed to Gorm, his shepherd, who came forward and lifted the reviving boy to his feet.

The dazed captive must be of noble blood, Meghan thought. The brooch that held his short cloak was surely gold set with jewels, and the belt and scabbard for his knife were encrusted with stones that flashed in the waning sun. But it was most of all his bearing that be-spoke high birth.

Surrounded by those who'd killed his kin and friends,

he must have expected a slow, cruel death, but he stood away from the shepherd's steadying hand and looked straight at Eldrid. No one understood his defiant words, though some of them sounded much like the Saxon tongue. It was said that long ago Jutes, Angles, Saxons and Germans had migrated south from the land of the Danes. There was no mistaking the boy's tone, though.

Eldrid cuffed him against the shepherd. " 'Tis a profitless boon you've won, girl." His gaze caught on Storm, outlined against the evening sun as he grazed in the high meadow. "Now, by blessed Cuthbert's otters! How came that stallion here?"

Meghan's stomach twisted. Her breath wedged deep in her throat. Then she glimpsed a way out. "Lord, when you came after the Northmen, the horse could have followed." Not a lie.

Eldrid still frowned, studying her with pale brown eyes. "That might be. Charlemagne's elephant could have been behind us and we'd have recked not. But how was it you rode that man-killer to the village?"

"I saw the ships, lord, and was so affrighted that I thought only of getting to you with all speed. Mayhap he was tamed by Mary Virgin."

Ulfric crossed himself. "That must be truth, Eldrid. Why will you niggle at deliverance?"

Hastily, Eldrid crossed himself, too. "Now praise God for our safety," he said in haste. There were more Northmen where these came from. It wasn't prudent to slight divine intercession. "Nay, Ulfric. I wondered only if the beast had grown gentle. I would fain have him for my mount. I'll send my best horseman to him tomorrow to see if he may be used." He said magnanimously to Meghan, "I give you leave to fetch away bones and scraps from the hall. Ulfric, you'll instruct the kitchen servants."

Ulfric grinned at Meghan. "I will, and gladly."

Eldrid looked at his men, most of whom bore some hurt. Many were supported by comrades. "Have your wounds tended," he ordered. "I bid you all to a feast tonight and a mass of thanksgiving first." He nodded at the heaped bodies. "Bear home our dead. I will pay for prayers to speed them through purgatory. As for the heathen, strip them and heave them in the river to follow their ships."

As the looting of corpses began, the Viking lad wrenched free of the shepherd and ran to the gold-bearded warrior beside whom he had fought, dead among a pile of attackers. Snatching up a knife, the boy stood over the dead man.

Meghan caught Ulfric's arm, imploring silently. He warded off the despoilers. "Eldrid, the boy defends his father or chief, as is meet. Would you not wish your sons to do the same?"

"Fiend take him!" Eldrid gritted. "Burn or bury the one he guards, then, but trouble me no more for his sake!"

The thane limped off, followed by those too wounded to seek spoils. Ulfric stared at the captive and scratched his head. "How's he to understand?"

Meghan spoke softly. She advanced as she would have to a desperate horse, holding out her hand. How to explain? Kneeling, she dug up a handful of loamy earth, then indicated the dead man and pointed again to the soil.

"Is it what you want?" she asked, though he couldn't understand the words. He took her meaning, though, and made a motion as if shaping a mound. Ulfric grunted and took the warrior's shoulders, dragging him away from the fallen.

"I'll have his arms," said Cynwulf, thrusting past Meghan. "And that great gold brooch."

"You will not, young master," said Ulfric pleasantly. "I claim his gear as my share." As Cynwulf glared

Ulfric added, "It does not become those who weren't forward in battle to be forward now."

Cynwulf went scarlet and stormed off. Ulfric took up a spade that had been some churl's weapon and began to delve. Not knowing how to ask such a favor, Meghan stammered. "Master Ulfric, would you leave the man some of his things?"

"He shall be buried with all," Ulfric said. "The heathen believe the dead need such gear for the next life—as did we before the priests came."

"Master Ulfric! God will bless you. . . ."

"I doubt God would approve," he said gruffly. " 'Tis plain and simple that I think we'd have to kill the lad or keep him chained were this chief dishonored."

Meghan glanced about and whispered, "Do you think anyone would dig into the grave?"

"I do," said Ulfric, still spading. "And that is why as soon as the rest wend home, I'll make this mock grave and we'll put the Viking elsewhere."

Thinking of the eroded hole near the hawthorn, Meghan said, "I know a place."

II

The bright-haired boy didn't weep as they made his father's grave beneath the hawthorn, not far from the hidden sword. Wrapped in his mantle, along with the lad's jeweled belt and scabbard, the warrior was covered with earth, heaped with rocks to keep out beasts, and these mounded with turf. With luck, the grass would soon knit over, and the Viking would be left to whatever was his portion beyond this life.

"Don't worry about the lad," Ulfric said as they walked homeward. "Gorm is a kindly man and his wife has no living child. She'll be glad of this one."

Meghan nodded. "But how frightened he must be." She glanced at the boy, who couldn't have been more than a year or two her elder. "And how alone—not a soul to ken his words, even."

Ulfric cast her a keen glance. "He lives. All else will mend."

"Good Master Ulfric, say a word for him to Gorm and Myra."

"Oh, ay. Be sure I will."

She thanked him, spoke softly to the captive though he couldn't understand. "May Our Lady comfort you."

"You must come to the feast this night," Ulfric called as she turned toward the orchard.

"Bless you for the thought, Master Ulfric, but I must stay by Gran."

He frowned, then shrugged. "As you will, but be sure to come to the hall tomorrow. I'll bid old Brynna save you some tasty morsels."

Again she thanked him, hesitated as she glanced at the boy. If there were some way to ease his burden! Or let him know that at least he had one friend, poor and outcast as she was.

Perhaps he did know. He took her hands, bowing low, and carried them to his lips. Ulfric said, nor was he laughing, "I think you have a champion, lass."

Meghan dreamed of dying men that night, woke often in cold sweat. She reminded herself of what the Vikings would have done to the village had they conquered, or to other hamlets had they sailed safe, but she was oppressed, as if the dead crowded in around her, invisible, but almost palpable, men like her father. Heathens though they were, she prayed for their souls, and for the boy in the shepherd's hut. At first light, while Gran still slept on the inner side of the platform that served as bench by day and bed by night, Meghan slipped one of Granfer's tunics over her shift, wrapped an old mantle of Gran's about her and hurried to the village.

Men were already going to the fields, though some of them looked as if they'd had too much of the thane's ale last night. None of them paid any attention to the ragamuffin figure whose face was hidden by brown fustian.

Brynna, a sallow woman of the old Pictish blood whose graying hair was hidden by a greasy coif, was supervising the day's baking, but she stopped long enough to give Meghan a reed basket.

"A bit of the feast for you and your gran," she said, coming as close as she could to a smile though it seemed to pain her. "You're a brave lass, though a ninny. Begging that whelp's life instead of getting a soft living for your poor old granny!"

A puppy blundered under her feet. She gave it a kick that sent it yelping against the wall. "Alf!" she called to a scullion. "Take this wastrelly tyke and drown him or bash his head. He's always in the way!"

The pup licked Alf's grasping hand. He was an ungainly little creature, white patched with black and cinnamon, with a fluffy tail and hopeful eyes. "May I have him?" Meghan asked.

"That's why some be poor," scolded Brynna. "Give them a few scraps and they must ay have a dog! But go on, take him!"

Alf, thin and carrot-haired, looked vastly relieved and gave the dog a pat as he placed him in Meghan's free arm. He wriggled up to lavish affectionate caresses with his tongue all over her face but quieted at her rebuke, and they slipped out of the kitchen.

Gorm and his wife were dark and gnarled as old roots, but their seamed faces were kind. Myra was famed as a midwife and herb-healer. They made Meghan welcome and Myra offered her a bannock. Meghan declined, saying she must get home to make Gran's breakfast, but she had wondered— This puppy, if she brought bones for him sometimes, could she give him to the Danish boy?

"Harald?" Myra smiled at him and gave him another bannock with a bit of bacon. "Why, yes, the lad might fancy a pet, strange as he is here. There's no need to bring food, lass. The pup can learn to help with the sheep, be'n't that right, husband?"

Gorm nodded his graying head. "Auld Tam knows his

business, but he's my dog and won't be much company for long days in the meadow. A good thought, Meghan.''

Crossing to Harald, who sat by the hearth set in the middle of the floor, she offered the puppy. ''Harald?'' His gray eyes were swollen. He had cried last night when no one could see. She touched herself. ''I'm Meghan. The puppy needs a home.'' Of course it meant nothing to him. She said, ''Harald,'' and put the small dog on his lap.

He sat quite still. The pup made an ecstatic sound and wriggled close, licking his hands. The boy bent forward, hiding his thin face in the pup's shaggy hair, but not before Meghan had seen a tear.

In these days after Easter, Meghan spent from dawn to dusk in the fields, striking together wooden clappers and moving about to scare off crows and rooks. At noon she ran quickly home to give Gran some broth and see that she was comfortable, snatched up a cold bannock and hurried back to her task. Other children, too, guarded corn, oats and barley and the long rows of beans and peas. Each villager owned certain rows in different fields, laid out carefully to get the best sun, but after Granfer's death, Meghan had found it easier to tend her own small patches.

The cornfield lay near the sheep meadow, and she always waved and called to Harald. There was a knoll with a view of the river. He often sat there, the dog in his arms, watching the way to the sea. Much of the time, of course, he was helping Gorm move the hurdles within which the sheep were folded. Their dung enriched soil used from ancient times, so it was important to shift the barriers daily. As the thane's shepherd, one of Gorm's privileges was to have the sheep folded on his own crop-lands from Christmas Eve till the eve of Epiphany, the twelve days of Christmas. Moreover, he had a Christmas

dinner of meat at the hall, and a loaf for himself and one
for his dog. Granfer used to say the folding was a way to
keep Gorm interested in his charges instead of wassail,
but Gran, then in her clear mind, had said even thanes
might show generosity on God's birthday.

Seeing Harald gaze off to the sea, Meghan's heart
misgave her. Did he wish she hadn't saved him? It was a
sad fall from roving on a dragon ship to shifting mucky
hurdles and making sure the spring lambs suckled suffi-
ciently even when they had for mothers flighty young
ewes who hadn't accepted their responsibilities. But
surely his heart must lighten when he saw the small creatures frisking and playing Lord o' the Hill, tumbling each
other down a slope. In contrast to their lugubrious elders,
the new ones skipped and rollicked, their only serious
urge being to search out their dams now and then and
feed, their bodies vibrating with eager jerks.

A flock of rooks was circling. They could clean out a
laboriously plowed, planted and weeded field right down
to the roots in a matter of minutes. Meghan rattled the
clappers and called out words Granfer had taught her:

"Rooks and crows, take care of your toes!
  For here come my clappers to knock you down back-
     wards!
  Holla ca-whoo! Ca-whoo!"

She ran along the rows, clacking raucously, whirled at
distant laughter, ready to confront tormentors from the
village, though these had left her in peace since the Viking raid. Then she laughed, gladly, for Harald had come
to the hedge that separated meadow from crops. The
rooks had flown off in search of unguarded food, but she
kept a wary eye on the corn and sky as she made her way
through tender plants to the boundary.

His clear gray eyes laughed at her as he made a

flapping with his arms and cloak, imitating a feathered
marauder. She sounded the clappers at him and they both
chuckled as the puppy, wildly excited, wriggled through
the hedge and jumped up on Meghan.

He had grown. His muzzle was losing its snubbiness
and his legs were getting long and gawky. Scratching the
black spot between his ears, Meghan said, "He's big."

Harald repeated, "Big." They beamed at each other.
He pointed at the big rounded clouds sailing across the
sky in a leisurely way. "Bee-ships."

"Bishops?" Meghan frowned. She cocked her head
doubtfully at the clouds. "Because they're fat?" She
mimed swollen sides.

"Bee." Harald vibrated his hand and made a buzzing
sound. "Ship." He pointed to the river and made a
smooth gliding gesture.

"Why a bee-ship?" Meghan asked.

With motions and the English he'd acquired, he finally
made her understand. When people died their souls
turned into bees and traveled in ships of cloud. Meghan
started to try to tell him that souls were in hell or heaven
or purgatory but decided against it. If he believed his father and companions floated in that bright world between
green earth and smiling sun, what was the harm?

To prolong the conversation, she bent to touch a
pasque flower that bloomed beside the hedge.

"Pretty," she said, then realized in dismay that the
flower was said to bloom only where Viking blood had
been shed. But he didn't know that.

"Pretty," he agreed. He was looking at her, not the
delicate lavender petals. "Like your eyes."

She blushed. A confusing but pleasant warmth tingled
through her, a feeling new to her yet like something
rooted deep, shared with all creatures and plants greeting
the summer after winter's chill.

She gave him a flustered smile and ran to frighten a

horde of crows, calling with more joy than the words merited, *"Here comes a stone to break your backbone— Ca-whoo! Ca-whoo!"*

During the time the sheep were folded near enough the corn for them to meet at the hedge, Meghan and Harald snatched moments to talk. Each day they could understand each other's meaning with less difficulty. Meghan was glad to see that Myra kept his garments carefully mended and sent bread and cheese with him for his lunch. When he noticed that Meghan had only a bit of bannock so hard she could scarcely chew it, he made her share his cheese along with his softer bread of pea flour, rye and barley.

When she asked if his mother would worry about him, he let her know that his mother had died the winter before and that was why his father had allowed him to come a-viking. His father, Hasting, had been of kingly blood and was a jarl, or earl, much greater, said Harald, with a lip-curl of contempt, than Eldrid thane. Someday, he'd win his way home and claim his heritage.

Meghan was sure he would and felt a stab of loss. He was her only friend. Still, she had learned enough of his nature to foresee that he couldn't reach manhood as a bondslave. When he heard that her father had been a Viking, his eyes sparkled.

"Glad I am to hear it!"

"Nay, Harald, it shamed my mother and has made a mock of me." She had to explain more slowly. His hand reached for the splendid knife that was buried with his father, clenched when it found nothing.

"No one will mock—" He stammered, searching out the words. "I will—stop mouths!"

She gave her head a frightened shake. "Words . . . talk . . ." She spread her hands and shrugged. "Nothing."

"It is *nithing* to mock you!" She already knew that meant shameful. Hastily, she changed the subject to her relief at his recent baptism.

His reply dampened her. He had consented because of Myra's pleadings and because his father and a good many Vikings, who were traders as well as plunderers, had been prime-signed by a priest at Hedeby, the great Danish trading center. This was the first step toward conversion and eased the consciences of Christian merchants who scrupled to do business with heathen. What was one god more to a Northman, especially when Christ seemed much like murdered Balder the Beautiful, who, it was claimed, would arise from the dead when the present world ended and rule a summer world of love and peace?

Northmen believed, too, that the world would end? she asked him.

Yes. When gods fought monsters in the last five days, raging fires would destroy even Valhall, Odin's great hall that was lit by swords. Even the gods would die. But the Tree of Life would endure, and within it, a man and woman to beget a new race.

"Our God never dies."

"He hangs on a cross. As Odin hung from the Tree of Life."

She crossed herself at the blasphemy. "Christ rose again."

"Odin tore himself loose after nine days."

"But you say he will die."

Harald shrugged and gazed out to the sea beyond the distant mouth of the estuary. Except for its dancing glimmer, it blended with the sky. "No god or man can escape his Wyrd."

She understood that. Wyrd was an ancient Saxon belief. What destiny, she wondered with a shiver, had brought them together? What would the end be? His escaping somehow, leaving her more lonely than before?

She blinked at the smart in her eyes.

His fair brows knit in concern. He touched her cheek, rubbing away the tears. "What's amiss?"

"I know you'll want to get away before you're grown up," she began bravely but then caught his hard brown fingers. "Ah, Harald! I shall miss you sorely!"

His hand tightened on hers. "Would you come with me?"

Dizzied at the terrifying but enticing thought, she held to him while the familiar world seemed to spin. This was real, not her old fantasy of faring off on Storm with the hidden sword. And those strange new feelings that mingled with spring and changes in her body—lengthening legs, narrowing waist and the blossoming of the small pink buds on her rounding breasts—these sensations gripped her till her knees weakened.

How handsome he was! Even though his face had not filled out, giving forehead, cheekbones and jaw a prominence that made his cheeks look gaunt. At fourteen, he was taller than most villagers, but coltishly rangy; long legs and arms seemed to get in his way. His hair was in between gold and silver and waved to his shoulders. He combed it daily and kept himself so much cleaner than anyone else that Meghan had started heating a little water and washing herself each night, a freak that it was just as well her grandmother could not notice. For all his frayed stained clothes, he looked a thousand times more princely than Cynwulf or Edmund, the thane's chubby, placid younger son.

Her heart raced to think of going away with him from this place where she had always been an outsider. Then she remembered.

"I can't leave Gran. There's no one else to take care of her."

He frowned but didn't argue. After a moment he said, "But someday—when she needs you no more . . ."

"I'll go with you. Oh, Harald, most gladly will I go!"

His smile was radiant as sun breaking through clouds. "Good. Then we have only to wait. Give me your other hand." She did, and he clasped both of hers in his big ones. "I will have no other wife than you, no other love."

It was joy now that brought her tears. "And I will take no other man, no other lover."

They gazed at each other in awed delight. It was with a boy's awkwardness that he bent to give her a first kiss. Their lips were shy and tentative but their spirits seemed to merge. Never in Meghan's heart would she be alone again—or a child.

Out of their will and longing and loneliness, they were betrothed.

III

Forty days after Easter came the Feast of the Ascension, and the three days before Holy Thursday were called Gangdays, for it was then the men of the village ganged after the priest to mark the village boundaries and pray for growing crops. Father Aiden led the way. Ulfric carried the cross, and other men bore banners and bells that sounded merrily. In order to make them remember the bounds, younger boys who rollicked in and out of the procession were tossed into streams and ponds and bumped smartly against rocks and trees that served as markers.

At certain trees, the priest stopped, led the group in prayer and blessed the fields and village. Though women weren't part of the procession, they followed along, laughing at the horseplay and joining in the prayers. Meghan walked next to Myra, enjoying the sunny day and proudly noting Harald's noble bearing.

Cynwulf must have noticed, too. Meghan couldn't hear his words but he seemed to be taunting the Danish lad, who ignored him. They neared a pond edging the river meadow, and though they were past the age for duckings and buttock bumpings, Cynwulf planted his leg in front of Harald's, caught his arm and plunged him into the water.

A roar of laughter went up as Harald floundered to rise from the mud. He rinsed himself as best as he could and rejoined the group. It was the kind of trick best treated as a joke, but Meghan's blood hummed angrily. She clapped with joy when, at a large rock, Ulfric swept Cynwulf off balance and jounced his rump soundly against the stone.

Red in the face, Cynwulf lunged at the steward. "I be no urchin for such lessoning!"

Ulfric held him calmly with one hand. "Nay, you be the thane's son. You more than any must know the bounds."

The procession resumed. Cynwulf kept a good distance from both Ulfric and Harald, but he sneered about hurd-yeds and pixie-blooded wights till Meghan longed to hit him. It was then that she resolved to show Harald the Viking sword.

On Whitsunday, Meghan came early with a great bundle of new rushes for strewing. This was one of the great feasts of the church, when old hay and rushes were swept out and the church floor spread with fresh ones. When she had scattered her offering, she hurried home to fetch Gran, for at Easter, Christmas and Whitsunday, Meghan would have thought it shame not to get the old woman to mass if it could anywise be done.

This meant frequent rests, for Meghan had to half carry her grandmother. They were at the edge of the copse when Meghan saw Harald with his foster-parents, wearing a fine blue cloak. Myra was proud of this tall new son and had worked to deck him bravely. He spoke some word to Gorm and Myra before he ran to Meghan and supported her grandmother on the other side.

"It goes better so." He laughed.

Gorm and Myra waited. They entered the church together, and because of Harald's care for her poor old gran, Meghan's heart glowed brighter than the candles that blazed on the altar.

Only necessary work was done during Whitsun week. There was dancing in the churchyard of an evening close by where the blessed dead slept on the sunny south side. On the shaded north lay unshriven sinners and those few who had made an end of themselves, despairing of God's grace.

Lads of Harald's age wrestled on the green, shot arrows at marks or contested each other with blunted staves, but Harald stayed aloof from this sporting as did Meghan. She was gathering faggots a few days after Whitsunday when she saw him outlined on the slope above the river, sitting there with his dog, Jarl, gazing toward where river ran into sea and sea into sky.

Heaping the faggots by the path, she hurried along the hedge bounding the field that had been last year in winter corn, grazed by village cattle till Candlemas and then plowed and planted to oats, barley peas and beans. The field that had lain fallow the year before had been sown last fall with winter corn and the field of spring corn would be fallowed through the next year, regaining its fertility as the cattle manured it. The order of crops and fallowing was as unvarying as the main church feasts that set times when certain tasks should be completed or begun.

What would this predictable round offer a Viking to whom summer weather brought faring forth in fresh-tarred ships, either for trade or plunder? She couldn't think that Harald would bide here his lifetime any more than a hawk would roost for long with chickens.

Stabbed by a foretaste of how lonely it would be without him, she slowed her pace. Why show him the sword, add fuel to his longing? True, he had sworn to return for her, but the seas were vast, boundless as the heavens, and full of storms besides. In spite of vows and wishing, when he left this place it was most likely she would never again see him. Nevertheless she felt she must show him the sword.

There was a bowl of ale and dish of meat on his father's mound; Harald had brought this share of the Whitsun feast for the dead man. Though she doubted that the pagan chief would welcome her prayers, Meghan knelt to say one before she scraped away moldly leaves and stones to reveal the cavern where the sword rested, amid twisted roots, swaddled in a ragged cloak of Granfer's.

She drew back, dizzied with the sweet smell of hawthorn, and said, "Harald, take it forth."

He cast her a puzzled look but leaned forward. A root had entwined the sword and he had to tug. The aged cloth ripped and clung to the gnarls as he brought out the blade, unfolding the remnants of fustian.

Rust had discolored the blade again and the hilt and pommel were tarnished, but Harald, eyes shining, rubbed with a will. After a time, the pommel showed silver dragons and the hilt gleamed with golden beasts and birds above tendrilled silver cross-pieces.

"How came you by this?" he asked sharply.

Meghan read his thought and flushed. "It came from no man's body. I found it almost where it lies, washed there by floods, surely. But I have thought—" Again she colored and dropped her gaze. "I have liked to think it was my father's."

"Then was your father of king's blood?" said Harald, laughing before he sobered, fingers tracing the ancient engravings. "This sword, I am sure it is Heaven's Gift, for I've heard its dragons and beasts sung of in ancient songs. Almost as famed is it as great Sigurd's sword, which Odin himself caused to shatter though it was forged anew for Siegfried Fafnir's-Bane. We Northmen often have a sword that goes down in a family and with it takes the luck and honor of that lineage. It is said this luck is a woman spirit in warrior's mail, a *fylgya*, who can be seen at times and protects the family or warns of danger."

Meghan glanced hastily about, relieved when she saw no towering woman in armor. "If this is true, what happens when a sword is lost, like this one?"

Harald smiled at her and clasped her hand to the hilt beneath his. "I would say the *fylgya* led you to it. Swords are often placed in a woman's keeping for bestowal on one she deems worthy. So, Meghan, Heaven's Gift is in your ward. The man to whom you give it, to him will pass the luck and honor of many heroes."

"To you will I give it."

As if burned, he dropped her hand and carefully wrapped the sword again, thrusting it into its hiding palce. "Say not so. I have not earned it. It may be the *fylgya* means it for another. Yet I thank you, my friend, for giving me sight of it. I will remember when I am with the sheep. And I am glad it lies so near my father, though he was buried with his own good sword."

When all signs of disturbance were brushed away, they wandered up the slope. Storm saw them and neighed, pacing toward them. Meghan called to him, plucked grass and offered it. He lipped softly from her palm, ignoring Harald, who laughed and said, "Folk still call it God's miracle or the devil's that you rode this one. Did you know Eldrid thane sent his best horsemen to try with the stallion, but he grew so wild and savage they durst not come near him?"

"I have heard it," said Meghan curtly.

The priest had gone on about that feat in confession till she was wearied and afraid, but she had sworn that never before the morn of the raid had she ridden the horse till he believed and convinced the thane it was God's mercy.

Since then, she had taken care to caress and talk to Storm only when they were beyond sight of the village.

Harald looked surprised at her tone. He had one secret; why not give him this other? She smiled and took out the small bag she wore always around her neck.

"Take this and let Storm smell it. I think then he will suffer your touch if you speak gently soft and praise him."

" 'Tis thus I've heard one wins a maid," laughed Harald.

Meghan twinkled back at him. "I think it none so different."

Storm snuffed the charm while Harald bespoke him. It was only when the stallion nudged his glossy muzzle against the boy that Harald made free to touch first Storm's face and then his shoulder. The horse accepted grass and herbs from Harald's hand and they were soon at ease.

"I believe he can never forget me now," Meghan said. "Keep the bag, Harald and wear it under your arm when you would come near him. Thus he will learn your odor mingled with the milt from his tongue when he was fresh born."

Harald shook his head. "It is as great a marvel as the sword—and yours, my Meghan."

Her lonely heart warmed at such naming, opened as a flower, tight-folded, does in the sun. "They are your secrets, too, Harald. I can give you naught else."

He laughed again, more deeply, and carried her hand to his lips. "Why, Meghan, here you have the most famed sword of all the Northlands and a pet of this stallion whom all fear! Methinks your treasures rare as you, and I vow if I live that one day you will sit with me on the high seat of my father's hall."

Dazzled, she sighed. "That seems too wild and proud a magic. It is enough, Harald, that you cheer my life."

He threw back his head, which blazed bright against Storm's sable hue. "Gorm and Myra are kind folk, but ask me not to stay all my years a shepherd-slave to Elfrid."

Meghan bit her lip. She said in a low tone, "I do not ask it. Yet keep the charm, I beg you."

After a moment, he bowed his neck. She slipped thong and bag around it, fingers brushing against his hair which seemed to cling to them. Storm followed them a little way, but when Meghan turned and bade him come no farther, he left off and went cropping at the springy grass.

If only we could ride away on him, taking the sword, she thought. But there was Gran. Still, who knew what might happen someday?

Two years passed, marked by holy days and the round of planting, tending and harvest. Sheep-shearing came and then Midsummer. On Saint John's Eve, bones and rubbish were heaped on the highest hillock beyond the village and burned to make a great fire. Brands lit from it were carried through the fields to ward off dragons who were abroad that night to poison springs and wells. A wheel of withies was set rolling down the hill, and young men whooped and shouted as they ran the course that showed that now the sun had reached its highest point, it must begin to sink.

Hay making took from Midsummer to Lammas on August 1, when loaves made from the first new grain were brought to church for blessing. After wheat was cut, it was time to reap the corn. Every able-bodied person, young and old, joined in the harvests that would feed them through the winter. The thane's fields were reaped first as a love boon from the folk, but as Gorm dryly observed, no one had ever failed to love the thane and refused to help.

Meghan worked behind the reapers, binding sheaves.

Harald was among the lads who formed them into shocks. The work was hard, but it was a time of joking and good nature from the first stroke of the Harvest Lord to the cutting of the final sheaf by all the reapers throwing sickles at it till the last stalk had fallen so that no single person killed the corn spirit. In heathen times, the one who cut the last stalk had been slain to restore the corn spirit's life, but now he was bundled in the stalks and roughly joked and handled while women made a corn lady from the last heads of grain and set the figure on top of the wagon bearing the end of the reaping.

There was a Harvest Feast in the thane's hall that night, and next day Meghan and other poor folk gleaned such grain as was left before first the cattle and then sheep were turned in on the stubble.

Harvest ended by Michaelmas at the end of September. After All Souls', swine were slaughtered and such beasts thought unlikely to live through the winter. Then came plowing and the sowing of the winter cornfield before Christmas. On Plough Monday, the day after Epiphany, a plough was brought into the church and solemnly blessed, though spring ploughing seldom began earlier than Candlemas, the Feast of the Virgin's Purification on February 2.

Spring corn should be planted by Lady Day, the Feast of the Anunciation, or certainly by Easter, and so the seasons passed.

Harald, at sixteen, was taller now than any man of the village, though Cynwulf was nearly of his height, and much heavier. Gran stayed the same, but Meghan's breasts curved ever more sweetly above her maiden waist and long, slender thighs.

Lads and young men began to look at her—some not so young. Nicholas, the hayward, whose task it was, under Ulfric, to overlook the condition of the meadows, fields, woods, hedges, keep a tally of each household's work for the thane and see that beasts were kept out of the crops, was a stalwart, well-favored man of about thirty whose wife had died in childbirth that winter, her babe with her. Next to the steward, he was the most important man in the village and much liked, though his position was one that often led to wrangles.

Maidens came much in his way, and the few young widows, for he had a good house, well furnished, and land and sheep of his own. Moreover, each may have thought she was the one to solace him. After his young wife died, his broad, squarish face had drawn tight and his light brown eyes were hollowed. Even his yellow-brown hair grew lusterless as a beast's on scant rations. He had ever a kind word and a smile for Meghan, so she thought little of his talking longer when they met, or that they seemed to meet more often. Belike he was lonely.

What she did notice was that Harald was seldom where she could see him from the fields and never came down to the hedge unless she waved and called to him. Perplexed and hurt at this coolness, she wondered if he fancied another maid. In truth, he had grown so handsome and strong that though he was a bondsman, single women cut their eyes at him almost as much as at Nicholas, but Meghan's close scanning after mass or other gathering times caught no sign that he favored any, though he was courteous and fair-spoken to all. Meghan had even heard it whispered that he bore himself more nobly than the thane's two sons—that Cynwulf could rage like a boar and was lustful, while Edmund, plump and pink as a pig, had girlish ways and held back from any danger or rough task.

In that autumn's harvest, Harald swung a sickle for the first time and greatly speeded his team so that it began to be first or second to finish reaping each row. Margit, the miller's daughter, a pretty though sharp-featured black-haired lass, watched him and whispered, with a little shiver, "See how the muscles of his shoulders move, how straight and graceful he is in the legs! A comelier lad was never seen."

"Ay," returned an older woman. "Next reaping, were he not a hurd-yed slave, 'tis sure he'd be chosen Harvest Lord."

Gratified at such praise of Harald, but jealous, too, of Margit, whose father was the most prosperous man in the village and who might, to satisfy a spoiled only child's whim, buy Harald's freedom, Meghan bent more zealously to the binding, which left sweaty chaff prickling beneath her garments. Her eyes stung. She pretended to rub out a speck.

What had changed Harald? Was he sorry for the promises they had made? He was not rude. He spoke her fair as he did all women. But if he could not do more than that . . . Her cheek burned. Unless he treated her as more than a stranger by the end of the harvest supper, she would seek him out and make him tell her. If he no longer had a mind to her, well, better know it than doubt and hope, hope and doubt.

Nicholas was Harvest Lord that reaping but picked no Harvest Lady to be second sickle. The last day of reaping, teams sweated and strove to beat each other to the end of the rows, and Harald more than once finished ahead of even Nicholas. Late sun gilded shocks and stubble when the reapers surrounded the last patch. Before Nicholas could signal for them all to throw their sickles, one man shouted, "The hurd-yed outdid us all! Let him cut the last sheaf!"

Nicholas frowned but others took up the cry. "The hurd-yed! Let the pixie-blooded one do it!"

"Are you willing?" Nicholas asked Harald.

In answer, Harald moved in with a long sure stroke, the grain falling over his blade like maiden's hair while his own shone silver-gold. As the last stalks fell, men and boys surged over him, swathing him in the corn, dragging him about the field while the women cheered them on with laughter and ribald cries.

"Bump his bottom all you will, but save what's in front for better ploughing!" called Margit.

Meghan was afraid. The dying sun painted the field red, and it seemed to her that the way the men yanked and hauled at Harald must hurt him; she could almost imagine the way such a crowd had once torn a man apart to appease the corn. And these folk had not forgot that Harald was a Viking.

Nicholas stood watching the horseplay. She ran to him and caught his arm, "Good Master Nicholas, they use him too roughly! Surely 'tis enough!"

He stared at her as if waking from a trance and passed a hand before his face. "Oh, ay! I mind me now you saved him on that day of the raid. Don't fear, lass. We be not heathens to rend him asunder."

But he made haste to gather some of the last grain and make it into a bundle which he held above his head, calling so loud and clear that it pierced the clamor.

"I have it! I have it! I have it!"

The men gave up their sport and turned. "What have ye?" they chorused. "What have ye? What have ye?"

"A Mare! A Mare! A Mare!"

A great burst of cheering went up. One young man snatched the Mare and ran off toward the village, hoping to claim a kiss from one of the serving maids could he win inside the great barn without being splashed by pails of water. The Corn Maiden was shaped by now, with plaited hair bound by ribbons and placed atop a wagon decorated with boughs and late autumn flowers.

Such men as were able climbed on top of the load while the other harvesters followed, singing lustily:

"Harvest Home! Harvest Home!
We've ploughed, we've sown,
We've ripped, we've mown,
Harvest Home! Harvest Home!

Meghan hung back to see how it was with Harald. He
had brushed off leaves and stubble and sang as loud as
any, but he could not disguise a slight limp. She was
starting toward him to urge him to seek a place on the
wagon when Margit merrily slipped her arm around him
and said he must lean on her—and if they fell together,
'twould make sweet falling.

They were near the copse now and Meghan turned
sharply down the path to her hut. Nicholas was suddenly
enough in the way that she must stop.

"Aren't you coming to the feast?"

"I must get home to Gran. She can do naught for herself."

"But surely you will come after you've seen to
her?"

"You must know, Master Nicholas, that I'm in the village only for mass."

" 'Tis pity, that, and you our fairest maid."

"Few think so. To most I am a hurd-yed's bastard."

"That was not your blame or your mother's either.
Most would be friends with you, little Meghan, did you
not hold yourself apart so haughtily."

She said with bitterness, "I was early taught to do that.
Children never pelted *you* with dung or called you pixie
brat."

His honest, haggard face reddened. "I call it shame we
older ones paid no heed or thought to what we deemed
children's play. But you are growing into woman's estate. Come to the supper and be at peace with those you
live among."

"It may be over-late for that."

He laughed chidingly. "Over-late? And you all of fifteen summers? Nay, Meghan, spite not yourself with urchins' fooling. I must go with the last load now, but if you come not within the hour, be sure I shall fetch you."

Before she could retort, he hurried after the wagon.

Gran craved only a little porridge and kept nodding off over it, so it was no great time before she was settled in bed and breathing slumberously. Meghan stood for a few minutes in indecision. How could she bear to see Margit hanging on to Harald, and he, from the look of it, not loath? But she was sure that Nicholas would do as he had said. The hayward was no harum-scarum jesting youth, but steady and sober, well known as a man of his word.

Meghan scowled. Why had he taken it into his head that she must join in village revelry? Wasn't it enough that she shared the work? But there was no help for it. She must go; and something odd in Nicholas' manner made her think it well to reach the barn before he haled her there.

She hurried to the river and swam to cleanse herself, unbraided her thick chestnut hair and rinsed it of sweat and chaff, gliding swift and naked back to the hut. Myra had helped her make the dress she wore for mass, but it had grown tight at the breast and short in skirt and sleeves, she had shot up so this past year. Meghan's glance fell on the chest, and she remembered her mother's handsome gown. Mayhap it would fit now, or near enough.

The red undergarment was a bit loose but the outer gown had a kirtle that brought it snug, and the full blue skirt reached just the tip of the fine leather shoes. An odor of thyme, southernwood and mint came from the clothes, faint and tangy. *Thank you, mother. I hope you wore this dress on many happy days before you died so young.* Meghan hastily combed out her damp hair and let it hang loose, fluffing it as she started out. It was curly, so she needn't worry much about it.

Nicholas was coming through the village gate as she went in. He took her hand and looked her up and down, a slow smile taking the weariness from his face. "Well come, Meghan. You look so fine you may be taken for a queen."

The dress was not that out of the way, but though his admiration turned Meghan shy, it made her carry her head higher and gave her the confidence to face the company and Margit. "Did Wat get his kiss?" she asked for something to say.

"Ay, he had the Mare inside before the wenches saw him," chuckled Nicholas. "But this night, few who crave kissing will be denied."

Trestles set up in one end of the great barn were heaped with platters of roast beef, stubble-fattened geese and pork. Loaves were piled in the center, and suet puddings steamed along the board, jostling bowls of frumenty—that delicious husked wheat soaked to a jelly—and dumplings of rye and pea meal. The thane's serving lads and maids passed up and down, filling bowls and ale horns. The thane, his lady and sons, Father Aiden, and the steward, Ulfric, and his wife sat at a table that faced the length of the others.

Children and young folk took their food and went out to eat near the fire where the ox had been spitted. Meghan saw Margit and Harald at one side, she chattering pertly to him so that Meghan's heart twisted. She numbly let Nicholas take her inside.

"Do you not sit at the thane's table?" she asked him as he made a place for them by Gorm and Myra.

"I sit where I please." He smiled.

He cut a loaf and covered a thick slice with meat for her, but she had small appetite and found a bowl of frumenty more to her liking. He shared his ale horn with her, and she blushed for it seemed he ever set his lips where hers had been.

It went beyond kindness, the way he was acting. The choice food turned to heavy uncomfortable globs in her stomach. When she finished the frumenty he'd put honey over, she said, "I'm weary, Master Nicholas. Fain I would go home."

"A maid your age cannot be weary at Harvest Home," he said. "The best is yet to come, singing the old songs and dancing."

"Never have I danced."

He looked startled. "Then 'tis more than time!"

"Pray, Master Nicholas—"

He touched her cheek. "You shall dance once. Then, if it likes you not, I'll see you to your door, for this is a night when lads and men have their fill of ale and gladsome turns quickly into mischief."

When most had eaten all they could, and some, from much ale, dozed in corners, the thane led in drinking thanks to God for the harvest, and then drank to the harvesters, who quaffed his health in turn. Then Ulfric, who knew many songs and had a true carrying voice, led the company in merry songs.

"For all this good feasting, yet art thou not loose
    Till ploughman thou givest his Harvest Home
        goose."

After a time, the trestles were taken up and folk went to dancing, inside and out, weaving in and out in circles, separating into pairs for a woman to pass under a man's arm, clapping the measure or singing it. Edmund stayed by his parents, but Cynwulf joined the frolic. If his hands made free with a woman, few would mind, and fewer say aught.

When Nicholas drew Meghan into the circle going

about the fire, her feet tripped, and she feared to blunder when he spun her away from him and back; but he guided her so that her missteps merged with right ones. She was almost enjoying the merriment when Margit drew Harald into the wide circle.

He needed little teaching. Lithe and easy, he moved with the skipping ring or spun with Margit. To Meghan he seemed not a stranger to the dancing, and she wondered in angry hurt if he had joined such frolics, with never a word to her, while she sat home with Gran. There might be cause for Margit's forwardness.

Brooding, Meghan was startled to find Cynwulf next to her. He still had his angel's face and waving golden hair a girl might envy, but his lips were too full and fleshy, and Meghan liked it not that a man should have so soft and white a skin, and liked less the way his bold green eyes played over her. "At first I took you for someone our hayward had lured in from town," the thane's son said in her ear. "But now I know you, Meghan."

"Well you might. You used to lead the cry that named me hurd-yed bastard."

He laughed. "Oh, that I have forgot and so must you." The dance parted them, but he called over his partner's head. "You must come more oft to our feasts, Meghan."

She did not like his forwardness or the way his fingers played as far they might up her wrist. Apart as she dwelled, she had heard rumors of this maid or that, and wedded women, too, that he had beguiled, Eldrid only laughing and providing in some sort for his left-hand grandsons.

Even less than dancing by him was she minded to watch Margit flaunt herself at Harald and smile up at him with small white teeth showing between red lips.

When the dancers stopped for need of breath, Meghan said, "You were kind, Master Nicholas, to bid me to the supper, but I must go now." At his crestfallen look, she added, "My head throbs. And I would be up early for gleaning."

Wishing him good night, she started off, but he overtook her before she reached the gate and gave her a basket. "Two loaves and some fat stubble goose for your gran," he said. "Thought you to be quit of me? I said I would see you safe within your house."

"It's ill for me to keep you from the dancing."

"Nay." She couldn't make out his expression in the dark but knew that he smiled. "I'm none so young as to dance for dancing's sake. But I hope that next time you will not be plagued by headache."

It was more her heart but she couldn't tell him that. He spoke of the harvest as they went along, and how the oak-apples, with sound clear kernels, betokened a good summer.

"And next summer, Meghan, will not your thoughts begin to turn on wedding?"

"No. Work enough I have for Gran without a husband, too."

"Jesus bless us, Meghan! A proper husband would smooth your life, not roughen it."

Seared by the memory of Harald bending to whirl Margit, Meghan cried, "I want no husband, proper or improper!"

Nicholas said nothing for a bit, but when he did, it was in such good nature that she was ashamed of flaring up at him. "The time will come when you think a husband not so irksome. But then they may all be wed to other maids if you hide yourself away."

"I will not cry for that."

''What a tongue!'' he chuckled. ''And I had deemed you such a gentle lass.''

She had no answer and was glad they had reached the hut.

IV

She slept poorly and set out for gleaning with heavy eyes and a heavy heart. As she gathered stalks missed by the binders, along with men too old for labor, widows and other village poor, she puzzled briefly about Nicholas, but misery over Harald soon crowded out all else.

Had he forgot those promises they'd made? That he would come for her when he'd gained his inheritance, and would have no other maid? Of course, that was over two years ago; if he thought on it at all, he could brush it aside as childishness. Perhaps he'd grown so fond of Margit that if her father bought his freedom, he'd marry her and aid his father-in-law, dream no more on the sea and his distant home.

But how could he forget the sword? If it shone and shimmered in the depths of Meghan's mind, how could it, to a Viking, not be a battle cry? The thought of Harald's working in the mill till he grew fat and grasping as the owner outraged her as much as if someone proposed to hitch Storm to a dung cart.

Smearing chaff and tears from her eyes, she was binding a sheaf with twisted corn leaves when a tall shadow fell over her. She glanced coldly at Harald and kept on working. He gave her a troubled look and began to glean.

69

"I never knew," she said snappishly, "that Gorm's household must pick at leavings with cripples and widows."

"You know that I have always helped you when I could."

"That was before you fancied Margit. God knows the miller's family need not glean! He charges so much flour for his grinding that many folk would liever grind in hand mills as I do."

Harald flushed to the roots of his silver-gold hair, which shone even fairer against his browned face and neck. The cloth of his tunic was coarse, but Myra had worked it around the border with hawks and hounds and dyed it the deep blue of a midsummer sky. Beside him, Edmund looked a placid clerk and Cynwulf a spoiled debaucher.

"I never fancied Margit. But when a lass is friendly— not like some I could name—am I to shove her away or hug my hands close by my sides?"

"That, for sure, you did not do!"

"Yet you came in with the hayward, sat by him and were his partner in the dance. Always you have told me you cared not for dancing."

"It would seem you do from your brisk hopping!" Tears threatened to overspill. "It cannot have been the first time you danced!"

"Ay, but it was, in this land."

It took a moment to take his meaning. She scoffed then. "Will you tell me that children dance in the Danish halls?"

"Not in the hall so much, but often we frisked in the courtyard. Especially we young ones loved to tread the Sword Dance, using wooden staves and chanting the words. There are many verses. My father taught me all of them. He was a rare dancer for so tall and mighty a man."

Wrath left her as she thought of all that he had lost, but that left her more forlorn. She bent to her gleaning. "If you bide in the village, Harald, 'twere better that you fancy Margit."

"Do you say so because 'tis best you smile at the hayward?"

"Shall I glower at a courteous and kindly man who goes in grief for his wife?"

"Not so grieved did he seem last night."

"He has lost a stone of weight since he laid her in the churchyard with her babe beside her."

Harald flung down the stalks he had gathered and turned savagely on Meghan. "Murrain seize this nattering of Nicholas and Margit! What I would know, Meghan, is how it stands with you and me."

She gnawed the back of her trembling lip. "Would you be quit of the promises we made as children? I deem such prattle means naught, but if you be tender of your word, I freely loose you."

He gripped her shoulders and shook her. "Devil take me, can you not say a plain word?"

Wildfire shocked through her from beneath his hands. His eyes probed her. Her knees refused support. Without knowing how it happened, she was close in his arms, his mouth seeking hers, finding it, as she, too, strove for that kiss. Beside that bygone children's pledging, this was full summer sun as to a timid spring day when faint beams hide among the clouds. When at last he raised his head, they both were trembling.

"I have no mind to be the miller's boy." His words caught in a small, breathless laugh. "So feel not over sorry for our good hayward. He has pick enough of widows and maids."

"I love you, Harald. Ever, only you."

She raised to kiss him but he held her away and frowned. "I see 'tis time and more I sought my own lands, if I'd come back to claim you before someone else does.''

She drew a little away. ''Even when I thought you wanted Margit, I never meant to have another.''

''Maids have been wed before against their will.''

''I cannot think such ill of Nicholas. And I am none so certain that he didn't favor me last night to ward off those eager to marry before he can forget his wife.''

Harald laughed. Something deep in his eyes made her blush. ''If you think that, Meghan mine, you are a child for certain. Ay, and Cynwulf. I saw how he left his place to come at dancing with you.''

''He thought I was from another place.''

''Would that he still did! What shift can you make if the thane's son woos you?''

''I hear he woos like a bull in the pasture. If he bothers me, I'll speak to Master Ulfric.''

''The thane puts great store in Ulfric's rede, but for all that he's only the steward.'' Harald smote his hand against his thigh. ''I should have gone with the summer, but it was easier to bide near you another winter. I told myself there was no haste. Now I see there is!''

Meghan shrank. ''You will not go with winter hard upon us? There must be fierce storms on the sea, ice and bitter sleet. . . .''

''No ships will sail before spring,'' he admitted. ''But I must be gone by Shrovetide and make my way to the nearest port. It may be I can work my passage on a Frisian ship bound for Hedeby, where merchants come from everywhere, even from trading in the Sea of Azov for silks and spice from China and Hind. I have mother's kin at Hedeby who will help me to my father's holdings.''

Such a long, dangerous faring. Who knew if he would safely cross the sea, much less win back to her? ''I fear for you, Harald,'' she whispered. ''If it weren't for Gran,

I would beg you to run away with me to the fells where no Christians go."

"But there is your gran. Besides, Meghan, I would have you beside me in my father's hall and by you have the sons to protect and guide the folk who look to my line for surety in these troublesome times when kings and jarls are ever at odds and seeking to chew up each other's territories."

She hung her head. "You come from princely blood. Your kinsmen, I think, will have a noble bride in mind for you."

"But for you, I'd be dead."

"That must not bind you." She took a long breath. "Harald, if when you come into your inheritance you find it well to forget these years, know I will not think you foresworn or blame you." He stared at her, eyes chilling, and she plunged on. "But if you keep a fondness yet must marry as your kinsmen bid, I would be your leman. Right gladly would I."

"Hush!" he said wrathfully. "You will be my lady wife, beside me in the high seat. If I do not come as soon as may be—though I fear that may be the summer after this—be sure that I am dead. But I will come. I will come."

Her heart brimmed with joy and went to dancing though she bent again to her labor. Whatever betided, she knew he loved her. And if he never came again, that knowledge would warm her all her life.

As she bent, she saw Nicholas striding away from the edge of the field. Had he seen them embracing? Her cheeks burned, but then she thought defiantly it was as well if last night meant more than kindness that he knew how it was with her. She bound the sheaf that Harald held toward her, laughing up at him above the ripe grain.

* * *

The day after Christmas marked the anniversary of the stoning to death of Saint Stephen. Boys beat each other with boughs of holly till the prickly leaves made them bleed, but none minded. Each drop of blood won the shedder a full extra year of life. It was also the day to bleed horses and oxen to increase their strength and keep them from sickness.

Granfer had sometimes grumbled 'twere best to leave the animals all their blood, but if it must be done, this was the best time since the beasts could rest till at least Epiphany and usually till nigh Candlemas before ploughing.

Storm had never been blooded, but this Saint Stephen's Day, Cynwulf, who claimed the stallion though he durst not get near him, insisted that he must be bled but gave the task to Harald instead of the thane's horsemen. Meghan heard of it from Myra after the Christmas service and at once sought Harald out, drawing him off to the cold north of the churchyard. "Why does Cynwulf want to get you lamed or killed?"

Harald grinned and shrugged. "Mayhap because I'm taller than he."

" 'Tis no matter for jesting."

"Would you have me sniffle and beg to be free of the chore?"

That would please Cynwulf but gain nothing. Meghan studied the sunken, unkept graves of suicides and notable unshriven sinners. "Between us, we could do it, Harald."

"And be called witches?"

"We could do it early before anyone stirs. When you bring blood to Cynwulf and he sees crusted blood on the cut, he can scarce fault you for doing his bidding. And if he makes you lay hands on Storm, you can do that in sight of all, taking any oath they like that there's no witchcraft in it."

His lips tightened but he turned it over in his mind. "I shall like not for you to mix in it. But 'tis a clever thought to do it before folks are abroad."

Cynwulf was watching them. Meghan said in a way that brooked no argument, "I will meet you in the river meadow about the time Storm begins to look like a horse, not part of the night. Make sure you keep the milt close under your arm. Have you a small sharp knife?"

"I'll borrow Gorm's. I helped with this last year, so I know how 'tis done."

Cynwulf was moving toward them, graceful and silent as a prowling cat. "Till morning then," Meghan said under her breath and quickly left the churchyard.

Storm flinched and stamped when the sharp small blade bit a vein in his neck, but he seemed to think himself stung by a bee or thorn from the tree near which they stood. Meghan soothed him with voice and hands while Harald held the clay pitcher. It took only a few minutes to have the blood that Cynwulf demanded. Then Harald put it to one side and pressed thumb and finger to stanch the wound and Meghan pressed on it a slice of the moldy apples strung in a corner to eat if she or Gran started a sore throat, or to press on cuts and bad burns.

"I'd like to see Cynwulf's face when you show him the pitcher," Meghan said.

"He'd like it better were I kicked to death. The sooner I'm gone from this village, the better. Else he'll think of some means to drag my head lower than his."

Gripped with fear, she caught Harald's arm. "Remember that you *are* going—that what he mocks and scoffs counts nothing. I pray you, Harald, bear you meekly."

"I have bit my tongue with him till I marvel I still have the use of it." Harald pressed her hand and took a swift kiss in the first pale light. "But have no fear. If I would live to claim you, I must dig my toes in dung and answer him with butter and honey.''

The blood had clotted. After they had caressed the horse and praised his patience, each went from the meadow by a different route.

Cynwulf would not believe Storm blooded till he saw the crusted nick on the smooth hide. Meghan, at the last, had not been able to keep away and had joined curious folk who followed the two young men to the river meadow.

''Show me how it is that you can get nigh him when none else may,'' growled Cynwulf. ''And swear may God strike you if you have used aught heathenish.''

Harald swore, his hand on the cross-piece of Cynwulf's ivory-handled dagger. Meghan prayed hard to Mary Virgin. *''Blessed Lady, 'tis from the tongue of the colt and a body's natural sweat. Can there be evil in that? Harald's mother is dead. Be you his tender mother; hold your hand over him!''* She cast about desperately for something to promise. *''You know we are poor, but guard Harald and I will cut off my hair and lay it on your altar.''* Meghan thought her long waving red-brown hair was the prettiest thing about her. Its rich luxuriousness did much to keep her from being too cast down at having no ribands or baubles.

The folk stayed well back while Harald approached Storm, who went on cropping as if in disdain of the creatures gawking from the hedgerow. The wind brought back Harald's croon. He walked with such easy confidence that Meghan thought he must have visited Storm before. The slightest pang of jealousy shot through her but she thought quick shame of that. 'Twas well if the horse and her lad were friends; it made neither less fond of her.

Her sigh of relief was lost in the astonished murmur of

the villagers when Harald stretched out his hand to
Storm, waited till the stallion snuffed at it and smoothed
and stroked the gleaming black hide.

Even from where she stood at the back of the group,
Meghan heard Cynwulf's strangled curse. He thrust his
dagger in his sheath and started forward. "Now, by Saint
Stephen's broken bones, shall a hurd-yed tame a horse
that I cannot?"

"Nay, young master," called Ulfric, hurrying after
the thane's son. "Hurd-yed or Christian's not to do with
it! 'Tis well known some have a gift for horses. Content
you—"

Cynwulf paid no heed, flinging his weight forward at
every step, carrying the pitcher of blood. While he was a
bow-shot distant, Storm whirled away. Breaking into a
smooth canter, he seemed to flow with the sea wind
along the high meadow and didn't stop till he was far
away.

Meghan couldn't hear what Cynwulf snarled to Harald, or Harald's response, but Cynwulf hurled the stallion's blood in Harald's face and struck him. Harald
smote back and a cry went up. That a slave should strike
the thane's son! The two grappled. Cynwulf's henchmen
ran forward, drawing knives, but before they could reach
the struggling young men, Ulfric had dragged them apart
and set his heavy body between them.

That blow couldn't be forgotten, though, a hurd-yed
bondman defying his lord. Cynwulf's comrades bound
Harald's arms with their belts and pricked him forward
with their daggers.

Blood matted his hair but Cynwulf was as smeared.
They looked a savage sight as they stopped before the
hedge. "These good folk can witness to my father how
you struck your master." Cynwulf spoke with difficulty,
for his lip was smashed and swelling. "You have earned
death. But I will speak for you to the thane if you do as I

have bade. Fetch yon beast and stay him while he's castrated. That, I think, will tame his fiery temper.''

Ulfric protested. "Young master, even if this stallion
can be thrown with ropes and held for cutting, it might
bring his death. He's no colt but in his prime."

"If I can ride him not, then let him die.''

"The thane may not be of your mind. The stallion has
sired enough fine colts to make up for his wildness.''

Cynwulf showed his teeth. "If he were wild to all,
well and good, Master Steward. But that he suffers this
pixie's hand and snorts at mine—that I will not bide.''

Ulfric said stubbornly, "Gelding so fine a beast is a
matter for the thane. And so, I wot, is what befalls this
bondman." Cynwulf glowered, but he knew, as all did,
that Eldrid valued his steward's rede.

"Then let us go," he said, "and hear my father's
judgment.''

Meghan stood at the back of the hall thronged with villagers as Eldrid heard his son, then stared at Harald with
light brown eyes. "A slave has no excuse for raising
hand to those above him. But plead what you will.''

"He struck me. No man has done that.''

"Then Gorm has been too sparing of you.''

Gorm pushed forward and knelt. "Ay, lord, that I
have. 'Tis my fault, not the lad's. But my good wife and
I—we have no child. We have loved this one well." He
gulped. "I pray you, master, punish Harald but grant his
life. I vow to lesson him in all the worship that he owes
you and your house.''

"Harald is no brawler," Ulfric put in. "He is diligent
in his tasks. This is his first mischance.''

Eldrid considered for a while. He had grown very stout
these last years; his skin was pasty and his straw-colored
hair was streaked with white. It was rumored that he had
upbraided Cynwulf more than once for acting as if he

were already lord. Pursing his small mouth, he spoke at last.

"You shall have mercy, slave, do you but prove chastened. You will fetch the stallion to the fallow field and there await my pleasure."

White about the lips, still smirched with blood, Harald asked, "My lord, will he be gelded?"

"By the rood, if I say it, he shall, and you also!"

Harald would have spoken but Gorm gripped him tight and cried, "Grant him this night, lord, to see his duty."

Eldrid's eyes gleamed and he chuckled. "Methinks we have here a slave unruly as that stallion. Easy it is to kill such but of more profit and glory to make them serve." He straightened, but even so his belly protruded beyond his chest. "Hear my word, Harald. You shall lie bound in the barn without food and water till you decide to bring hither the stallion or till you die."

Myra turned to Meghan, whispering through tears, "God be thanked! When the lad has time to cool, sure he will not die for a stallion's balls."

Meghan believed he would. But she comforted Myra as Harald was jostled past. As she murmured soothing, hopeful words, her mind flew from one side to another of the trap enclosing Harald and returned with the same answer. She must get him away while he was strong, and it were best he took Storm with him, not only for speed's sake but because the stallion might be punished in the man's stead. And she would give her love that other treasure, the hidden ancient sword.

The village gates were closed at night, but no guard was posted since there was no danger of Viking raids this time of year, and there had been, for a generation, peace with Wessex and East Anglia. No one was abroad as Meghan entered, for in these nights between Christmas and Epiphany, spirits wandered and the Wild Huntsmen thundered along on black stags and horses with their pack of brimstone-glaring hellhounds. Though she crept through the village in dread of discovery, Meghan was at least free now of the eerie terror that had gripped her with each howl of the wind as she prepared for Harald's escape.

While there was still some twilight, she had carried Granfer's old saddle and bridle out to the river meadow, showed them to Storm and slipped the bridle on him. He had champed at it and fidgeted, but she talked him to acceptance, led him to a log and climbed upon his back. He tossed his head nervously but he carried her about for a while. She had no time for more. If the stallion would let Harald mount him, that would be best. But if he wouldn't, she meant to coax Storm far from the village that night and leave him in the wilds, out of Cynwulf's reach.

She had tied to the saddle a bundle of Granfer's feast-day clothes, apples, bread and dried fish. It was a pity she couldn't ask Myra for cheese and meat, but Harald's kindly foster-parents must be able to swear they'd no part in his flitting. She took cloak and knife and went to fetch the sword.

Would the Viking's ghost seize her? Or the spirit of whoever had owned Heaven's Gift? Trembling with cold and fear, her scalp prickled at each snapping twig, each moan of the rising wind.

She crossed herself as she delved among the roots, whispered to thickening darkness which seemed full of watching presences. "Chieftain and you whose name I know not, I take this sword for Harald. If it may be, protect us in this night. Help him gain his own land."

Something touched her arm. She shrieked, nearly fainting, expecting to look into a skeleton face, but then she found 'twas only a branch of hawthorn, moved by a chill gust from the sea. She tugged Heaven's Gift from the entangling roots and fled across the meadow, daring not to look over her shoulder. Leaving the sword with the other things, she hurried to the village, keeping to shadows and backways till she reached the barn.

There was no watch on Harald. Who would trifle with Eldrid's will? But she flinched as the door creaked, thinking it must resound through the village. It seemed that someone must surely hear her pounding heart, which, in her own ears, muffled all other sounds.

There was no alarm. The doors stayed shut, and there was the glow of a fire or rush lamp through only a few windows sealed with oiled hides. Propping the door ajar, Meghan stole inside. There was a scurry of mice and she heard a stirring.

"Harald," she whispered, groping toward the sound.

"Meghan? What do you here?"

"I've come to get you away."

He was still a moment. Then he said, "I've no mind to catch you in this moil."

"None need know."

"Eldrid may blame Myra and Gorm. 'Twould ill repay all they have done for me."

"They can swear on the cross they knew not and are such pious folk that Eldrid must believe them."

"But if you're thought of—"

"Why should I be?" She laughed to give him heart, though she was clammy with cold sweat and her entrails twisted with fear. "Nay, Harald, Storm will be sped, too. The tale will get about, I trow, that the Wild Hunt took you both."

"But—"

"You must both be gone—best gang together!"

Feeling along his arms, she slipped the knife beneath the hide ropes and sawed them away before she freed his wrists and ankles. "Trussed like roast boar," he muttered, rubbing his feet. "We must take the ropes hence."

"And sweep behind us with straw till we're well away from the barn and our tracks mingle with all." She put Granfer's cloak about him and gave him the knife. Till now she had not really thought to manage this, but now hope filled her. Harald stopped her wild soft laughter with a kiss, and then they were away.

He drank deep at the brook. They scattered their sweeping straws as they walked, but she kept the ropes to add to Harald's bundle. Storm lingered near the things that held her scent and whickered as they made out his dark form against the night.

Meghan fed him an apple, rubbing her cheek against his, putting her arms around his neck. "Good-bye, beauty. I have loved you since you were born—such a little sprawly thing and look at you now!" She swallowed hard, overcome at losing both Storm and Harald at once. "Bear my love safely," she whispered.

Then she bade Harald breathe in the stallion's nostrils, caress him from muzzle to hoof, talking the while in a careless, gentle, teasing way as one beguiles a maid. Granfer had said it was much the same, that a man with skill for horses could win his way with any woman did she but let him speak and touch her.

The stallion danced a bit when Harald put on the saddle, but Meghan soothed him. She held Storm by his long thick mane while Harald clasped her to him, their embrace the only warmth in the chill blast. They cleaved together, her softer body molding to his lean one, their kiss so wild with yearning and grief at parting that when he tore himself away, it was as if their flesh had joined and was most cruelly severed.

"I'll come back for you," he said thickly. "Be sure, sweeting, I will come. If your gran bides so long, she shall sail with us."

He led Storm to a ledge and eased lightly into the saddle. Meghan handed him the sword. " 'Tis Heaven's Gift—and mine, too," she said. "My dear love, fare you well. If you cannot win back, I will not blame you, but I will love you all my life and pray for your good."

"If I do not come, pray for my soul as Christians do, though I hope these years of hearing mass will not bar me from Valhall, where my father feasts—and sure, my mother, too, for among us we deem a woman dead in childbirth should share the warrior's glory."

He bent again to kiss her. They clung for a moment. Then horse and rider moved away as sleet began to sting against her face, melt and mingle with her tears.

She cut her hair that night, to lay on Mary's altar.

V

Gorm and Myra were indeed questioned about Harald's disappearance, but they were so clearly amazed—and glad, in spite of the peril to them—that the thane must needs believe them innocent, even before Ulfric said that he had watched their door that night in order to stop them if they thought to free their fosterling, for he'd had no mind to lose so good a shepherd.

Some folk must have remembered that Meghan had once ridden the stallion and had saved Harald's life when the other Vikings were slaughtered, but it was not dreamed that a young maid, even had she dared demons and spirits abroad those nights, could have contrived such an escape. The priest said 'twas like the devil had taken the black horse for his own and borne the hurd-yed off on him—good riddance to both, for though he had prime-signed the youngling, never had the scamp come into full communion. The village was well quit of killer horse and pixie Dane.

When Meghan came to mass on Epiphany, though, Cynwulf overtook her in the churchyard and stalked her to the side, green eyes narrowed as he searched her face.

"Do you know how it is, Meghan, if one helps a slave escape?"

"How should I know such things?"

She tried to answer boldly though her knees turned to water. Then she heartened herself by thinking it was ten days since. Harald was well away. He might have to wait some months for a ship, but he could pass for Saxon, and in a busy port town, one more stranger would scarce be heeded. She'd had no single coin or jewel to send with him, but he was sure to find work enough to feed and lodge him. He wouldn't sell Storm, she was sure. If he couldn't take the horse with him, he would turn him free in some forest.

In spite of these thoughts, she grew afraid as Cynwulf's full red lips curved down in mockery and his gaze moved along her throat to where her mantle draped over her breasts. How could he make her feel so, as if he saw through her garments? Shamed heat rose to her face and he laughed softly.

"So shy a maid, Meghan? Yet you are fair, though you have shorn your curls."

"Young master, let me pass.

"Not till I've told you the dues I think you owe me." He was like a great cat toying with a mouse. "Who gives a slave a spear or sword, should that slave escape, owes the master half the slave's value. But to give a horse—oh, then, Meghan, needs must the guilty pay the slave's whole price."

"It pleases the young lord to jest."

She spoke coldly though her heart tripped so hard and fast she thought her tormentor must hear. What if he knew she had given a bondsman both sword and horse? He could not know; he only sought to plague her, trick her into unguarded speech. She started around him. He caught her wrist, passed his hand slowly up her arm beneath her cloak.

"Perchance others have not eyes, but I have marked how you and that Dane looked on each other. You saved him from me—the first man I might have killed—nigh three years past.''

''Oh, ay, 'tis a sad chance for certain, to be kept from taking a *lad's* life!''

''I am but a year or so the elder.''

''Still, 'twere no great deed, to slay a boy when all his friends were dead.'' Greedy fingers curved above her elbow now, brushing the side of her breast. She tried to wrench free. Failing, unwilling to make a scene in the churchyard, she hissed at him, ''And to have starved a man to death that would not tole you in a horse for gelding—that were scurvier yet!''

He gripped her brutally. His eyes had widened and the centers contracted to tiny black points. ''By God's wounds, 'tis a marvel to be chided by a Dane's bastard!''

She showed her teeth. ''Now are we back to when you named me that as a child—a spoiled vicious one you were and will ever be!''

''Children we are not.'' He laughed again, temper fading as he sensed her fear. ''Nay, Meghan, I will not claim the slave's price in goods and work—methinks you would needs become my bondmaid! But I will have a kiss of you the first time that we meet alone.''

Nicholas was coming toward them, broad face impassive though his mouth was drawn tight. Cynwulf let her go and turned to banter with the hayward about preparing for Plough Monday. Meghan returned Nicholas' greeting, avoiding his troubled eyes, and hurried away. If Cynwulf was bent on her, what could she do, alone with an old woman who drowsed mostly, or wandered through any year but these last ones? Storm and the sword were gone with Harald, the secrets that had given her pride and comfort. She bowed her head and sobbed in helpless fear. Oh, if only she might have fled with Harald! Even if he came again, what might happen to her first?

* * *

Gran fell ill a few days before Candlemas, fevered so that it seemed her frail, bleached body must wither to nothing. Sometimes she smiled and talked with her dead husband till Meghan glanced about and crossed herself. Or, when Meghan lifted her to pour gruel or water down her throat, Gran weakly clasped her hand and called her Maire, Meghan's dead mother's name. It had been long since Gran had been aught but a care, her mind straying uncannily from her childhood to the last times she was capable, but she was Meghan's only kin. It had seemed she would live forever. Now Meghan saw she was dying and felt it in the roots of her being along with a certain bitterness she could not chide away.

It was at Candlemas Harald had purposed to be gone; had he been able to tarry she would have gone with him once Gran was sped. If Gran had passed at Christmas— Oh, that was wicked! Meghan crossed herself and prayed and tended her grandmother with loving gentleness, but still she felt chance had played her a cruel joke.

She must fetch the priest before Gran's life flickered out, but the sick woman was so restless that Meghan feared to leave her. She was full of gratitude when Nicholas came on Sunday, thinking something was amiss since she had brought no candle to the mass for blessing. He sent the priest straightway and came back himself with Myra and Gorm. While the others knelt, Father Aiden prayed and then anointed Gran with oil on her eyes, ears, nose, mouth, on the backs of her thin hands and on her feet, covering the sins wrought by the senses, by hand and word and going aside from the right way, though indeed Gran could have sinned little since her last shriving. As the priest departed, he glanced about the bare, clean hut.

"It is not meet that a young maiden dwell alone. I will bespeak the thane, daughter, that he give you service in his hall."

Near Cynwulf? Meghan started to protest. It seemed Nicholas would, also, but Myra spoke quickly, crossing to take Meghan's hand in her gnarled brown one. "We would have Meghan bide with us if she will."

Gorm nodded. "Ay, we have already spoken on this, my good wife and I."

The priest shrugged. " 'Tis kindly done. And the girl should earn her bread, I trow."

He left then, with his serving lad, but the others watched with Meghan that night, taking turns to sleep a bit. It was Nicholas, toward dawning, who roused Meghan from a drowse. "She passes soon," he murmured.

Gran struggled now for breath. Rasps sounded in her throat. Meghan lifted her up. The old woman said, "Maire, my daughter . . . ," smiled waveringly and died.

In company with her old gossips, Gran lay in holy ground, where the sun fell warmly. Meghan did not think she would tarry in purgatory, for her life had been that these last long years. Even now, most like, she was with Granfer and Maire and all the blessed who joy in the smile of God. For all that, Meghan wept sore and often, more than she herself could understand.

True, Gran had been her only folk, and Meghan reproached herself for the persisting thought that had she died more timely, Harald would not have fared out alone. Feeling oddly useless, without reason to get through the days, though she helped Myra with all diligence, Meghan was comforted most by Jarl, Harald's patch-faced dog, who kept close by her and warmed her feet at night. He had almost starved himself after Harald left and even now seemed to listen for his step.

One Sunday before mass, Meghan brought some snowdrops to place on Gran's grave, Granfer's and her mother's. She knelt between raw mound and grassy ones, praying for their souls' bliss and wondering if she would lie beside them or if it might be she would find her rest by Harald in his far country.

Tears streamed down her face, as they did all too easily these days. She tried to cheer herself by thinking that Harald would soon be sailing toward his home—but oh! Much might befall. He could die or wed someone of his kin's choice and she never know it—though she could not think he would do that last, even to save his heritage.

"Nay now, Meghan." She started and wiped hastily at her eyes, rising to meet Nicholas. "Would you wish your poor gran back in so doleful a state? She has no pain or grief now unless she sorrows that you do."

Meghan saw his young wife's stone from the corner of her eye and thought he must have oft counseled himself thus. "You speak truth, Master Nicholas." Meghan swallowed and tried to smile. "I cannot wish Gran back, yet—she depended on me. Ever since I was a child, she has been my charge. I still am like to think I must hurry home and feed her or 'tis time to change her garments— and then I remember that neither she nor any needs me."

"Ay," he said roughly, eyes darkening with pity and something other. "A heavy burden have you borne all your years. The habit of nurturing is one hard to break— and 'twere ill you turned flighty and careless."

At that Meghan did have to chuckle faintly. He laughed, too, then colored to his light brown hair and looked her in the eyes. "You are young to wed, Meghan, but not so young as some." She stepped back, lifting her hand to ward off what she guessed he would say, but he spoke on doggedly. "Could you like me for a husband?"

"Master Nicholas!" He had been kind. Though the mason wouldn't say who had paid for Gran's stone, she was sure it was he. But marry him or any other she could not, even if Harald never came back. "You stand next to the steward and have your own land. I am no fit bride for you. There are widows of substance and maids well dowered—''

His mouth slanted down. "Think you I am not old enough to know my mind?''

"You do me too much honor.''

"I would do you honor before another does you less,'' he said grimly. "When your grandmother died, I thought to ask you even in that sad hour, for surely you must see the thane's son means you evil. Then Myra spoke and it seemed well you had some time for rest and thought.'' His smile was tender. Though he was not and could not be her man, that look sent trembling awareness through her. "But it seems you are too used to cares to thrive without them. A home of your own. A man to hold you . . .'' His voice deepened with laughter and her heart beat wildly. "Why, my Meghan, if 'tis cares you must needs have, I offer them in plenty!''

"I thank you for your kindness but it cannot be.''

"Kindness it is not.'' His look made her drop her eyes. "I had seen you had a softness for young Harald—and I never thought it was the devil took him—but you cannot pine your whole life. If there's one in the village that you like, I have not marked it, and I have watched you Meghan, more than you have known.''

She shook her head. "Nay, Master Nicholas, I have a mind to no one here.''

He set his hands behind him. "But Cynwulf has a mind to you. For fear of his father, he durst not debauch a virtuous wife, but an orphaned girl? Would you bring ruin on Gorm if he tried to protect you?''

That was a danger she had not thought on, though she knew Cynwulf had bastards by serving girls. It was rumored that more than one maid had given him what should have been her husband's, though it was not said he had used force. When the handsome thane's son flattered and wooed, it wasn't hard to see how a simple girl might be coaxed to yield.

Meghan spoke more bravely that she felt. "I scarce think Cynwulf would force even an orphan girl if she fought and cried out to make it scandal. Neither of us would be well served, Master Nicholas, if I wed you from fear of him."

Nicholas crimsoned but said hardily, "I do not say that Cynwulf would rape you in church. Still, many a lass has come to love the man who gives her her own hearth and holds her in his arms at night."

She could think of nothing to answer but gazed down at the pale white flowers wilting on the graves. Nicholas sighed. "I see 'tis early to talk of this. You are too heart-sore for your gran and maybe, too, for the Viking lad. But, Meghan, he is gone as sure as the Wild Hunt had swept him off. It boots not to yearn after what is lost."

His voice dropped on the last words and he looked to where his dead love lay. Meghan's heart was wrung for him. She knew not how to tell him that she could no more cheer his bed than that poor dead woman beneath the soil. She was glad that the sexton began to ring the bell for mass.

Thane Eldrid sickened during Lent. Gorm said he often did in order to be granted the flesh food he scarce knew how to live without. But when he grew no better after Easter and kept his bed, folk thought he must have the wasting illness that had devoured his grandfather and two uncles in their prime. The villagers neither hated Eldrid nor loved him. He was not cruel, he was not kind; he was the lord. Edmund, the younger son, was deemed to be like him. But Cynwulf—Gorm was not the only one to shake his head and frown.

He was nigh twenty. Many had heired their lands as young and made creditable thanes. But Cynwulf cared only for the hunt, of beasts and women. He was high of temper and used to having all his will, especially since his mother, a gentle lady who had ruled him somewhat, died two winters past.

"Were we at war, he might be worth something," muttered Gorm to Nicholas when the hayward had stopped one evening to ask how many helpers were needed for the shearing—and perchance, as Myra teased, to fill his eyes with Meghan. The chief shepherd drained his ale and squinted at Nicholas. "The best we can pray is that rash one fares off with horse and hounds and hawks and leaves the management of all else to you and Master Ulfric."

"I trow he will do that." Nicholas grinned. "Can you imagine him caring or knowing if the fields lie fallow in proper turn, or how they should be planted?" He lowered his voice. "I fear me, though, when he is lord, that few fair maids will go virgin to their husbands. The priest has not the backbone to gainsay him. 'Twill be, I ween, a swinish rule in the hall."

Myra glanced nervously at Meghan. "There are light wenches enough and lusty widows who throng to Cynwulf's beckon. 'Twere plain wickedness for him to seduce honest maids."

"It is the hunt," said Nicholas, jaw hardening. "He is such a one as glories in running down a free wild thing rather than poleaxing an unthrifty ox that cannot last the winter." The hayward's gaze touched Meghan. "Were I a pretty lass, I would make haste to wed me while Eldrid lives. Father Aiden, weak as he is, cannot blink at adultery, and even Cynwulf, so far as I know, has yet to harass a married woman."

When Nicholas was gone, Myra took Meghan's hands in hers and peered with earnest dark eyes into her face. "Meghan, you know we are blithe to have you with us.

But we dread what may chance. Nicholas is a most goodly, proper man.''

"Have you a mind for him,'' put in Gorm, leathery face earnest, ''we will make a feast for you such as had you been our daughter, and Myra will help you sew a fine bride dress.''

Meghan looked from one kind, worried visage to the other. She knew, without their saying, that they would protect her as well as they could against Cynwulf's constraint. But how could she bring ruin on these good people, who had fostered Harald, too? If it came to such a pass, she'd run away though that must dash what hope she ever had of seeing Harald unless she might somehow reach a port and earn passage to his country.

A terrifying thought, but it held a slender hope and raised her spirits enough to smile a little. ''Master Nicholas deserves a woman who can give him all her heart.'' She hesitated and then decided that she owed them the whole truth. No one was like to come seeking answers now of how Harald got away. ''I love Harald. We plighted troth while we were children.''

Myra paled. ''But Harald—who knows what's happened to the lad? Will you ask the Wild Hunt to carry you away?''

''Harald rode off on a black steed, right enough.'' Meghan laughed. ''It was not the devil's horse, but the stallion who grazed in the river meadow.''

''That one was the devil's beast!'' said Gorm and crossed himself. But Meghan twinkled at him.

''No, foster-father. I have known that horse since he was born. He has ever been my friend, and he grew Harald's, too.''

Myra started up in fright. ''Was witchcraft in it?''

''No more than in any horseman's ways—a thing my granfer taught me, and you know he was a Christian.''

"Ay." Myra took a breath of relief, but her eyes were big with wonder. "Tell us. How fared Harald forth?"

"I fetched him from the barn and had some few things ready in the meadow. He would seek a port and ship."

"But, lass, can you hope to keep that troth you plighted?" Gorm moved his graying head. "It joys us to know our foster-son rode with your love, not snatched by the dark huntsmen, but he cannot come back."

"He has sworn he will."

Both stared. Then Myra took her meaning and her face blanched. "Do you mean—as he came that first time? In a dragon ship?"

"He will not plunder. But long ago he swore to fetch me to his hall. If he lives, I believe that he will do it." Meghan's voice broke. "Except for Gran, I would have gone with him Saint Stephen's night. But you see why I cannot wed Master Nicholas."

Myra beamed in spite of her apprehension. "God send it falls out well for you two young ones." She sighed. "But we shall miss you sore, you both." Gorm clenched his bark-brown sinewy hands together.

" 'Tis better we should miss them, wife, than other things befall. Best pray that Eldrid tarries—and that Harald tarries not! It's been a mild winter. By God's grace, if all ran smooth, he might win back before the winter storms." Gorm's smile was crooked. "Now may I have no ale at Whitsun if I thought ever to hope to see a Viking ship thrust up the river!"

They all laughed but quickly sobered. None had to voice what ran in their thoughts, that much might befall before Harald might in anywise contrive to claim her.

On May Eve, many young folk frolicked the night away in the forest and brought in the May next morning with garlands and flowers. Meghan had never gone a-Maying, but since she was a child, she'd gone out before dawn to gather dew from the hawthorn flowers and wash her face with it. Gran had said it brought luck and beauty. She had a cup to fetch some home to Myra and was shaking leaves over it, when she heard horns winding and distant merriment as young folk trooped in from their revels.

Taking cover behind a hedgerow, she saw that Margit must be May Queen, for she bore a branch of flowering hawthorn and was garlanded with more of it. The May King was Ulfric's eldest son, Tam, a sturdy, dark-haired young man who could not stop kissing Margit. She kissed him back in a way that made it seem likely more than kisses had passed between them in the night. Among those who joked and urged them on was Cynwulf, who had a girl on either arm, kissing and fondling both at once while they laughed and tucked flowers in his hair. Meghan gasped. Had Eldrid been in strength, a son of his would never have sported in this way; how should a lord have respect and honor from his folk if he behaved so?

As if her shock pierced his jollity, the thane's son glanced toward the hedgerow, then stared. He loosed the girls and shooed them on when they would have waited. Meghan scarcely breathed and dared not move. Perhaps it was a bird he'd spied, or a hare. She felt a trapped creature herself, praying he would move on, but when the roistering procession was well ahead, he came straight to her. Meghan rose to face him but did not give back his smile.

"So here you are instead of helping us bring in the summer," he accused gaily. He noticed the cup. "Do you gather May dew? You need it not." His green eyes smiled into hers, though there was no warmth in them. "For sure, Meghan, you already are too fair to be as unkind as you seem."

"Such dew is good for health, as well as beauty." She had a sudden thought. "Pray take this to your father for his washing. At the least, he might be glad to think of the flowers it came from.''

''He has water enough.'' Cynwulf shrugged. He drew near the hedge. Meghan stepped back. ''What's this? You will not greet me with one kiss even on May morning?''

''You have had many kisses this dawn, young master.''

''Yet it is as none, since none was yours.''

She was glad the hedge was between them. ''My lord, these be not decent words from you to a village lass.''

He laughed softly. ''You, a village lass? Nay, you are a witch, riding that killer horse when you were but a child, slipping out on May morn to bathe in dew.'' His eyes burned over her. ''Rather would I have seen that than made free with scores of wenches.'' His golden brows knit. ''Why do you, of all, give me cold words and few?''

''In seemliness, little aught can pass betwixt us.''

She started along the hedge. He, on the other side, matched pace with her. ''More must pass. I cannot cease from dreaming on you.'' She said nothing but walked faster, hoping to be in sight of folk before there would be a gap in the hedge. He seemed to speak his thoughts aloud. ''That hurd-yed who sired you must have been a chief, you bear you so proudly though you have been poorest of poor, and butt of your age-mates' jesting. Meghan, I would do you such honor as I may but you know I cannot wed you with a ring at the church door.''

Startled that he would even think of it, she said quickly, ''Indeed, I know that.'' Bitterness edged her voice. ''I have never thought anyway to be wedded at this church where the hide of a man like my father frays on the door like a pegged beast's.''

''None here is meet to husband you.'' He took a long breath and said in a rush, ''Be my love, Meghan, and you shall have your own good house with servants and the best of all that is mine. I will treat you as my heart's wife, though one day I must marry to get lawful heirs. But your children shall have favor and advancement such as they could never win otherwise."

"Yet they would be bastards, even as I was—though that were no blame to my poor ravished mother."

He crimsoned. "And 'twould be blame for you?"

"Who'd call it else?"

His eyes glittered like shards of Rhenish glass. "Take care that you yield not as a bondmaid what you deny in such good will and fondness as I show you now."

"I am no slave."

"You owe me one for him you helped away." He smiled mockingly and his voice was hard again, not cajoling. "I think you have no other body to pay me but your own. It would go better with you, Meghan, if you came to me in love."

"That cannot be. I love you not, nor ever will."

Then it was well there was between them the broad thorny hedge. The black centers of his eyes swelled to cover the green and the curve at the back of each nostril showed white. "You're o'er-haughty, Meghan, with me that will be your lord. When you think well on what I've said, you may have a different answer."

He strode toward the village. As she took the way to the shepherd's house, her hand shook so she almost spilled the dew. Cynwulf was far more set on her than she had guessed. If Eldrid died, she must away, and quickly.

VI

Thane Eldrid had himself brought to Lammas service on a litter. His skin was like a rind of old cheese, and he was so fallen off in weight that the men hoisted him as they'd have borne a child. None thought he could live long.

Nicholas was Harvest Lord again. He asked Meghan to serve as second scythe. There were four or five women who reaped faster and better than she, so she refused, though she knew it was in his thoughts to raise her in the regard of the villagers. He was her trusty friend. Had she not loved Harald, she could have liked him well.

Three days past Lammas, all able-bodied folk were at harvest when the bell began to toll outside the accustomed times. Nicholas stopped, and as he crossed himself and prayed, so did the harvesters, for all were sure what must betide even before a lad came running from Ulfric.

The thane was dead. The steward bade them pray for his soul but go on with their labor. Those who would might wake with the corpse that night, but harvest must go forward, so the burial feast would be held on Sunday.

Everyone knelt and prayed for Eldrid. He had been thane as long as most could remember and people were used to him. "Better that Edmund were heir," muttered the man next to Meghan.

His wife answered, "Belike Cynwulf will leave the ordering of all to Steward Ulfric, and then will nothing change."

But for Meghan it had changed already. Cynwulf could do now as he would. Not even he would brazenly take a woman till his father was decently buried. Go she must, but it were witless to haste from the field this moment when it might cause remark or hindrance. That night, though, she must take herself far from the new lord's reach.

Nicholas overtook her as she wearily left the field at sunset. She stumbled. He caught her and did not release her hand but held it between his big round ones as if it were something precious he would fain protect.

"Plight me your troth, Meghan," he said urgently. "There can be no weddings till the thane is buried, but if we have made agreement, it is a covenant in the eyes of Holy Church; Father Aiden must stand between you and Cynwulf then, will he, nill he."

Sweated and grimed as he was, the hayward smelled of earth and harvest, a man laying up provision for the winter. He was solid and honest—real, not a dream, an impossible hope. Yet Meghan did not hesitate, though she dreaded the future.

"I told you, Master Nicholas. I love another."

He answered quietly, brown eyes steady. "I would not make you my true wife, little one, till 'twere your wish, too. You will ripen as grain does. I trust to that and the cheer we shall have together to win you in good time."

"It would not be fair—"

"Devil take fair and unfair!" His grasp turned bruising and he gave her a shake. " 'Tis the only way I see, lass, to keep Cynwulf from you!"

Meghan bowed her head and brushed his work-toughened hands with her lips. "I will not let you peril yourself so. God and His mother bless you for your care and bring you the woman you deserve."

She slipped away from him and hurried to her foster-parents' hut. A henchman of Cynwulf's, Brice, the feckless youngest son of the thane whose lands lay closest on the north, rose as she stepped inside the door. He had bold pale blue eyes, a chin set back to his throat nearly and was thin as a winter-starved nag, though it was said he was marvelous skilled in swordplay and second in the hunt only to Cynwulf.

"I have come to fetch you to your master's house," he said, showing yellowed teeth. He jerked his head toward Myra and Gorm. "I have told these good folk you owe both horse and servant to the thane. Unless you can pay the hurd-yed's price, Meghan, you must come up to the hall."

"None can witness to the new thane's claim," rumbled Gorm. He knotted his fists against each other.

"Will you dispute your lord?" Brice's tone was silky, but threat gleamed in it like a blade through woolen skeins.

Meghan's mind raced. She would not drag Gorm and Myra into her troubles, but if she could put Brice off—steal away in the night . . . Sun and hot work always made her dizzy and somewhat uneasy in the stomach. She didn't have to feign much to lean against the door and make as if to retch.

"What's this?" growled Brice, stepping away.

She sank down on a bench. "I—I am not well, sir. The heat and . . ." She hid her face as if ashamed.

"Is this true?" Brice demanded of Myra, who came to hold Meghan's head and wipe her face. "Is she in the way of women?"

"That she is," said Myra. "And an ill time she ever

has of it. No service will she be in the hall till this be past."

"Yet she worked in the harvest—"

"It came on me in the afternoon," Meghan said faintly. She began to retch again.

"Pfaugh!" Brice retreated outside. "I must learn Cynwulf's mind. What use a woman is in this state. . . ." He went off grumbling.

"Is it so with you?" Myra asked, bringing a beaker of water.

"I'm sick enough to think of going to Cynwulf. But no, I am not in my course." She knew men often slept apart from their wives at that time, half in fear, half in disgust. It gave her a desperate hope. "Myra, you know much of plants and herbs. Can you not give me something to make me ill in earnest?"

Myra stared before her face wrinkled deeper with amazed laughter. "Ay, few men can wreak their will with a maid vomiting on their shoon. 'Tis a rare good notion."

"Except she can't keep it up for long without ruining her health," put in Gorm.

"That's true." Myra frowned.

"Why should I go ill at all?" asked Meghan with sudden inspiration. "Why not make Cynwulf sick? Can you give me something, foster-mother, that will not taste in ale?"

After a dumbfounded moment, Myra said, "There is a smut that grows sometimes on rye. It can bring frenzy and delirium, or that great burning itch of the skin they call Holy Fire. A bit of the smut, if I can find some in the rye, would set the young thane's mind on things other than ravishment."

Gorm's head moved worriedly. "But if Cynwulf takes you to him unwilling and at once is stricken—'twill smack of poison, and child, uncanny rumors have been noised about you before.''

"I will swear by anything they ask that I am not a witch. It cannot go on long, this dosing Cynwulf. I have no mind for murder. But he may grow frighted with his wickedness, thinking God sends his ills, or it must surely chance that I can get away unless he shuts me in a prison room.''

He took his first step toward this by sending a retainer with the message that the thane's bondmaid need not come to the hall till she was in health, though she would be borne thither if her legs couldn't carry her, after Thane Eldrid's funeral. This burly man-at-arms made himself an unwelcome guest, so that Meghan could not help Myra but must needs lie on the bench. That night, he stretched out in front of the hut.

Thane Eldrid's bier was borne to the church in the direction that the sun moves for it was bad luck to go withershins. Meghan did not go to the service with Myra and Gorm, but after they were gone awhile, she told the guard that she thought she was able to go to the hall and would liever walk there on her own than be fetched.

The burly, scar-faced man yawned and scratched himself. "Then let's be on our way, girl. But first give me a loaf and another of the good wife's cheeses.''

If only to stop his fattening from Myra's and Gorm's food, Meghan was ready to face whatever might chance in the hall. Best have an end, however it fell out. After she fed the guard, she made a bundle of her few belongings, carefully tucked in the bit of linen Myra had wrapped around the fragile brown rye smut and started for the village, the retainer crunching and munching at her heels.

* * *

The hall was emptied for the burial, though preparations for that evening's final feast had begun. Meghan paused at the odors and turned to her warder. "As you know, I've been too disordered to eat but the walk has bettered me. I hunger. May I find myself a morsel?"

"Why not?" The other grinned. " 'Tis certain Cynwulf wants to bed no skeleton. I myself could fancy part of an eel." With the knife he wore at his side, he speared an eel stewing in its own juice out of the pot and cut off half of it, eating with relish as the juice dripped sputtering on the coals. Meghan filled a bowl with frumenty and honey, found a horn spoon and ate so slowly that her guard said impatiently, as he wiped his hands on his tunic, "Come along. You can finish your nibbling in the thane's room."

Dread twisted through her. "Nay, shall I not lodge where the servingmaids do since the thane will have it I'm a slave?"

The scarred man grinned. "You know well 'tis not to turn the spit or change bed straw you've been haled here. The thane's brother has the bed closet in this room, but Cynwulf sleeps aloft." The retainer laughed hugely. "If can be called sleep the sport he makes there."

Outside stairs led to the upper chamber, which was low on the sides, but the center pole was high enough for the tallest man to stand beneath. Walls and ceiling were richly tapestried or draped, carpets and furs softened the floor. Weapons, mail and hunting gear leaned against the wall or were stowed under the eaves. A silver candlestick stood on a great carved chest. Clothes were tossed carelessly here and there amid bones, dirty dishes and half-drunk beakers.

A bed filled the middle of the loft, a little straw showing beneath coverings of fine linen, wool and bearskins. The room put Meghan in mind of the lair of a beast. The guard leered at her and the bed, sighed resignedly and said, "I will bide at the door till the thane comes. But first let me gather up these toys lest you prick your pretty fingers."

He took swords, spears, daggers, a battle-axe, even the feathered arrows, and bore them out with him. Meghan sat near a small window which spilled light into the luxurious den. She ate a few more spoonsful of the gelatinous honied wheat and then stirred in the smut. If she couldn't lure Cynwulf to eat, she'd swallow it herself.

She couldn't keep from shrinking under the eave when he called to the guard and ran up the steps. Sun set his hair ablaze as his eyes swept the loft, settled on her and gripped like the talons of his hawk.

"Huddled there like a coney!" He laughed and drew her up but frowned at her unkempt hair, dirty face and the stained dress she had worn for harvesting. "By Cuthbert's otters, you cared not how you came to my hall, Meghan."

"A bondmaid needs no feast decking, lord, to scour pans and empty slops."

"You recked right well 'twas not for that I called you! Holy Saints, your hair is knotted as an old cow's tail and your face smudged as a blacksmith's. Had I never seen you before—" He cocked his head and laughed deep in his throat. It seemed the purring of a great cat. "You cannot put me off in this wise, pretty! Women shall tire you for the feast where I will break the fast I've held for my father's sake, and after that my long fast for you shall end."

"My lord fasts? But sure, this little dish of frumenty—"

"I like it not." He released her, caressing her hip and back as if she were already his. "This night I shall have meat and Rhenish wine—and you."

He stepped out to shout at the serving women. Meghan

prayed Mary Virgin not to let her die, and ate the smutted frumenty.

Edmund liked it no better than Meghan that Cynwulf made her sit by him and drink from his horn. She could not eat the tidbits he pressed on her, though. She was truly ill, either from the smut or the shame of his watching as he lay among the bearskins while women washed her hair and body, anointed her with scented lotions and clad her in fine garments. They combed out the mass of red-brown hair that curled into ringlets as it dried. Then he sent the women out. She trembled, but when he drew her down beside him, he only toyed with her hair and stroked her without disordering her clothes.

"Do you not see, Meghan, that I love you well and would have your friendship?" He kissed her and rose. "Think on it, sweetheart. 'Tis not so sad a fate, to be the thane's love."

"I would rather be your lowest scullery maid and sleep among the hounds!"

His eyes glittered. "Best you learn courtesy, Meghan. Do not, and I will use none. That could go ill for you."

He had gone out then and she hadn't seen him till he had her brought down for the feasting. Before that, she thought the rye smut worked in her, for her flesh crawled and tingled, she began to burn and it was all she could do to keep from scratching madly at herself. Was she badly poisoned? Would she die? The worst would be that she'd never see Harald again.

Candles wavered before her and so did the hall and everything in it, the people rimmed with rainbows, the hearthfires curling into serpents. One writhed toward her— No, it was Nicholas, craving the thane's leave to speak.

It was granted. The room steadied a bit for Meghan as

she looked into the hayward's eyes. A warning there? A plea?

"I fear me, lord, that something is amiss," said Nicholas clearly. "Beside you sits my handfasted maid." Edmund looked up eagerly and Father Aiden rubbed his chin, but Cynwulf flushed. " 'Tis the first I've heard of it," he said tightly. "But it boots not. She is my bond-maid and cannot marry without my leave."

"Then, lord, I beg you let me pay her worth."

Cynwulf made as if to joke. "Nay, Master Hayward, have you made yourself rich from looking to my fields and cattle?"

Nicholas did not smile. "The thane must know that I have a freeholding, sheep and a few cows."

"Keep your mangy beasts," began Cynwulf, but Edmund protested, "Brother!" and Father Aiden cleared his throat. "My lord, with handfast couples—sometimes it goes that neither can in good conscience ever wed another."

Cynwulf paled. His nostrils swelled and he whirled to Meghan. "Be you handfasted to this man?"

A way out. But she could not cause Nicholas to forfeit his estate and the thane's favor. Through weaving delusions and towering flame-edged creatures, she gripped the edge of the bench and spoke in a voice she meant to carry through the hall. If she were dying or running mad, at least she would declare her love first and let it rest on Cynwulf if he denied her plighted troth.

"I am handfasted, but not to Nicholas. Harald, the Dane, and I have sworn to wed each other."

"Harald—the hurd-yed?" "The pixie lad?" "But Satan bore him off on that black devil horse!" Cries and murmurs ran round the room.

Cynwulf gripped Meghan's wrist. "So you did help him get away!" he said under his breath, then called above the uproar, "Mayhap the Dane bewitched an honest maiden. But he is gone—"

"Nay, he is here."

Silence fell. From the back of the hall strode a tall man. Meghan cried out with recognition even before Harald threw back his hood. Her distorted vision spun webs of gold about him and the dozen fair-haired giants in mail coats who stood at the entrance with swords and battle-axes. She stared at the sheathed sword Harald had at his belt, and it shone with white blinding light. Heaven's Gift.

Standing before Cynwulf, Harald said, "I have come for my bride."

Cynwulf sneered. "And to pillage, belike!"

Harald laughed as at a peevish child. "My men are sworn to peace on this voyage unless it needs be otherwise. Give me my lady and not a single hen will be missing. But I have a score more stout fellows outside."

Edmund said, "Sure, brother, there's no choice. Give him the wench!" But Cynwulf heaved up, face ridged with fury, dragging Meghan up.

"He shall not have you!" The jeweled dagger flashed before Meghan's eyes. Then she heard a singing sound, and the hand that grasped her loosened. Heaven's Gift had gone through Cynwulf, held him for a second against his high seat, before his weight tore it free. Harald wrenched the trestles aside and caught her in his arms as all blazed up and she slipped into blackness.

Blood seethed in her as if she'd been hollowed out and filled with molten lead. Her thirst could not be quenched. When her brain cleared a space from visions, she was aware of a gentle rhythmic motion.

"Your ship . . ." she panted to Harald.

"Yes." His cool hand smoothed her face, and she ached for the fear in his eyes though he spoke cheerfully.

"My kinsmen were faithful men, right glad to give me all my rights when I fared home on Storm from Hedeby. Many sailed with me to claim you, though they knew there'd be no prize but you. Glad am I that only Cynwulf fell." Harald held her close. "Why did you take the poison?"

"Cynwulf would not." She tried to smile. "I hoped only to be sick enough to give him disgust of me—but thought if I should die, 'twere better than lying in his arms."

"It's driven Myra near wild to think you drank the stuff she meant for him."

"Myra? I have dreamed she tended me."

"Not dreamed." He laughed tenderly. "She and Gorm chose to come dwell in my hall. And look, 'tis Jarl, craving to lick your hand."

"Good Jarl." She let her hand rest on his head and drifted into sleep.

In a few days, she could eat, and Myra took the bandages off her hands that had kept her from clawing herself. Gorm was so seasick that he vowed never to set foot off solid land again, but once Meghan began to mend, she felt no qualms, so that Harald laughed and said it was her Viking blood. She slept with her head on his shoulder in the pavilion rigged for her on the deck and he stroked and kissed her fondly but left off when she moaned and went soft and eager, wanting him.

"Nay, love," he whispered. "We will hold our wedding feast so all know you come as wife, not captive, and nobles' wives shall deck our marriage bed." His voice dropped even lower as she quivered beneath his long, sure hands. "Also, you must be well and strong before our child roots in you—mayhap a lad to carry Heaven's Gift and ride a son of Storm's."

And so they waited. Perhaps in greater happiness than if they had taken all, for there was still that to be longed for. On a bright nooning, the warriors oared and sang their way to shore. Meghan threw her arms around Harald's neck as, Jarl splashing beside them, he carried her ashore. She knew she had come home.

Book III
The *Fylgya*
Sweden
970

I

The incised, red-painted runes on Kati's mother's stone proclaimed that "Ragnfrid was the most skillful woman in Uppland." Folk still praised her ale and fine weaving. Her husband's pillar said, "Olaf fared south. He fed eagles with his foes but died himself in Serkland."

Old Gyrd, Kati's grandfather, often lamented that had he insisted Olaf bear Heaven's Gift, the heirloom sword given Gyrd at their wedding by his beloved first wife, a Danish lady, their son would not have fallen in those southern countries whence came spices and silks. Ragnfrid had been taken by a fever the year after Olaf's comrades returned without him. Kati remembered neither of her parents, though she sometimes dreamed of being rocked and sung to in a sweet voice. That sweet voice, that kindness was never that of Thorhild, her aunt and foster-mother.

Thralls whispered that Thorhild was so sour her babes died young from being pickled in her womb. Sigyth, her husband, a prosperous merchant, was usually away on trading voyages, exchanging furs, amber, and hide ropes for the luxuries of Serkland, so Thorhild's formidable energy went into running the estate on the mainland across from Birka, the great trade city.

"You act as if you'd just come out of the mountain, girl," Thorhild would scold when Kati snarled the wool she was carding into a hopeless mass or burned the bread or poured yeast into the ale before it had cooled enough. "You must know how to do better than your serving women or you will be a mock to them and your house will fall to disorder."

Kati tried harder after these outbursts but such work was dull compared to Gyrd's tales of distant lands and roistering adventure and, best of all, stories of those who had owned Heaven's Gift, especially her great-grandparents, Harald and Meghan.

Lacking a grandson, when the old Viking came to live with his daughter, Thorhild, much to her disgust, he had taught Kati the skills learned by boys of free families—shooting with bows and arrows, fighting with sword and shield, throwing spears, jumping, running, skiing and skating. The two companioned each other. As long as Gyrd lived, Kati had been happy when with him; but last winter, when Thorhild was upbraiding her for some mischance, the old chieftain had shaken his white-streaked yellow hair.

"You rule your household with a harder hand than ever I used on my ship when I went a-viking."

Thorhild, her single beauty of waving red hair knotted tight beneath her white linen coif, moved so the keys at her broad waist gave an impatient jangle. "Belike, father, had you not been such a boon drinking companion and giver of gifts, you would not now feed at your son-in-law's table."

Gyrd flinched as if struck by an invisible shaft. Then he said slowly, painfully, "You know well, daughter, that I gave your Sigyth his first ship and cargo. Never has he bespoken me with aught but friendship and reverence."

Thorhild colored to the edge of her prim coif. "Nay,

father, you know that you are welcome! Forgive me, only understand that I am sorely tried. This girl is in my charge, but you are turning her into a regular Valkyrie! What good is such a one at the loom or in the brew-house?''

She whisked off hastily to see if the cloth she was dye-ing had reached the right hue. Gyrd gave himself a shake as if waking from a strange dream. His drooping shoulders straightened, and he roared after his daughter, ''Those dried-up dugs of yours might as well have been on a wild boar! You're such a troll that I swear 'tis you, not Kati, who was changed at birth by Those Who Dwell in the Mountain!''

At Kati's scared look, he embraced her bearishly and said, ''The sword is yours, lass. Guard it well, for you are the only hope I have of this family!''

''Grandfather—''

The clumsy caress of his horny palm tangled the heavy fall of wheat-colored hair that he said was like her mother's and grandmother's, though her eyes were not blue like theirs but had the warm sheen of amber.

''If I have done you wrong in teaching you as I did Olaf, forgive an old man, my Kati. These last years, you have been my joy.'' She clung to him and he gently released himself, smiling as he raised her chin and looked long into her eyes. ''Don't weep, child. My old companion, Trygve Eyolfson, has long asked me to share his hall. Best I go thither. But never fear, my lass, I shall come to your betrothal and to your wedding feast.'' He winked prodigiously. ''And I'll drink to your son's health when water's poured over him.'' Till this was done, or till a child was given suck, it could be exposed to die of cold or thirst, the usual fate of deformed babes or those born to poor folk in lean times.

Gyrd set forth on his skis that very day, propelling himself with a pole as agilely as any youth, but he was

never seen again. Thorhild wailed guiltily when her messenger to Trygve brought word that her father had not
reached him. She vainly sent out searchers, and it was decided he must have fallen into a great fissure along the
way.

Kati was sure it had been no accident. She was grim
and still with Thorhild, but at night, huddled in the loft
with her cat, Scota, she cried herself to sleep.

She was as relieved at Thorhild then, when she was
chosen to serve Frey in the famed temple at Uppsala.
When a new priestess was needed, a delegation searched
all Sweden for a maiden of beauty and intelligence. Frey
shared the temple with Thor and Odin, but he was best
loved of all Swedish gods, for he brought fertility to
earth, animals and humans, and it was under Frey's
Peace that outlawed men found sanctuary on the temple
grounds.

Each ninth year, for nine days, a man and male beast
of each principal kind was offered and their bodies hung
in the sacred grove. This sacrifice took the place of the
king's death, for Frey himself had been a king who died
for his people, and after him, kings were sometimes slain
for the good of the land.

Kati felt more devotion to Frey's sister, Freya, who
loved cats and traveled in a chariot drawn by them as she
searched earth and heaven for her lost lover, weeping
tears of gold. Freya and Frey were children of Nerthus,
or Niord, and both blessed fields and the generative fury
that brought together all living things.

"It's well you'll be the god's wife," Thorhild sneered,
"for you could never manage the household of a mortal
man and keep him clothed and fed. Frey's image is marvelous, they say, and able to speak, but you won't have
to fill his belly nor must he needs spew out your wretched
brewing."

Being rid, with honor, of a freakish and unhandy niece

dissolved Thorhild's stinginess. She feasted Frey's messengers royally and delved into chests to outfit Kati with chemises of wool and pleated linen; gowns of red, leaf-green and blue, the red one with richly embroidered sleeves so wide and flowing they hung almost to the ground; shoes and hose; a pair of gold brooches with a festoon of amber beads to hang between them when they were fastened above each breast; and two cloaks, one of red silk for summer and a thick shaggy woolen cloak from the Western Isles.

Kati was delighted to be given her mother's best girdle, wool worked in gold and silver roses with a purse of the same pattern hung from it along with a jade-handled knife and carved ivory needlecase that held the bronze needles Ragnfrid had used. Though she knew her aunt's generosity sprang in part from not having to dower her, Kati was grateful enough to bid her a seemly farewell and give thanks for her fostering.

She would have preferred to ride like Aun, the big bald-pated priest who was in charge of the delegation, but he insisted that she travel in an elaborately carved and painted sledge drawn by a pure white horse. Tucked in among silk cushions and furs, Heaven's Gift scabbarded and wrapped in the scarlet cloak, Scota nestled against her with sapphire eyes peering inquisitively over the sables, Kati waved a last good-bye to her aunt and the household folk and turned her face eagerly toward the north and her new life. She didn't want to marry anyone, but if she must, a god was less likely to mind her deficiencies.

It was early summer. Through freshening leaves of alder thickets, fed by springs and melting snow, the river sparkled, rushing like an impatient lover straining to reach his beloved. Young corn almost hid rich brown plowland, and meadow grass dipped and swayed softly to the wind's wooing beneath slopes yellow with wild mustard. Haze softened the hills. Anemones made wine-red carpets beneath the birches and apple orchards were in lacy white bloom.

Though the sledge runners slid with more ease than wheels could have through the mud, the horse was splattered to withers and haunches; and though thralls groomed and grained him when the four horsemen stopped to rest their mounts, he was soon so splashed and smeared that it was hard to guess his color. The high sides of the sledge protected Kati from most of the mire, but she would have preferred to ride the horse and spare him the sledge's weight.

They stopped that night at one of the king's many estates and were feasted by the steward, Kati being given the closet-bed where the king slept when he progressed from one holding to another with his court. The sheets were silk but the bed straw was musty and crumbled. Kati had a much better rest the next night at a big farm where herbs sweetened thick grass beneath the bedding and the pillows were plump with feathers.

Kati sighed when Aun told her it was three more nights to Uppsala and the next two would be passed wherever they found shelter, for their way now stretched through a wild, forested region, little traveled except by woodcutters and hunters.

The pines grew so thick and tall that the light that reached the mat of slushy needles was faint as if filtered through water. Kati pulled the furs closer about her and Scota, whispering to the cat's wondering meow of complaint, "Never mind. We'll be out of the forest tomorrow, and in Frey's temple there must be many crannies to explore and lots of ledges where you can sun yourself."

As if returning the comfort, Scota gave Kati's hand a few licks with her rough tongue, yawned and settled into a dozing ball of gray-violet softness. Kati beguiled the monotonous miles by remembering the tales Gyrd had told her of Heaven's Gift, the women who had held it in trust, the men who had wielded it. Would she ever find a man worthy to use it? Much rather would she have been Gyrd's grandson and worn it at her own side.

It was the time of year when the sun set late. Its light blended with dusk to glow in a deep blue twilight that lasted far into the night. This closed in about the travelers before they reached the abandoned wood-cutter's hut where Aun had said they'd stop.

Kati drowsed, cheek against Scota, who had nestled against her shoulder. She was suddenly roused by a violent jerk of the sledge, shouts and the clash of steel.

It was like waking into a nightmare instead of dreaming into one, which for a moment she thought she had done. One of her escorts lay still, blood pumping from a severed arm, Aun had been dragged from his horse and the other two servants were fleeing as fast as their mounts would go from the brigands who had swarmed out of the trees.

Ignoring Aun's threats and the dying man, a dozen robbers closed in around the sledge. Two restrained the white horse while others hacked away at the harness.

A squat, heavy-shouldered man laughed as he came close enough to see that Kati was a woman. "Look what we have, comrades! A pretty little bird in a furry nest!"

"She is Frey's!" squealed Aun. "And I am his priest! Have you no fear of the gods?"

"Not a nail-paring's worth of fear," growled the other. "Especially since neither of you will live to accuse us. Lads, before we sport with Frey's wench, shall we see who can send a spear through this croaker's thick body?"

The men holding the priest let him go and joined the ring around the wretched man who sank to his knees, calling on Frey. No one was watching Kati. As the robbers jeered and feinted with their spears, tormenting their captive, Kati freed Heaven's Gift from its scabbard, drew her knife and put Scota to one side. It was to Freya she called, not to Frey, as she struck the leader down and sprang in front of Aun, shearing off one brigand's hand. It fell, still grasping a spear.

Shouting, Scota beside her, she advanced on the nearest enemy. He cried, " 'Tis Freya herself! See her cat?'' He took to his heels. The others were not far behind, even the wounded one, who ran as he twisted a belt around his stump.

Kati howled after them for a way, brandishing the sword, which seemed as light in her hand as if it propelled itself. She even thought it sang, like the highest note of a harp, and she seemed to hear Gyrd laughing.

As the battle fury ebbed, she was seized with a wild glee over so many sturdy thieves fleeing a girl and a cat. Leaning against a tree, she laughed till her sides ached. Deciding there'd be no more trouble, she picked up Scota, who was rubbing against her leg, protesting the whole unseemly brawl with indignant mewling.

"Well," said a voice behind Kati, "I thought you a Valkyrie, or Skadi, the huntress wife of Nerthus. But you laugh as my sister did when she bested me in a game."

Turning slowly, sword ready, Kati stared at the tall man, who could have disarmed her from behind. Burning at her carelessness, she demanded, "If you're not a thief, why didn't you help us?"

"When I heard swords clang, I came fast as I could, but you had already put the rogues to flight." He spoke with an accent she took for Norwegian. In the strange azure light, she saw a lean face framed by black hair. Dark eyebrows arched above deep-set eyes that seemed to be blue or gray, though they borrowed the color of the twilight as well. Sobering, he bowed. "If you must rely on yon trembling priest for protection, though, it were best you let me see you out of the forest.''

Rankled at his patronizing amusement, Kati tossed her head. ''How do we know you're not a robber?''

His teeth flashed whitely. ''Robber I am not, unless you call all men of Norway robbers.''

''Why have you left your own land?''

He was silent for a moment, then said curtly, ''Let it suffice 'twas not for murder or maiden rape. Whether you will or not, I shall see you to a main-traveled road.'' His voice dropped. ''No matter that you grip that sword like one of Odin's maids and laugh when you should sob with fright, I take you for mortal—and very woman.''

Before she could retort, Aun's tremulous cry reached them. ''Kati! Kati Olafsdotter! Be you living?''

''All's well,'' she called and hurried back to where he had sunk down on the sledge.

He huddled in his fur-lined cloak while the stranger leaned over the dead servant and robber. ''Shall I bury these among the rocks, priest?''

'' 'Twould be well done of you.'' Aun got shakily to his feet. ''The others?''

The black-haired man chuckled. ''They took the lass for Freya, or at least a *fylgya*, a family sword spirit. They won't be back.''

''All the same, it would show piety for you to see us safe to Uppsala,'' pressed Aun. ''As you see, one of my men is slain and the other knaves fled.'' At the next discovery, he wailed. ''They had our provisions in their saddle packs!''

''I have some food,'' said the stranger. ''Tomorrow I can fish for us if we reach no dwelling.''

''Then you'll take us to Uppsala?''

''With the greatest pleasure.'' The man gave Kati a cool smile that made her grit her teeth. ''I had stopped at a hut a little farther on when I heard the fray and Valkyrie whooping. Do you proceed and keep the fire going while I bury these men.''

Kati took off the hammer of Thor necklace that she wore and slipped it over the head of Frey's slave. ''May you feast this night in Valhall,'' she whispered.

''Slaves go not thither,'' sniffed Aun.

''He was brave.'' She gave the priest a look that made him shrink in spite of his bulk. ''All gods love the brave.'' She took the headstall of the sledge horse and led him forward, Heaven's Gift still in her hand.

When they fared forth next morning, Kati insisted on leaving the sledge in the hut and riding the white horse, using the saddle of the dead servant whose horse carried their belongings. Eirik Haakonson easily controlled his blood-bay stallion with the new sort of bit and bridle copied from the Magyars, those fierce hordes that had taken over much of eastern Europe and were pressing against the Germanic kingdoms. He used Hungarian stirrups, still scarce in the northern countries.

In daylight she saw he was older than he had seemed by dusk. Lines were graven at his mouth, and small ones showed at the edges of his fjord-blue eyes when he smiled, which he did often, for in spite of the way they had met, he treated her with no more seriousness than he did Scota. When the road permitted, he chatted knowledgeably with Aun about Kiev where he had traded with Swedish merchants, and of Byzantium, that fabled city where Northmen served in the Emperor's guard. From the easy way he spoke of Norway's noble houses, it was clear he came from one of them.

True to his word, he caught fish for them that night. He said nothing when Kati charred them, though he smiled in an aggravating way. But Aun spat out the burned bits and made a face.

'' 'Tis well the high priest, Hedin, will not have to eat

your cooking, girl, or I would soon be hunting for a new priestess.''

Eirik laughed. ''If Frey mislikes this battle maid, for sure she must serve Odin.''

''Nay, she is Frey's,'' snapped Aun. ''If she suits him not—or Hedin, which comes to the same thing—the god's wife may early go to join him.''

A chill shivered down Kati's spine. She knew that occasionally virgins sacrificed more than their maidenheads to Frey, but till she heard Aun's sinister words, she had not dreamed that could happen to a priestess. Aun sensed her shock and gave her a thin-lipped smirk.

Mastering her fear, she smiled disdainfully. ''A strange worship must it seem to Frey, sending him a wife he does not want. I had rather sup with Freya.''

Aun's small dark eyes bored into her. ''You have been chosen. You are Frey's forever.''

She laughed though dread gripped her as she understood, with a sensation as if the ground had given way beneath her, that what she had deemed deliverance from Thorhild's dour chiding meant that her very life depended on the favor of this Hedin.

If he was like Aun . . . Eirik was watching her with an unreadable expression. She turned so he couldn't see the trembling of her lips.

The temple lay outside the city, surrounded by a grove of mighty ash trees and many fields and farms that supported the service and splendor of the three great gods. When they paused at the road to the temple, Aun started to thank Eirik for escorting them.

The Norwegian raised a disclaiming hand. ''Nay, priest, I will seek my thanks in taking sanctuary under Frey's Peace.''

Aun's jaw sagged and Kati stared in amazement. ''You are outlawed?'' demanded Aun.

"A small disagreement with my cousin and king." Eirik shrugged.

"It must have been more than small to send you into Sweden," Aun retorted.

Eirik grinned hardily. "The upshot came to more than words, but when his temper cools, our boyhood friendship will count for more than his royalty-swollen head. However, to keep him from doing something he'd repent, I thought it well to go a-journeying."

"Ay," grumbled Aun. "Every outlaw and traitor in Norway takes refuge in Sweden!"

"Call you me traitor?" Eirik's hand was on his sword. No hint of laughter softened his taut-angled face.

"I spoke not of you," said Aun pettishly. "And Frey shields all, can they but reach his temple."

He reined his horse, and all three rode along the thoroughfare that led through flowering orchards to giant trees girding the huge edifice of staves, its doors and windows carved and brightly painted, the many gables ending in dragons' heads like the prows of ships. Parts of bleached skeletons dangled in the grove, though not from the biggest tree, a great ash that towered above the temple. Kati tried not to look at them.

Thralls hurried to hold their horses. Eirik swung from his saddle and lifted Kati down. Hard-muscled hands pressed hers and the blue fire of his eyes lit singing flame within her so that she felt strange and dizzied as if she'd been long in the warmest sun drinking strong wine.

"Farewell, my *fylgya*," he said so that none else could hear. "I will not be far away."

A resonant voice behind them said, "It is not well for mortal man to touch the god's wife."

They both turned. A silk-garbed man whose regal bearing made him seem taller than his middling height watched them keenly from eyes as polished a dark green as the jade Kati's uncle brought back from Serkland. He had moist red lips, an outthrust jaw, and glittered with gold from jewel-studded fillet to the gold-embroidered bands edging his green mantle.

Eirik's face hardened but he inclined his head. "Forgive a stranger seeking shelter under Frey's Peace."

"Sanctuary must be granted to all who reach this place." The voice was the most evenly beautiful that Kati had ever heard. "But you must earn your keep or pay for it. Have you brought gold?"

"None I wish to part with. But I am a rare hand at shoeing horses."

"Our blacksmith can use your help." The man who could only be Hedin nodded, then turned a freezing stare on Aun. "Where are the servants? Where is the priestess' sledge?"

"Noble Hedin," stammered Aun, "we were set upon by robbers. The servant who fought was killed and the others ran away."

"Then, in Frey's name, who delivered you?" Hedin's lip curled. "I know that you did not, soft hulk that you are. Was it the stranger?"

Aun sent Kati and Eirik a warning glance. Such a rescue spared his pride more than admitting a girl had fended off the thieves. "You have the right of it, Holy One. We left the sledge because the priestess preferred to ride. She is fair, but by the gods of the grove, she had better been a man."

"Then why did you pick her?"

Aun said bitterly, "My lord, these six months have I traveled the land, but all the comely maidens were betrothed. The unbetrothed ones were such trolls they would send Frey's wrath upon us and make his worship a laughingstock to all who saw one."

Hedin scanned Kati head to toe as he might have a

beast brought for offering. In his manner there was not a trace of the man-woman awareness that Kati unconsciously expected to cause in any man from her indulgent uncle to thralls. Hedin was a glittering hardness protecting a core of power. His slash of a mouth curved slightly.

"What is your name, girl?"

"Kati Olafsdotter."

"No longer. Henceforth you are Frey's wife and his priestess." His gaze caught on the edge of the scabbard showing beneath her cloak. "Can that be a sword?"

"Yes. It has been long in my family."

"You have no family, only your husband-god. Swords and weapons may not enter his temple."

"But it's my heritage!"

"Aun, why did you not tell her weapons are forbidden?"

"I didn't know she had it until—" He checked and offered sullenly, "A thrall can carry it back to her home."

Kati gripped the hilt. "I will not yield it! Rather will I fare back to my uncle's hall."

"Once chosen, a priestess does not leave the god." Hedin's mocking voice chilled Kati. "But some join him quickly in the afterlife."

"Let me keep the sword," Eirik said. "It will not be far away." Kati glanced at him hopefully and then despaired.

"But when your outlawry is over, won't you return to your own land?"

"I won't go for a while, and who knows? By the time I do, you may have found someone you trust to keep it."

As Kati hesitated, unwilling yet seeing no recourse,

Hedin said, "If I allow this, will you put away your freakishness and serve the god with wifely submission?"

There was no choice. "Yes," she said and put Heaven's Gift into Eirik's hand.

II

The great temple was dark as a forest, dimly lit by small windows in the high eaves that faced all four directions, so that the gold ornamentation seemed to glow of its own richness. Thor's throne was in the middle of the hall. His life-size wooden image clutched a hammer which he seemed ready to hurl. Sacrifices were made to him if there was danger of plague or famine. Odin was on one side, his ravens on his shoulder. He received offerings in time of war.

Frey sat on a golden throne, phallus erect beneath his golden robes, his boar crouched at his feet. When a marriage was celebrated, he was given gifts and every day it was Kati's task to bathe him with ale and smear fat on his lips. She did this gingerly at first, thinking he might complain about her ministrations, but as days passed and she never had the feeling that the famed image was anything but painted, gilded wood, she carried out these duties much as she had polished furniture in her foster parents' home.

Frey made all things fruitful. Kati reverenced that power but was increasingly sure it did not dwell in the figure on the throne. It seemed pointless to sing to him as Hedin taught her, clapping her hands or ringing small golden bells.

128

She was the only woman in the temple except for servants who silently brought food to her room and attended to her needs. Odin and Thor had no resident priests. The noblemen among their worshippers were priests themselves and able to offer sacrifice here as well as at the temples on their estates.

Frey had many such high-born devotees, but since his perpetual good will was necessary for life to continue, he was constantly attended by a priestess-wife, chief priest and several priestlings like Aun, who painted their faces like women's and danced before the god, tiny bells fastened to their wrists, ankles and girdles, as they writhed in obscene supplication. They would caress the god's phallus and pretend to thrust themselves upon it, swooning in feigned ecstasy that revolted Kati as she stood chanting beside Hedin who took no part in the mime except for sounding a great brass gong when it was time to begin the show, which was put on as often as there were worshippers.

At first Kati had reveled in being rid of household chores, spinning, weaving, brewing ale, making bread, but after a few weeks, she found herself missing the bustle of a place where people lived and worked. She even missed Thorhild's chiding tongue.

Had it not been for Scota, who shared a small, luxurious chamber just off the God's Hall, Kati would have been miserably lonesome. Scota adored the temple with its hundreds of rafters and eaves that ascended to a peak at the very top. Hedin grumbled about her, but since cats were loved by Freya, his god's sister and sometime consort, he had to put up with Scota's giving him a tap as he passed a pillar where she lay in ambush, or her staring at him long and unblinkingly from a pedestal.

Though she mourned the loss of Heaven's Gift, it was well Kati didn't have to confront the ancient blade with its memories of the men and women who had cherished it, the tales old Gyrd had told her. How could she be worthy of that heritage, imprisoned in a temple?

Worst of all, she had been forced to give the sword into the keeping of an outlawed foreigner, a man she scarcely knew! Adding to her restlessness was the fact that she couldn't shut him out of her mind or stop wondering how long he would stay in the sanctuary. When he left perhaps he would have the decency to take Heaven's Gift back to her kin—though it would surely rust in Thorhild's and Sigyth's hall.

Kati was not allowed to go beyond the temple courtyard, but the sacred tree stood there, ever green, towering higher than the dragons' heads of the temple eaves, great gnarled roots spreading to nourish it. The trunk was as thick around as five or six stout men, and it was easy to believe it had grown from a sprout of Ygdrasil, the Tree of Life on which Odin had impaled himself, suffering nine days and nights to learn the runes.

One of the roots made a comfortable low seat, and there Kati often sat with Scota, listening to the birds, watching them and the frisking squirrels. She felt as if she were waiting. But waiting for what?

Frey's priestess must always be young and beautiful. What happened when she began to age? Could she go back to the real world then? One day Kati asked this question of one of the withered beldames who brought her food.

The woman stared at her bleary-eyed before she said in a voice that cracked from want of use. "I was the god's wife. So were we all."

Kati's heart stopped. She was more afraid than when she'd faced the robbers. "You—you had no kinsmen? No place to go?"

A twisted smile revealed worn yellow teeth stumps. "When the high priest spies the first gray strand in your hair, the first small line in your forehead, you will have your choice. Live as a temple drudge or join the god quickly.''

''How—is that done?''

''The god enjoys your virginity—that is, you are skewered on his phallus. If that doesn't send you to him, the potion given to dull the pain of consummation certainly will.'' The old woman's shoulders sagged. ''I have seen a few go that way, but most cannot part with life while still young and strong. I would blithely do it now but Frey disdains such husks.'' She gave Kati a glance in which there was more pity than envy and shuffled out. Kati shuddered.

Was that all she was to have? Glittering boredom till she had to choose between death or years of cheerless slavery?

She rebelled at either fate and most especially when she remembered Eirik's brilliant blue gaze, his crooked, strangely attractive smile. Bitter to think a son of his might bear the sword which should have belonged to one of hers, but that was not the only reason he haunted her thoughts and dreams.

Reluctantly, she was having to admit that even if she hadn't faced such a joyless future, she would rather have been his wife than Frey's or any god's at all. She tried not to think of him. He would return to the real world, love someone and have children, while she anointed the god, chimed bells and waited for that first slight wrinkle, that first white hair.

The ceremonious monotony was broken by worshippers who came to ask boons of the gods of the Hall, or by marriages noble enough to command Frey's direct blessing. During all this time, the image had not vouchsafed a word. Kati was beginning to think its vaunted power to speak was only a tale spread by drunkards or priests, till, at midsummer, a rich farmer came to ask Frey's advice in selecting an heir since he had no close kindred by either blood or marriage.

Cutting the throats of the ram, cock and boar, each splendid of its kind, Hedin let their blood splash Frey's throne, laved his hands in the spurting jets and raised them toward the image.

"Oh Frey," he intoned as the animals twitched in their death throes. "Accept thy servant Ord's offering and grant him thy wisdom! Speak, Lord, we pray thee!"

There was wild jingling as Aun and the other priests danced and exhorted Frey in whining wails. Sickened by the blood, Kati was glad her only role was to ring a circular brace of many-sized bells and invoke Frey's name.

Hedin pitched forward, lay with a hand grasping the god's gold sandal. A fearsome voice resounded through the hall. Kati quaked at her earlier doubts, but as the god spoke on, there was a naggingly familiar ring to the deep tones.

"I am pleased with your gifts, Ord, and I will favor you with fine harvests and fecund beasts the rest of your life if you name as heir my beloved priest, Hedin."

Ord had fallen on his face at the first words. Trembling, words muffled by the stone, he pledged himself to do as the god advised, but remained prostrate till Hedin rose and lifted him with a bloodstained hand.

"Frey will show you favor, Ord."

It was then that Kati recognized Frey's voice. Of course! It was Hedin's magnified somehow to boom throughout the hall.

There was a wry taste in her mouth. She still believed in Frey's power, but it was not to be found within this temple. Her service was a sham.

Summer ended. It was time for Frey to make his annual journey through the countryside, feasting with harvesters, blessing farms and answering his worshippers' questions. The god's image traveled in a gold-inlaid cart awninged with silk. Kati and Scota occupied cushions at the god's feet. Hedin rode behind the wagon and was followed by a mass of Frey's devotees, who sang, shouted and rang bells.

Close to a hundred folk chanted Frey's praise from Uppsala to the first stop at one of the king's estates. The wagon bed was lifted off its base and, with joyous clapping and incantations, was carried through the fields. That night, in the hall, while Frey's retinue was unstintingly feasted, Kati stayed beside the image, offered it ale and rubbed the painted lips with fat.

The enthroned god sat near the door of the hearth room and a bed was made up for Kati close beside him. Hedin was given the steward's closet-bed at the other end of the chamber.

The women of the household withdrew to the spinning house and such men as could slept on the long benches on either side of the hearth while others sought a place in lofts and stables.

The unfamiliar hall and the strangeness of being among so many men kept Kati awake for a time and then the loud snoring did. Trying to muffle the sounds with pillows, she hoped the whole journey wouldn't be like this.

She was drowsing when a hand closed tightly over her mouth. "It's Eirik," came a soft whisper. "Come out, my *fylgya,* and talk with me awhile."

Her heart pounded. Eirik! Frey's wife was not supposed to walk with a man, much less alone at night, but she had only scorn now for her duties and a great happiness at seeing Eirik, whatever the reason.

She gave a nod of assent. He took his hand away. Because of the men in the room, she had only removed her girdle and shoes. She pulled on her shoes now and slipped her mantle around her, snuggling the sleepy Scota under the bearskin and sheets.

Embers glowed in the long fire, casting ruddy light on the sleepers. Kati feared that opening the door would rouse someone, but Eirik shielded her with his body and urged her, with a hand beneath her arm, to enter one of the chambers built on the sides of the main hall. From the smell, this room was full of stored furs. Eirik had left the door ajar and they soon stood in the courtyard, but since the outbuildings were filled with worshippers from Uppsala, Eirik drew Kati along the path that led to the fields.

The warmth of his strong hands sent a glow through her. She realized with a certain shock how seldom she had been touched by anyone since Gyrd disappeared, and not at all since arriving at the temple. She missed the simple physical closeness of another human being, but that didn't explain the wildly delicious exhilaration that sang in her blood. Then she remembered his outlawry and stopped in her tracks.

"What are you doing here, Eirik Haakonson? Why have you left sanctuary?"

There was a timid new moon. In its light, she could just make out the white flash of his smile. "Since the gods gave me protection, it seemed I should show my gratitude by joining his escort." His voice deepened with a timbre that started a tremulous melting within her. "The truth is, Kati, that I had to see how my battle maiden fared. Often I have come to the wall around the temple court hoping for a glimpse of you. Once I saw you by the great tree, but though I called loudly as I dared, you didn't hear."

"A good thing." Her spine crawled at the thought of his being one of the sacrifices hung in the grove. "Eirik, it is dangerous for us to walk like this! It cannot be."

"You like it well, then, being the god's wife?"

"My foster-mother truly said I lack the skills to be a man's," she jested to conceal the hurt his scorn caused.

"Skills! Think you it was for her skill at weaving that Frey burned for his bride and in wooing lost his magic sword that will leave him defenseless at Ragnarok?"

She thought of Frey's erect phallus and was glad Eirik could not see her hot blushing. "Men seek wives who can direct their serving maids in all needful things. I can ski and skate and throw a spear, draw a bow and use a sword . . . but I burn the porridge and ruin the ale."

He chuckled. "A plight easily mended. Leave such tasks to the innumerable worthy women, like my own good sister, Helga, who find in such things their pride and reason for living. Housewives are many but *fylgyas* are few." He took her face in his hands, long fingers caressing her temples, the angle of her jaw. "You are the only woman I can wed, one to companion me—one who can love as fiercely as she fights."

He kissed her mouth. She stiffened, arching back, but he held her with tender strength, kissing her eyes and throat till a flickering sweet warmth in her center spread to loins and breasts and fanned throughout her body. She could not have stopped him had he drawn her down in the field, but after swooning moments, he raised his head and gave a husky laugh.

"Let us away, then, this very night."

Sobered as by a dash of icy water, Kati freed herself. "We would be caught. Hedin would never allow such an insult to Frey."

"I thought you brave."

"Brave is one thing, stupid another. No one would help or shelter us from fear of Frey."

Silence grew like a wall between them.

"And I took you for my *fylgya*," he marveled bitterly. "I thought you bore the luck and honor of my family and yours, even before you gave into my keeping that peerless sword.''

''I had no choice,'' she said in a voice turned harsh because she strained to keep it from breaking.

He flung aside his mantle and unbuckled the scabbard that held Heaven's Gift. ''If the sword could speak, what would it tell you?''

She wanted to clasp her hands around his that gripped the hilt, wanted to run with him and indeed trust to their luck. But a vision of his broken body rose before her, dangling in the sacred grove after cruel rites. For herself she would have risked flight, but she could not bear what would fall to him if they were taken.

''The sword speaks not to me,'' she said in dulled tones. ''Return to sanctuary, for there would be none, anyplace, for this madness.''

He was still as the thin moonlight. She fled, and encouched again at Frey's feet, she wept against Scota's sleek body, deep into the night.

Next day, seated in his wagon, Frey listened to the woes and problems of the neighborhood and gave his judgments in Hedin's mellifluous voice. Kati didn't know how the priest, who was standing beside her, managed to project the words so that they seemed to come from the carved wooden lips, but he did it, and each person who asked the god's advice brought a gift which Hedin sent back to Uppsala with the worshippers who were returning that day. People from the present region would conduct the god to his next audience, and so it would go to the end of his progress, although his most devoted followers—or those, Hedin growled, who seized this chance for feasting—might accompany the god the whole time.

Kati did not see Eirik that day or in the morning when they set forth, but several men of the procession were

hooded. She scanned them closely but decided that none
of the fat, short or hunched men could possibly be Eirik.
She told herself that she was glad. There was nothing else
she could have done, but she felt forlorn and deserted as
the wagon rumbled along.

Frey, she said under her breath, addressing the real
power, not the grotesque image which she was beginning
to loathe. *We are told how you longed for your bride—
how you thought you could not endure your waiting. Will
you not pity and help me, you and your sister Freya, who
weeps for her love? Free me from this mockery and let
me, with the man I love, celebrate your true rites, those
of life and loving.*

She did not think he heard.

Most hay was mowed by the time they had left Uppsala, the ripe corn was being harvested and beasts, fat
and thriving, were being brought from high summer pasture. As the god traveled through stubbled fields, trees
shed their leaves, baring screes on the mountains beneath
dark forests. Yellow leaves clung here and there to
birches. Alder thickets showed faded green along the
streams, but most color came from the red-brown leaves
of the rowan about clusters of bright red berries so thick
that farmers said they presaged a winter of heavy snows.

Many farms, many feasts, and often Kati danced on
threshing floors which had horseheads underneath the
packed earth that reverberated as the flails sang. She
danced before Frey's image, but it was really to Eirik that
she stretched her arms and swayed as she arched breasts
and pelvis, offering her body. Above bells and clapping
she could hear the groaning lustful breathing of the on-
lookers and spun tauntingly near them. Since she could
not have her desire, she took perverse pleasure in arous-
ing hunger. The panting worshippers could sate them-

selves with each other while she lay alone at the god's feet.

Kati was accustomed now to Hedin's profiting from putting words in the god's mouth. He was indeed Frey's priest, so she thought it mattered little if he benefited from offerings made by those who could afford it. It troubled her, though, when she learned that Hedin accepted bribes to weight the god's decisions in matters that seriously affected people, such as betrothals, inheritances and disputed boundaries. She felt like his accomplice, and when the god's rulings struck her as unjust, guilt pricked her till she remonstrated.

"I thought the widowed mother had the right of it," she argued. "Her work built up the farm. It seems hard now that her son and daughter-in-law exile her to a small loft as if she were a worn-out thrall."

"What can you know of such things?" Hedin's dark green eyes drilled into her. "Dance and hold your tongue, or Frey may require a new wife much sooner than usual."

But there came a time when she could no longer stay silent while he worked his trickery. A great estate with many farms had passed from a jarl to his son by his wedded wife, but he had two fair young children by his leman—a girl of fourteen and a slender, handsome lad a few years younger. The jarl's concubine had loved him so that she died by her own hand when she learned of his death. Now the trueborn heir, Sven, purposed to possess also the small but prosperous farm the jarl had bestowed on his love with the provision it should go to their children.

The night Frey's cortege arrived, Kati heard the serving maids whispering about it and casting pitying glances at Hilde and Erling, the brother and sister who stayed close to each other, their golden heads gleaming and their eyes the shade of bluebells. It seemed they had kinfolk in Birka who hadn't been told of their mother's death.

If they favored her, Kati thought it no wonder that the jarl had loved her better than the pursed-mouthed woman who scowled at them from under heavy dark brows like her son's. Servants hovered as protectively near the children as possible, but what could thralls do if their new master decided to give them a difficult life?

Sven sat before Hedin, who occupied the high seat, and the two of them talked long and softly after everyone else had gone to bed. Kati scarcely slept, though she supposed that at least Sven would have to see that his father's children were properly reared and given a decent start in life.

Early next morning, Frey was carried through the fields and set down on the threshing floor amid heaps of white fennel and blood-red berries and bronze leaves of the rowan. Sven knelt before the god, a somber jackdaw with scraggly black hair and beard, swathed in dark garments.

"Great Frey," he twanged nasally. "The care of my young half brother and sister weighs heavy on me lest they be tainted with their mother's weak mind. In your wisdom, tell me what is the best provision I can make for them? I would fain do my duty, though they are a feckless pair and a thorn in my honest mother's side."

Kati saw how Erling flushed and his hand went to his jeweled knife before his sister caught it and whispered. They both wore green and shone in that wintry place as if they were the Elf King's pride, just come out of the mountain.

Grim would it be for them, with such a foster-mother and -brother. Thinking of this, for a moment Kati could not believe the cadenced words that were coming from Frey's mouth.

"I will take the young ones into my service. The girl

may serve in my temple and the lad await the solstice. I
will call him to me then, for he is comely.''

An exiled girl was no threat to Sven; but Erling might
be in a few more years. So Hedin would geld him, cut
his throat and hang him on a tree. Kati's mind spun.
She sprang up and stood before Frey with outspread
arms.

"Lord husband, you cannot want the life of this fair
boy and the weeping of his sister!" she cried. "Only last
night you told me they should receive in gold the value of
their farm and go to dwell with their kinsmen in Birka.
Sven's good ale may have clouded your mind but surely
you now remember!"

She gazed straight at Hedin. He looked thunderous but
understood that unless he let the god agree, she would ex-
pose his deceit to the people. She would suffer for this if
they got back to Uppsala; now she must escape at the first
chance, perhaps into Norway. If only she had fled with
Eirik!

Frey's voice had a hollow sound. "You are right, my
priestess wife. The children shall go to Birka."

"You said they must set forth today with the servants
of their mother's household."

"Let it be done," said Frey in a choked voice.

With his neighbors looking on to see the god's word
was fulfilled, there was nothing Sven could do but hastily
prepare the brother and sister for their journey. From the
joyous looks of the serving men and women who hurried
to accompany them, it was clear that they would take
care of their young master and mistress.

Anything Sven did now would cause scandal, even
outlawry.

It was with relief that Kati saw the children depart,
escorted by their mother's steward and other servants,
but her blood turned to ice when Hedin looked at her.
Frey needed a priestess on this ritual progress, but if,

at one of the halts, Hedin spied a virgin of suitable beauty and birth, he might not delay his vengeance but dispose of Kati and celebrate the god's nuptials on the spot.

III

They journeyed on next day. Hedin said not a word to Kati beyond the necessary. This terrified her more than threats and raging. It was as if he saw her as a living corpse, one needing only to be buried.

Snow fell the day they left Sven's estate. Because of that and Sven's displeasure, no one from the region joined Frey's procession. Only a single hunched hooded follower from Uppsala accompanied the escort of temple servants, who now, wearing snowshoes, spent more time pushing the cart through snowdrifts than in chanting and chiming.

When the wagon stalled, Aun and Hedin didn't whip the pair of chestnut horses pulling it, but they lashed the thralls cruelly. One slipped and fell beneath the wheels, his chest so mangled that it seemed he could not live.

Hedin ordered him dragged to one side. When Kati realized that the man would be abandoned, she sprang from the wagon.

"He cannot be left like this!"

"There's no room for him in the cart." Hedin shrugged.

"He may have my place."

Eyes like frozen stagnant water dwelled on her. His fleshy mouth curved down. "Very well, priestess. Let's

142

see how long you'll flounder through snow to stretch out whatever life's in this crows' bait."

Kati bandaged the wounds as well as she could. The sturdy red-haired man seemed to be past pain and could not speak, but she saw thankfulness in his gaze as his fellows eased him onto her cushions. Several of them cast her quick glances or muttered gratitude as they helped cover him with furs and rugs.

They had taken off his snowshoes, and now Kati fastened them on, pulled up her furred hood and could have laughed, had matters not been in such a pass, at Hedin's amazed stare. Flounder she would not, in fact she could travel faster than the horses whose hoofs caked with snow to slippery masses that thickened till they fell off. Their shoes were studded with little spikes so they could keep their footing on ice, but this did not help in soft new-fallen snow. Desperate hope sparked in Kati.

If she saved her food . . . If she waited for the right time . . . Neither Aun nor Hedin were used to snowshoes and she was sure the thralls wouldn't rush in pursuit. Night fell early, but the snow reflected starshine.

Hugging Scota to her beneath her mantle, she thought, *We might win free. To Norway, Eirik's land.* Better to try than wait till it suited Hedin to do away with her. But she would feel so much braver if only she had the sword.

They labored on, sheltering by night in *seter* huts or wood-cutters' shelters. Kati tended the hurt thrall, who was fevered and called her "Mother" when she fed him gruel, though once his delirium lifted enough for him to grip her hands.

"Priestess—you won't leave me for the wolves?"

"No. Soon you'll start to mend."

"You know I will not," he said, pain twisting his face at each word. "What I fear are wolves—before I am dead."

"That fear you need not have," she promised and made him sip more ale.

Stealthily, she had been hoarding cheese, dried meat and fish, a few apples, dried plums and cherries, hazelnuts—anything that would keep. She secreted these in a skin bag kept under the cushions. At the end of a week, she had enough saved to venture striking out, but the injured man still lingered. She heard Aun tell Hedin that they could not be more than a few days from a large farmstead where there was a budding girl who might by now be ripe for priestesshood. Dread sickened her.

If only the wretched thrall would die! Skeleton fingers gripped her heart as she thought that the doomed, broken man might outlive her unless she seized her first chance to steal away.

Much as reason and a young, healthy creature's love of life urged her to be gone, she was unable to desert him. If only she had the Heaven Sword! Then she might die fighting and be counted worthy to join old Gyrd in Odin's spear-raftered hall where the god sipped wine and fed his wolves from the warriors' banquet. She took some cheer from knowing Freya welcomed maidens, and since the goddess loved cats, Scota might come to share that afterlife. But it was bitter, bitter, to die without having lived as a woman.

She, who had scorned wedding any man, now regretted more than all other things that she had not spent even one night in Eirik's arms.

The cart lodged again in the snow. The hooded man from Uppsala helped shove and so did Kati, but no matter how they and the horses strained, the wheels only sank deeper. "The god must be taken out till the wagon's free," decided Hedin. "Lift the thrall down, too. The horses have all they can do without dragging carrion."

"Have mercy on him," Kati implored.

Hedin ignored her. The servants, as gently as they

could, laid the man on the rugs Kati hurried to spread on the snow.

"Don't—leave me!" he pleaded.

Sinking down, Kati cradled him in her arms, shielding him from the piercing wind. "I won't leave," she promised, wiping away cold sweat that rose on his face from the hurt of being shifted.

The high priest heard her and turned with a terrifying smile. "So you wish to stay with the slave, priestess? Very well. But first you must give your husband-god the gift of your maidenhood."

The men who were lifting out Frey turned motionless as the image. "Put down the god," commanded Hedin. "Uncover him for his bride."

He and Aun came toward her. Scota arched her back and hissed. Kati put down the dying man and glanced about for any kind of weapon, in desperation drew the small jade-handled knife she carried at her girdle. The priests halted, then rushed at her from either side. Kati swung her mantle to confuse them and leaped toward Hedin.

It was not her knife that cut him down but a hacked ancient blade that sung in its arc, the flash of its pommel dazzling her.

Almost without a pause in its sweep, the sword drove into Aun's fat neck. He sank like one of the kine he had so often sacrificed.

In their astonishment, the thralls had let Frey's image topple in the snow. None of them made a move against the Uppsala devotee whose hood had fallen back to reveal black hair tousled about a thin tanned face.

"Eirik!" Kati choked.

His arm closed guardingly about her as stern eyes searched each of the men before them. "Well?" he asked. "Will you fight for those who drove you or will you join with us till the time when you can seek your freedom?''

"We will serve the priestess," one man said. "Speak your will, lady. You trust this man?''

She would have fallen except for his support. Joyous amazement rang in her laughter. "I trust him. Let us plan what we must do.''

Frey's splendid garments were taken from him and the likeness tumbled into a chasm with the bodies of the priests, so deep down they would never be found. Eirik donned the golden robes, for he had hit on the daring plan of posing as the god while they traveled toward the Norwegian border.

"But you are outlawed there," Kati protested.

"No," he said with a crooked grin. "I had words with my cousin-king, right enough, but he didn't exile me. It was my own choice to travel for a while and let him think better of his haughty ways with those of birth as good as his.''

Kati frowned. "Then why—?''

He laughed tenderly. "Because of you, gooseling. Claiming sanctuary was the only way I could think of to be near you, and I hoped to win you away during the progress. When you wouldn't come''—he gave her a severe frown—"I well nigh made for my own land then. But when I looked at the sword, I saw you holding it again and knew you were my *fylgya,* my luck and my love.''

He did not kiss her in front of the men, but she trembled at his caressing voice, the way his gaze seemed to note and delight in everything about her. He was here, he loved her and they had a chance, at least.

The mangled thrall was carefully put back among the pillows, and the servants joined their voices to Eirik's in urging Kati to ride and tend to him. A makeshift harness was fastened to link the priests' mounts to the wagon team, Eirik helped dig away the banked snow barrier, and without the weight of the image and with the extra horses, the wagon creaked, grumbled and rolled onward.

Kati slept that night in Eirik's embrace, but though they stroked and kissed and thrilled wildly to each other, he sighed at last and placed the sword between them.

"You are my heart's wife," he said. "But I will not have all your sweetness till we wed in the world's eyes. If aught should chance to me, I would not have you bear a fatherless child or be shamed because of me."

"If aught chanced to you, I would not care what came to me," she whispered, but he only held her close, the blade hard against their flesh, and would not kiss her anymore, groaning as she tried to reach his lips.

"Nay, Kati mine. You'll not have such a marriage bed."

"I have no kin to blame us."

"All the more need that I must guard you in a brother's place. Sleep, love. Be my honor, the way that I have dreamed you."

Their hearts beat tempestuously for a long time, but finally they slept.

The thrall died about midmorning, rising in Kati's arms in a last attempt to capture his fleeting life. Strength drained from him. His face turned to a boy's as he pressed it against Kati's breast, heavily, and was gone.

They gave him as good a burial as might be, scraping snow away from a rock ledge and walling him in, wrapped in an extra cloak of Eirik's, hands crossed over his knife, a bowl of ale beside him, with gifts from all of them and Thor's hammer amulet about his neck to commend him to that mighty lord of thralls.

That night they reached the great farm. Eirik had

snowshoed behind the wagon till they could see the distant cluster of buildings. Then he climbed up beside Kati and crossed his arms majestically.

"Well?" he grinned. "Am I lordly enough?"

"That black hair won't do." She frowned. "But this cloth-of-gold scarf will make you a handsome headdress-crown." They went through Hedin's accessories and added gold armbands, rings and chains, so that only by those disconcerting hazy twilight eyes did Kati know he was her love and not a glittering deity.

The master of the fields, a sturdy brown-haired man of middle years, came to meet them with his household. One of the thralls whispered that his name was Torkel Aamundson. Among his womenfolk was a lovely girl just flowering into womanhood. Kati shivered to think how close the young maid had come to assuming the priestess' robes.

"Greeting, Torkel Aamundson," intoned Eirik. "I bring you blessing."

"My Lord!" cried the master, leading his party in obeisance. "Your likeness has always had the gift of speech but now, in truth, you have imbued it with your living spirit!"

"I have," Eirik smiled, "because my wife-priestess is so fair that I would consort with her in fleshly form, not as a god."

Torkel gazed on Kati with wondering admiration. "No wonder, Lord. You shall have my own bed, spread with silk over new straw sweetened with herbs. We will feast this night and tomorrow make sacrifice." He looked anxious. "Will you require the same number of beasts as last year? I lost several of my best heifers this year and—"

"I will claim no beasts at all," said Eirik, "if you can give us provision from your stores."

Torkel's weathered face relaxed in a smile. "Gladly

done, Lord. But can you give us your wisdom without the blood of sacrifice?''

Eirik took Kati's hand. "For this season, my own hot blood suffices, friend Torkel.''

The feast that night was especially merry since the farm folk knew they would not have to yield up their precious animals. With jesting and earthy good wishes, Frey and his bride were escorted to the closet-bed and shut within to enjoy the luxury of silken sheets and the scent of fresh hay and thyme.

As always, when they were alone, they cleaved together like longing, separated parts of one body, intoxicated with each other, seeking to yield all, have all. At last, shaking, Eirik drew away.

"This bed is dangerous in its comfort,'' he muttered huskily. "We had best lie in all our clothes this night. I fear me that without encumbrance, I might take you in my sleep as I often do—but 'twould not be a dream.''

"Eirik . . .'' she breathed, swollen, aching with her need of him. "Oh, love, let us! I know you will not play me false.''

"Not if I lived. But I will get no child on you while all stands unsure for us.''

He put the sword between them and moved till his hand only touched her hair. In spite of Scota's nestling behind her knees, Kati felt abandoned, yet she knew he did it for love of her. Marvelling at all he had undergone for her sake made her feverish need gradually subside till it was replaced with overflowing tenderness, and she took his hand and kissed it.

She would be his luck as he was hers. She would be his honor. But one night— *Oh, Frey, you true force, not the wood deception, let us, in all honor, have no sword between us.*

* * *

They rested three days with Torkel, blessing the fields and beasts. Folk, both rich and humble, came from all the region to behold this wondrous god who had assumed flesh for his wife's delight and to lay their disputes and problems before him.

Kati was astounded at Eirik's searching questions, deliberations and rulings so sagacious and fair that even those on the losing side of a question could scarcely grumble. He accepted no sacrifice of beasts, but if a well-to-do worshipper left gifts of gold or cloth or foodstuffs, Eirik had these distributed among the poor except for coin that he gave to Frey's thralls so that they would have the means to start anew in life once the progress ended.

The fame of this walking, talking generous god who could feast and joke like a man, spread over the countryside. Eirik had to ride in the wagon to the next estate because he had become so popular with Torkel's folk that a score of them insisted on honoring him with their attendance.

"A damned nuisance," swore Eirik, grimacing as he settled himself resignedly amid the cushions. "But the village we'll reach after two more manors lies on the border. There, my *fylgya*, we'll take to skis or snowshoes and be in my own hall within a week."

"I can't believe it," Kati sighed, tears of grateful happiness filling her eyes. "But Eirik, are you sure you won't later wish you'd married a notable housewife?"

"Now, if I did, how would my sister spend her time?" he teased. "Nay, love, let Helga rule spinning room and kitchen while we hunt cloud-berries or train young horses." He laughed softly. "Before long, there'll be the training of our children, too. I'll warrant that will prove a task for both of us!"

In spite of the snow, folk traveled from outlying farms and hamlets to feast with Frey and seek his counsel. The ardent, tender passion coursing between Kati and Eirik was so powerful that she believed it truly touched those around them, that the imposture held more of Frey's real blessing than Hedin's greedy use of the image.

This sharing of joy with the countryfolk would have been a triumphant celebration of her release except for the hunger that besieged them so relentlessly that Eirik dared not kiss her now or hold her in his arms.

The burden of restraint fell all on him. Kati had long since lost will and strength to dam the surging force that demanded fulfillment. Oh, let them gain the border! Quickly, quickly!

It seemed forever, but at last they reached the village, followed by singing people from the last halt, met by folk who hurried out to hail this marvelous Frey. Housed in the nearby manor, Eirik performed the usual rites and handed down his judgments.

"When this is over," he said to Kati after they were resting on the second night in their closeted bed, "we will forbid worshippers to accompany us, and as soon as we're well away, the thralls may go wherever they will, but you and I, Kati, we'll speed for our home."

Our home. How wonderful it sounded to one who had never hoped to find a place where she could belong. She pressed his hand to her cheek, and though her body yearned for his, that was the lesser part of the way she loved him.

Next day, he held court in the village. Impatient as he was to return to his own country, he pondered each request or grievance, and it was midafternoon when the last supplicant approached the chair that had been placed on an improvised dais.

This man was swathed in a shaggy cloak with a hood that shadowed his features. He moved with grace and confidence, and though he knelt, he did not incline his head, but watched Frey with a curious smile.

"Great Frey, all have heard what a blessing you've brought to earth and beasts this progress, but it would seem you have given so freely of your vital gift that you have not made fruitful your own fair wife—a pity, since 'tis for her you took on mortal shape. If I am right, this is the last place you must visit. Now, before you make the hard journey back to Uppsala, I invite you to sojourn with your bride at one of my manors just over into Norway."

He threw back his hood. Golden hair gleamed brightly as a crown and blue eyes sparkled at Kati as he held out his arms to Frey who hastened to embrace him, murmured something in the stranger's ear and called out to the people: "Good friends, not even a god can refuse the King of Norway when he comes with such a gracious invitation! Come, wife, let us make ready!"

Frey's servants, now free men who had chosen to stay with Kati and Eirik, were at the wedding feast when the king himself placed their hands in each other's, but Kati felt their true marriage was when, for good this time, she placed Heaven's Gift in her husband's keeping.

"This night," she whispered, "we will not sleep with it between us."

He kissed her before king and that proud company. A great cheer went up, and in the glad tumult, old Gyrd's spirit-hailing rang loudest of all.

Book IV

The Empress' Nightingale

Lappland, Sweden,
Rus, Byzantium
1014–1017

I

Spring was finches and thrushes, the cuckoo singing from rustling new birch leaves, night calls of the loon from the snow-melt swollen lake below, and most of all to Rana, the joyous melodies of the bluethroat nightingale.

She wove his tunes into her own but could never match them. His improvisations were as varied as the *joiks* hummed and trilled by Sameh herdsmen as they rested after the long journey from the wintering grounds and rejoiced in watching young calves follow their mothers as the reindeer feasted on tender grass and juicy lichen exposed in ever-widening expanses while the snow shrank with each day.

When the band had first reached this spring-autumn camp, the only one with permanent buildings, snow had still covered everything. It had been good to settle snugly into the turf *kåtor*, or lodges, as soon as these had been aired out, old twigs cleared away, and new ones scattered before skins were spread over the floor. And what a feast there had been from the autumn slaughtering, meat frozen and stored in the *njalla*, the strong shed supported on a single post that was thick as a tree, higher than Rana's head, and polished so slick that even the wolverine's formidable claws couldn't find a grip.

If the band was weary of their dried, tough winter meat, other creatures were famished in this time before the earth stirred and new life burgeoned. It was during one of the last snowstorms that Rana, gathering wood, had come upon a vixen with her paw caught in a cleft-log trap.

The bait that lured her there hung on the central spike between the two deep slits—a few succulent bites of offal that might mean the difference between life and death, between having the energy to breed or having no pups that spring. The fox was white as snow except for yellowish eyes and black nose. She looked thin in spite of her thick coat.

She didn't struggle as Rana approached. Perhaps she had already exhausted herself in trying to free the paw which battling only fixed more inexorably. For whatever reason, the fox watched Rana.

Unthinkable to tamper with someone's trap. Furs paid the taxes exacted by Swedes and Norwegians and were bartered at trading fairs for kettles, utensils, knives and jewelry. But the animal's eyes spoke to Rana. Of the hard winter, of how sweet it was to be alive in the spring, and Rana shivered as if she, too, were gripped in a trap, waiting the club that would end the fight that any creature's life was here in the northland.

Rana took off her thick shawl. She dropped it over the fox's head, hoping it would keep her from biting. The animal was quiet as Rana forced a stone into the cleft, easing pressure on the trapped paw. As gently as possible, she worked the furry foot upward and out of the slit.

The fox fell sideways. The paw was bleeding and left crimson spots on the snow. Rana swept away her shawl. The vixen blinked those golden eyes. For an instant, Rana thought she would speak. Then she was off, limping but swift, moving white against still white.

Something made Rana turn. Fenn stood there, her

foster-brother, son of Suki and Votar, who had raised her from infancy. Nine summers the elder, he had taken care of her ever since she could remember, leading the *härk*, or gelded male, she rode on till she could guide her own mount, carving her first small skis, telling her about the creatures that shared the lands traveled by the Sameh as they followed their herds through the eight seasons that made the year.

Like many Sameh,. Fenn had a broad face that narrowed at the jaw to a pointed chin. Short and sturdy, he was now not quite Rana's height, though the big red wool tassel on his Four Winds cap made him look taller. He had light brown hair and eyes, and Suki's dimples showed in his cheeks as he gave Rana, even now, that warm, glowing smile he'd always had for her.

"Fenn! It was your fox?"

He shook his head. "No. It was yours, small sister. I meant to make you a sledge robe of such white fur, but I think now you would not like that. Is it so?"

She thought of the vixen. "It is so. But, Fenn—"

He laughed softly. "No, don't say you're sorry. It may be the fox spirit will help you sometime. But you had better hurry with the wood or Mother will be cross."

That had been before the calves were born. Now they were able to travel. It was time to move to higher, cooler ground, away from swarming midges and gadflies, time to move out of the turf *kåta* and get out the summer lodge.

Rana had helped Suki bundle the hide covering, the four curved support poles, cross-spars that stretched between them, and the cooking-pot rod into two burdens that could be attached to either side of a reindeer's pack saddle.

The *kåta* wasn't heavy, so the copper kettle and traveling chest were packed on top. The other household goods were fastened on the pack saddles of two more reindeer.

One of these was Sefni, a new *härk*, unused to such work. He reared up, striking out viciously with his forefeet, but Fenn had strapped the load securely, and now talked soothingly to the animal as he gripped the rein and took hold of the fresh horn stumps that were sensitive to pressure.

While he controlled the reindeer, Rana deftly fastened a strap to the saddle and ran it around the animal's chest to keep the load from slipping when going uphill. Then she secured another strap around the *härk*'s rear to steady the pack saddle when heading downhill.

"Can you hold this beast while I fetch Grandmother?" Fenn asked.

"Of course I can," Rana sniffed. "Didn't I hand-feed him after his mother died?" Taking the rein, she let one hand rest lightly on a budding antler.

Sarvar, or bucks, lost their horns early in the winter: gelded males, some months later: and *vajor,* females, kept their sharp little horns till spring. Fenn said this was so a *vaja* could forage under the snow for the food she needed to nourish a calf within her or after it had dropped. No hornless male could force her away from her grazing place.

"Well, Sefni," she said to the reindeer, who did seem to remember her a little and ceased his frightened trembling. "Are you glad you'll graze peaceably this winter while the *sarvar* wear themselves out fighting and rutting? Or would you rather carry on like they do even if you couldn't hold your head up after a couple of weeks?"

She swatted at a gadfly that buzzed near his velvety muzzle. She had seen reindeer cough and choke to death from inhaling the tiny larvae, contained in sticky liquid hanging like threads from the animal's nostrils. A sting on the back deposited larvae that burrowed through hair and skin to cause boils and live off pus till the next year when they tunneled their way out, leaving an open, fes-

likely, she was nursing a dozen or more pups in a den dug into some ridge or riverbank. Rana smiled at the thought as Fenn glanced back and grinned at her. No blood brother could have been kinder or dearer. She wondered fleetingly why he hadn't married, and then frowned, wishing she could remember something about the tall, blond young couple who must have been her natural parents.

Rana hadn't realized she was different, not Sameh, till other children started teasing her for her pale hair and light eyes, calling her a troll-changeling. Votar had quickly put a stop to that, but Suki said it was time Rana knew the truth.

She was their sun-child, their beloved treasure, but not born of their short, dark bodies. One autumn as they had moved to their wintering grounds a terrible storm engulfed them. They quickly set up their *kåtor* and weathered two days of driving snow, but when they moved on, they found a beautiful young man and woman who had not been so lucky. It was too late to revive them, but the baby, snuggled inside her mother's clothes, sucking the drained breast, wailed from nothing worse than hunger. Rich milk from a *vaja* had soon righted that.

Touched by the couple's sad fate and obvious love—the man had shielded the woman with his own cloak and body—the Sameh had raised a cairn over them and buried them with their rich garments and ornaments, though the Sameh had no cause to love tall, golden Norse folk who demanded from them levies of bear, marten, otter and reindeer hides, feathers and ropes of sealskin.

Clasping the lovers' hands, Votar placed between them an ancient iron sword, its blade hacked and worn though the hilt was of intricate workmanship. The cairn was near a *seite*, one of the weird stones worshipped by the Sameh time out of mind. Twice a year, as the band passed it on their migrations, Rana brought food to the

cairn and stayed by it for a while, trying to imagine what
her parents had been like and why they had died so far
from home and kinsmen, but mostly hoping that their
spirits were together, that they were happy in the other
world.

Votar didn't like questions about his journeys to the
spirit realm, but once she had summoned up courage to
ask him if he had ever seen her parents there. After a startled glance, he stroked her hair. "All is well with them,
and very well."

"Did they tell you where they came from?"

"Little one, where they dwell now, it doesn't matter."

Rana still wondered, though not because she was dis-
satisfied with this life of constant moving after the reindeer. She loved the way seasons blended and changed on
the journey that took them across Sweden to the smiling
fjords of Norway and back again.

As they moved up the valley, climbing gradually, all
was quiet, except for the crackling, clicking sound that
came from the stretching of a tendon in the reindeer's
toes. At every step, it tensed across a small bone. In a
storm, or at night, Fenn said, this sound held the animals
together, as did a scent made in their hoof glands, and the
white of pale tail tips. The people's shoes, leather with
grass-filled soles, were noiseless as Fraxi's pads.

The caravan's silence made other sounds seem louder.
An avalanche crashed down a mountain, and the thunder-
ing echoed up the valley as a buzzard screamed in the
sky. Ptarmigan made chunking cries from the scrub. A
lemming squeaked as if pounced upon.

Mile after mile, mountains lowering ever higher around
them, they moved to the rhythmic sound of the reindeers'
stretching tendons. It was past noon when they stopped in
a meadow and unloaded the *härkar*, tethering them to
willows.

Rana scavenged for dead branches and twigs while

Suki got a fire going to make their herb tea. The family drank birchwood cup after cup of this brew and devoured hunks of dried meat. Grandmother could no longer chew it, so Suki shredded some to stew soft in a small pan. After resting for a while, they reloaded the reindeer and traveled a few more hours before camping for the night.

And so the days slipped by as they wended through passes and valleys, often crossing small brooks, now and then having to ford a stream swollen by melted snow into a frothing current that obscured the slippery, uneven rocks. At these places, Fenn took Grandmother on his shoulders, just as other men carried small children and babies or anyone too weak to wade the swift rushing water.

The younger women held up their skirts and edged into the icy, swirling force that soon came above their knees and then their hips. Rana, like the others, used a staff to help find her way through the treacherous stones. Fraxi and the dogs swam desperately, swept along like toys, but they clambered ashore downstream and shook themselves before trotting up to their masters.

Led by their reins, the reindeer crossed quite easily, their weight stabilized by four feet instead of two, hoofs sliding less than wet leather shoes. Since nearly everyone was wet and chilled, fires were built to brew tea while people changed clothes and took the grass out of their shoes to dry.

Often it was possible to see the dark spread of the reindeer herd high on a mountain snowfield, safe from stinging insects. And now the caravan was nearing the *seite* and the cairn of Rana's parents. The *seite* occupied a ridge, a great stone set up by the ancient ones.

There was no way of telling whether its resemblance to a human figure was natural or carved by long-dead hands. Great hollow eyes and a gaping mouth watched the travelers, and each family hastened to pledge offerings of food before it.

After camp was made and Rana had brought firewood and water, she gathered forget-me-nots, globe flowers and blooming heather, and took them to the cairn heaped at the other end of the ridge.

Mother. Father. I have come to see you again. Please be happy in Saivo. They say that everything there is much like this world, only made perfect—

What was that? It sounded like a moan of pain. Rana had never been afraid of her parents' spirits, but now the back of her neck prickled. She spread the flowers on the rocks and edged around the heap.

Buskined feet and legs looked real enough, especially the one bent at a strange angle. Rana moved to where she could see a man lying on his face, arms stretched out as if he had been crawling before he collapsed.

He was dressed like the Northmen who came to the Sameh winter camp to collect levies and looked very tall. An engraved ring showed on one hand, and his hair was a thick mass of curling golden brown.

Rana dropped to her knees, turning his face. Golden eyelashes flickered, then opened, and she gazed into eyes the color of a high mountain lake that reflected only the sky. His face seemed long compared to round or triangular Sameh visages. His nose was straight and his hollowed cheeks burned with fever.

He shaped a word Rana didn't understand. Slipping her shawl beneath his head, she touched his mouth gently and gave him what she hoped was a cheering smile. "We are friends. Don't move. I'll be right back."

It was simple enough for Votar to set the broken leg and splint it, simple to make broth and spoon it into the stranger's mouth. But the willow bark tea did not reduce his fever and Votar muttered that the splintered bone, jolted by the man's crawling, must have created poisoning in the blood.

"Can't you suck out the evil?" Rana implored. She had seen Votar do this, drawing out whatever caused illness in the form of pebbles or wads of hair.

Her foster-father shook his head. "Not this kind. I think he will die."

Rana caught Votar's hand. "Please, father! If you went to the spirit world, maybe you could find out how to heal him."

Votar's dark brow wrinkled. "Why should I do that for one of these tall folk who harass and tax us for ranging on lands we roamed long before they thought to claim them? It takes much power to visit the spirits."

But Suki had been watching Rana. Her brown eyes were sad, but she spoke with a firmness her husband, mighty sorcerer though he was, never disregarded. "Perhaps the spirits of Rana's golden parents guided her to this man. You must help him, husband, if you can."

Fenn had been silent. He said now, "If finding a cure leaves you exhausted, father, I will lead your string tomorrow. You could ride till your strength returns."

"Like an infant or old one?" Votar grunted. His shrewd eyes considered Rana, who watched him pleadingly. "All right," he grumbled. "What can a man do with his whole household against him? But I warn you. I am tired. I'm not sure I can reach the spirit world."

He got his drum out of its fringed, painted case. The hide cover was stretched over a round frame as wide across as the length of his arm. With red alder-bark juice, he had painted all the gods, those of sun, storm and wind; guardians of animals, birds and fish; the Mothers who watched over home and children and aided women in childbirth; and symbols for all things a sorcerer might need to ask the spirits about.

Suki spread his white polar bear hide, and Votar sat

on it cross-legged, eyes closed, his carved drumstick, shaped like a flattened double-headed hammer, resting lightly on the magic symbols.

Slowly, he began to drum, a faint tapping that seemed to Rana like her own heartbeat. Gradually, the beat increased, now thumping four times to each throb of Rana's heart. Votar seldom required privacy to consult the spirits, but after a time that could have been long or short, Rana could not tell, his eyes opened and he scowled at them.

"Don't you have something better to do than stand around gaping?"

Fenn went for more wood. Suki attended to the stew, and Rana carefully raised the stranger and got more willow tea down him, more of the strong broth. He choked out what sounded like a curse, glared at her and cried out what was surely a reproach or accusation.

"It's all right," she told him. "We're friends. Friends."

All that evening, she gave him broth and tea, bathed his hot face and throat, talked to him soothingly when he raved. What had happened to him? Why was he in this place where only wild things and Sameh wandered?

He was so tall, but wasted now from hunger. The features that had seemed strange to her at first were now becoming familiar, like something remembered from a dream. He was of her blood people. She wanted to save him for that, but even more because he was alone.

Votar did not eat with the others. After rousing from another unsuccessful trance, he told Fenn to go around the camp and bring back the hearts of any birds or animals that had been killed that day. After a time Fenn returned with a bowl of things Rana could not bear to look at, though she heard Fenn enumerating them.

A *härk* had broken its leg and had to be slaughtered; a ptarmigan and mountain plover had been taken by some boys who had also snared a hare. Not a very impressive collection, so Votar gave Suki a little powdered bear and wolf heart to add to the dish she would cook for him. The bear was great magic. When skinned, he looked so human that he was called Old Man of the Woods and Grandfather as well as the Honey-Pawed One.

Surely, after partaking of this strongest magic food, Votar would reach the spirits! But though he drummed on long after Fenn and Suki slept, he never dropped the stick or became transfixed as he did when he had ascended to the other world. At last Votar gave a shuddering sigh and put the drum aside.

"It is no use."

"But, father—"

"No use." Votar's head drooped on his breast from his exertions. "Some sorcerer has made thick, heavy spells around the stranger's soul. I cannot reach it."

At Rana's cry of protest, Votar added wearily, "We can carry him with us till he dies if you want, but it's a waste of trouble. He doesn't know what's happening and must die soon of the poison in his blood."

"I won't let him! There has to be a reason that I found him by my parents' grave."

Votar said ruefully, "In the soul of the universe there are flashes of what we call reason, but mostly it seems chaos to us because it is vast and eternal. Perhaps when this man's spirit leaves its mortal shape, it will help you because you pitied this present husk."

She didn't want some spirit's help. She wanted the man, the one whose face rested on her breast. She wanted him to look at her with those deep blue eyes and know her, speak to her in words she could understand. But she knew her foster-father had done all he could.

Easing the stranger's head to his couch of furs, she brewed a restorative tea for Votar, who drank it slowly, relaxing, and retired to his place by Suki.

Rana gazed down at the sick man. Was there no way to

help him? What could she do against a witchcraft that even Votar was powerless to overcome? In desperation, she wrapped her cape about her and went out into the glowing blue night, making her way to the cairn.

Mother. Father. Did you send the stranger? Can you help him?

There was no answer, but she felt impelled to sit down by the cairn. She pictured the stranger, and she must have been light-headed with exhaustion, for it seemed as if he lay in her arms. There was no time, no weight to him, and suddenly she could see herself holding him, though she still inhabited a body that stood a little distance away.

A white fox trotted up and nuzzled at the knee of this second self of hers. It had a mangled paw but moved without a limp, and she wondered why it hadn't shed to its blue-gray summer coat.

Without words it said to her, *Get on my back. I will take you to the spirits.*

"You're too small."

The fox seemed to laugh. *Try it and see.* Whether the animal grew or she shrank, Rana didn't know, but she was on its back, holding to the thick furry neck. They sped through emptiness that echoed into howling winds, flaying cold, blasts that threatened to hurl her from the fox into icy pinnacles and bottomless chasms. She clung tightly, closing her eyes, fixing her mind on the stranger's need, and they were suddenly in a green forest where birds of every color flashed and sang in fruiting, flowering branches. All the animals she had ever seen, and many she had not, gathered to make her welcome.

We will help you, they told her wordlessly. *We will help you because you helped our sister, the fox.*

Then they were out of the beautiful forest, soaring through a void which ended as they met murky heaviness, a stifling spongy mass that seeped into Rana's nose and mouth and ears, filled and paralyzed her body with stinking cold slime.

Hold to me, the fox warned.

Dizzied, invaded by the unseen enemy, Rana clung to the animal and held the stranger as fiercely in the shelter of her core-being. He must not die! He must not—even if she did.

The invisible substance blazed. Within her, outside her. Seared till she thought she must fall like singed rubble from her mount, Rana kept blackened, bleeding arms about the fox and called on the spirits.

The flames ebbed. Spent, huddled against the vixen's neck, she looked down at the world and had to endure the agonies she saw—bearing a child that thrust, doubled, through her body; thirsting in deserts; writhing under a lash; wracked by fever or the torturer; drowning; bleeding from grievous wounds. At any time, the power contesting her whispered, she could escape by releasing the stranger.

Let him go. He will die anyway.

But she hid him deeper, folding the essence of her soul around him, a shield from malignancy that grappled her in many shapes, engulfed her as water, fire and avalanche. Now other creatures surrounded her, buoyed her in the flood, absorbed the fire, broke the crushing impact of masses of rock, earth and snow. But she was dead. There was nothing left of her. Only the tiny kernel that held the stranger.

Into this nothingness, this incredible stillness, came the song of spring's first nightingale. He was joined by all the birds that fly, even the mountain owl, and as they sang, Rana became whole again, unmarked by all she had suffered, embracing the fox, who turned golden eyes to her.

It is well. I can devour the sickness.

In a flash they passed through the wonderful forest of

animal spirits, through winds and piercing cold, through bleak nothingness to the cairn, back to the body that held the stranger's form.

The fox nosed at his leg, began to tear at it. Rana cried out, but the fox sent a message. *Trust me.* Rana watched, unbelieving, as the fox ripped away masses of hideous flesh, green with corruption, till only the bone of the leg remained. Then it licked the bone. Slowly, flesh massed again, layer after layer, till the leg was whole.

Here is your man. The fox glanced up at Rana, yellow eyes lambent. Then it turned and slipped into the willows beyond the cairn. Rana looked down.

The stranger wasn't there. She must have dreamed it. Dreamed it all. And yet she was so tired . . . Her body fell bruised, held the memory of burning, of freezing. As she tried to rise, her numb legs gave way, hummed painfully, but at last she was able to creep back to the lodge, defeat sour in her mouth.

Of course she had dreamed it. No fox had whisked her to the spirits and then removed the poisoned flesh and blood of the stranger's leg.

Without looking at the doomed man, she built up the fire to make him more tea and heated the broth. It was only when she started to bathe his face that she noticed that he burned no longer. His breath came easily without the laboring gasps. He even seemed less haggard.

Scarcely daring to believe her senses, Rana pulled back the covering and examined the leg. It was still broken but much less swollen. Whatever the reason, his fever was gone.

She gave him tea and broth, covered him warmly and brought her bed close to his. As she took off her outer clothing, several white fox hairs fell to the rug.

II

Fenn repacked his *härkar* so one was free to draw the light sledge hastily contructed for the stranger. Votar looked sharply at Rana when Suki delightedly announced that the man was better, but he asked no questions and Rana attempted no explanations. She herself wasn't sure what had happened.

All that mattered was that the man was getting stronger. When the fever left him he was still too weak and starved to do more than look his thanks for the careful tending Suki and Rana gave him. He slept most of the time, in his sledge or, when they stopped, in a *kåta*. But after a few days, he could sit propped up against a pack and feed himself. When the stranger tried to communicate, Votar's cousin Paavo was able to understand him.

Rotund, red-cheeked, with a sinew-thin drooping black moustache, Paavo talked with the sun-haired man, stopping now and then to translate for the others.

Jørun Leifsson thanked them for saving him. He was a Norwegian noble who had been spending a few years in Iceland when his old father and three brothers were trapped in a blood feud with equally powerful neighbors. The quarrel started over slurs a Ruriksson made about Jørun's sister after she refused to marry him.

One of her brothers had killed the vilifier and was killed in turn. Jørun's father had wished to bring the matter before the *thing*, a large yearly gathering where lawsuits were brought and decided by all free landholders, but the mother of the first-slain cried shame on her men to think of accepting silver or gold compensation for her son's life. She upbraided them till the Rurikssons collected their many tenants and supporters and rode to the enemy manor.

Starkad, eldest of the Rurikssons, was in command. When his men surrounded the principal buildings, he called on the trapped people to send out their women, children and servingfolk. As for the men, they could come out and die fighting in the open or perish in the flames of their hall, as they chose.

The Leifssons sent out their servants with the children. The youngest of the three Leifsson wives was afraid to die, so she went, too. They were allowed to shelter in the barn farthest from the hall. The Leifssons held off the attackers with arrows, killing several, but Starkad himself shot a flaming arrow into a heap of old bed straw stacked against the timbered hall. As the building burst into crackling flames, the aged Leif and the women lay down on their beds and covered themselves with hides so they would suffocate before they burned.

Jørun's sister? Feeling she was to blame for the battle, she chose to die, though she was still a maiden, little more than a child. She was found with her father and mother, their bodies unmarked by fire because of the big oxhides stretched over them.

The rest of the Leifssons and their retainers fought till the ceiling timbers began to crash around them. Then they leaped through the door, charging their enemies. They took heavy toll of Rurikssons before they were finally cut down.

Jørun heard the tidings almost the moment his feet

touched his native soil. He rode for vengeance, but Starkad and his brothers, called the Burners by then because of their horrible deed, had been outlawed and fled the country.

Jørun's long mouth twisted as he made his count. He had found one Rurikssøn in the Dane king's court, another with the Jarl of Orkney, a third in Iceland. He had killed them all in fair fights. But Starkad had gone to serve in the Varangian Guard, an elite corps of mercenaries who guarded the Byzantine emperor, a common resort of Northmen who found it advisable to leave their own countries.

He'd been on his way to take ship in Birka for the journey to Byzantium, traveling on snow shoes, when he slipped over a snow-covered precipice and broke his leg. Seeing the cairn, hoping it might be some kind of dwelling, he'd crawled there before losing consciousness.

Where were the Sameh going? he asked.

He frowned when he learned they were bound for the high mountain valleys, but Votar, through Paavo, pointed out that their guest was in no condition to take ship for that long journey through the Baltic to the lakes and rivers that led to fabled Byzantium. While Jørun's leg knitted and he regained strength, he'd be better off in the high country.

Jørun thanked them. When he said he hoped he could somehow repay their kindness, his eyes rested on Rana till she blushed and went back to working on the summer shoes she was making for him. His pack had been knocked off in his fall and buried in the snowslide, so he had only the clothes he was wearing, the knife on his belt and a bag of gold and silver. Most of all, he lamented the loss of his sword, a gift from his father when he'd left for Iceland.

His jaw hardened. But swords could be bought, good enough for killing a man who'd burned women.

Rana dared to ask, "Would it not be better to keep alive your family's name? Supposing you, not Starkad, fall in Byzantium?"

Jørun gazed at Rana. She looked back at him, meeting those lake-blue eyes. A shock went through her, as if he had touched her naked flesh, as if the lights that blazed in the northern sky had entered her body, filling her with shimmering, radiant fire.

"There are my brothers' two sons," he replied. "Only boys. If I do not settle this, they must, in honor. I would spare them that. Besides, I have no mind that Starkad breathe the bright air my brothers cannot."

She knew he would not be swayed, but she ached in protest. As they journeyed onward, her feelings of tenderness and longing grew stronger each day.

Surely the powers had brought him to her. He would be dead if she hadn't saved him. Then where would his vengeance be? But that was something she couldn't tell him. With his notions of honor, there was no guessing what he'd think he must do. If he ever returned, she wanted it to be because he loved her, not to pay a debt.

By the time they reached the summer camp, an immense plateau with mountains on every side, and set up the *kåtor* near a beautiful small lake, Jørun was able to get around a little with the stick Fenn carved for him. One part of Rana rejoiced, but she dreaded the time he would go, not only because of the danger, but because she couldn't imagine how she'd get through the days without seeing him, hearing his voice, treasuring the smile that took the bitterness from his face. She wished she could smooth his face with her hands and lips, erase the cruel memories, but at least his face grew younger when she sang for him her nightingale song.

He was much with Fenn and began to pick up the language. This was a lazy time for the men because though the herd grazed on the moor and slopes in the morning, the midges that came with the warming day urged them to the eternal snows that never melted, even when the sun colored the peaks during the short night.

The men repaired gear, fished, whittled bone and wood into useful objects, and talked just as much as the women did while they tended to their never-ending chores.

The only major task that had to be accomplished during summer camp was earmarking the calves so there would be no disputes over ownership. During one long vibrant twilight, herders and dogs drove the reindeer out on a neck of land protruding far into the lake. The way back was sealed by fastening the dogs to staves thrust into the ground. Then, as quietly as possible, owners moved through the animals, searching out their *vajor* with young.

Rana could use the braided leather catching rope with its bone slip knot as deftly as most men, another of Fenn's teachings, but she was usually able to grasp a calf by a hind leg, force it down gently as she talked to it and quickly cut her mark in its ear. From the *vaja* Suki had given her when she was old enough to lead one, calves had come, and calves born of them so that she had, counting the five she marked now, eighteen reindeer.

The calves were so surprised they didn't struggle, but the instant they were let up, they ran off with little gruntings till they found their mothers and comforted themselves by suckling.

Jørun was watching from beside Fraxi. When Rana had finished helping Votar mark his and Suki's beasts and started for the *kåta* with her string of ear snippets, Jørun fell in step beside her. He still used the stick but his limp was almost unnoticeable.

She was glad and sorry. Glad he would not be crippled; sorry he would soon go away. "Is there anything you cannot do?" he asked.

Puzzled, she glanced at him. "All Sameh women do these things."

"But you are not Sameh."

She shrugged. "Their ways are all I know."

"You are happy? Always wandering, without a home?"

Amazed, she said, "Everywhere we stop is home." She indicated the broad plain, the peaks crimsoned from the glow of the sun beneath the horizon. "This place is for summer. Soon we will start for our autumn camp, and then move lower still for winter. I love all my homes and the journeys in between."

He watched her intently. "Could you be happy in one place—a camp for all the year?"

The idea was so strange that she halted to think about it. "How can that be? The reindeer . . ."

Jørun laughed caressingly. "We have no reindeer, but our cattle do go up in the mountains for the summer and come down in autumn to feast on harvest stubble. Would a small migration like that satisfy you?"

"I don't know." She could not imagine such a life. "What are your lodges like? What do the women do?"

As he talked, she frowned with the effort of picturing log *kåtor* many times the size of any Sameh storehouse; a hearthfire that never moved; beds built permanently against the walls of these lodges; horses, cows, pigs and goats instead of reindeer; planting seeds in a certain place so crops would come up.

"But some things are much the same," he said as if to reassure her. "Women make cheese—cows give much more milk than *vajor*—and sew clothing and cook the food." He added softly, "And they have babies to love and tend."

"If there are no reindeer, do mothers always carry the baby's cradle?"

"Our cradles are too big to carry."

"Then what good are they?"

"Our cradles stand on the floor," he said patiently, "or hang from the ceiling."

"And the babies are left alone? Don't they cry?"

"Babies always cry," he said after a blank stare.

"Sameh babies don't. Only if they're hungry or cold or need fresh moss." She made a lulling motion. "Babies rock to and fro from a pack saddle or the mother's shoulder. When she puts the cradle down, she props it so the baby can see her and not feel lonely."

His straight brown eyebrows drew together. "A child has to learn that it can't have everything its own way."

"Sometimes there's no milk for a Sameh baby, mother's or *vaja*'s. Often the wind stings. There is much we cannot protect babies from, but we can keep them close so they'll know we love them."

"If you didn't move all the time, a baby would know where it was."

She could still, in half-sleep, seem to remember the sway of her cradle's moving with the *härk*, the soothing motion of Suki's shoulders. "My baby will be with me," she said determinedly. "The Sameh way is good."

"But what if you do not marry a Sameh?"

Could he mean—? She glanced up at him, hope fluttering like a winged thing in her throat.

He touched her face as if he could not help it, withdrew his fingers as if they were burned. Had he felt that shock, that joyous rush of blood that hummed through her like the spring song of all nightingales?

"Of course you will marry a Sameh," he said harshly. "A good man who has no blood on his hands."

He went off as swiftly as his broken pace would allow. Rana stared after him. The happy flame died. What had he been about to say? If he cared for her as she did for him, she would follow him anywhere; live in those strange *kåtor*, sleep in those fixed, high beds.

But she *would* have a Sameh cradle for their child.
Yes, she would.

Then she had to fight back tears because he was going
away, and even if he lived, who knew if he would ever
return? Blindly, she moved onward. She would not marry
a Sameh. Or any other man. Only Jørun.

Shedding reindeer looked as if they had mange and
were a scruffy, shabby sight, but their new coats were
coming in and their horns seemed longer each day. Now
that the calves were grazing for much of their sustenance,
a sort of bit was placed in their mouths in the afternoon so
their mothers could be milked in the evening. Few gave
more than a cup, squirted into a large birch scoop, but
this was so thick and rich that what wasn't used fresh
could be made into cheese with scarcely any left as whey.
Some milk was poured into kegs and mixed with leaves
of mountain sorrel. This would be a delicious change
from dried meat the next winter.

On all the vast moor, the only trees were scrub willows
growing thickly about the lake, no taller than Rana. Their
dead branches were used for fuel. As the nearer supply
was used up, Rana went farther to collect faggots and one
day noticed a bright green hillock some distance from the
lake. Moving around, she saw that it was indeed a fox's
den, verdant on top from their dung. There must have
been a score of holes going in and out of the hillock, facing the rising sun. A dozen slate-blue foxes basked or
played in the sun, and the half-grown ones set up a yap-
ping as Rana approached.

She gazed into the golden eyes of the largest fox. Its
tail thumped, just like Fraxi's. Could it be the same one
Rana had freed that spring? Rana half expected it to
speak. When it did not, she called softly, "I am glad to
see you well, glad you found your mate. Thank you for

taking me to the spirits to save the man I want to father
my children.''

The fox yawned benignly and rested its pointed muzzle between its paws. One of them was scarred.

Like Suki, Rana carried much of her equipment on
a brass belt ring—awl, needlecase with sinew thread,
spoon and knife. Men might spin yarns and play wolf-
slayer on the back of a cutting board, using reindeer toe
bones for dice, reindeer and wolf; but women, though
they enjoyed stories and jokes and might join in with
some of their own, had unending tasks. Root fibers had
to be plaited into water flasks and baskets, clothing
made, and Suki was skilled in sewing beautiful bands to
adorn garments and harness, some of them embroidered
with silver thread. And then the sedge grass for stuffing
shoes had to be dried, pounded and combed and rubbed
to softness before it was twisted into rolls for later use.

One afternoon while Rana was working at this, Jorun
ruefully surveyed another nicked finger and tossed aside
the wood scrap on which he was trying to emulate Fenn's
carving. "I can at least pound grass," he said to her.
"Let me help you."

Paavo, who was visiting while working on a knife
sheath, looked startled and then bent forward so that his
stringy moustache hid a smile. Rana protested, "This is
women's work."

He took the mallet from her. "Was it women's work
when you saved my life?" he asked in a tone no one else
could hear. "Votar has told me he could do nothing and
went to sleep, expecting to see me dead next morning.
He thinks that you went to the spirits for me, and since
you are no sorceress, it was a marvel you returned."

"I had a guide."

She told him about the fox. When she had finished, he
said, "I will never kill, or let my tenants kill, another

Wanderer of the Woods, however many fat geese one makes off with.'' Her arm brushed his as she pulled a long-toothed bone comb through the matted grass.

Slight as the touch was, awareness of him consumed her, thrilling to every part of her body but concentrated in warm languorous sweetness in her loins.

She loved him. All the time, she loved him. But when their eyes met or they touched, however fleetingly, this overwhelming need surged up, hunger to know his mouth and arms, be lost in him as she welcomed him into her. Yet fiercely as it pulsed, this longing was different from the frenzy that drove *sarvar* to rut till they neither rested nor ate while they mounted *vaja* after *vaja,* often serving them with one swift thrust. She desired Jørun with her every fiber, yet she craved to know his heart and mind even more than she yearned for his straight, graceful body.

''My leg is healed,'' he said to her now, still speaking for her ears alone. ''I must start for Birka.''

She felt as if an icy shaft had driven into her and quivered in her center. ''Can you not travel south with us? We must leave soon, before the storms begin.''

He hesitated, then regretfully shook his head. ''I must reach the Dneiper before the waters leading to it freeze. It is a long journey to Byzantium.'' Don't go! she wanted to cry. But she knew he must do this thing before he would believe his life was his own. She wished she had something to give him, a talisman to guard him.

Suddenly she thought of her father's sword. If her parents knew how she loved Jørun, she was sure they would want him to have the heirloom. But it was in the cairn, and she could not delay him from what he felt he must do.

''You—you will come back?'' she whispered.

His gaze met hers. She felt as if she were drowning in that deep lake blue. ''If I live, Rana, I will come.''

"I will wait."

His eyes blazed joyfully before he said, "The way is dangerous. Starkad is a mighty warrior. Don't wait for me too long."

"I will wait till you come."

"No," he said strongly. "I owe you my life. To ruin your young fresh one would be poor thanking. If you can be happy with a good man, don't put him off and waste what you can have."

She didn't argue but vowed in her heart, *You are my man. I will have no other. If you do not come, I will stay in my foster-parents' lodge for all my days.* A daring thought exploded in her mind. *Or—I will come to find you.*

With that hope, she managed to smile at him. It was as if they were alone in the *kåta*, alone together in the whole great world.

Jørun left next morning, shouldering a pack of provisions, wearing grass-lined shoes Rana had made for him. Votar was offended when their guest tried to leave silver, so Jørun slipped a pouch of coins to Rana and asked her to have Fenn, when they were near a market, buy gifts for Votar and Suki.

"And this is for you," he said, slipping off his golden ring. "It's too big for your fingers, but you might wear it around your neck."

She nodded, unable to speak. She would wear it till she could give it to their son.

He brought her hand, palm up, to his lips, and kissed it. "Be well and happy, Rana."

"Travel safe," she said and beseeched him with her eyes. Come back. Come back.

Fenn was going to guide him out of the trackless moors to where he could find his way to the coast and Birka Island. As they set off, Rana watched till they were tiny dots against the hazy mountains.

She worked furiously till bedtime, scarcely pausing to eat, gathering wood, making cheese, pounding sedge grass, dashing away the tears that blinded her.

If this day could be so long, how could she get through the countless ones before she could even begin to hope he might return? Suki and Votar watched her sympathetically but didn't try to cheer her. She was grateful for that.

III

The sun sank lower, no longer crimsoned the mountains throughout the short Arctic night. For a few days, clouds enshrouded the camp, misty grayness hiding the reindeer on the ridges above. It was time to start for the spring-autumn camp before an early storm swept in.

Grandmother shivered, even among the furs they heaped on her. "I am so tired," she murmured. "Children, let me stay here, where I was happiest, where I met your father."

"You'll come back again next summer," Suki chided. She made her mother some hot tea and she and Rana resumed the packing. Next morning early they must be on their way.

When they woke, no one noticed the old woman was missing till Rana went to wake her with a bowl of mashed cloud-berries and pounded meat.

"Here you are, grandmother," she said, forcing cheer into her voice. She drew back the covers.

Nothing.

Votar found his mother-in-law a little way up the mountain. She had climbed till her aged heart gave out. She looked peaceful and happy.

They buried her in a rock fissure, face turned to the rising sun, placing all her belongings about her, with plenty of food. Furs were heaped on the pack saddle strapped to the gentle *härk* she had ridden, and Votar cut his throat in a swift, merciful thrust so the animal could carry her to Saivo, her husband, and a fresh new body.

It was strange without her, but she had chosen her place to die after a long, busy life. A happier end than many. Still, a sense of losing a familiar part of things nagged at Rana as she helped secure the *härkar*'s burdens, and she was glad to lead her string across the mist-enveloped plain as the caravan moved out.

How far ahead was Jørun? At lower levels, the migrations of centuries would leave a track he could easily follow unless snow fell. The threat of winter pressed down with heavy fog that made the group move in an unending phantom mist.

Plodding onward, Rana caught her breath as, above the layers of cloud, a mountain reared into sun and sky, seeming to tower much higher than when one could see the whole expanse.

Endless day.

It struck her in revelation. Above the storms and weather of the earth, there was always brilliant sky, beaming sun. It might be on the underside of the world, but it was there.

Breath rushed into her lungs. For a moment, she was illumined with joy. The love she felt for Jørun overflowed to all creation. Whatever happened to them in this life, that love would be always there. Like mountain, sky and sun.

Her afterglow of exaltation lasted after low-hanging clouds again hid the peak. That moment of clear seeing had taught her more than her dimly remembered journey to the spirits. It must be what Votar had told her lay at the center of the universe, beyond the winds and chasms of his shaman's flights. Perfect peace.

But she was still very much in this world, in a body that ached for Jørun's. Sleet began to sting her face. She lowered her head, half shutting her eyes, and knew that winter, for her, had already come.

Votar drummed that night, asking the spirits of wind and snow to withhold their fury till the Sameh were safely through the passes. The powers must have listened, for no storm broke, though the weather was sullen. Some streams were so swollen by glacier-melt and rain that the reindeer had to swim across, their fine new antlers a low, moving forest of leafless trees. Their thick new coats helped buoy them up, and the whole herd, dark gray shadows in the lighter mists, had vanished ahead with their herders by the time all the people had rowed across in the three small boats that were left in the willows from year to year.

How good it was to see the first birches, bent into human dancing shapes by the winds! As they passed the cairn of Rana's parents, the clouds lifted, and it was possible to see far through the mountain passes to the broad valley where they were bound.

Fenn joined them that night. He had given Jørun more provisions from those stored in the permanent camp. Jørun would likely reach Birka in time to find passage southward. Fenn spoke to them all, but his light brown eyes rested on Rana with a kind of wistful sadness.

Night frosts turned leaves every subtle or brilliant shade of crimson, yellow and orange. The birches by the lake blazed with a gold that reminded Rana of Jørun's hair. Under the clear autumn sky, the lake reflected the blue of his eyes.

Where was he? Did he remember her?

The upsurge of passionate life before winter, the fever that possessed the *sarvar* and prepared the *vajor* to wel-

come them, burned in Rana. If only Jørun had made love
to her—if she had at least known that! As antlers clashed,
as bucks reared up to sheathe themselves in females,
Rana kept as far from the pasture as she could. She was
glad when the weeks of fervid coupling ended and it was
time to move toward winter camp.

The bucks, so strong and splendid a few weeks before,
were gaunt and exhausted. Antlers loosened and fell from
their sagging heads. They were a dismal sight beside fat
härkar, whose horns were as impressive as ever. Even
a *vaja* could now intimidate, with spiky, sharp little
horns, the buck who had mounted her only days before.
Most of the *vajor* carried in them the start of calves that
would be born when they returned to this camp in the
spring.

It was impossible that Jørun would be back by then.
How many seasons must she wait?

The spirit lights, sometimes great arcs of rays, sometimes a diffused glow, reflected green, yellow-green and
sometimes rose, on the snow as reindeer, connected by a
strap that ran between their hind legs to light, sturdy,
boat-shaped sledges, pulled them through days that were
scarcely brighter than the starry nights, and darker when
there was a full moon. Sefni drew Rana's sledge, and she
guided him with a single rein, drawn to one side or the
other.

The sun shone wanly from beneath the horizon, but the
brightest noondays now were darker than midnights at
the height of summer. The herdsman skimmed along on
skis. When storms shrieked in, the reindeer huddled together for warmth, and the *kåtor* were quickly set up.
There was still good grass under the new snow and moist
soft lichen of every color from ivory and pale gray-green
to yellow. When the caravan reached a favorable spot,
camp was set up on a snow-cleared hillside and the herd

fed richly while the men cut and chopped wood to fuel hungry fires that kept lodges snug no matter what the cold outside, and on which simmered delicious stews and warming herbal brews.

According to the carved calendar stick of reindeer bone, the caravan spent fifty-eight days on the journey to the pine forests of the winter camp. The herd spread out over the pine-covered upland pastures to feast on succulent lichens waiting beneath the snow, and the people camped near a spring bubbling up from the rocks on the edge of the forest. The water was icy but still so much warmer than the air that vapor rose from it.

Though marshes and streams were frozen, there was almost no wind in the great pines, and it seemed much warmer than the exposed moorland they had crossed. Less than a day away was a settlement of river-Sameh who never ranged far from home and kept sheep as well as reindeer. Votar, Fenn and the other men went there with excess reindeer and such furs as wouldn't be demanded in taxes to be traded for wool, blankets and a few luxuries from Norse traders who came to the settlement to exchange their wares.

Determined not to brood or mope, Rana often went out on skis to see the winter world and sometimes took Fenn's turn at herding. Then, though it was winter, she sang the nightingale's tunes.

Snow after snow had fallen, so that the reindeer had to dig deeper to reach their food and their heads disappeared in the holes as they grazed. Knowing they must be wary, they looked up frequently, alert for danger, before they went back to foraging. In spite of this vigilance and that of dogs and herders, an occasional animal was lost to a lynx or wolf, or the fiercest marauder of all, the wolverine, who crept stealthily up on a grazing beast, sinking into the snow when it raised its head, till it could make a final spring and sink crushing fangs into the reindeer's neck.

On their skis, men hunted wolves, too, bringing back their pelts for clothing, and pursued the lynx, whose urine was said to form amber. The lynx's beautiful fur was valued beyond ermine, the snowy winter coat of the stoat, but these were dearly bought. The men took only one lynx that year. It had thrown itself on its back in its final battle and of the seventeen dogs attacking it, killed three, maimed two so badly they had to be slain, and crippled ten more.

Bears slumbered, but other creatures had to eat. Though both ptarmigan and hare changed from brown summer appearance to autumn gray and then to white, this disguise often couldn't save them from the same hunters who relished reindeer, or from fox and ermine who had turned as white as their quarry.

The moon had been full three times since the Sameh reached winter camp and was now swelling for the fourth time as the days grew lighter and longer. Snow thawed enough in the day to freeze at night, layers that kept the reindeer from reaching their food. Herders felled trees with the heaviest growths of beard lichen to feed the herd, and were debating whether to move closer to the coast for easier grazing when the western spring winds started blowing.

The reindeer faced it, sniffing, restless to move. In less than a day, the sledges were packed, and as *härkar* pulled them away from where the *kåtor* had made such comfortable shelters, only smoldering hearth ashes were left of the winter homes.

IV

The spring-autumn camp in the broad valley was where the calves were conceived and born and where most males would be slaughtered or castrated. It was strange to Rana that so many creatures could have come into being and passed back into the spirit world or begotten their own kind while she still waited. New babies had been born in the *kåtor*, too, and Paavo's son had married. It seemed to Rana that life flowed around her as a river sweeps around an embedded stone.

She had known Jørun couldn't return the first year, but as the second one wore on, as the summer sun painted the snowy peaks above the moorlands, she grew increasingly restless. As the band prepared to start for the autumn country, she told her foster-family that she would go in search of Jørun. Votar sighed but didn't look surprised. Suki's eyes widened in distress.

"My heart, how will you travel that long perilous way among strangers who will not help you as Sameh would, but who may hurt or rob you?"

Votar put his hand comfortingly over his wife's. "We have always known," he reminded her, but the wolverine scar was more livid than usual. "I will talk to the spirits, daughter, and ask them to protect you."

"Thank you, father." Rana hesitated. Fenn had not said anything but the sadness in his face made her ache for him. "Will you ask the spirits another thing?"

"What is that?"

"If my parents would grant it, I would like to have the sword that lies between them. For Jørun. For our son, if we have one."

Votar considered. "I will ask, when we reach your parents' cairn."

As they made their way through mist-obscured moors and valleys, Rana led her reindeer, but she felt detached from all that happened, as if her spirit was already questing ahead, straining to find her love.

She mourned with the camp when Paavo's brother-in-law was swept away by a flooded river but was glad that the widow, Unno, a plump, round-faced woman with kind eyes, chose to move into Votar and Suki's lodge rather than become part of Paavo's household.

Unno was Votar's cousin and had always gotten along well with him and Suki. Her son, Durre, a merry-eyed, long-legged boy of fourteen, was already a good herds-man and a champion at playing wolf-slayer, often de-feating both Votar and Fenn on the same evening. His lively presence and Unno's good-natured sharing of the work relieved some of the tension caused by Rana's im-pending departure.

At last the rock gnarl of the *seite* came in view, and the heaped rocks where Rana's parents slept. Her heart pounded as the caravan approached, and as soon as the *kåta* was pitched, she took a bowl of milk soured with mountain sorrel and hurried to the cairn.

This was where she had found Jørun. Where she had entered the spirit world on the back of the vixen. Placing the bowl on a ledge, she tried, as she had so often, to summon up an image of the young blond foreigners who had died shielding her against the storm.

Mother. Father. I love Jørun as you must have loved each other. Help me find him. Give me your blessing. And if you can, send good to Suki and Votar and Fenn.

She pressed her face against the cairn, and the stones did not feel cold. In the dark cave of her mind she saw a sword blazing with the shimmering glow of the Spirit Lights. It gave itself into her hand and she knew her parents had heard her.

That night Votar drummed beneath a larch near the *seite*, one of the special trees by which he sometimes ascended to the other world. Those inside the *kåta* heard the rhythm grow fainter till it was scarcely more than a heartbeat. It ceased altogether.

"He is with the spirits," Suki murmured.

She hurried to give Votar tea when he came in and a bowl of soup, for he had fasted all that day. He sipped the steaming brew gratefully and smiled as he looked at Rana.

"It is well, daughter. Your parents give you the sword for the man they guided to their cairn. And they welcome you to take any of their jewelry. The sword is the luck and honor of your line. They want it used." He began to eat the soup. "Fenn and I will move stones, but you yourself must enter the grave and take the sword."

When Votar had rested, he and Fenn went with Rana to the heap of rocks. She held a pine knot while they shifted aside the great stones that closed one side of the shallow cave dug into the slope. Votar made incantations and Fenn held the torch while Rana ventured into the shadows and paused, heart thudding, till her eyes could see by the flickering light.

She was stabbed by the memory of Jørun when she saw golden hair escaped from beneath furs heaped over what had been bodies. She was not afraid of her parents, she knew they blessed her undertaking, yet she flinched and trembled as she carefully shifted the rotting furs above where she thought their hands would be.

Gold gleamed dully on white finger bones, small and large ones, closed together on the handle above a rusted blade, a weapon that was not at all the glorious one of her vision. And to touch those skeleton hands, unclasp them—

Rana's scalp felt as if it were shrinking and her spine chilled. But those golden beings of her prayer rose before her. *We are not the bones. They are no more to us than the shed antlers of a sarv are to him when he has splendid new ones. Our sword is for the living, child. Take it.*

Gently as she could, she lifted the hands with one of hers and drew away the sword. She saw a gleam of ornaments, the torch reflected green and crimson flames, but she did not want them.

Mother, father, thank you. She kissed the bones, the strong ones and the delicate, placed them together beneath the furs and backed away from the grave.

It was fine weather when they reached the autumn camp, so fine that Suki said, "There's no snow, daughter, so you can't travel by ski or sledge. Why don't you wait? Go with us to winter camp and reach the coast from there."

Rana dreaded striking off by herself, but the ease of the journey was the least of her present fears. She was daunted at the prospect of a port city, at trying to bargain for passage south. She didn't speak the language. She didn't know the customs. But she thought of Jørun and clung doggedly to her resolution.

"If I don't hurry, mother, ice will close the rivers, and I'll not leave a port before spring."

"That's right," said Fenn. "I'll take one of my *härkar* to carry our provisions and traveling *kåta.*"

Rana spun toward him. "You—what do you mean?"

"Of course I'm going with you."

Vastly relieved, overwhelmed with gratitude, she caught his hand and squeezed it. "Oh, Fenn, if you'll just help me get to Birka and find passage!"

"Passage for us both." He grinned. "Can you think I'd let my—sister travel alone to Byzantium? Even we Sameh have heard of that city's splendor and wickedness."

Neither Suki nor Votar looked surprised. Fenn had evidently told them his resolve or they had guessed it. Yet Rana's heart misgave her. "Who will look after the herd? Help our parents?"

"I'm far from helpless," Votar grunted. He rested a hand on Durre's broadening shoulder. "Between us, we can manage, can't we, lad?"

Unno already did so much of the women's work that Rana had to hunt for things to do. And Paavo would lend a hand when necessary. Still, Fenn was an only son, not just a good worker.

"Please, Fenn," Rana urged. "Just find me a place on a ship . . ."

Suki pressed Rana's hand to her cheek. "Daughter, it is hard to let you go, though we have always known you must. We will worry less if Fenn is with you."

"I will help with the slaughtering," said Fenn. "Then we will go."

Besides the small *kåta* designed for one or two people, the *härk*'s pack saddle was loaded with supplies and belongings. Another *härk* carried furs, some wrapped around the sword, and a bag of amber that should pay for the journey. The amber was partly a gift from Suki, but most of the tawny transparent lumps had been saved for Rana, wherever they were found, since she was a baby. Rana gave her ten reindeer to her parents and Fenn gave six of his best *vajor* to Durre and authorized Votar to do as he judged best with the rest of his string.

After some consultations, it was decided that it would be much safer for Rana to travel dressed like a man. Nothing could be done about her eyes, but Suki cut her hair so it could be tucked up inside her cap and plaited the cut-off remainder of the silvery mass into a thick braid that she put in a chest with her silver wedding collar and other treasures.

It was hard to say good-bye. After exchanging farewells with Paavo and all the people she had known since childhood, Rana knelt before her parents, pressing their palms to her forehead.

"Thank you for saving me, for loving me, for bringing me up." Her voice choked off and she blinked at hot tears. "I can never pay what I owe you, but I will love you all my life."

They drew her to her feet and embraced her. Suki held her longest. "You have been the light of our *kåta*. We know your life cannot be with us, but it would give us joy to see you now and then if that may be. To know you are well . . ."

"If I live, I will come to see you," Rana vowed. "Jørun told me he has holdings not too far from here. Maybe, in spring and autumn, we can bring our children to see you. When they are old enough, I'd like for them to go with you to summer camp. My children must know the ways of the Sameh, for you will always be my people."

"Your children!" Suki smiled through her tears. "Ah, my heart, we will look forward to that happiness!"

"Till then," said Votar, "we will ask the spirits to guard you."

Fenn hugged his parents, whispered something in their ears to make them chuckle, and then, each leading a *härk*, he and Rana set out through the golden birches.

* * *

Fenn sang much as they traveled, short half-hummed verses breaking into trills. He sang of brilliant foliage, of good grass and plump lichen for the reindeer, of animals and plants preparing for the freezing months ahead. Some *joiks* had no words, but all resonated with content and often with delight.

"I don't see why you're in such high spirits," Rana said a bit grumpily one night as she spread their shoe grass to dry and got out sinew and awl to mend a worn sole. "Everything was soaked when we crossed the river and that ptarmigan you shot at got away and—"

He laughed. She glanced at him and the radiance in his light brown eyes made her turn quickly to her work.

"I am with you," he said.

"But—"

"I know," he cut in. "We're hunting for Jorun. But I don't think about that as we travel. Only that we are together. At night I can stretch out my hand and touch your hair."

"Oh, Fenn!" she cried in regret. What was she doing to him, this dearest, trusted friend?

"Don't be sorry." He spoke in a deep, certain, man's voice. "I love you, Rana. Let me be happy."

But his *joiks*, after that, often made her sad. He deserved much more from her than this shared journey. One night, without speaking, she slipped beneath his covers. He held her close for a while, face buried in her hair, but at last he groaned and turned away.

"Go to your bed." His tone rustled like some creature struggling in high, dying grass.

She obeyed, but it was a long time before either of them slept.

Birka was an island. Fenn sold the *härkar* at a settlement on the mainland and bargained with a ferryman to take them across. Fenn knew a little of the southern language from traders at the winter market fairs, but it was still amazing to Rana that he was able, mostly with gestures, shrugs and incredulous smiles, to get the ferryman to reduce his charge to a small part of one of the silver coins they had received for the reindeer.

The famed trading center spread along the palisaded waterfront, and wooden platforms ran out into the water. Long ships were hauled onto the beach, and there were four small harbors where bigger ships lay safely at anchor. Fenn explained this, though he had never seen a ship before, either, and was wide-eyed with wonder. An earthen rampart of a tall man's height surrounded the city at the back. Tall wooden structures were built into it at intervals, and there was a walled hill overlooking the town.

The ferryman tied his shallow craft to a post on one of the plank platforms and tossed their packs onto it while they warily disembarked. Rana hadn't liked that short, bouncy trip across the lake—it seemed unnatural not to have earth or snow beneath her—and she shrank from the prospect of the unimaginably long voyage before them.

And the city! Not even during the periodic lemming swarmings had she ever seen such density of living creatures, in every kind of costume, it seemed, except that of the Sameh.

Most of the people were tall and fair, but there were stocky yellow-haired ones and a mingling of dark-skinned elegantly clad men wearing cloths wound high about their heads and secured by feathers or bright stones. Jewel-hilted curved swords dangled from their belts, and one imperious, black-bearded man was followed by a boy whose dark brown skin was set off by robes that gleamed with golden threads. Unacquainted as she was with them, Rana could tell many languages were being spoken. Trade was conducted everywhere, along waterfront stalls, beside the ships and in wood-paved streets curving among the buildings packed within the walls.

If Fenn hadn't been beside her, Rana was so bewildered and dismayed that she might well have despaired of her quest, but instead of being confused by the bustle, Fenn's eyes shone and he laughed gleefully.

"There are no furs in sight half as fine as ours," he exulted. "They should bring at least twice as much here as traders give us in the north."

While Rana labored under both their packs, he had staggered along with the baled furs. Dealers were already flocking about them, and one spread what looked like a ship's sail on the ground, motioning for Fenn to display his burden.

In leisurely, caressing fashion, Fenn spread out bear and otter skins; glossy marten pelts, thick, beautifully patterned lynx hides; shaggy wolf skins; snowy ermine—all of magnificent quality, a many-hued treasure. The eyes of potential buyers gleamed with ill-concealed avidity.

The burly red-haired man who had spread the cloth fended eager hands off the lustrous heaps and said in the tongue of the Sameh, "Well, friend, what is your price?"

"My brother and I seek passage to Byzantium."

Strong teeth flashed in the curly red beard. "You're in luck! I myself am sailing for there just as soon as I fill out my cargo." He studied the furs and nodded. "Yes, For these, I will take you all the way to Byzantium."

"And give us coin enough to pay our way back," Fenn said casually.

Pale blue eyes rounded. The merchant scowled. "Why such a trade would beggar me! Are you an honest Sameh or a thief from Bagdad?"

I don't know where or what Bagdad is, but I know our

passage will cost you nothing besides our food," Fenn
retorted.

He turned from the red-haired man and spread his
hands to the other dealers with an inviting grin. Pointing
to the ships, then indicating himself and Rana, he said,
"Byzantium." Then he took out the coins they'd received for the reindeer and pointed at the ships again,
making a flowing motion. "Byzantium—Birka."

The most imposing dark-skinned trader took a bag
from his brown servant boy and poured a glitter of gold
on the furs.

"Don't trust him," growled the first merchant. "He'll
sell you both when he gets you to the Black Sea."

Other men were offering coins, jewels, rolls of fine
wool or shining cloth, knives with ornamental handles, a
dazzling wealth that made Rana's head whirl. She had
never dreamed such things existed. And to see them all at
once!

She would have struck a bargain quickly, just to get it
over, but Fenn considered each offer, rubbing his pointed
chin, while the fire-bearded big man kept telling him
some bad thing or other about each of the traders, the
most common being that they dealt in slaves and would
certainly add Fenn and Rana to their human wares. This
shocked Rana. She could scarcely believe people bought
each other like reindeer.

"And you?" Fenn asked with a raised eyebrow. "Are
we to believe you are the only honest man in Birka?"

The man threw back his iron-muscled neck and roared.
"I probably am—which doesn't say a lot for Birka. But,
my young Sameh, I like the way you handle yourself, and
I've a kindness for your people who nursed me one
winter when I was hurt in an avalanche and lay like one
dead for many weeks." He placed one hand on his sword
hilt and the stub of an arm on a hammer-shaped amulet
that hung about his neck. "I'll swear by Thor, Frey, the

White Christ or any god you will, that I'll land you safely in Byzantium and either bring you back myself or pay your passage with some trusted friend of mine.''

"Give me the gold or silver now.'' Fenn smiled. "And I will pay it back to you when we leave the south.''

The light blue eyes gleamed with respect. "Done.'' He got out a small scale, weighed gold coins in it, then put them into a leather pouch and handed it to Fenn, waving the disappointed contenders away. "I'm Holger Sweynsson, and my ship is that fine one there with the raven figurehead and red sail.'' He sighed. "Of course, no merchant vessel can be as beautiful as a dragon ship after its prey, but I'd trust my *Raven* to sail you even to the New World that Eric the Red's son, Leif, discovered over a dozen years ago.''

"The New World?'' Rana frowned. There was more than this? Than Byzantium?

"Time to talk about that while we're voyaging,'' Holger said. "Will you help me stow these furs aboard? I want to make a deal for walrus tusks, maybe some sealskins. As soon as that's done, we can start.''

The *Raven* seemed huge to Rana. Bundles and chests were heaped under heavy cloth coverings on the raised wood floors at either end and the open, lower space between. Holger gave an order to Björn, a lanky boy of about Durre's age whose hair was as silvery as Rana's. Small brown spots were dusted across his nose and he had a wide grin. He covered the furs with heavy cloth and shoved them as far back under the half-deck as he could.

"Stow your packs where you can get at them,'' Holger advised. "We sleep on the decks, but there's an extra leather sleeping bag that'll hold the two of you and keep you snug.'' He set a hand on his sword belt and flourished his stub. "*Raven*'s made of the best oak. The keel's fifty feet long, shaped out of one tree with straight grain, and the planking's just as sturdy. The ribs come from trees I found myself, growing where they had room to spread and form the strong parts naturally." Another flourish toward the collapsed sail. "Made of the best, tightest wool from Iceland. No wood pegs in the planking to let in water through their holes, but good iron nails. I saw to it myself that every overlap was well-caulked with tarred fleece. She's just had a new coat of pine pitch and—"

"Thor help us, Holger!" What had looked like a heap of clothing rose from a pile of leather ropes, proving to be a skinny, very tall man with a weathered, pitted face; graying black hair; a big, broken nose; and dark, mournful eyes. "The *Raven*'s a good stout *knorr*, but your bragging won't make her a warship, any more than it would change a good, homely housewife into a battle maiden."

He spoke Sameh even better than Holger did. The merchant glowered at him a moment, then grinned reluctantly. "Skarp, old comrade, if you've no taste for glory, why do you twang sagas on your harp? You can't forget we were Vikings any more than I can. Quit your grumbling and meet our passengers." He scratched his head, squinting at them. "I forgot to ask. What are your names?"

Fenn gave his name. There was no time to consult. After a glance at Rana, he added, "This is my brother, Rand."

For the first time, the big red-haired man really looked at her. It was hard to meet his keen pale gaze. "Is the lad mute? He's said not a word. How'd you come from the same mother, him with those gray eyes and fair skin?"

Skarp laughed harshly. "Comrade, you shouldn't be amazed at a light-eyed Sameh. It would be a wonder if, in that village where you wintered, there's not a child or two with your fiery hair, though let us pray they be not so ugly. Fenn, Rand, welcome to the *Raven*.''

Sitting down on the ropes, he seemed to forget all of them as he drew an arched instrument of wood, carved with birds and beasts, out of a skin case. Holding it as lovingly as he might have a woman, he touched the strings, which gave out music powerfully reminding Rana of wind in the birches. A lump swelled in her throat.

What were they doing so far from home? If Birka was strange and frightening, what would Byzantium be? What hope did she have of finding Jørun? And if anything happened to Fenn, it would be her fault.

''You may stay here,'' Holger said, ''or wander through the town. Be careful though. Slaying of foreigners and men of other districts is punished here—such protection has made this a great trade center—but a pair of young Sameh might look fair game to certain rascals.''

He swaggered off. Fenn and Rana exchanged glances. Fenn's eyes sparkled with excitement. ''Let's eat,'' he said. ''And then let's see the city.''

V

Before they left, Rana burrowed out a place for the sword among the furs and wedged it there in its hide cover. She was more used now to the bustle, and with their passage found, curiosity overrode her timidity. She liked Holger and intuitively trusted Skarp. It would be good to hear his music. And what rare luck to be on a ship where at least two men spoke Sameh! She intended to learn Holger's language, though. It was well to understand what was being said, and besides, that would be a fine surprise for Jorun. If he lived, if she found him—

She pushed such thoughts away. He *had* to be alive. If he had gone to the spirits, surely she would have sensed it. As they climbed over the edge of the ship, Skarp called, without looking up from his instrument, "Have a care, younglings. Best come back here before dark, and don't let painted women coax you into their huts."

"What do you think he meant by that?" Rana asked as, holding hands so as not to be separated, she and Fenn made their way through the teeming crowds on the waterfront.

Fenn ducked his head and wouldn't look at her. "I have heard that in cities some women have no husbands

202

or family to care for them. They take strange men to bed in order to buy food.''

Rana stared disbelievingly. "Can't such a woman just move in with a family and work for her keep?''

"Cities are different, especially a place like Birka that doesn't raise much of its food. Of course, there are a lot of woman servants, but there are many of those women Skarp mentioned." As if uneasy with her questions, he pulled her along so fast that she had all she could do to keep up with him.

"Look at that high stave building with the big cross in front! That must be a temple of the White Christ the King of Sweden worships. Shall we peek inside?''

They did, but Rana was so appalled at the image of a tortured man bleeding on crossed pieces of wood that they retreated before a long-robed man with dark hair fringing a bald head and a big silver cross hanging around his neck could rise from where he was kneeling and catch up with them.

"Was that Odin?" Rana whispered. "Jorun told me how the All-Father hung from a tree.''

"That was the White Christ, and those who believe in him call Odin and the other Norse gods bad spirits.''

"Like Stalo?" He was a stupid giant whose favorite food was Sameh children, though he'd settle for adults if they were all he could find.

"I guess it's something like that." Fenn chuckled. "Who cares what these people say? The real powers are the ones painted on father's drum.''

Rana shivered with foreboding. "Those powers rule in Sameh Land. But, Fenn, it could be different here.''

He looked astonished. "There's still the same moon and sun, the power that sends rain and snow, the spirit of fire. No, Rana, we reverence what is true, what is real. These other people have made gods out of dead men and women. Look at the cakes that old woman is selling! Let's buy some.''

They had a marvelous time wandering from stall to stall, admiring leather work, carved objects of bone and antler and admiring vessels of every kind from copper and bronze to a transparent substance that looked like thin ice and was sometimes as clear though it was more often of dazzling green or amber hue. Rana longed to touch the different rolls of cloth, some almost fine as cobwebs, other sorts heavy with gold and silver embroidery. As they moved along the wood-paved streets, heady fragrances came from a few houses. Some smelled deliciously of food, others of smoked fish or tanned furs.

They stopped to watch a craftsman taking from the same mold what Fenn whispered were Thor's hammer and the cross of the Christians, both in gold. They caught a glimpse of Holger drinking from one of the cone-shaped transparent containers they had seen earlier, in a crowded little hut from which poured a confusion of tongues and a sour odor of sweat.

Fenn wrinkled his nose. ''The traders used to bring ale to the market fairs and try to get us to drink so much of it that we'd give our furs away,'' he said. ''I got a very bad headache from it. Holger had better find his walrus tusks before he has too much of that nasty stuff.''

Most houses were of logs, though many were mud-and-wattle. Though they were jammed close together, some had fenced pens for goats; fat, short-legged animals which Rana didn't recognize; horned beasts bigger than reindeer; and large birds that didn't fly and behaved even more foolishly than ptarmigan. There were countless dogs, though none were as handsome as Fraxi, and smaller animals who sunned in doorways or on top of sheds and looked like miniature lynxes. These looked so soft that Rana longed to touch one.

Twilight was gathering, so they hurried back through the town and neared the building where Holger had been drinking.

A man suddenly flew through the door, followed by a second and third. As they struggled in a heap of arms and legs, Holger burst outside, shaking off several attackers, kicking one against the house across the street, crashing a mighty fist down on another.

Roaring, he was wrestling his sword from its scabbard when a big man clubbed him from behind. His knees went out from under him as might a slaughtered *härk*'s. Getting to their feet, his downed enemies swarmed toward him.

Fenn jumped over Holger's body, drawing his knife. Rana was instantly behind him, guarding his back, her blade ready. The six assailants prowled warily about, swords and knives flickering. Rana would have given much to have her parents' sword.

Someone shouted Holger's name. Two gigantic yellow-haired men came running with raised swords. Holger's foes took their heels. The newcomers stared at Rana and Fenn, shouting questions, but subsided as Rana knelt and lifted Holger's head, feeling the scalp carefully.

There was a contused bump but no blood. He made a grunting sound, opened his eyes, scowled and blinked. The rescuers' anxiety dissolved. They doubled over with laughter, hooting derision and bawling out remarks that Holger dismissed with a crooked grin. Rising as if his head might break, he gave Fenn and Rana a mighty hug, turned to tell his friends about them, and then explained in Sameh that these enormous twins, Aasmund and Thorri, were the rest of his crew. It was lucky they had been in a tavern just up the street when he got into an argument with that passel of Danes. Just because Sven Forkbeard, their king, ruled part of Norway, they had swelled notions of their prowess, but he reckoned they'd had a lesson.

He gave Fenn and Rana another bear hug and swept them down the resounding wooden walk to a house where their party feasted on all manner of strange and appetizing dishes which Holger said were cooked in the Arabian fashion, for many Arab traders visited the town. He and his men drank wine that he explained was from the same Rhine River whence came much of the transparent ware, glass, from which it was drunk. Fenn sipped from his cone-shaped beaker, but Rana didn't like hers and gave it to Thorri, who swilled it down as if it were water.

The three Norwegians threw arms over each other's shoulders and staggered to the ship, singing in a way that made the sounds of a reindeer herd seem melodious. Skarp hurried to meet them. When he saw Fenn and Rana, he chuckled in relief.

"I was about to come looking for you, but no one would bother you while you're with these ugly brutes!"

"*They* rescued me," corrected Holger with ponderous solemnity. A great arm draped around each of them, he told the story.

Skarp praised Fenn and Rana, but his tone sharpened as he said to Holger, "Did you get those walrus tusks?"

"Walrus tusks?" Holger rubbed his head with his stump. "I'll get them in the morning."

Skarp sighed. "I've dragged out the sleeping bags. Can you get into yours, Holger?"

" 'Course I can," huffed the merchant. But while he was trying, he collapsed and began to snore. Skarp sighed again and with help from the twins got their chief inside his shelter.

Rana hesitated at getting into the one she was to share with Fenn. Then she reminded herself that she had slept within a few arm-lengths of him all her life. Still, by silent agreement, they folded their outer garments, used some for pillows, and placed the rest between them. Rana was so exhausted that she sank instantly into sleep.

Very early, Skarp went with Holger to get the walrus tusks. Thorri and Aasmund had headaches and drowsed partly beneath the half-deck that provided soothing darkness. Rana signed to Björn that if he wanted to leave the ship, she'd stay to watch. The boy grinned his thanks and hurried off to enjoy the sights.

Fenn returned first. With a smile of triumph, he spread out a length of incredibly soft, light wool dyed a lovely shade of gray-blue. On top of it he placed two bronze needles and skeins of blue thread.

"Boy's clothes are good for the journey," he said, "but you'll need a nice dress when you find Jorun."

She fingered the wonderful cloth with delight, then shot him a worried look. "But this must have cost more than the coins left from selling the reindeer." His splendidly worked antler-handled knife was gone and so was its handsome scabbard. In its place hung a plain leather sheath and wood-gripped blade. "Oh, Fenn!"

"You must have a dress," he said stubbornly. "One like city ladies wear. Can you make it?"

Hadn't she noticed with great care the garments of the women she'd seen yesterday and those who'd come near the ship that morning? She couldn't duplicate the panels that hung front and back over the long-sleeved undergown, but there'd be enough material for a sort of overtunic.

"Oh, Fenn!" she said again, and pressed the cloud of thistledown to her face.

Holger and Skarp returned with a cartload of walrus tusks and oaken kegs of honey. When these were loaded on the *Raven*, everyone pushed till the boat slid into the shallow water. As soon as the end with the rudder floated, they all clambered aboard. Holger took the rudder while Thorri and Aasmund plied the oars at the back and Skarp and Björn adjusted the square crimson sail to swell with the breeze. The long ships that passed them had from twenty to sixty men rowing, but Holger, expertly managing the rudder with his stub and good hand, explained that merchant ships relied mostly on sail and used oars only when necessary.

As soon as they were well under way, the huge twins laid down their oars. Aasmund went to stand near Holger, keeping sharp watch, while Thorri shaded his face with his mantle and went back to sleep. Tightly caulked as the *Raven* was, water splashed over the side, especially at the lowest middle part. Björn got down in the space between the half-decks and scooped out water with a copper bowl.

Rana faced south. The sun glittered on the lake. One beat of her heart sang: Jørun! And the next whispered mystically: *Byzantium!*

They camped that night on the shore of the mighty lake, and the men cut down trees and trimmed them to serve as rollers for moving the *Raven* across a neck of land that separated the lake from the Baltic.

Next day, they launched into the Baltic and steered for the rising sun. It was days before the waters began to narrow as they sailed through the land of the Finns. Finally, they touched land again, at a Swedish merchant outpost on an immense lake, where they traded for fresh provisions before turning south.

It was necessary, too, to leave the *Raven* in care of a friend of Holger's at the post and transfer the cargo to two smaller boats that could pass down narrow channels and be portaged across land stretching between lakes and rivers. Rana stored the sword carefully among the furs. Sometimes they could use a sail, but often Rana and Fenn had to join in the rowing. When it was calm enough, she cut and sewed pieces for the blue gown.

It was usually possible to camp on shore, and as they rested around the fire, Skarp often played his harp, or Holger expounded on his adventures, switching back and forth from the Sameh tongue to Norwegian, which Rana was beginning to understand better each day, though Fenn was much faster in picking it up.

Several hundred years ago, Holger said, the warring tribesmen of the region sent to the Swedes, whom they call Rus, and asked them to rule over them and stop the eternal fights. Three brothers came, but Rurik was the greatest. He established Novgorod, and his son later ruled in Kiev, where the main trade route from the Rhine met the route from the Baltic to Byzantium.

It seemed that Holger had been everywhere: to Iceland, Greenland, the Orkneys, Ireland and London, and even to the dazzling Caliphate of Cordoba, for on several occasions, Vikings had sailed around Spain and into the Mediterranean.

The fireside entertainment wasn't all Holger's yarns or Skarp's tunes and sagas. The Northmen delighted in hearing Fenn's *joiks* that reflected the moods of the changing year and the herd. Closing her eyes, Rana could see the Spirit Lights that must flicker now above Sameh as they journeyed to winter camp, and her heart swelled with homesickness for Suki, Votar and the caravan.

At Fenn's urging, she sang *joiks*, too, using the weird plaint of the loon, the call of the mountain owl, melodies of thrush and finch and sparrow as well as that of Fenn's favorite bluethroat. She had trained herself to keep her voice low when speaking but her singing was so clear and sweet that Skarp looked at her strangely.

"The only lads I've heard sound like you either hadn't grown whiskers or had been gelded so they could warble praises to the White Christ."

"Oh, many Sameh sing like that," Fenn said. "It comes from imitating bird songs."

Skarp still looked thoughtful. Rana evaded his dark eyes. She trusted her companions now and was sure they wouldn't take advantage of her womanhood, but it was better that they treat her like one of them, especially when they stopped at a farm or settlement for provisions, or encountered other travelers.

After Novgorod, a prosperous city with a large domed church, timbered streets and block houses, fortified against attack, the next place of note they reached was Gnezdovo, where waterways led to the Volga and the Caspian Sea, the fabulous caravan routes of Arabia and the five-thousand-mile China silk road. There were countless burial mounds here, and Holger left beer at some of them for dead comrades.

Here, too, the travelers learned momentous news. Byzantines had been warring for years with Bulgars, ferocious warriors who were a mixture of Turk, Hun and Ugric. Basil II would henceforth be known as Basil the Bulgar-Slayer, for he had recently defeated the Bulgars, taking fifteen hundred captive. These he blinded, leaving one man in each hundred a single eye so that these could lead their companions home. Samuel, the Bulgar ruler, had died at the sight of his maimed hosts and his kingdom now swelled the Byzantine emperor's domains.

Holger shook his head over the frightful tale. "Vikings are called wolves from the sea," he muttered. "But it is *nithing,* dishonor, to cripple prisoners who were only fighting for their lord."

Men were hired to help carry the boats overland to the Dneiper. As the boats were shoved into the silty waters, Holger shielded his eyes to scan the plains. "Two weeks to Kiev," he said, "Then six weeks more to the Great City. You won't believe the rapids till you see them, lad—and believe me, that's just as well."

But Rana lilted her nightingale *joik* as they oared along. They were finally on the Dneiper! The very river that would take them to the Black Sea. And on the other side lay Byzantium.

VI

The walls of Kiev glowed golden rose on the high west bank of the river. Rounded domes and towers showed above the fortifications, stretching along the river and spreading far back toward the plain. From here the Swedish-descended Grand Duke of Kiev ruled Rus, all the lands they had passed through since leaving the Baltic.

They stayed in Kiev two days, sleeping in the boats and taking turns guarding the trade goods. With either Holger or Skarp, Fenn and Rana wandered through the eight marketplaces where tribesmen from the steppes haggled with perfumed merchants from Bagdad and where it seemed that everything in the world must be for sale—Chinese silks, spices and rugs of India, glassware, jewelry, weapons, all manner of cloth, birds and animals and human beings. These, mostly fair-skinned and blond, often girls in their first bloom, were, according to Holger, largely destined for servitude among the Moslems, some for harems. Rana pitied them, not only for being wrenched from their homes, but because they would have no choice of what man could claim them.

The Emperor Vladimir's hand showed throughout the vast city, most notably in his great palace where seven hundred people dwelled and which had attached to it many workshops where magnificent work was done in all kinds of metals, including intricate silver and gold images and vessels to adorn the many churches he had caused to be built on the sites of pagan temples razed at his command.

It was beyond Rana's wildest imaginings, but knowing that they were only six weeks from Byzantium made her feverishly impatient. She was glad when Holger concluded his trading and they started for the mouth of the river.

The nightingale song rose to her lips, but what it really called was *Jørun! Jørun!*

There were seven rapids important enough to have names in the Norse language. Rana thought that Gelandri, the Yelling, and Leanti, the Laughing, especially deserved their titles. At the worst rapids, the boats were hauled aground and borne past the wild waters. At shallower ones, the cargo was taken off and carried to where the skillfully steered boats could resume their burdens.

A storm struck as they hit one turbulent stretch. Björn was swept overboard. By the time Holger and Thorri hauled him on board, he had stopped breathing, but Holger draped the lad over his arm so that water gushed from his nose and mouth and then knelt above him, setting his mouth over the boy's while pinching his nostrils, breathing heavily through his nose and expelling the air into Björn.

Björn's face was blue and he seemed dead, but Holger persisted and after what seemed a long time, Björn stirred and began to cough. Holger leaned back, cradling the boy while Skarp gave him wine. Color flowed back to Björn's cheeks. They wrapped him in furs, and by the time the storm passed, he seemed as good as ever.

Holger said that way of breathing could sometimes re-

store victims of other mishaps but it didn't always work.
"Worth a try." He shrugged.

Next day, they sailed into the Black Sea.

Kiev's splendor had astounded Rana. Byzantium awed
her. The city's walls reared from the water, guarding the
whole peninsula, and above them rose the tiled domes of
churches with crosses that gleamed golden in the sun. On
the ground that formed a spine for the city rose what
Hólger said was Hagia Sophia, reputed to be the most
splendid church in all Christendom, seat of the patriarch
who ruled eastern Christianity as the Pope held sway
over western Europe.

Under sail, Holger and Skarp steered the boats around
the point to one of two harbors. The opposite shore was
heavily fortified. Holger waved his stub at the myriad
ships sailing into or resting within the walls that circled
out into the waves to protect the harbor.

"The Golden Horn!" he cried. "In time of attack,
there's a huge chain fastened across the channel to keep
out enemy ships. None have ever broken through, though
they've tried often enough."

As he went through the formalities of gaining admit-
tance, Rana stared at the ramparts in numb consternation.
At Novgorod and Kiev, she'd had a foretaste of the rash
enormity of her quest. Now she was overwhelmed.

How could she find Jørun among such multitudes?
And if he had succeeded in avenging his family's murder, would Basil the Bulgar-Slayer be tender of a man
who killed one of his famed Varangian Guard?

She looked at Fenn. His sober expression echoed her
dismay. She trembled with anxiety and regret. What had
she dragged him into? All too soon, the boats were
moored, and Holger squinted at his passengers.

"Well, my younglings, here we are. The Great City
you've come so far to gawk at. I expect to be here the full

six weeks merchants are allowed, staying in the Monastery of Saint Mamas just outside the walls." He must have noticed their bewilderment, for he said kindly, "You can stay with us, if you want."

Rana turned to Fenn, who read her questions and gave a slow nod. She took a deep breath. "Friend," she said to Holger, "I must tell you something."

In their monastery chamber, Holger held the sword in his hand, eyes glowing. He tested the edge reverently but with a warrior's discernment and looked at Rana with much of the same respect.

"So a lass raised by Sameh now owns the Heaven Sword! 'Tis the most famous blade in all the Northlands, and it was believed lost forever when Sigurd Thorsteinson, who had it from his mother, the daughter of a priestess of Frey, fled with his betrothed maid into the wilds when her brothers would have forced her to break faith with him and wed a rich old merchant who'd pay the debts. I met Sigurd once at a *thing*. He was a goodly man, and as for Ingunn, his bride, 'tis said she shone beautiful as a young Freya."

Skarp said in his dreamy *skald*'s voice, "I have made a song of them. And one of Jørun Leifsson, too, and how he tracked down the Burners. So he came here to kill Starkad?" He shook his graying head. "Rand—lady, you must be ready to learn your Jørun is dead. Starkad was commander of the emperor's Varangian Guard. Even if Jørun made shift to slay that man of blood, 'tis likely the emperor would have him executed."

Rana shivered. Fenn took her hand protectively. "My sister must know, one way or the other. If you could help us learn if Jørun lives . . ."

"We can do that," Holger assured them. He gave the sword back to Rana and patted her shoulder awkwardly.

"If Jørun's here, we'll do all we can to win him free."
He glanced at his crew. "Is it not so, men?"

The twins roared gusty assent, and Björn's face
flushed red at the delight and terror of being called a man.
"Ay, we will!"

"But first," said Holger, sobering, "we must find out
if Jørun found Starkad—and if he did, what happened. I
have an old friend in the Varangian Guard. He'll know."

"I have some fine amber," Rana said. "If gifts would
help . . ."

Holger grinned. "Bribes may come later. Thorkil will
tell all he knows for a beaker of wine, which I would buy
him in any case. Will you and Fenn bide here or will you
come into the city? I can leave you in the Forum of Constantine, which is the biggest public square and market,
and meet you at the statue after I've seen Thorkil."

Rana was overcome with wonder as, from beneath the
rose domes of Hagia Sophia, the church she'd seen from
the harbor, Holger pointed out the adjoining sprawl of the
Palace of the Emperors with its great hippodrome for
horse racing and circuses, the baths, quarters of the Varangian Guard, a polo ground, and innumerable courts
and terraces that led down to the ramparts and lighthouse
on the sea.

More people must live in that rambling complex than
in a good-sized town. Was Jørun among them? Holger
guessed her thought and gave her hand a comforting
squeeze. "Skarp will take you to the square. I'll be back
as soon as I can."

Thorri and Aasmund went off to seek a wine shop, but
it was young Björn's first time in the city, and he was almost as wide-eyed as Fenn and Rana. They passed
through an arch to enter the great circular place loomed
over by the figure of a beautiful, almost naked man on a

pedestal of purple-red stone, with golden rays shining from his hair.

"That's Con—Constantine?" Rana asked.

"The emperor is sculpted as the Greek sun god, Apollo." Skarp smiled. "He made the city his capital centuries ago, but it was here a thousand years before him, founded by Greeks, enlarged by Romans." He indicated the shops set up between the columns of the porticoed buildings circling the statue and a great fountain. "Shall we see what's for sale?"

Rana glanced toward the palace. Skarp watched her sympathetically. "Come along, lad—lass, I mean. Holger can't join us for at least an hour, and I'm betting it's more."

The goods were as varied as the people selling them, as the dozens of languages heard on every side. As Kiev's market had been to Birka's, so was Byzantium's to Kiev's. Unguents from Trebizond, Syrian silks, finest linen, Greek alabaster, Persian vases, carpets, jewelry, weapons and ornaments from the farthest reaches of East and West. And through another archway, the colonnaded avenue ran to other public squares till, Skarp said, it reached the Golden Gate, which was used only by triumphal armies or for solemn state occasions such as coronations.

"But that's no problem," laughed Skarp, "since the city has fifty gates." When Rana asked why there were so few women, and they obviously servants, Skarp said that Byzantine women of good family were restricted to their homes except for church-going. Richer families had private chapels so the women had not even that reason to leave their seclusion. "Almost as guarded as Moslem females." Skarp shrugged.

Over by the fountain, a young man tossed balls in the air and kept them moving, bouncing the brightly colored spheres from his nose, head and shoulders. Constantine-Apollo gazed benignly down on a cluster of half-grown children who were shaping their supple bodies into incredible postures, interlocking with each other, forming pyramids and towers from which the smallest one dived to a catcher, seeming to fly, then sweeping a deep bow before running about with a cap into which the crowd tossed coins.

A man with a turban sat cross-legged on a rug and fingered a long instrument with holes in it, coaxing out a shrill sweet melody to which a pair of large serpents swayed as if they were dancing. Rana and Fenn were watching them in fascination when Holger loomed beside them, dropped a coin on the gaudy rug and smiled reassuringly into Rana's pleading eyes.

"Your sweetheart's alive, lass. And he must love you well, for he could be the empress' chamberlain or head the Varangian Guard if he would consent to be her lover."

"The empress?" Rana echoed.

"Basil is an able ruler and great commander, but a dour, sour husband. He either doesn't know or doesn't care that his wife consoles herself, especially with Northmen. She fancies their strength and blondness."

The empress and Jørun? The Forum spun around Rana. Blood seemed to drain from her. She would have fallen had Fenn not breathed her name and held her up.

"It's the wonder of the barracks how daft the woman is for your man," Holger went on. "He slew Starkad in fair fight, but Basil was minded to have him blinded and tortured to death for killing his most redoubtable guardsman. However, the empress intervened, claiming him for a slave, and Basil yielded rather than endure her shrewish tongue."

Rana moistened her lips. "What—what has she done with him?"

"He's locked up somewhere in her apartments."

Despair clutched Rana. An ordinary prison would be bad enough! But an empress' private one! "Has—" She swallowed but was still unable to speak.

Holger reddened. "Lass, barrack talk is that when Jørun would not oblige her, even under threat of death, the empress had her physicians drug him, both with potions to cloud the mind and those used by Moslems to enable one man to service a harem. Jørun never knows when they'll be in his food and drink. She uses them only when her blood is unbearably heated, for she hopes he'll yet return her passion."

"Then they have—he's made love to her!" Rana felt pierced by a curving blade that seared and froze at once.

"If you could call it that," said Holger. "She's had his mindless body. That only."

Rana fought down jealous poison that made her physically sick. It wasn't Jørun's fault. But the empress! Rana hated her lover's jailer with wholehearted ferocity till she remembered that without the woman's intercession, Jørun would be miserably dead.

"How can I see him?"

"It must be round-and-about, lass. But I have a plan. The empress constantly seeks new diversions. Thorkil thinks she would make quite a pet of a girl from the Sameh country."

"But I can't speak Greek. Or Latin, either."

"No matter. What she'll want are your bird songs. If she likes you enough to make you one of her attendants, it shouldn't be impossible to sooner or later have speech with Jørun."

"I still don't see how we can get him out of the palace," Rana despaired.

"There may be a window, someone to bribe—who knows?" Holger lifted an eloquent shoulder. "Figure how to free him, and we'll smuggle him off in a boat. Now, from what Thorkil tells me, our best plan is this. . . ."

VII

For the first time in her life, Rana was not dressed like a Sameh. Concealing Jorun's ring, she wore the gray-blue dress of soft wool she had fashioned and thought so fine until she beheld the glittering fabrics and jewels worn by the courtiers and even the servants. Hugging the bag of amber, she stood by Fenn, grateful for his closeness, in the congregation of spectators who were being allowed to watch the celebration of the ninth of the Twelve Days of Christmas. Thorkil had won them entry as visitors from the Sameh folk who were bringing a gift for the Empress and wished humbly to entertain her.

Watching the small dark woman who sat on a dais in a thronelike chair beside the emperor, Rana tried to guess what kind of soul existed behind the huge painted eyes, white face and red lips, but it was as impossible to discern an essence beneath the mask as it was to speculate on what kind of body was covered by the jeweled, gold-encrusted garments.

The empress glittered from crown to sandal but Basil II, Slayer of Bulgars, lord of an empire that continually fought off a swelling Moslem tide, wore royal purple without ornamentation, though his purple shoes were embroidered with pearls. His diadem was also set with pearls and surmounted by a cross formed by elongated ovals. His swarthy bearded face was cast in such grim lines that Rana couldn't believe he ever smiled.

At the left-hand entrance, the Admiral of the Fleet stood with flute players, some of his officers and Varangian guardsmen, these last fierce-looking in furs worn hairy side outward. At the right door, the commander of the Varangian Guard waited with a detachment of mail-clad warriors. A court official motioned, and the Varangians, tall, splendidly built men with fair or red hair, rushed into the hall. Thorkil was almost of giant height with brownish yellow hair.

When Holger had told him why they had come, Thorkil, who turned out to be a distant relative of Jørun's, joined enthusiastically in the venture. When Rana protested at his running risks, he laughed hugely.

"Life has been dull since we came back from whipping the Bulgars. My term of outlawry from Norway is over, and I was planning to leave as soon as I could. No, lass, if I can help my bold kinsman out of the empress' arms, 'twill be my pleasure!"

Now the Varangians struck their shields with their spears and shouted, "*Jul! Jul!*" till they reached the dais. The admiral's party ran in from the other side, and the men formed a double ring, circling the thrones three times before dividing again, army on the right, navy to the left.

The fur-clad guardsmen and other Varangians chanted a song which Rana could not understand, and then all joined in a long hymn which Thorkil had said praised the emperor before they went to stand behind the dais.

The official who had signaled the *Jul*-bringers now approached the spectators. With his ivory staff, he touched a silk-turbaned man on the shoulder. Followed by a black servant lad, the visitor went forward and bowed his head to the dais while he was introduced and the golden casket borne by his slave was opened to show a dazzle of precious stones.

Backing away, the man was followed by richly garbed men dressed in every fashion Rana had ever seen and some she hadn't, travelers, the chamberlain announced, that came from Venice, Samarkand, Athens, Rome, Mainz, London, Paris, Cordoba.

Their gifts were so magnificent that Rana's hands sweated against the ermine-fur pouch that held the amber, and her stomach shriveled to a tight kernel. The amber was splendid but in its raw form, lumps that ranged from pale yellow to dark honey. Beside the elegant filigrees and designs of the world's most skilled artists, she was afraid her gift would be too rustic. The empress had just yawned over a necklace that sparkled green and ice-crystalline.

When the official tapped Fenn's arm with a supercilious smile at the Sameh tunic and close-fitting trousers of reindeer skin, Rana's knees were shaking. Glad of the concealing gown, thankful above all for Fenn's presence, she made a quick prayer to her parents and the spirits.

An image of the white fox flashed before her. It seemed to say: *You are descended from those who wrought valiant deeds with the sword you've brought for Jørun. For him, you rode on my back to the Other World. Can you not brave rulers of this one?*

Still, if not for Fenn at her side and the image of the sword glowing in her mind, she could never have reached the space before the dais, especially after hearing a low ripple of laughter from the courtiers. Her cheeks burned as she handed the amber to the chamberlain and knelt before the thrones, eyes on a level with the empress' gilded sandals.

The chamberlain said a few words. At a command from the empress, he beckoned Thorkil, who made obeisance to the rulers and said in the Norse tongue, "The empress would know something of your country and customs. No Sameh has visited the court before. You will wait for her in her apartments.''

The empress gave a further order. Thorkil bowed again and said to Fenn and Rana, "Come. I will escort you and be your interpreter.'' He led them through long corridors, passing through several courtyards with fountains and gardens, and brought them into an exquisite room spread with soft carpets in tones of rose. A couch was draped with rich purple. Cushions of rose and gold silk were heaped on it and about the floor. Tables of brass or carved wood held bowls of flowers, but their scent was lost in the empress' oppressively spicy perfume.

A hundred treasures gleamed from niches and chests: figures of the Christians' holy folk, gold and silver boxes wrought with jewels, musical instruments inlaid with ivory or gold. The walls were azure and on them flew birds of every hue and shape, some so fantastically plumed and brilliant that Rana was sure they could not exist. She recognized owls, hawks, cuckoos and finches, but there was no bluethroated nightingale.

Swept with a wave of homesickness for the Northland, for Votar and Suki, their *kåta* and the reindeer, Rana caught Fenn's hand. "Oh, Fenn, I'm afraid I have brought you into great danger! Our parents expected to lose me sometime but not you. Get out of this palace while you can!''

He closed his other hand strongly over hers, calming its trembling. "I will not leave you. Not till Jørun has you in his charge.''

Thorkil sank down on a silken pallet and spoke to several beautifully dressed young women who had come in from another chamber and stood as if waiting for orders. Bowing, they backed gracefully from the room. Rana started after them.

"Sit down," Thorkil said testily. "I know you're

eager, lass, to find that passage to your Jorun, but it won't do to search now. You must win the empress' favor so that she'll want your company. After you're accepted, you'll learn where he is."

"But how can we get him out of here?"

"That, too, must wait till we know about his prison," Thorkil said.

The serving maids returned with silver trays laden with fruit, honied pastries, goblets of sparkling wine and more of it in a graceful pitcher. They placed these on a low brass table and retired at Thorkil's dismissing wave.

Rana had scarcely been able to eat that day. Her stomach was still cramping with anxiety, but she knew the round golden fruits were juicily delicious, for Holger had bought her one in the market. She ate one and nibbled a date before trying what Thorkil said were apricots and figs.

Though she sipped the wine with caution, her head was light by the time the empress finally appeared, dropping to the purple couch with a relieved sigh. One of her ladies took the crown and placed it on a high cushioned stand. Another knelt to slip off her golden sandals, and they had not finished these tasks before the maids brought wine and refreshments. Thorkil had risen, motioning his charges up at the empress' approach. She seemed not to notice them till her feet had been bathed in scented water and she had eaten a cake and savored a goblet of wine.

Ignoring Thorkil, she looked at Fenn and Rana with a wearied frown. Rana's heart stopped. Would the woman dismiss them, perhaps forget to call them back? Rana's throat was tight and her tongue clumsy but she threw back her head and trilled the bluethroat's song, its greeting to spring, its mate and the quickening world.

She seemed not to be in the luxurious room at all but could almost see greening birches about the lake, smoke drifting from the *kåtor*, new calves nursing from their mothers who feasted on tender lichens and the first sweet grass. Rana shifted from the bird's melody to a *joik* of longing.

> "How beautiful the mountain! Bursting from ice.
> How swift the river! But not so swift, not so wild
> As my heart yearning toward you . . ."

In between the words that only Fenn could understand, she wove the plaint of the loon, silver gossip of finches, sparrows' chatter, but always returned to the pure, lilting ecstasy of the nightingale.

She did not control the song. It possessed her. And when it was done she felt emptied, saddened. She did not know if she had done well or ill. Fenn and the Varangian stared at her in amazement, but whether this was for her song or dismay at her daring, she could not guess. Paralyzed with hope and dread, she ventured to look at the empress.

Tears were running down that white face, streaking it with black coloring from the eyelashes. The crimson lips, thin beneath painted outlines, had softened. Dabbing her eyes with a wisp of linen, the empress smiled. When she spoke, her voice was kind.

Thorkil answered several of her questions in Greek, the empire's aristocratic tongue, and turned to Rana. "The empress is pleased with her Sameh bluethroat. She invites you to join her retinue. You will sleep at her feet. When she cannot rest, which is often, you will be her nightingale."

So faint with relief that she could barely keep her feet, Rana knelt and murmured her gratitude. The empress' earthy chuckle sounded incongruously from that face where artifice struggled to preserve remnants of great beauty.

"The empress says that unless you fall in love with a courtier, she knows you won't stay forever so far from the land you sing of with such longing. When you wish to depart, she will send you away with gifts that will perhaps, when you are in the North, make you sing, with some affection, of Byzantium."

Glancing at Fenn with a slight wrinkling of her straight, long nose, the empress spoke briefly. Thorkil turned to Fenn. "You may share quarters with Her Magnificence's male servitors who dwell on the opposite side of the courtyard. One of the tailors will make you suitable garments for this climate."

Rana suspected the empress had said something about Fenn's smoked-leather-and-sweat odor. She flushed angrily but Fenn bowed and smiled his thanks.

"The empress will clothe you, too," continued Thorkil. "Her ladies must beguile her eyes and you must wear blue and gray like a nightingale. But if there are things of your own that you wish to have, Fenn may take servants to fetch them."

Rana repressed a grin as she pictured what the empress would think of *her* Sameh clothes. "All I want is the sword."

"I will bring it," Fenn said. His light brown eyes were at once sad and joyful. "But I had better keep it with me. May the powers guard you, my Rana."

"May they protect you," she echoed.

As he bowed and went out with Thorkil, she realized this was the first time in all her life that she would sleep without the comfort of Fenn's presence. The empress motioned her to sit on cushions by her feet. When one of the servants poured some wine, Rana was glad.

To serve as translator, the empress often requested the attendance of the wife of one of the courtiers who was of the princely Swedish house of Kiev. Ladya's Norse was thick with words borrowed from Slavic dialects, Greek and Latin, and she was too vain to say when she didn't fully understand Rana's words or know how to relay the empress' questions. Rana suspected that the plump, middle-aged lady made up a good deal on both sides while gorging on sweets and sherbets. Heaven only knew how she received and conveyed Rana's explanations of Sameh life as they followed the reindeer, or told of the glimmering Spirit Lights during the months when the sun was never seen.

Whatever tales Ladya improvised, they must have been diverting, for the empress laughed often and clapped her beringed hands or shuddered and gathered her silken robes closer about her. She frequently waved Ladya away and smiled at Rana, speaking the Greek name she had given her.

"*Philomele.*" Nightingale.

Then Rana would sing, and since her *joiks* were in Sameh, it was safe to voice her love for Jørun, her longing to see him. Tears sometimes came to the empress' cynical eyes and at such times Rana thought how strange it was that they both might be thinking of the same man. Then the wondering pity she often felt for the aging lonely woman would turn to outraged disgust.

To keep a man prisoner, drug him to have his body! It was as perverted and unnatural as this glittering, overcivilized court about which Rana was learning appalling things. Though it was banned as sin by their religion, many noblemen enjoyed slender boys more than their wives. And the women thus abandoned fondled a servingmaid or trembled with lust as one did her bidding.

Mercifully, such entertainment didn't appeal to the empress, though she was massaged every day with perfumed ointments, her thin body reminding Rana of a plucked fowl's, sighing with indolent pleasure as two Moorish female slaves rubbed and kneaded her from toe to scalp. Then her hair was carefully dressed, she was arrayed in one of her resplendent costumes, and performed her only serious duty of the day, conferring with the cooks, for she understood her imperial husband's dyspeptic taste. She dined with him only on state occasions, however. By mutual consent, the royal pair saw each other formally and seldom, Basil preferring the company of his military commanders and she preferring—what?

Rana often wondered, and dimly understood the emptiness that drove the childless, virtually husbandless woman to seek at least physical closeness with comely young men, command the imitation of love.

Did she try to assuage her need for Jørun when, in the night, she left the room where Rana and one of the ladies slept, and entered the adjoining curtained chamber? The moans, gasping and muffled cries sent heavy fire through Rana, making her clench her hands and tense her legs and thighs against strange feelings that spread from her loins and prickling breasts.

Ladya, who enjoyed scandalizing Rana, especially after the younger woman had evaded the Kievan's overtures, said that the empress' chamberlain was responsible for keeping the room next to the empress stocked with strong, handsome and, above all, virile men. She usually never even saw the face of her servicer, though occasionally she would notice a new guardsman and send for him.

Though Rana detested Ladya, these leering disclosures gave her, for the first time, an opening to seek information about Jørun.

"The empress has never favored one man over the others?"

Ladya's green eyes narrowed. Her pointed red tongue touched her lower lip as if tasting something corruptly delicious. Glancing about to be sure they weren't over-

heard even in the language no one else of the empress'
household spoke, she grinned viciously.

"Long ago there was a beautiful Frank, but he died.
Of fever? Or poison, when he was smitten by a fair
maiden of his own years?" Ladya's voice sank even
lower. "Those who remember say the empress' love for
him was nothing compared to her passion for the Northman she's caged for over a year."

Rana's heart thudded oppressively and her palms were
clammy. "A Northman?"

"Ay. Ungrateful, that one! The empress saved him
from blinding and dismemberment, so you'd think he'd
employ those spared organs to thank her. Not a bit of it!
Her physician's potions make him rage hot as a bull,
'tis said. When she visits him, she creeps back haggard
and sated and the chamberlain can wait four or five
days before bringing her a fresh stud." Ladya crossed
her hands over her heavy bosom and rocked with mali-
cious laughter. "But that's not what Her Magnificence
craves. After all, can't she command the best pricks in
the empire? She wants the man to love her! Can you believe it?"

"I believe it." Selfish and trifling as the empress was,
she had treated Rana with kindness, and she was growing
old without a soul who truly cared for her. It was impossible not to be sorry for her while remaining inexorably
determined to wrest Jorun free.

Rana's manner silenced Ladya but only for a moment.
"The servants say he's still handsome and fit. His cham-
ber is large. He runs around it many times each day and
practices leaping and other stunts as if he were a tumbler.
The empress plays chess with him; supplies him with
Latin books, which he can read; and allows him a harp.
He no longer tries to escape by attacking the servants
who bring him food and tend his needs. The empress is

never alone with him, of course. No strangling her and making a break for it.''

"But if he keeps himself strong, he must hope to escape,'' Rana said fervently.

Ladya raised a lazy painted eyebrow. ''Oh, hope.'' She shrugged.

Without hope, Rana could never have endured being near Jørun yet unable to see him, or the excruciating night when the empress went, not to the young man in the next room, but somewhere else. Rana followed in a few minutes, but when she peered down the dimly lit corridor, the empress had vanished, and a dozen doors and archways opened off the central hall that led through the maze of the empress' quarters, which were a palace in themselves.

Rana ventured down several turnings but encountered more doors. She could scarcely investigate every room. Next time she must risk following quickly. Pressing her face to the marble wall, she fought twisting nausea that shook her at the thought of those painted lips kissing Jørun, that scrawny white body entwined with his. She tasted blood. If her hands had been on the empress' throat that moment, she would gladly have strangled her.

It was useless to try to sleep. Going back to the reception room, Rana slipped out into the courtyard. The flower-sweetened breeze cooled her burning face. Throwing back her head, she watched the stars and wondered if they were the same ones that shone down on the Sameh winter camp.

Beside her, Fenn said, ''Can you not sleep, my Rana?''

She saw him nearly every day, usually in this courtyard, though sometimes the empress wanted to hear his *joiks* and invited him to a meal or refreshment. Just knowing he was nearby helped Rana endure, though her guilt increased with each day. She could never repay him. And should he not return safe to his parents, how could Suki and Votar keep from hating her?

All this shot through her mind, and then the wretchedness that had driven her to the garden overwhelmed her. "Fenn! She—she has gone to him!"

Fenn made her sit down on a stone bench beside a splashing fountain and drew her against his shoulder, letting her sob and stroking her hair as he had when she was a child. "That means he is alive," he said after she quieted.

"But I can't find out where! I tried to follow tonight. There must be fifty halls and doors along that corridor!"

"I know where he is."

"You do?"

He drew her to her feet. "Come. I'll show you."

A gate at the end of the court opened into a smaller one that curved around the wing that housed the empress' rooms. Moving carefully in the darkness, Fenn led the way to a tower at the end. From a small slit of a window high above their heads came a yellow beam of light.

"Up there," said Fenn in an undertone. "One of Jørun's guards lives in a room next to mine. I treated him to wine last night, and in his cups, he lamented the boredom of watching beside a door to which only the empress has a key and the obscenity of having to stay in the chamber to make sure the drugged man doesn't hurt the empress."

Except in the way she desires, Rana thought savagely. "That window's too small for a child."

"Yes. Jørun will have to come out by the door." Fenn rubbed his pointed chin. "If there were a way of knowing when the empress would visit him, I could bring the guard a bowl of wine that would make him sleep, hide him and dress in his clothes. Then, when the empress unlocked the cell—"

"Since the potions are put in his food, someone in the kitchen must know," Rana pondered. "I'll find out."

"If you let me know, after the guard's out of the way, I can tell Jørun not to eat or drink that evening. We could never handle him in the maddened state the empress' drugs induce."

"Is there a way out of the back part of the wing?"

"There's a small entrance the guards use so as not to come through the empress' apartments. I'll spy out the best route to the Bronze Gate that opens to Hagia Sophia. It has a guard, but probably Thorkil could arrange to be on duty there. So long as no alarm is raised, he, as a Varangian officer, should be able to get us through the city gate. Holger has finished with his trading and is ready to sail on short notice." Fenn chuckled. "We may have to say there's plague among us to be allowed to leave the Golden Horn by night, but once out of that fortified harbor—"

"There are so many ifs—so many things that could go wrong!" Rana gnawed her lip. "I hate for you and the others to run such risks."

"Can you think of anything better?"

She couldn't. It returned to her with renewed force that without Fenn's help she could never have hoped to free her love. She brought his hands to her face and kissed them, weeping, unable to express that passion of gratitude that filled her. He flinched and jerked his fingers away.

"Let me know when you learn that the empress will go to Jørun," he said almost coldly. "I'll have to tell Thorkil and hope he can get word to Holger. Meanwhile, I'll keep cultivating the guards. We can't talk much but they like my *joiks,* and good wine breaks the monotony of a long watch."

"Can Jørun hear you?"

"I think not. The door is solid. I've never heard a sound from him."

Rana thought of Jørun behind that door at this moment, maddened by philtres into doing the empress' will. Only hope of escape could have kept him alive; he'd be better off dying in an attempt to win liberty. Rana was ready to die with him. She only prayed that no one else would suffer.

She thanked Fenn and told him good night. Back on her silken pallet she could not sleep but writhed in torment as she clutched Jørun's ring and tried not to imagine what was happening in the tower.

VIII

On pretext of being curious about Byzantine food, she got Ladya to take her to the kitchens. Helping herself gluttonously to sweetmeats, Ladya put Rana's questions to the cooks and translated their replies. Rana had already eaten many of the dishes, of course, using the forks and spoons affected by the court, but in the big kitchens that served all the empress' retainers, she was amazed anew at the many kinds of food. The Sameh had added wild game and fish to their main diet of reindeer flesh, but in addition to beef and mutton, ham, all manner of game, pheasant, doves, pigeons, chicken, goose and a great variety of fish, the royal household ate oysters, milk-fed snails and fine wheat bread, vegetables, fruit and a fantastic array of flaky pastries as well as honey, almond, and date confections, and fruit and yogurt sherbets. They drank the best wines of Greece and Italy.

Much olive oil was used, but otherwise, according to Ladya, many of the recipes went back to the days of Roman rule, especially the fermented sauces that were served with all meats. Liquamen was the empress' favorite, a clear golden fluid made by salting anchovies or mackerel and fermenting them in an earthenware jar for several months, stirring occasionally and adding wine.

After learning what it was, Rana understood why a sprinkling was all she could tolerate in spite of the empress' urging.

Alert for substances that could be drugs or disguise them, Rana professed honest wonder at the shelves of spices and seasonings. Flattered at her interest, the chief cook, a rotund Syrian, named them for her and explained some of the ways each was used.

One recipe going back to a first-century gourmand named Apicius was for a sauce using pepper, lovage, parsley, celery seed, dill, asafetida root, hazelwort, caraway, cumin, ginger, pyrethrum, liquamen and oil. A dressing for pheasant called for dill, garlic, mint, tarragon, mustard, vinegar and boiled-down grape juice. The cook lifted a large jar of cinnamon bark and set an assistant to grating it, filling the corner with fragrance that temporarily overcame the pervading pungence of liquamen and olive oil.

"Cinnamon comes from India by way of the China silk route," Ladya began, but Rana didn't hear the rest. Her gaze had fixed on a small alabaster container that was usually hidden by the cinnamon.

Nodding in pretended interest, Rana waited for Ladya to stop and then asked offhandedly, "What's in the little jar? It must be rare and powerful."

Ladya's green eyes widened. She gave a soft laugh and spoke in a ribald tone to the cook, who gave her a sly wink and laughed though he gave a noncommittal shrug.

"What is it?" Rana persisted.

Ladya popped a date nougat into her mouth and licked her fingers. "I'd swear it's the stuff used to change our reluctant Northman into a rutting bull." She leered at Rana. "I'd like to slip a taste into your wine, my little icicle. Maybe it'd thaw you out."

Rana evaded Ladya's touch but heartfelt sincerity sounded in her thanks. All she had to do now was drop by the kitchen frequently enough for the cook and his helpers to take her for granted. And some evening, the Syrian would reach for the alabaster jar.

A week passed. After returning from Jørun bruised and scratched, so satiated she slept for a day, the empress had not gone to the men in the adjoining chamber, but as her tossing increased, called on Rana to rub her temples and sing to her.

"Philomele," the woman would sigh. Sometimes she went on in a rush of words Rana caught only a fraction of, but often she spoke with deliberate care, obviously needing to unburden herself. "I am afraid, nightingale. Afraid of growing old. I am afraid of dying."

In such moments, smoothing the veined dry flesh, Rana pitied her as much as she'd hated her when she was with Jørun. The empress had no friends, only courtiers. The single thing she shared with her husband was a throne. She had no children. Her life was a glittering charade. No wonder she tried to find something real for herself even if it was the commanded lust of young guardsmen, the drug-provoked bestiality that was all she could have of Jørun.

When Rana tried to comfort the empress in her broken Greek, the older woman would hush her. "Sing, nightingale. That's better than words."

So Rana would, ironically, sing her love for Jørun along with the call of the birds, and eventually, the empress would sleep. At the end of the week, she went to the waiting soldier but returned quickly and asked Rana's attendance.

After that, Rana could not sleep till her mistress did. She almost felt the empress' enflamed yearning, her humiliation and torment. Rana had to respect the woman's struggle even while loathing her.

"It can't be much longer," she told Fenn when they met in the courtyard.

She had already told him about the alabaster jar and that she was becoming accepted in the kitchen. The cook was glad to be appreciated and always urged her to taste some special treat. She complimented him on them all, though some, like lamprey roe, were more than she could force down.

"Thorkil's managed to change his duties to night guard at the Bronze Gate," Fenn said. "Holger comes past each evening and Skarp's making sure the twins don't get too drunk to sail."

Rana shivered. "So many things can go wrong,"

Fenn held her hand between both of his. She felt steadied by his sureness and strength. "Don't worry about that, my Rana. I'll be here every day at this hour. Just let me know when that potion's used."

"You'll bring the sword for Jørun?"

"Of course. It's burnished and sharpened." Fenn smiled. "Think of it when you get frightened. Your parents gave it to you, it's the luck and honor you must pass on to your children. Fix your mind on it."

She went back into the incense-cloyed rooms but Fenn's counsel was wise. Strung to the screaming point, she found a quiet center, a vision of the sword, and though it was an ancient scarred iron blade, it shone like the sun.

Three nights passed, three more long days. The empress seemed to wither before Rana's eyes, staring hauntedly at her mirror, scolding the servants who arranged her hair and painted her face. On the fourth day, after she had bathed, been massaged and had her face creamed with rare ointments, she waved off the girl with the kohl for her eyes and the vermilion for lips and cheeks.

She stared fixidly into the polished bronze mirror. A bitter smile curved her lips. Then her hand began to shake, her eyes rolled back and she gave a cry, toppling from the ivory stool.

Ladya and the other ladies screamed. The servants stood agape. Dreadful as the woman's convulsed struggle was, Rana felt a wave of relief. The empress' face was purpling; it was clear she could not breathe. When she died, it should be easy to purloin the key, and during the clamor over her death, make good Jørun's escape.

Yet those frail limbs moved so pitifully. And the woman's terrified gaze caught Rana's, implored. Rana could almost hear her saying, *I'm afraid to die.*

Kneeling beside the empress, Rana suddenly remembered how Holger had brought life back to Björn. The empress' case was different, but Rana knew of nothing else to try. She shrank from touching those shriveled, pallid lips, but she set her own over them and blew strongly, then drew her breath back in a sucking fashion, repeating the forced respiration till a fetid slime flushed up from the empress' throat. Rana spat it out, cleared the empress' mouth with her fingers, and clamped her lips again over the dying ones.

Now she thought she could detect a fluttering in the breast beneath her own, a sensation of faint breathing responding to hers, but she was afraid to stop till breath from the empress' nostrils stirred her hair, till the heart began to beat, lurchingly at first, then with increasing regularity.

As Rana fell away, exhausted, the physicians hurried up. But the empress' dark eyes fixed on Rana and her fingers stretched out feebly.

Rana took them.

In a few days, the empress was restored enough to talk. Rana had not left her, for the woman clung to her so that Rana had to move her pallet alongside the royal couch so that the empress could touch her in the night. It might have been a perfect time to steal the key except that the physicians were sleeping in the chamber until their mistress was clearly out of danger.

During these days and nights, Rana thought of Jorun and sometimes regretted saving his jailer. It made no sense. She was ready to kill the empress or anyone who got in the way of freeing him; to have let the woman expire naturally would have been the easier, safer way.

And yet . . . *I'm afraid to die!* No, there was nothing else Rana could have done and been worthy of the sword. From what Holger and Skarp said, its owners had used it valorously in battle, but it had never spilled innocent blood or taken a defenseless life. But when she thought of Jorun in his prison, thought of the way this woman had used him, Rana burned with fury, the more because Fenn's plan couldn't work till the empress visited her captive. The physicians warned that her heart had been severely weakened by the seizure and she must avoid excitement or exertion till her strength returned.

How long would that be?

With each day, the empress looked less like death. She ate with better appetite and often asked Rana to sing. One day the emperor sent word that he would pay his wife a visit to congratulate her on her recovery.

The empress had herself dressed splendidly and her face artfully powdered and painted. She received her husband propped among cushions. They kissed formally, Basil made polite inquiries, complimented her on her appearance and retired in less than five minutes.

His wife stared after him with a weary smile. Then she gave a small shrug and turned to Rana, taking her hand.

"I have little enough to live for, nightingale." By now Rana could understand the gist of what was said in

Greek. "But I am grateful that you saved my life. No matter what the priests say, I fear the darkness."

"Lady, do not." Rana faltered for the right words, not wishing Ladya to interpret. "I have been to the other world. There are terrors on the way, but the heart of the universe is perfect peace, perfect light."

"Nightingale, it may be so for you. But mine is a wicked soul."

"That is part of the terror on the way. If you move toward the light, you will surely find it. It is endless day."

Tears streaked the woman's cheeks with runneled kohl and powder. At last she forced a smile. "I will pray you are right, child. You comfort me more than all the priests." She wiped her eyes and sat more erectly, assuming the proud mien of a sovereign. "Still, I am glad to be here, and I owe that to you. Ask what you will. It shall be yours."

Rana's heart stopped, then leaped wildly. Did she dare? The empress did not have to keep her promise. In her passion for Jørun, what might she not do to a rival? Searching behind the empress' mask for her spirit, Rana spoke softly.

"Lady, grant me that key you wear always on your body."

The empress recoiled. For a moment, Rana feared she would be smitten again, but then the woman sat even straighter, bending an imperious frown upon her.

"The key? Do you know what it is for?"

Rana threw back her head and the steel of her parents' sword was in her tone. "It imprisons my love."

"What are you saying?"

Rana repeated the words. The empress called for Ladya.

When she had heard the whole story, except for the part played by Thorkil and Holger and the plot to get

Jørun away, the empress was silent for an oppressively
long time. Ladya's green eyes darted back and forth between her and Rana, and a wondering spiteful smile
played about her lips. Whatever happened, Ladya would
enjoy it, would revel in spreading the tale about the
court.

Hope began to die in Rana. The acridity of defeat was
like metal on her tongue. Her own life—well, she had
gambled, given the empress a chance to do a good thing.
But she had no right to place Fenn in peril.

"Magnificence," she pleaded. "Do as you will to me,
but I beg you not to punish my foster-brother. He is here
for my sake, he's not to blame—"

The empress raised her veined hand.

"You shall have the key." Her lips twitched. "For
such a story, I would almost give you your Jørun even if
you had not saved my life. Anyone can cause death but
few can bring happiness. I will be glad that I can do
that."

She sank back on her pillows. As Rana knelt to kiss
scrawny ringed fingers, the empress said, "Sing one
more time for me."

Fenn, carrying the sword, went with Rana to unlock
Jørun's cell. That was fortunate. Her fingers shook so
frantically that she couldn't turn the key. Fenn did it for
her and pushed open the heavy door. Rana stepped into a
room where the empress' scent lingered, where one high
window glowed on the gold-brown hair of a man who
glanced up from a book. His jaw dropped. Those dark
blue eyes grew wide.

"Rana!"

Then they were in each other's arms.

Her joy was so great that Rana had no idea how much
time passed before Jørun at last took his mouth from hers

and kissed her eyes, her throat, her hair as they mingled tears with laughter.

"You have been so often in my dreams," he whispered, holding her back to look at her. "Are you really here? Is it true?" His face twisted suddenly and he pulled away. "Or are you the empress? Is this some foul magic?"

She told him all. And then she took the sword from Fenn and placed it in his hands. "My parents gave me this for you, and for our children. Let us go now, my love." Glancing about the sumptuously furnished room, she said hesitatingly, "The empress bids you take as a gift anything in your quarters."

His eyes blazed. "Can she think I would have aught of hers?" He glanced at his rich garments. "Even these things I will send back if I can borrow clothes from one of your friends."

They left the palace by the door used by the guards. Only when he stepped aboard one of the small ships did Jørun seem to believe what had happened. Holger, Skarp and the others greeted him heartily, as did Thorkil, who had come ahead with the astonishing news. He was sailing with them, back to his own country.

Only after the boats had rowed about the point and their sails were rigged to catch the wind, only when Byzantium became a glittering phantasm on the horizon, did Thorkil move to where Rana sat with Jørun, too blissful to even speak.

"The empress hopes you will keep this in memory of her," he said to Rana, unwrapping azure silk from about something that flashed blue fire. "A nightingale for a nightingale. She will pray for you and asks that you will sometimes send a song to her spirit."

Jørun's lips tightened but he only shrugged at Rana's questioning glance. " 'Tis a pretty bauble—and will serve to prove this story to our children should they start to reckon it all a fairy tale. Shall we be married in your parents' camp before we go home to my hall?''

Rana nodded and smiled with the radiance of love. "And we'll tell my parents, won't we, that each fall and autumn we will visit their camp?''

"We will, most gladly.'' His look sent sweet flame through her. She thought of a night that was coming soon, a night when they would sleep on shore, and in each other's arms.

A song swelled from her heart through her lips. She poured out a melody to the sun and Fenn's *joik* answered from the other boat as the craft skimmed northward.

Book V
The Dark Mirror

Norway, Iceland,
Mexico
1067–1071

I

Kyra's legs were numb from kneeling over the mill, and she stumbled in her haste to carry the flour to Ulvhild, the broad, freckled woman who ruled the kitchen.

"Put it in the kneading trough," Ulvhild grumbled.

Before the thick-waisted matron could think of another chore, Kyra poured out the flour and left the kitchen, catching up her skirts to run along the hewn logs that formed a walkway around the buildings facing the court-yard. Her father, Jarl Ragnar, was home. When he crushed her in his bearlike embrace and held her head against his chest while his laughter rumbled comfortingly in her ears, Kyra was so happy she wished she could stay there forever—that this only person in the world who had ever shown her love would never go away again.

He always did. But he was here now! A gate between stable and kitchen led to the farmyard with its barns, pig-sties and byres, and beyond these, near the river where there was small chance of their fires spreading, were the smithy and bathhouse. Kyra was going in the other direc-tion, though, for the great hall was near the steward's house which guarded the entrance to Jarlsholm.

In spite of her haste, Kyra smiled up at the men's faces carved on the eaves of the hall. She liked them, though

Ulvhild said they were heathen devils like the heads carved on the poles of Ragnar's high seat. In this year of 1067, after mass conversions forced by the king who became Saint Olaf, Norway's patron, after his death in battle against Canute in 1030, all Norway was Christian on the surface, though many, like Ragnar, rubbed ale and fat on the gods' carved lips and left ale, milk and bread at the grave mounds of ancestors or at certain stones.

Kyra hesitated at the door. Ragnar's men would be sleeping on the benches that lined the walls on either side of the long-fires that ran down the middle of the great timbered room. At the far end was the high seat and table with closed beds on either hand. Ragnar had one and his sons shared the other. Hoping none of the men would be awake—for ugly though she was, Kyra had learned to be wary of men, especially her half brothers—she was using her weight to pull open the heavy door when fingers dug into her shoulders, jerking her around.

"Sneaking off from your work, you worthless slattern?"

Gudrun shook her as a dog might shake a bird. A tall, powerful woman, Gudrun was still handsome and fair-skinned, though her large jaw was flabby. She wore many gold bracelets, jeweled brooches fastened the richly embroidered panels she wore over her wide-sleeved undergown, and she carried the keys to every chest and storehouse of the manor on the brass ring fastened to her girdle. The hair that showed beneath her pleated linen coif was tarnished gold. So were her eyes. These reminded Kyra of Ragnar's great Iceland falcon's, except that the falcon's fierce gaze softened for Ragnar and she baited for him, disgorging her prey, offering her kill to her master in affection.

Not so Gudrun. Young as Kyra was, she knew her stepmother despised her father. When Gudrun spoke to him, her voice was like a chisel shaping runes in stone.

She had so left her mark on that mighty chieftain that he spent little time at his principal manor. He had returned only last night from his estates in Halogaland, bringing with him a foster-son.

Gudrun shook Kyra again. "Get back to the kitchen!"

"But, lady, I've ground the flour—"

"So you want to sidle in among the men like your bitch mother before you!"

Such naming of her mother and being kept again from her father set off wild madness in Kyra. Accustomed though she was to her stepmother's slaps and pinches, something flamed in defiance. If Gudrun killed her, so be it. No longer would she meekly endure abuse.

She sank her teeth in Gudrun's wrist, tasted blood, bit deeper. With a strangled curse, Gudrun set her free hand in Kyra's hair and wrenched her head back. Kyra saw the flash of the jeweled knife Gudrun wore at her belt, but a brown hand checked it in midair.

"Nay, Lady Gudrun," said a deep, pleasant voice. "The maid perchance is at fault, but sure she cannot merit death or maiming."

Furious as Gudrun was, Kyra could feel her response to the young man who had intervened and now steadied Kyra as Gudrun abruptly let her go.

" 'Tis a sly jade that tries me sore." Gudrun gazed at the stranger in helpless appeal, though she was well nigh as tall as he and almost as broad in the shoulder. "I thank you, foster-son, for checking me—her rat's teeth in my wrist made me forget myself. But enough of that! Come walk with me and tell me how you find Jarlsholm."

She slipped her arm through the tall lad's, for a closer look had shown Kyra that though he was well grown, though his voice was resonant, he had a smooth face and was probably no older than Egil, who was sixteen. He even resembled him, though the very likeness made the newcomer shine.

Where Egil's red hair was frizzy, his was tawny gold and waved thickly about a face that was thin and sensitive with a nose that was slightly beaked. Instead of making him ugly, it gave him a hawk look that made straight noses appear negligible. His firm mouth had tenderness at the edges and his eyes were the gray of a thundercloud, not a washed-out pale shade like Egil's.

Though Gudrun impatiently tried to draw him with her, Kyra's rescuer regarded her in a way that brought blood to her cheeks. What he must think if he'd seen her bite Gudrun! But there was almost a smile on his lips as he gave her a small nod and moved off with Gudrun. Kyra stared after him.

So that was Ogier, the fosterling Ragnar had fetched from Halogaland, Land of the Aurora! No wonder Ulvhild and the other serving folk had declared him handsomer than Egil and Hrapp together! Odd that Gudrun, instead of being jealous for her sons, seemed of a mind to show him favor.

A pang shot through Kyra as Gudrun kept hold of Ogier, laughing as they proceeded up the walkway. She still wanted to see her father, but the encounter with Gudrun had bruised her eagerness. Subdued now, she opened the door and sped like a wraith past the slumbering men on the benches to her father's ornately carved and painted bed closet.

Since the hall was lit only by the vent hole above the fires, open now though it could be closed against rain with a piece of transparent bladder, only dim light revealed Ragnar's countenance when Kyra opened the door of the enclosed great bed, big enough to hold three or four people.

Gazing down at Ragnar, Kyra felt shock at the way he had changed since she last saw him, almost a year ago. His once-flaming hair and beard was dulled with white, his many scars showed livid on arms, chest and seamed, weathered face. *He is old,* she thought in terror. *He looks so tired.* She fought back tears as she bent to kiss the cheek ridged with an old wound.

His eyes opened. Joy sparked in their green depths. "Paala!" He caught her to him, but Kyra knew her mother's name.

Full of pity but frightened at his embrace which was not a father's, she set her hands against his breast and whispered, "Father! It's Kyra."

His arms loosened. He flinched back. Shaken to realize that after all these years, he still loved a dead woman, remorseful at having caused him pain, Kyra put her arms around him and pressed her face to his shoulder.

"Aren't you glad to see me, father?"

A sigh that could almost have been a sob shook his huge frame. He patted her head and buried his face against her hair. "You are my dearest sight left on all this earth, child."

He brought up her chin and stared at her, proud delight mixed with longing in his eyes. "You're no longer my little maid, but will soon be a woman with your mother's grace and beauty." He frowned, lifting her hand. "What is this? Burns and cuts! 'Tis not thus a gentle-born maiden's hands should look."

Kyra got the servants' leavings and had seldom satisfied her hunger. At fourteen, when some girls were wedded and mothers, she had the thin, wiry body of a child and reached only to Gudrun's shoulder. Her form, like her black hair and slanting dark eyebrows, must have come from her mother, but her eyes were the luminous, almost crystal blue-green of water that formed where a glacier had melted a little in the fervent sun.

Witch-eyes, Gudrun called them, and she never tired of reminding Kyra that no man higher than a thrall would ever want someone with such dark, ugly skin even if she hadn't been the bastard of a sluttish witch who had fortunately died in childbirth before she could completely ruin the jarl. Not wishing to cause strife between Ragnar and his easily angered wife, Kyra drew away her fingers with a careless laugh. "I help in the kitchen. Lady Gudrun says that a girl should learn how to do everything so she can guide her household when she becomes a wife."

"A wife?" Ragnar scowled in earnest, then tugged at his beard. "By God's Wounds, you do well to jog me, lass, for 'tis sure I must make you a suitable match and see you in a sound man's keeping before I die. I fear me Gudrun will not trouble to seek out a good and honorable marriage."

Kyra flushed. "The lady says that since I am . . ." Floundering, Kyra couldn't meet her father's gaze. "She says I cannot hope to wed into a noble family."

Ragnar was very still. Then he growled irefully, "If it's your wish to be a knight's lady, a part of my lands in Halogaland would get you any number of impoverished nobles. But I thought rather to give you to some upright franklin who tends to his farms rather than hanging about Olaf the Silent's doleful court."

Until she saw Ogier, Kyra had dreamed of marriage as a way of escaping Gudrun, vaguely picturing a husband who'd resemble a young Ragnar. Ogier's faint smile had changed all that. But he was noble, or he would not be Ragnar's fosterling.

"I have no mind to wed at all," she said in a low tone. "Good my father, let me stay with you so long as that may be."

He laughed in a tender rumbling, smoothing her hair back from her forehead. "It must be your mother in you loves me, lass, for I have been neglectful. Wishing to see you when I could, I have kept you under Gudrun's hand when I should have given you into the charge of friends or good nuns to be properly reared. Gudrun knows only boy cubs, and I think she has never forgotten that though she is my wife, your mother was my love. I cannot trust her with your future.''

He sounded so grim that Kyra caught his hands. "Lord father, do not force me to wed!''

"I will not force you,'' he said heavily. "You are yet scarce-grown. But before I visit Halogaland again, I will see you betrothed or in the care of folk I trust more than my wife.''

Kyra didn't argue with him. After that morning, she knew she could bear Gudrun's abuse no longer. If Ogier had not been there . . . Still, so long as Ragnar was at his manor, and Ogier with him, she feared no one. Her heart swelled with love for both of them, and something like worship for Ogier.

This worship grew, till she could not trust herself to look directly into those eyes which were the color of storms where Thor's flung hammer thundered and his bright beard flashed lightning. Hrapp, a slight blond youth of Kyra's years who had a girlish delicacy of feature, got on well enough with his foster-brother, but Egil glowered at him sullenly whenever their father's back was turned.

Glower was all that Egil dared, for in swordplay, wrestling and archery, Ogier excelled the jarl's best warriors. It had to be as gallingly clear to Egil as it was to everyone that in their contests, Ogier won without exertion. Never did he strut or boast. He was respectful to his elders, courteous to women and served his father at table, yet a flock of urchins pursued him when he set foot in the courtyard.

"He minds me of Harald Hardrada, God save his soul,'' mused Arne, a grizzled man-at-arms. "If you stood our Ogier beside him, methinks they could scarcely be told apart.''

Ragnar crossed himself. "God save King Harald's

soul. Hard-Ruler he was called when he came to Norway's throne, but he was valiant.''

Harald had fallen only the autumn before in England, defeated by Harold of Wessex, the English king who died three weeks later, battling William, the conquering bastard of Normandy. A great fiery-tailed comet had marked these fateful events. Folk were glad when it vanished.

Ragnar glanced at Ogier, who was playing draughts with white-haired Flossi, the *skald*. '' 'Tis no wonder they favor. The lad is Harald's grandson, though not by way of his wife, the daughter of the ruler of Kiev and the Rus. That was a rich marriage of state, but Harald's real love was of the noble Swedish line that founded Novgorod. He brought her back to Norway with him but she died young. Her only child, a little maid, was reared in a convent.''

His voice softened. Gudrun watched him as a falcon does quarry too formidable to seize. ''Harald's daughter is dead?'' asked Arne.

''Ay,'' said Ragnar, quaffing the silver-inlaid drinking horn to the dregs before he spoke again. ''Many years is her sweet face and loveliness turned to grave mold.'' He stared at Gudrun with baffled, furious eyes. '' 'Tis ever thus with the good and gentle. Kyra, child, come here and sing to me.''

''You have a *skald* for that,'' Gudrun protested, her nostrils pinched white.

Ragnar shook his head. ''I am too sad for tales of war and heroes.'' He smiled at Kyra, sewing a new shirt for him, looked ruefully at Mork who was curled in her lap. Only a kitten when Ragnar fetched him home in his mantle as a gift, Mork was Kyra's only solace when her father was away. Mork purred in her arms or, when she wept from a scolding or loneliness, he sympathized, scrubbing her tears away with his rough tongue. He had beautiful gold-green eyes and was the terror of the dogs. Gudrun called him an evil spirit. Her kicks always missed him, though he never fled her but moved with haughty dignity. "Bring that monster-cat, daughter, and sing the song I heard you giving Ogier this morning."

" 'Tis but a lullaby, lord father."

"That's not amiss," he chuckled. "I'm sleepy enough."

Lifting Mork, who stretched and yawned, showing his pointed berry-colored tongue, she went to sit on the footstool at her father's seat. Gudrun's angry stare made her throat go dry, so she ignored everyone but Ragnar, singing the words she had learned from mothers with their babes, for it had never been crooned to her.

"Sleep, child, sleep.
  Father guards the sheep.
  Mother shakes the tree.
  From it drops a dream.
  Sleep, child, sleep.

The stars are little lambs . . ."

"That a jarl should listen to such peasant stuff!" snorted Gudrun. "Flossi! Bring your harp and play something worthy to be heard!"

The white-haired bard rose from the board with a laugh. "I had best play harp better than draughts," he said. "Ragnar, your fosterling has trounced me thrice within an hour. What have you brought among us?"

Shaking his head in mock despair, he took his seat beside the jarl and ran long, skilled fingers over the strings of his harp. Kyra loved to watch him almost as much as she loved his music.

The pedestal of the instrument was carved in the shape of a woman whose flowing hair streamed back to form the graceful arch, most beautifully gilded. Flossi's face was unlined but weather-darkened so that his silvery locks and hazel eyes were in striking contrast. Gold chains of Ragnar's favor were about his neck, shining against leaf-green mantle and tunic, and a great emerald blazed from his finger as he began. Though he obeyed Gudrun's behest, yet did he not annoy his lord with sagas full of split skulls and lopped arms and legs, but sang of a maid enchanted by her stepmother.

> "She then to a sword-blade shaped my form,
> And bade me flash in battle's storm.
> A sword-blade I was, keen and bright,
> And dear to squire and valiant knight."

Ogier had come over to listen and called his approval with the others when the ballad ended with the girl redeemed by her lover, but he whispered in Kyra's ear, "I liked your singing best."

She blushed, overcome by his nearness, his smiling eyes and his voice, which reached into her heart and warmed it till she felt the glow must show outside. Her fingers fumbled and she pricked herself. A drop of blood stained the linen shirt. Dismayed, Kyra glanced toward Gudrun. Those molten eyes were fixed on her with such hatred that Kyra's joy at Ogier's attention was seared as if by withering heat.

Had this stepmother the power to transform her, it would not be into a sword but a doe for the hunting. And now not all because of Ragnar's favor, but because Ogier had smiled on her. Kyra's love made her aware that loathly and forbidden though it was, Gudrun had conceived a passion for her foster-son.

Ragnar was at Jarlsholm through most of the summer, hawking or riding about to visit his tenants. The hall, not used while he was gone, resounded with jesting and Flossi's harp. Kyra thought her father looked a very king, in his carved high seat with the red wool tapestry behind him, embroidered with Saint Olaf's deeds in gold and silver, blue and green. There were blue hangings over the benches where the warriors' shields hung above each place, and two rows of massive pillars supporting the vaulted roof were carved with birds and beasts entwined with flowering vines and trees, all bravely painted.

With wool or flax twined around the distaff Kyra tucked beneath her armpit while playing out thread to the spinning distaff wheel, she spun on the stool beside her father, or sewed, or carded wool. She was busy, but at tasks suiting a lady. When Gudrun scoffed that her stitches were like troll-tracks, Ragnar said he would blithely wear garments from his daughter's hand. Then Gudrun held her peace, but her hard eyes promised that Kyra would pay later for this time of bliss.

Folk were harvesting the silvery ears of barley when a messenger came hot-haste from Ragnar's steward in Halogaland. A neighboring estate's men had slaughtered some of Ragnar's reindeer that they claimed were trespassing, and it was clear the new heir of that property thought to enlarge his lands at the expense of Ragnar's. It behooved the jarl to come at once and show the upstart that his holdings would be protected.

Ragnar's wounds showed livid, though he calmly bade Gudrun see to the messenger's refreshment. Turning to Ogier, he said as if to an equal, "We must leave at dawn—teach that cockerel that he cannot crow on my earth."

Ogier nodded but he said something under his breath. Ragnar glanced at Kyra and slowly nodded. Egil stepped forward and had he not stood next to Ogier, he would have seemed a rarely handsome lad.

"May I not ride with you, my lord father?"

Ragnar hesitated. "Stay here and guard this manor and your mother," he said at last.

Egil colored darkly. "How shall I ever be a knight if you leave me at home when there's hope of a battle?"

"When you have as many scars as I, my son, you'll laugh that you ever had such a fear." Ragnar spoke kindly and dropped his hand on Egil's shoulder. "No glory waits in the north, only chastisement of a wet-eared cub."

Casting a jealous glance at Ogier, Egil demanded, "Then why do you take *him?*"

Ragnar's heavy graying brows rushed together. " 'Tis not for a stripling to question his lord and father, pup. Till you learn that, Saint Olaf strike me if I take you on any weighty emprise." Egil looked so shamed that Ragnar's tone softened. "I take Ogier since he was nurtured in Aurora Land, knows the boundaries and folk of my estate and can be of use. Just as here, you would be my aid."

At that Egil looked less sulky, but Gudrun's gaze fixed on Ogier with sudden blazing and her face went white. She rose and swept from the hall. Egil followed her after a moment. Ragnar sighed, shrugged and turned to Kyra.

"Lass, though you never complained, I think your stepmother has not used you gently, and now you are becoming a woman, she will like you even less. I can leave you in the convent at Nidaros or with my kinsman Halvard and his good wife, Inger. Oft has she asked about you and said she longed for a daughter."

"Take me with you, father," she begged. Already her heart had shriveled to a small painful knot at the thought of his leaving. And to lose Ogier, too!

"I cannot, lass," Ragnar said sternly. "I go to a struggle, not a feast."

She choked back a plea. It was no time to plague him. She had never met Halvard, but she knew he was a bastard grandson of Ragnar's grandsire and had inherited the good farm with which his noble father dowered his leman when he wed her to a franklin.

"Think you Inger would let me keep Mork with me?" Kyra asked.

Ragnar laughed and tousled her hair. "So long as your sooty creature makes no alliance with the rats, I'm sure Inger won't grudge him his milk and fish. She'll be at the *seter* now with the cows and will be glad of your help."

Kyra had seldom been up in the mountains, and it would be good to be busy. "Have you garments enough?" Ragnar asked. "A mantle?"

"You brought me that fine shawl from Nidaros," Kyra said. She wore an everyday dress of gray wadmal and wool twill, and would not have had another had Ragnar not insisted that she have red wool enough out of Gudrun's stores to make herself a gown for church and feast days. When she told Ragnar this, he frowned. "Never mind, we shall take linen and wool enough to outfit you in proper style. Inger will help you sew, and she shall have material enough to dress herself, too."

"But Lady Gudrun—"

"Fret not yourself about her, child. Get your other things together. We leave at first light."

Kyra went to the loft where she now slept with the serving women and began to put her few belongings into a bag. A pair of Hrapp's cast-off bone skates, an extra petticoat, an ivory comb that had been Ragnar's gift. She would wear the fine red gown with the silver brooches, embroidered girdle and amber beads Ragnar had given her on her birthday that month, the new shawl and soft leather shoes.

Mork watched her with a half-open eye from his perch on the balcony. "Mayhap Inger will give you cream sometimes." Kyra told him and whirled guiltily as Gudrun almost filled the entrance to the upper storey.

"Cream, indeed! Better she drown that devil cat! But belike you'll fool the poor woman with your soft, sidling ways!"

Heaving herself up the ladder, Gudrun threw a cloak made of the softest fleece from the Orkneys into Kyra's face, along with a dark green dress that had been the feast-day apparel of Hjördis, her favorite servant who had died two years ago and been a very small person. "Here! Your father commands that you be gauded out as if you were his true-born get!"

"I thank you, Lady Gudrun."

"Thank me not!" Towering over Kyra, the mistress of Jarlsholm obviously struggled to control herself. "You and your whining tales! You with the witch eyes! Mark me well! If you return to this manor, it will be at your peril."

Coldness raced down Kyra's spine, fingered her bones. She feared those hands that had so often struck her, but she remembered that she was Ragnar's daughter.

"I will go where my father wills," she said.

Their gazes locked. Gudrun's face puffed with rage. Her fingers made claws. Kyra stood her ground. After a breath-held moment, Gudrun spun about. In an instant she was gone, but Kyra, shivering at such malignancy, picked up Mork and hugged him.

It had been a happy summer, the best of all her life, but she knew, if she wished to live, she must keep clear of Gudrun.

The *seter huts were small, of logs and turf. A few half-grown lads* helped with the work when they weren't frolicking in the meadow or fishing, but for the most part, this summer place was a woman's world, while in the valley far below, men hayed and harvested. When the cattle and goats came down, they could feed fat on the stubble before they were closed in their byres for the harsh winter. Even though the weakest were slaughtered, many that survived till spring would have to be carried out of their shelters and helped to the grass that would renew their strength.

But now they grazed contentedly in lush green pastures watered by streams grown about with buttercups and angelica, coming to be milked of an evening at Inger's melodious *lokk*, the special calling song she'd learned from her mother and taught now to Kyra.

Kyra enjoyed filling a birch bucket, resting her head against a cow's warm side as her fingers rhythmically pressed the teats that released copious spurts of creamy, frothing milk. Now and then a restive cow set her foot in the bucket or switched a heavy tail in Kyra's face, but there was usually a sort of peaceful communion between human and animal. Kyra loved the moist, soft herb-scented breath of the cattle and thought the calves, who still got all the milk they wanted, looked like deer with their big ears and eyes and comparatively narrow muzzles.

She was not as fond of skimming the great vats or churning the cream to butter, but Inger was so kind and beguiled their toil with such interesting stories that Kyra was happy except for missing Ragnar and Ogier.

When they were not busied with making cheese or butter, Inger wove on a polished birch loom set against one wall of the hut, and so deftly did her fingers ply the shuttle that the soapstone weights tied to one end of the warp threads scarcely vibrated. Mork loved to tap these long oval weights with his paw and would lie on his back, disporting himself in kittenish fashion, when the loom was not in use. Gudrun had said Kyra was too clumsy to weave and had never taught her, so that she'd never had the satisfaction of forming cloth from the wool and flax she'd laboriously wound on the spindle. Inger showed her how, and it gave her a sense of accomplishment to watch the material for Halvard's winter cloak grow on the web while Inger stitched at one of Kyra's new gowns and talked of *huldre*-folk, those shadowy unbaptized children of Eve who, mostly unseen, shared the earth with mortals.

"*Huldre*-maids are fair," said Inger, snipping a thread with the scissors she wore fastened to her girdle. Much younger than her husband, she was still fair herself, with tranquil blue eyes and unwrinkled skin. "But they have a cow's tail. However, if a man will marry one, she loses the tail and becomes as good a Christian as any. My granny was *huldre*."

There was the *nøk* who lived near cloud-berry marshes and streams so that if someone drowned it was said, "The *nøk* has taken him away," and there were men who put on wolves' skins at dusk, and hung them up in the morning, the muzzles red with blood. Kyra had heard such tales before, but here in the mountains they actually seemed likely to be true, and she was glad to have Mork snuggled against her on the fragrant grass pallet, though it was never really dark.

Glaciers had always whitened the mountain peaks, but now they were often hidden in clouds, and one day these lifted to show snow halfway down to the meadows. The days were shortening. Halvard sent men with mules to carry down the summer's yield of round cheeses, butter in birch boxes and panniers of sour milk and whey.

Kyra was sorry to leave the bright, high world but glad that the time was nearer to Ragnar's return. Each morning and night, she had prayed for him and Ogier and often in between. Though it was presumptuous fancy, she pictured dwelling somewhere with Ogier and Ragnar— mayhap in the Land of the Aurora?

Ragner was not home at Yule, and though Kyra helped prepare the food that was bountifully served through Epiphany, she was often so overcome with disappointment and worry that she had to flee to the loft or frigid storehouses to weep.

Candlemas next and snow lay thick. It was hard to believe young plants would soon be starting. By the beginning of Lent, Kyra was so distraught that Halvard said he had a mind to ride to Jarlsholm and see if Ragnar had gone home another way. Kyra, heedless of Gudrun's menace, begged to go with him, and they were preparing for the journey when Arne, the old warrior who'd fought under Harald Hard-Ruler, rode in on a spent stallion.

"I'm to fetch you home to your father, lass," he said when they clustered about him. As he warmed himself by the hearth and ate and drank, he told how Ragnar had not only drubbed the trespasser from his lands but claimed damages enough in furs, hides, antlers and walrus tusks to fill a ship. This he had left in Oslo, the city founded by

Harald Hard-Ruler, bidding Ogier take the cargo to sell in Gotland, the island that had dominated the rich Baltic trade since the decline of Birka.

Ragnar's victory had cost him dear. A spear wound in his thigh had not healed and he'd been carried by litter from Oslo to Jarlsholm, arriving there on Saint Lucia's Day, the thirteenth of December. He had hoped to keep Christmas with Kyra at his kinsman's farm, but though his wound was closed, he grew daily weaker in spite of Gudrun's constant attentions.

Kyra's heart faltered. "He is very sick, my lord father?"

Arne looked sorrowful. "Each day, he has wasted and he has much pain in his bowels. Lady Gudrun says perhaps his blood was poisoned by the spear."

If only Ogier were with him! "Let us go early tomorrow." Kyra urged. "Are you able, good Arne?"

"Ay, but my horse is not."

"Leave him to rest," said Halvard. "You may take my best mount."

Kyra went with Inger to make ready, but she could not sleep that whole night long.

Guide stones had been set up to mark a safe path across marshes and fords so that folk might go to mass or the priest bring blessing to a departing soul. Some of these pillars were gray, striped with glittering white crystals, others dark rainbows of green, rust, red and yellow. Following these when fog obscured their way, Kyra and Arne pressed for Jarlsholm as fast as their horses could travel without hurt and reached the manor in four days.

Gudrun sat by the hearth in the hall, weaving a tapestry that showed the death of Ragnar Ladbroke in the King of Northumbria's snake pit where the Viking chief had died true to his gods rather than accept the White Christ. She dropped the shuttle, unraveling a serpent's fang as Kyra ran past the great pillars toward the bed closet, and stretched forth a hand as if to restrain the girl, but the long-fires were between them. Kyra, panting, flung open the enclosure.

A sickly, fetid odor filled her nostrils, but she drew the white head against her breast and kissed the sunken cheeks. Ragnar's eyelids fluttered. She breathed his name. The green eyes opened to look at her, hazed at first, then quickening. To her vast relief, he did not take her for her mother, but said huskily, pausing with each syllable, "Child, you have come. Sorry was I to send for you with snow still on the ground—"

"Nay, father! Would you had sent sooner." She was horrified at the way flesh had left him so that he seemed aged parchment stretched over bones. But he was not fevered. His mind was clear. Kyra took hope and forced a heartening smile. "I have learned some tasty dishes from Inger. They'll put strength in you. Why, by Eastertide, you'll be good as new!"

A waxen hand lifted to her hair. "I am weary, sweeting. If Ogier would but come so that I might leave you in his charge and see his face, I could go blithe to my Maker." His eyes closed, and his chest rose and fell with the effort of speech. "I cannot fight again as I did in Halogaland."

"You have earned peace, lord father. Your sons can defend the estates."

"My sons?" His face twisted. His gaze fell on her again and he spoke more strongly. "I see by your gear you have just come. Rest and eat, daughter. Then sit by me."

"I will eat if you will."

He smiled faintly. "And you were once so biddable! Well, bring some porridge and I will do my best. If you wish, you may leave your monster-cat at my feet." She put Mork there and hurried to the kitchen.

Gudrun stood at the loom, shuttle stilled in her fingers, her face a frozen mask.

Ulvhild was cooking sour cream into *rømmegrøt*, a sort of thick pudding. Kyra filled two bowls with it, grated cinnamon on top and carried them to the hall. Gudrun was gone but Arne had built the fires and was stretched on the bench beneath his shield and sword, already sound asleep. Flossi, on the settle beside the bed, played his harp softly.

He greeted Kyra with pleasure and yielded her his place. "I watched by my lord all night," he said. "By your leave, I'll sleep now. But first let me fetch you wine."

She protested that a servant could do that, but he said beneath his breath, as if the walls might hear, "Young mistress, do not eat or drink, or let Jarl Ragnar, except from what is used by everyone and from a hand you trust."

For a moment, she didn't take his meaning. Then she quailed. "Sir, you think—"

He cut in, "I have seen your father before this recover many times from grievous wounds. He is too long in mending. Perhaps he has that crab illness that consumes from within, but it costs nothing to be careful."

He helped her doff her cloak and brought beakers of mulled wine before he went to his place, so near the loom that it cast a shadowy web across his face. Kyra set down her own food and roused her father.

Beguiling him with tales of the *seter* and what she had learned from Inger, Kyra fed him the whole bowl and cradled him against her while she held the wine to his lips.

" 'Tis good," he whispered, sighing. "Wouldst sing for me, lass? That childish song, that lullaby—"

She sang, and when he slept, color in his cheeks,

breathing more steadily, she ate her own pudding, drank the spiced fruit wine and then carefully lay beside Mork at her father's feet.

Whether Kyra's will that Ragnar live empowered him, or whether Flossi's half-phrased suspicion was true, the jarl thrived now on food prepared by his daughter. Within a week he was able to sit up and a few days later took a meal in his high seat. To Kyra's surprise, Gudrun spoke her fair and praised her care of Ragnar before the servants and retainers, but Kyra remembered that first look from her stepmother as she entered the hall, nor had she forgotten Gudrun's farewell last summer.

"I shall bide here this summer," Ragnar said to Kyra. "When Ogier comes, we'll hawk and hunt, but I have had enough of battle, my blood and other men's."

In those weeks before Easter, he was content to rest, in his seat or against heaped pillows, while Flossi sang of heroes and Kyra worked at the loom she'd asked to have set up near the bed. She had begun a coverlet for him, patterned with Ygdrasil, the Tree of Life, birds and animals in its branches, the tree that survived the dying of the old gods to repeople a brighter, better world. Gudrun, saying the light was bad, had removed her loom to the weaving house.

These were peaceful days, Mork drowsing on Ragnar's lap or batting at the warp weights. "When think you that Ogier will come?" Kyra ventured one day as she shared wine from her father's gold-mounted horn.

"It depends on if he reached Gotland before the winter storms," said Ragnar, rubbing the beard Kyra had trimmed that morning. It was pure white now, as was his hair, but otherwise he looked almost his old self. "If he wintered in some trading city, we can't expect him before Whitsun or even harvest."

"Would he might ride with us to mass at Easter," Kyra said wistfully.

Ragnar laughed. "You will have me in the saddle then?"

"Ay, my lord father."

He smiled at her confidence and drew her close, stroking her hair. "Ah, my child, had you not come to stuff me with puddings and fish soup, I think I would rest now in the churchyard. No doubt you will have your way and I must e'en gallop with the best. But 'tis time I gave you something of your mother's. I have learned that I can die, and this gift must not be lost, for it carries with it the luck and honor of many noble men and women."

Putting Mork aside, he reached over to move a panel that opened to reveal a long, narrow cavity. He drew out something swathed in crimson silk and handed it to Kyra.

At a gesture from him, awestricken, heart pounding, she drew away the scarlet cloth, stared at the hacked, pitted blade, the silver dragons on the pommel, a golden hilt with birds and beasts so intertwined they could not be separated. Somehow, though she had never seen it, she recognized it as if from having held it in many, many dreams.

"This was my mother's?"

"Ay. 'Twas her last wish you should have it."

And then, as Flossi and Arne listened in amazement and Kyra trembled in wonderment, Ragnar put the sword back in its hiding place and told all that had happened to Heaven's Gift since Frey's priestess brought it to Norway.

"Ah!" cried Flossi. "What a song I shall make of Rana and her Jørun! What became of the sapphire nightingale?"

"Belike 'tis in Sweden," Ragnar said, weary now.

"Fenn's son wed Rana's daughter. Two of their children stayed with the Sameh, a son became a merchant in Upp-sala and—" His voice failed but then he reached for Kyra's hand. "And your mother loved me."

III

Ragnar *waxed stronger with each day. He rode to Easter Mass* with all his folk, and Gudrun, in thanks for his recovery, gave a splendid altarcloth to the church. She behaved so fondly to him that Kyra was fain to believe that his illness had made the lady realize his worth. If Ogier would come, all would be near perfect; except that Egil had become a curse.

He was always coming in her way, making her squeeze past him, or catching at her hands. His blurred likeness to Ogier made her detest him all the more.

"May I not salute my sister?" he asked with irritating slyness.

"Indeed, you have never acted like my brother."

"You were before a scruffy, soot-streaked bony little thing." Opaque blue eyes strayed over her breasts and hips. "A year has changed you,"

"Belike 'twas enough food," she said dryly. "Nay, Egil. Let us be friends for our father's sake, but 'tis not seemly, this kissing and caressing."

"Were I Ogier, I think you would not say so." Egil's laugh was scornful. "You were ever at his heels like a bitch puppy." His gaze narrowed. "Methinks you would not deny our foster-brother anything he sought—and if you got a bastard, how would it be called, the bastard of two bastards?''

She slapped him, cutting her hand on his teeth, bringing blood to the sneering mouth, and ran outside before he could capture her. After that, she took more care than ever to avoid him.

At Saint John's Mass, Ragnar feasted his manor folk and tenants. It was at this midsummer merrymaking when fields were thick with grain and meadow grass came to his stirrups that Ogier rode home, accompanied by a dark, bow-legged little man whose name was Isaac. His black eyes adored his young master who had bought him from a Syrian trader who had flogged him close to death.

Tears came to Ragnar's eyes as he embraced his fosterling. Beside the young man's hair of tawny gold, the jarl's seemed winter-faded. Unable to sell the ship at a reasonable figure, Ogier had brought it back to Oslo and left it in charge of a merchant friend of Ragnar's.

'' 'Tis your vessel,'' Ragnar said, when he heard the price Ogier had gotten for the Halogaland tribute. ''And you shall have a share of the profits of that cargo.''

''Nay, my lord,'' Ogier protested, but Ragnar overvoiced him.

''You must have a start in life, and you have earned this, lad. Before harvest, we will journey down to Oslo and stock the ship for another trading voyage, but this time, we will hire another captain. I would not have you from my side for such a time again.'' The jarl's glance fell on Egil, who was watching all this with a lowering face. ''Egil, 'twould not be amiss for you to see something of the world. Wouldst take a ship to Gotland or to Novgorod?''

''I am no trader,'' Egil said flushing. ''I am your eldest true-born son, heir to this manor.''

''Had your forefathers not been traders and Vikings

both, there'd be no manor,'' Ragnar said. ''Whelp, I was knighted at the king's own hand but never did I think shame to use a scythe in harvest or match wits with those Baltic thieves! He who thinks himself too noble to learn how wealth is made may soon have none.''

Gudrun came between, proffering ale to her husband and Ogier. Her eyes were like polished brass as she looked at her husband, but when she turned to Ogier, they softened with a longing that made Kyra chill with foreboding.

Ogier was man-grown now, stunning in his beauty as the warrior-saint from whom he was descended. Could Gudrun restrain herself? Kyra trembled and beneath her joy at Ogier's coming rose a slimy-cold quagmire of fear.

Nothing untoward chanced, however. Ogier at his side, Egil trailing sullenly, Ragnar rode about his lands, regaining strength and color. In the long, radiant evenings, he played draughts with his foster-son, and Kyra, busy at loom or with her distaff, ached with tenderness for them both. She did not seek to be alone with Ogier but was content to watch him. It seemed his flesh had stored the sun's warmth and brightness; there was a shine about him, and she did not think it was all in her dazzled eyes.

Gudrun was busy at her loom, too, once again set up in the hall opposite Kyra's. The torment of Ragnar Ladbroke was finished, and serpents writhed about him on the tapestry that hung over the jarl's sword and shield that were ranged above his high seat. Kyra did not like to see it there; but it was most artfully worked, and Ragnar had praised his wife's skill.

''Almost I can hear those serpents hiss,'' he chuckled. ''I am a Christian man but think the more of that chieftain for cleaving to his gods. May he feast in Valhall!''

''He is in hell,'' said Gudrun.

''Nay, wife, I am not so sure. Or about those Odin's

men and Thor's who would not renounce their faith for all of Saint Olav's coals on their bellies. Methink the King of Heaven must respect their fealty, for it was pledged before they learned of Him."

Gudrun's lips curled. "Yet thy grandsire was prime-signed in Birka the better to sell his goods."

Ragnar only laughed. "Well, now that you have punished that bold heathen, what weave you next?" His brow furrowed as he studied the pattern on the loom. "Can it be roses? In the years of our marriage, lady, you have wrought curious designs, but never do I mind me that they were flowers."

Gudrun's face reddened, darker for the stiff white coif with its fine gold embroidery. "Is there a law says I cannot try something new?"

"Sure, 'tis handsome stuff. That heaven blue and blossoms rose and silver with green leaves and stems all twined. Is it for Kyra?"

Shoulders stiffening, Gudrun kept her face hidden. "This is a tunic, husband, for our foster-son. Have you not marked how tight his things have grown?"

"A kind thought," approved Ragnar. "So fine a tunic is for feast days, wife, or weddings. What say you, Ogier? Wouldst make a bridegroom?"

Kyra fled. Mork bounded ahead of her, up to an oak-shaded rocky outcrop above the fields where once there'd been sacrifices to the old gods. Freya-grass grew thick beneath the bushes around the ancient stone, delicate tiny white blossoms with blue veins and a blue-brown center. 'Twas said a brew of it would turn a man mad for a woman he had hitherto disdained.

A marvel, Kyra thought bitterly, that Gudrun slips it not into the wine she serves Ogier! Oh, her roses and Mary's pure blue when she is like those adders she wove about the Viking lord! Can Ragnar see nothing?

Pressing her face against the sun-warmed stone, Kyra

wept in helpless outrage, heedless of Mork's attempts to rasp away her tears. Her mind was telling her something she could scarcely believe! That withering, flab-jowled woman with the fresh, unblemished lad—a sin against nature if not against God!

Lost in misery, Kyra heard no footfall. She jumped when Ogier said, dropping down beside her, "How now, little Kyra, what moil is this? You fled as if a swarm of bees were after you."

She drew away from him. "You can stand quiet for Gudrun's measuring and let Ragnar make your marriage without my presence in the hall!"

"But I cannot, that last." He brought her chin up. His gaze overwhelmed her. Soft, thrillingly sweet fire played between them. She was consumed by it, melting in his hands. "You are young," he said, voice catching, "but you must know that I can make no marriage without you."

She stared, hoping, yet afraid to believe. She cried out his name. His mouth found hers. They were in each other's arms and it was like reclaiming some lost, beloved part of herself.

Ogier said he would speak with Ragnar that night, totally disregarding Kyra's conscience-stricken protests that her birth kept her from being a proper match for him. "You are the child of Ragnar and a lady he loved well," Ogier shrugged. "No, it is you I will have. Ragnar may well bid us wait a year or two—you are scarce fifteen, I know—but methinks he must be glad."

Kyra could scarcely eat for nervousness. Her stomach twisted itself into the sort of snarl Mork made of her yarn when he had a chance, and when, after the meal which had seemed interminable, Ogier asked Ragnar to walk out with him to advise on the imping out of a falcon's broken wing feather, she thought she would be sick.

True, Ragnar loved them, but he was a noble and powerful man. Who could say what plans he had made for her or his foster-son? In this anxiety a hard core of purpose took form, quieting the worst of Kyra's apprehension.

Ragnar was her lord and father. He had been all-powerful in her eyes, his will as ungainsayable as God's. But if he forbade the marriage, so long as Ogier desired it, she would be his.

Strange calm descended on her with that decision. She needed more flax for Ogier's shirt and started to the storehouse for it. As she passed through the anteroom to the courtyard, she heard a fearful cry.

Running out in the blue dusk, she saw Ogier and Ragnar beneath the balcony across the way. From which of them had come that wail? Transfixed, Kyra stood there. Their speech came to her on the little wind, gusted, shattering.

"It cannot be!" Ogier.

Then Ragnar, so low she could barely make out the words, could not believe them when she did: "Alas, boy. I would gladly die to make it otherwise. But you are my own dear son. Kyra's brother by my blood. Kyra's brother."

Twilight swirled about her. She tried to move forward, but her knees dissolved. Then all was flame-shot darkness.

She was being carried. Carried by someone who stumbled, who was gasping. She didn't want to wake up. There was some awful knowledge waiting. She would rather stay in the deep black nothing. But the wavering steps—the labored panting . . . She stirred just as she was almost dropped on a hard surface, her bearer collapsing beside her, arms gathering her close to a heaving chest.

"Kyra," said her father. "Kyra . . ."

Then she remembered. Starting up, she glanced wildly about, searching the hall's shadows. "Ogier?"

A sound of hoofs was her answer. She struggled to rise but Ragnar's clasp restrained her. " 'Tis best he go for a time, lass—till you and he understand this love between you—" Ragnar's voice broke off. He hung his massive head, so that she loathed and pitied him at once, though she felt she must die from her pain. "You heard?" he muttered.

"Ay."

It was all she could say. Hard, glittering.

He raised shamed eyes to her. "Child, forgive me! When I saw you grow fond, I was glad, thinking you would friend each other after I am gone. Never did I dream that this would chance." When she was silent, he pleaded, "Still, lass, I think it is that—brother-sister love. When you grow used to it, you'll see the truth."

"The truth is that we love."

"Ay, but in a different sort than what's 'twixt man and maid."

At that she laughed cruelly. "It seems you know well that kind of love, lord father. Your wedded wife. Ogier's mother. And there was my own."

He stared at her, dumbstruck, and she could not stem her wrathful grief. "You plucked each flower you saw! And now you say we must not have each other!"

He grasped her hands. "You have a right to chide but try to understand. My father wed me young to Gudrun. I was fain to have a bedmate but never was she more. Ogier's mother I burned for and her husband was old. She died young of the wasting illness and when her husband died, I put the lad in my steward's care, for I knew well that Gudrun would not brook a rival to her sons. Your mother . . ." His voice dropped. "I loved her with my body, heart and soul. Women I have had in plenty, so many, in so many places, I cannot remember even their names.'' His face set in harsh lines. ''Say what you will to me, save this—that I loved not your mother.''

''What boots it if you did?'' blazed Kyra. ''If she sees us—knows what you have done—think you she will not curse you for my sake?''

Ragnar choked. He drew back his hand, struck Kyra so that her head smote against the wall. She lay half-stunned but struggled up as his face purpled. Veins bulged terribly in his neck and temples. He pitched forward with a strangling cry.

Fury swept away in dread, Kyra slipped to her knees and tried to raise him. There was great commotion. She realized for the first time that there were other people in the hall. Flossi, Arne, bending to help their lord.

And Gudrun, trying to hide a smile.

Like a tree lightning-struck on one side, Ragnar lay in his bed, one eyelid sunken shut, that half of his mouth sagging. Yet there was in that side of his face an innocence that erased years, so that Kyra saw how he must have looked when young.

He could speak, but with thick slurring. Most of the time, he rested quietly, peaceful so long as Kyra stayed by him, holding his nerveless hand between both of hers, trying to give him warmth. When she was overcome with sleep, she lay for a time at his feet while Arne or Flossi watched in her stead.

Gudrun did not try to tend him. She had unraveled the fair blue wool with its silver buds and blooming roses. In its stead she wove a web of somber hue, the color of ashes, death without the majesty of black. Her shuttle flew to shape the Fenris-wolf, burst from the chains from which he had so long watched bright Valhall, triumphant over Odin now, grim jaws fixed on the god.

One day Ragnar was so still Kyra feared that he had died. But when she called his name, chafing his hands, bending to feel the faintest stir of breath, his eyes opened.

"Ogier." The ruined mouth formed the word rather than spoke it.'

Kyra's heart lurched. She knew then that her father was dying. "Arne," she called beseechingly.

The old soldier rose from the pallet where he had rested like a hound close to his master. "Shall I seek the lad?"

The room swam before her. Gudrun's face seemed to float mockingly in the light from the hearth. But Kyra bowed her head and pressed her father's hand.

"Find him, good Arne." She bent and kissed Ragnar's pallid cheek, dewing it with her tears. "Make all the speed you may. Fetch hither my—my brother."

She watched by Ragnar all that night. In the dawn, he seemed to rest more peacefully. His eyes opened, lucid and clear. The good side of his mouth smiled on her tenderly.

"You . . . must rest, child. But first sing me that old song . . . that lullaby . . ."

". . . Mother shakes the tree,
    From it drops a dream . . ."

She was singing when he died.

IV

Ragnar's funeral was held with great pomp, and his grave-ale lasted for a week. Kyra besought her stepmother to keep the jarl's body above ground as long as possible in case Ogier came in time to see him, but Gudrun gave a savage laugh in reply. " 'Tis enough to endure one of his bastards at my husband's bier!' She held up her hands and Kyra saw the small white scars her teeth had furrowed in Gudrun's wrist.

"Lady Gudrun—"

"You weep, yet you killed him," Gudrun hissed. "He struck you and that toppled him. Though his fist has loosed more than one tooth in my head and he grinned to see *me* spit blood." Stained gold eyes flickered like candles swayed by the wind. Tight lips curved in a smile. "Yet even a bastard may mourn her sire. And your bastard brother, if he comes, may mourn you both at once."

As Kyra stared, unbelieving, Gudrun seized her, and when she struggled, shouted for servants.

"The girl has run quite mad. Bind her. Then put her in the brew-house with a pallet."

The folk obeyed, pityingly, trying to soothe her. "Flossi!" she cried as they started to bear her from the hall. "Flossi, you heard—you know I am not mad!"

Gudrun watched him narrowly. He shook his head. "Poor lass," he said, fingers straying on his harp, evoking a quivering plaint. "Poor, poor lass! Rest as the lady bids. Perhaps 'twill clear your mind."

Arne was gone, Isaac fled with Ogier. Now that the *skald* had failed her, she had no friends at Jarlsholm. Gudrun could work her will. Kyra indeed lost her sanity for a moment, screaming pleas and accusations, but she was bundled along and dropped on the straw pallet someone had fetched to the brewing house.

The moment she was freed, she clambered up in spite of bound hands and feet, but she was thrust back, staggering. The door slammed, barricaded from without. The smell of all the ale ever brewed in that small shed filled her nostrils. There were no windows, only the smoke vent above the cold hearth through which she could see a patch of overcast sky.

No way out except through the door. Kyra braced her shoulder against it and pushed with all her might. It only moved a fraction before it was stopped by whatever had been put to hold it. And the hampering leather thongs! Kyra sank to the pallet and worked her teeth to unloose her hands, but the knots seemed to get tighter. She was luckier with her ankles, untying them after manipulations that left her wrists raw from the way she had strained her fingers.

Now she could walk. It made her feel a bit less helpless. She scanned the room for a knife or sharp edge that might cut the remaining thongs, but there were only a few ladles, sieves and measures, nothing that would serve.

No water, either, or food.

"Your bastard brother may mourn you both at once." The gloating words sounded in Kyra's mind. She stiffened with fear.

Gudrun meant to do away with her, that seemed sure.

But Ogier, would she kill him, too, if Arne found him? Or did she hope to win him yet, the beautiful young man who was no older than her son?

If there were a way to warn him—Kyra thought despairingly of Flossi. Would he help Ogier? She couldn't have faith that he would after the way he had either believed Gudrun's cry of Kyra's madness or had pretended to preserve his own skin.

Amid Gudrun's lies had been one bitter truth. It seemed indeed that Ragnar's heart had burst when Kyra's upbraiding made him strike her. Father, she mourned, forgive me. I know you loved us well, both Ogier and me. It was Wyrd, not you, that made us love each other. If you have come to heaven, beseech the Blessed Mother and her Son to protect Ogier.

She saw a flash of Ragnar's face, the way he had looked, mighty and flame-haired, when she was a child, and felt a little comforted.

Above, there was a scuffling at the horn vent cover, and a black paw appeared through the opening. Then Mork peered down at her. He gave a questioning meow.

"Oh, Mork!" Tears filled her eyes and she held up pinioned hands. This old friend was all she had left. It was a far drop to the hearth. But after much complaint, he sprang down, sending up a puff of ashes.

She knelt to hug him to her. He patted her face, bit her gently with his love-greeting and purred, telling her that now they were together all was well. It wasn't, but she hadn't slept more than in fitful snatches since the terrible day of Ragnar's seizure. Cuddling Mork's soft warmth to her, she lay on the pallet and fell into heavy slumber.

A grating sound woke her, but she didn't remember where she was and why until a darker shadow loomed over her from those in the dimly lit room.

Gudrun's foot stirred her. "So your cat found you—

not that your familiar can help you now, even if you be witch like your mother!'' Seating herself on the room's single bench, Gudrun spoke almost pleasantly. ''You have a choice, Kyra.'' She extended her hand with something that gleamed. ''This wine will bring you sleep, swift and kind, from which you'll never wake. Or I will accuse you of murdering your father by witchcraft. The servants can all swear that he fell the moment that he struck you. Will you have a quiet end and be honorably buried beside your father, or will you be sewn in a bag and drowned?''

Kyra's heart stopped, but amazement was almost equal to her horror. ''You must die one day, stepmother. Have you no fear of God?''

Gudrun laughed. ''I shall die in my bed with ample time to be absolved.''

''But you would send me to hell—make *me* a suicide!''

''A witch's death is even more cursed.''

''I am no witch. You know it well.''

''I think you are.'' Gudrun rose. ''I will ask you again tomorrow.'' Pausing at the door, she said, ''Sour milk and porridge are in the basket on the bench. But how can you be sure they are not poisoned?''

The door closed. The barriers were set in place. Even if the servants weren't convinced that she was mad, they were too afraid of their mistress to help Kyra. She could not even hope that Arne might fetch back Ogier, for Gudrun might murder him.

As if sensing Kyra's woe, Mork scraped his tongue across her hand. Kyra had barely eaten for days. The savory smell of the soup made her nostrils wrinkle and stirred a rumbling in her stomach. She was also very thirsty.

''Mork,'' she said, ''there's little to choose between being starved or poisoned. Shall we venture it?''

She could feed him and know the food was safe if he

lived, but that seemed an abuse of his loyalty. Carrying him to the bench, she gave him bread dipped in sour milk while she spooned up the soup, which was warm and tasty. She left him some, with several chunks of meat, and stroked him as he fed.

"My sweet good friend," she told him, "we will die together or live at least a little longer." She prayed for Ogier and their father's soul, and that she might escape. Then she lay down with Mork, hoping that if they'd had poison, there'd be no pain, but they would wake in heaven beside her father and the mother she had never known.

She woke in the brew-house. Mork, as was his wont when he thought she slept overlong, was marching up and down over her, bringing down his paws as if stamping.

The food had been wholesome, then. But there was no way of guessing when it might not be. Another of Gudrun's torments.

Kyra shuddered at a sudden horrid fancy—Gudrun's face on a body of a great spider, spinning a web in which Ragnar hung dead and Kyra struggled. It chilled her more than that saga which told how Valkyries had woven a bloody web, men's heads for weights, their entrails for weft and warp, gory spears for heddle-rods and an arrow for the shuttle.

Fighting to banish the evil vision, Kyra rose. "I can tell you stories, Mork. I can sing. And I will dance, too, and leap up and down—why, I'll be your tumbler as if you were a king!" She danced, trying to vanquish her fears, but Gudrun-spider seemed to fill the room.

The sky through the vent showed the glowing jewel-like blue of summer night, dimly lighting the chamber, when Kyra roused at the stealthy noise outside.

Gudrun, perhaps deciding a dagger thrust could also pass for self-murder? Kyra sprang up and hid in the corner by the door. If she had a weapon—but there wasn't even a piece of firewood.

The person without entered, bolted the door softly and moved toward the pallet. Even in near-darkness, Kyra saw this was no woman. She shrank to the wall as the figure bent and she recognized Egil's furtive tone.

"Kyra—" he began and then broke off, springing up and peering around. "Where are you? Art indeed a witch to go through that smoke-hole?"

Still as she could hold herself, Kyra prayed he would be too unnerved to look closely into the shadows but he gave a relieved chuckle and crossed to her in a long stride, taking her shoulders in his hands. "What, my lovely! No greeting? Methinks you'd welcome a man who brings you hope!"

Her heart leaped, but she said coldly, eluding his hot, moist fingers, "What hope?"

"Why, if you're kind to me, I'll spirit you away this very night." His chest puffed out. "Mayhap, when mother dies, I can bring you back to Jarlsholm."

She realized with shock that he was now the successor to their father. And not a sliver of manhood to him! Yet he *was* the jarl and her plight was desperate.

"You cannot mean this, brother." Never before had she called him that. "Ragnar was father to us both. For our shared blood, I ask my freedom."

He grunted, trying to twist her closer, jutting forward that part of him that swelled hard against her thighs. "Freedom? It is your life we speak of! 'Tis no light thing to thwart my mother. Not for old Ragnar's blood will I do it, but for your fair body."

"Are you not the jarl?" she scorned.

"I will hide and keep you," he retorted harshly. "But not for blither-blather of kinship." He wrestled her to him, searched hungrily for her mouth, hands rough on her breasts and loins. She brought her knee up, with all her might, against that obscene rigidity he pressed on her.

He yelped and bent double. "Bitch! Would you geld me?"

"Gladly would I!" she gasped. "Get hence or I shall scream the walls down! And tell your mother!"

Those child's words for such a deadly case.

Still bent over, he moved for the door. She tried to reach it first but he knocked her across the room. By the time she could get to her feet, he had braced the door tight.

Many times in the next few days, she told herself she should have deceived him, made shift to gull him till she had a chance to get away. But he would not have waited. No. At the end of that road, she always knew she would rather be dead than possessed by him.

She grew sick and clammy at the thought. But Ogier was the same kin. What was the difference? With him, she felt not this shamed disgust, but as if her sundered self, raw and bleeding, was healed, made whole by him.

Had Gudrun accused her yet? Ulvhild said nothing, only brought food and drink. Each time she tasted anything, Kyra thought how easy it would be for Gudrun to poison her. Spider, in no hurry to pounce, knowing that her victim could not escape her web.

Kyra fought the despairing apathy that made her want to simply lie on the pallet. She danced and ran the length of the room, over and over, sang to Mork and told him stories.

The one that heartened her most was the tale of the Heaven Sword, the heritage of her family. She pictured them, comely men, beautiful women—English Meghan and her Harald; Kati who left Frey's service to be Eirik's wife; Rana who had sought her love even in Byzantium.

But when Kyra endeavored to imagine her own mother, that brought up Ragnar. She tried to remember his peaceful death, but the memory of that moment when he reeled back, stricken, haunted her.

She clung then to the image of the sword. Whatever chanced with her, she would try to be worthy of those who had owned it. But what loss, what pity, if it stayed hidden in that secret place! Her span must end soon or late, but the sword had lived for centuries. It waited now for him that would take it up. How she wished that man might be Ogier.

She made a mark with a bit of charcoal each morning on the wall. Five of them, though it seemed eternity. That evening Gudrun came.

"Well, Kyra? How will you have it? Quick draught or witch's death?"

"I will not slay myself."

"Then you shall be accused."

" 'Tis you must answer for that. They say that dead men walk sometimes, but Ragnar sure must be in Paradise or he would strangle you."

Gudrun paled. "Is this witch-speaking?"

"It is a natural wish enough." Kyra took a deep breath. Something burned within her, a force that made her speak without volition, as if voice and words came through her lips but were of someone else. "I curse you by my father and my mother. May you die eaten by your sins, may your own web snare you, may you have the end you would give me. May your sleep be nightmares, your best wine poison, may there be not one soul whom you can trust—"

"Slut!" cried Gudrun, backing away. She stared not at Kyra but at something behind her. "Witch-whore! Oh, you shall die!" She fled the room.

Kyra shook herself, coming out of that curious spell, frightened, but elated. Good, good, to see Gudrun cringe, feel something of that terror she liked to cause others. Still, it was with a prickling of the scalp that Kyra turned to look behing her.

Only the wall. Only dusk shadows.

Kyra laughed, so wildly exultant that Mork rumbled in protest and rubbed against her legs. She scooped him up and did a whirling circle, wondering if indeed a witch might feel that same glee in routing a foe.

Whatever it cost, that moment had been sheer sweet power. Devil, ghost or God, she thanked the granter.

She was eating the food Gudrun had left, when there came the sound of the door props being moved. She gave Mork a final tidbit, her own meal suddenly a roiling knot in her stomach. Well, it was not to be expected that Gudrun would wait long—not after such a fright.

But it was not Gudrun who entered. It was Flossi. "We must away! The lady is writhing on the floor. She cries that a witch strangles her. But when her women would lift her, she snaps like a wolf and foams at the mouth."

Kyra's spine chilled. She stared at the wall Gudrun had watched but still saw naught.

Flossi threw a hooded cloak around her, gripped her arm. "Gudrun took this fit as she was beginning to denounce you as having slain Ragnar by witchcraft. It will not take long for Egil to raise a cry against you. Come, bring the cat an you must, but keep your face hid!"

"The sword!" she breathed, hanging back.

" 'Tis with the horses, and such gear of yours as I could find." She hurried with him then and, muffled in the cloak, Mork hidden under it, moved toward the stables in the farmyard while Flossi shifted the door props in place.

Courtyard and farmyard were deserted. Folk must have flocked to the great hall at news of the mistress' sudden illness. Flossi helped Kyra into the saddle and touched the long leather bundle tied between pack and cantle.

"There is your sword. I have it and all things ready, but I hoped Arne might return with Ogier and help steal you away."

Kyra pressed his hand, the long slim fingers with their bard's callouses. "That is why you seemed to think me mad!"

He laughed shortly. "What else? Could I, dead or poisoned, help you? Now let's ride! Morning at latest there'll be men after us." Vaulting to the saddle with surprising agility for one of his age and profession, he gave his mare her head.

"Lass," he called over his shoulder, "if you have aught of magic, cause Gudrun's henchmen to weary fast, or let us soon meet Arne. And Ogier, if that may be!"

If that may be.

Oh, let it!

Breathing a prayer of thanks for her deliverance, she tossed back her hood and let the wind rush wild-free through her hair.

V

They came safe to Oslo and found Arne, Isaac and Ogier at an inn near the Mickle Yard which Flossi knew Arne favored because the owner was an old comrade. Arne had only found Ogier the day before when he'd started to board ship for Iceland. They were preparing to start for Jarls-holm.

Now at the tale of Ragnar's death and Gudrun's afflic-tion, the men crossed themselves, except for Isaac, who was a Khazar, Turkish by race but Jewish in faith. Kyra did not tell Ogier of Egil's lusting. She wanted no ven-geance, only to get far away from him and the danger of being killed for a witch.

Hand on his sword, Ogier looked at her and growled, "I would fain make Gudrun eat her lies in the sight of all."

"Belike she is past that," Flossi said. "Nay, lad. Let God have her. If you fair young ones had staunch and powerful kinsmen to uphold your rights, it might serve to stay in Norway and battle for the goods and properties I know that Ragnar left you. But the manner of Ragnar's death and Gudrun's seizure look ill for Kyra. The ship is yours, Ogier. Let us take it and fare forth!"

Kyra stared at the white-haired *skald*. "But, Flossi,

you need not leave. A bard like you will be welcomed in many a noble house.''

"You are my lord's children, both.'' Flossi's hazel eyes were determined, but he laughed, nodding at his carefully wrapped harp. "Besides, I think I will get better songs from you than from pasty Hrapp or skirt-chasing Egil.''

"After . . . what passed, I had not thought to keep the ship.'' Ogier did not look at Kyra. On meeting, there had been a stiff embrace, his swift kiss on her forehead. Since then, he had spoken to everyone but her. "I wanted naught of Ragnar's.''

"Will you spite the dead?'' Arne grunted. " 'Twill ease your father to know you had somewhat of all he had intended for you.'' He whistled the air of a bawdy song and squinted drolly. "I hope I won't be seasick.''

Ogier looked at his father's friends and laughed. "Kyra, my sister, it seems we must be sailors, will we, nill we! You, Isaac?''

"I am your slave,'' said the small, hunch-shouldered man.

Ogier frowned. "You are not. I freed you as soon as I had bought you from that brute.''

Isaac smiled. "Just so, master. That binds me twice.''

The ship was already provisioned and laden with trading goods from Ragnar's estates and most of a crew hired. All the men of the party were able to lend a hand with sails or rowing. Flossi sold their horses to a knight of his acquaintance who was kind to his beasts. They spent that one night at the inn and sailed with the tide.

North Star was a merchant ship, but Ragnar had chosen the oak to make her and had a hawk carved on the curving prow. Her sail was blue wool, and every part, from nails to rigging blocks, was of the best.

Gunnar Eyolfson, the brawny, yellow-maned, fierce-moustachioed captain, was a longtime man of Ragnar's.

He got so drunk at news of his death that he'd had to be carried aboard, but once on *North Star* with the salt wind in his face, he quickly revived and took over from Baard, the stocky, red-haired Swedish helmsman. The other three crew members were brothers—Leif, Kol, and Uni, youths from Halogaland, the youngest of whom, Uni, was about Kyra's age. Tall and high-spirited, with clear blue eyes and flaxen hair, they hoped to make fortune enough to buy a farm and settle there with their widowed mother who was now living on a son-in-law's grudged charity.

The men slept on deck in hide sleeping bags large enough for two, covering themselves when it rained with skins or sails, but they made a cozy nest for Kyra under one of the half-decks among bales of wadmal. She shared her sleeping bag with Mork and Heaven's Gift, the blade wrapped in soft leather and silk but the hilt exposed so she could touch it when lightning rived the sky and *North Star* pitched violently. The sword was such comfort in night and rough weather that she was almost glad Ogier had refused it that night in the inn.

"It's for your husband," he said, trying to smile, though his eyes were dark with pain. "Or your son."

"I will have neither." *If you cannot be my lover, if you cannot give me sons.*

"Of course you will," he said firmly. "And you will name one lad for me."

"As you will name your daughter for me?"

He flinched and she felt his pain herself. "Nay, Kyra, you're little more than a child." He took her hands, held them relentlessly, compelling her to meet his gaze. "You are my own dear sister. Let us be thankful to have each other and not bewail the rest."

Thankful for the torment of desiring what must not be? Bitter words rose to Kyra's lips, but she forced them back. She should indeed be thankful—and she was. Not only for her life, but for being with Ogier. She bowed her head. "You are right. But I shall never marry. Someday you must have the sword."

That she and Ogier traveled on the ship Ragnar had given them made it seem that their father's love was with them still, that he knew they loved him though he had unwittingly wrought them such grief.

They would winter in Iceland. The late summer nights were still too light to navigate by the North Star, but Gunnar was a *kentmand*, "one who knows." Besides all his knowledge of birds, fish, seaweed, what kind of trees driftwood came from, and the currents, he had a table compiled by Stjerne-Oddi, an Icelander, which gave the sun's altitude for the entire year, and another table showing where along the horizon the sun rose and set. With his sunboard, divided into half-wheels, Gunnar regulated their course each noon when there was enough sun.

On cloudy, foggy days, he had to rely on experience, and during storms, the crew had all they could do to stay afloat. At such times, Kyra helped bail out the water that threatened to overwhelm *North Star*, and then life seemed sweet indeed, even without her love.

During one especially wrathful storm, Gunnar made sure that everyone on board had a gold coin. "If Ran takes us to her hall, she will feast us better if we're not empty-handed," he said. At Kyra's startled look, he shrugged a heavy shoulder. "Of course, I pray to Mary Virgin. But Ran still casts her net for handsome, strong men to lie in her bed. In her realm, it boots not to be Christian."

They began to smell a different scent than that of ocean brine and sighted, after three weeks and over five hundred miles, the fjord-chewed coastland with dark lava headlands and snaggle-toothed hills climbing from the green land to glacier-whitened mountains.

No wonder the Irish monks who had fled here from the

Vikings, had thought themselves safe until the first Norwegians landed in 860. They had not stayed, but their report brought other settlers, especially after Harald Fairhair set out to break the power of his jarls. Many outraged nobles loaded the pillars of their high seats on ships full of cattle and other belongings and set out for Iceland.

By the time of Harald's death in 930, Flossi said, thousands of settlers had taken up small kingdoms in Iceland, building their halls close to where their high-seat posts drifted ashore, raising temples on hallowed ground fetched from Norway. These chieftains needed much land for pasturing sheep and cattle, planting barley and locating bog iron; each great farm had salmon preserves and coastal lands for hunting seals and fishing.

Because of bloody feuds between these powerful men who had not brooked a king, they agreed to be ruled by a law code first read out at an assembly of all free men meeting at Thingvellir in 930. Here, each June, representatives of all the districts came to settle disputes and make judgments. It was at such a parliament in the year 1000 that Iceland received Christianity, though allowing private worship of the old gods.

North Star came to calm anchorage at Horn Fjord on the south shore, where fertile green fields stretched away from the black sand of the beach. To the southwest was a wide, peaceful valley, and here among forest and meadows lay the farm of Flossi's uncle and foster-father, Ottar the Black.

Ottar's dark hair was streaked with white and his eyes dimmed with age, but they filled with joyous tears as he greeted Flossi. His storehouses bulged with supplies; it was pleasure, not hardship, for him to have guests through the winter.

It was a mild autumn thus far, with snow only far up along the peaks. Kyra loved to wander through the mead-

ows, all walled with red and black lava, or visit the little
church, made of red-brown brick framed with driftwood,
grass-covered roof slanting to the ground, that stood
among mountain ashes and pale-trunked birches on a
slope above the farm building where Ottar's grandfather
had made an alter to Thor. Iceland's trees were neither
large nor plentiful enough for much building. Even the
hearthfires were made mostly with driftwood, and soot
covered the ceiling of Ottar's hall where, to beguile the
lengthening nights, Flossi played his harp or Ottar played
his two-stringed *langspil.*

All the men slept in the hall, but Kyra had a pallet in
the weaving room where wrinkled old Margit presided
over the women of Ottar's house. These were Ulva, a
strapping blond young widow who shared Ottar's box-
bed when he needed night warmth, and Ramborg, the orphaned child of a tenant, with soft brown hair and gentle
manners who blushed and dropped her eyes when Uni
looked at her.

Kyra helped with endless women's tasks, carding the
black, brown and white wool of Ottar's sheep or spinning
it into yarn.

Food was plentiful, if monotonous, and much was familiar. Grain didn't grow well here, so flour was imported and costly, but some was made from moss and
lyme grass and red seaweed.

There were two things that Kyra could not eat. One
was sheep bones dissolved in sour whey and fermented.
Mork adored it. The other was Ottar's favorite dish,
hafkal, or sea cabbage.

The stench was like carrion permeated with urine.
Shark meat smoked or pickled, then aged in the earth,
looked like spoiled bacon and tasted the way it smelled.

Ogier made Kyra and himself skates from cow bones,
and when the weather was fit, they skated for hours with
the Halogaland brothers and Ottar's younger folk, skim-

ming across frozen lakes and rivers, seeming almost to fly in that chill white world that blended into the pallid sky. As Ogier soared past or swung around her in a circle, Kyra wished they could glide on to the end of the world—reach a haven where their shared blood didn't matter, where they could love each other.

There were few travelers abroad in this season, but at Yuletide, Ottar gave shelter to an old comrade, Halfdan Curt-Leg, a grim-visaged rust-haired chieftain of middle years, outlawed last summer at the Althing. He had thought to defy what he felt an unfair judgment—after all, the man he slew had struck him first, but powerful kinsmen raised such an outcry, refusing money payment and demanding vengeance, that they had won their suit. When Halfdan stayed at his farm, they had sent word that if he didn't leave the country for the decreed three years, they would burn his house around his ears, and everyone within it. To spare his parents and folk, Halfdan had set forth in foul weather and would take spring's first vessel bound from Iceland.

With him were other tidings. The last ship of autumn to reach the western coast from Norway had brought news that Egil Ragnarsson had offered thrice the atonement price for a jarl's death to whoever would deliver to him Ragnar's bastard daughter. He accused her of murdering Ragnar by witchcraft and of bewitching Lady Gudrun so that she must be shut in a small cell where she screamed that she was stung by vipers and that her food was poisoned offal.

Kyra dropped her spindle, heart pounding wildly at this evil news, but Ogier handed her the carved wooden stick and said softly, "Don't be afraid, my Kyra. *North Star* will leave these shores before word is noised about that we have been with Ottar."

And that was so. As brilliant sun began to melt the

snow off black lava and green grass, as soon as the harbor
was free of ice, the ship was loaded with provisions exchanged for part of the cargo, and with much gratitude
and some tears, the *North Star* hoisted sail.

Ogier had invited Halfdan to go with them to Greenland, and the outlaw was glad to embark before his foes
had excuse to plunder his holdings. He took the place of
Uni at the oars because the lad, with his older brothers'
consent, had decided to stay with Ottar. The chieftain
promised to send for their mother that she might take
charge of his hall.

North Star reached Greenland in four days without
ever losing sight of Iceland's glaciers. Pastures reached
down to the sea, and sheep, cattle, pigs, ponies and goats
fed around the sprawling farmsteads. Northmen had been
coming here for a hundred years. Erik the Red had
founded the first lasting colony and the good land was
taken.

Ogier didn't mind work, but he had no mind to be a
tenant. Vinland, a land of grapes and timber, briefly col-
onized and then abandoned, sounded so inviting that
Ogier questioned the Greenlanders with whom he traded
iron goods for supplies. Why had Northmen, always
seeking good and fruitful lands, not persisted in a place
that abounded in game and fish, with good soil and, most
wonderful of all to those born to long dark winters, a
place where the sun always rose by midmorning and
shone at least six hours?

That alone would have inclined Kyra to fare there. But
the bloody tale of Frøydis, Leif the Lucky's half-sister,
made her shudder far more than warnings of the coppery-
skinned Skraelings who had on occasion raided the infant
settlement.

Frøydis had persuaded some Greenlanders to make an
expedition with her to bring back timber and grapes, but
when the work was done, she ordered her partners slain;

and when her men would not kill the Greenlanders' wives, she took an axe and murdered them herself. She then sailed back to Greenland, enriched by robbery and murder.

Kyra grimaced. ''I would fain taste grapes and have sun in winter, but Ogier, let us not go where such horrid deeds were done.''

''Where shall we go, then?'' Ogier asked a shade impatiently.

Kyra had no answer, but Halfdan stroked his ruddy beard and said, ''There are stories of lands even farther west and south, fairer than Vinland, with brighter sun.'' He laughed, throwing back his big shaggy head. ''Three years I am outlawed! I would as soon spend them seeking new lands as wandering through old ones!''

Ogier looked at Kyra, who nodded, then turned to the other men. ''What say you? Any who would rather find passage elsewhere is free to leave us here. Leif, Kol, would you go back to Iceland? 'Twould gladden your mother's heart.''

''She has Uni,'' the young men chorused, blue eyes sparkling. ''And once she has charge of Ottar's household, she'll have no time to worry about us.''

Gunnar pointed his yellow moustache and grinned. ''Would I trust another captain with *North Star?*''

''No more would I leave her rudder to another helmsman,'' said Baard stoutly.

''Then west it is,'' cried Ogier, and Kyra's heart swelled. Last winter, winged on ice, had she not dreamed of going far beyond the world?

VI

Only the North Star, never wavering, assured them that they were still in the world and not in a boundless universe of ocean and sky. When there were no clouds or fog, the star shone brightly, for as the ship sailed south, there began to be real nights, and instead of becoming colder, the winds grew ever more balmy and the sun beamed with heat that left them sweating in their woolen clothes. The men who had linen garments put them on. The others went bare-chested. Kyra put off her overgown, but the under one was hot enough, though fortunately it was of linen rather than wadmal.

During the most intense heat, they rigged hides to shield part of the deck. The sour milk and ale they had replenished in Greenland were gone. Except for storms that buffeted them sometimes for days on end, they would have died of thirst, but every possible receptacle was set to catch rain water and this was poured into cleansed hide bags.

They were sick of dried or pickled fish and meat. The stony flat unleavened bread had to be soaked before they could chew it. Mork had long since caught all the ship's mice. His coat lost its sheen, and he spent most of the time sleeping as far back in the half-deck as he could get, close to the sword. Everyone had bleeding gums, and though they suffered neither dire thirst nor hunger, weeks of confinement on the ship was telling on them all, though Ogier bore himself cheerily and spoke eagerly of the good land they would find—one surpassing the old world by far.

Kyra slept with her hand on the sword each night, and ever they were borne farther and farther south.

"Land!" cried Baard one morning.

Kyra thought at first that she was dreaming, but when he shouted the joyous words again, she scuffled out from under the half-deck and peered to where he pointed.

A dark green fringe appeared beyond the waves, merging into clouds. Sea birds winged against the sky, shrill calls a gladdening welcome.

Rushing to their places at the oars on either end of the ship, the men helped the billowing sail. *North Star* flew over the water as if longing to rest on the white beach sparkling along a deep crescent. If this was an island, it was immense. There was no visible end to the coast.

Would there be people? Civilized but exotic like Chinese? Or Moslems? Savage hide-clothed folk like Vinland Skraelings? Cities or only forests? It was truly a green country, but these were not pines, oaks, birches or any trees they knew. These trees had straight naked trunks, double or triple a man's height before long, plume-shaped leaves sprouted from the center. And the shore—that vast rim of fine sand! Kyra felt a wave of homesickness for the rocky coasts and fjords of the north. But at least it would be hard to wreck a ship on this shore.

Ogier came up to her. His hawk nose seemed even larger in his thin, browned face, but his eyes glowed like the sunlit waves. "Get the sword, Kyra. You shall be first to set foot on this land!"

Mork, in fact, was first, jumping from the lower midpart of the ship as soon as its keel touched. But Kyra took the Heaven Sword from its coverings and prayed to God and all the spirits of her ancestors who had held the blade. *Be with us in this strange place. Grant us courage.*

The men stretched a plank from deck to beach. It took both hands to hold the sword aloft, but she did so as she led the way.

What a blessing to walk on earth once more! Kyra could not stop kneeling to touch it, crumble it in her fingers. It smelled moist and fertile. And the water of the spring Baard found was deliciously sweet and cool, trickling from mossy rocks above a reedy marsh.

Beyond these flat lowlands, swamps and thick vegetation, stretched dense forests that climbed toward peaks that disappeared into clouds—or was that snow on top? How wonderful it would be to have sun like this, yet live in sight of mountains as majestic as those above Jarlsholm! The others had the same thought. It was decided to march toward the gleaming summits as soon as they had rested and made a shelter for *North Star*.

The ship was dragged and pushed to a knoll and turned keel-side up among willows, the first familiar growing things they had seen. Kegs and tubs were filled with sails, ropes and the hide sleeping bags, and heavy garments were left in the sea chests. All these were arranged beneath the hull and a thatched shelter erected above it.

They feasted on grilled fish and fruits that birds were eating. There were no ill effects from the unfamiliar fruits. Some of the birds were brilliantly colored, crimson, green, yellow and blue, and one had a huge yellow bill bigger than its head and neck put together.

The wadmal they had brought for trading was too heavy for this climate, so with knives and Kyra's scissors, sleeping cloths were cut for each person.

Up early after a restless night because of winged pests,

they secured their bundles with pieces of leather rope and started off. Till they were sure that water would be plentiful, they carried bags of it, along with what was left of their dried meat. All had weapons. Kyra had belted on the Heaven Sword. Mork alone carried no burden. He flashed through the brush, lurking, then chasing butterflies, birds and creatures that resembled elongated frogs with longer tails. He pursued strange creatures that looked like hairy little men with withered faces and tails they used like hands. They chattered at the humans and taunted Mork, who futilely chased after them.

It was difficult traveling through high reeds, grass and marshes, or tangled thickets of trees, vines and shrubs, but no one complained. It was unspeakably good to be on one's legs again.

By evening they had reached the heavily wooded foothills. The next days took them higher and higher, the weather growing steadily more temperate as they passed from dense forests to an upland plateau looking toward distance-purpled mountains. After some debate, they decided to push onward.

Kyra was less interested in what sort of country lay over the mountains than in whether there were people.

There were no other women in their party. Even if some of the men chose to stay and colonize with her and Ogier, the colony was doomed to die out. Unless she became wife to one of them, and that was unthinkable. No, if their lives were to become more than barren exile, they would need to find other people. Yet remembering how Skraelings had driven out the Vinland settlers, Kyra dreaded as well as hoped for the sight of human beings.

Through mountain passes and valleys, they found fowl, rabbits, deer and fish in streams and placid sparkling lakes. They saw huge bears and several kinds of lynxes, wolves and badgers. There were wheeling hawks and eagles. Owls called at night. These familiar creatures and the pines, spruce and oaks, made the travelers feel more at home. The feeling increased Kyra's hope that people lived there.

They reckoned it was near Michaelmas. Snow fell on the mist-shrouded peaks and sometimes flurried around them. They followed a river that squeezed through narrow gorges, spilled in rainbow waterfalls, and swelled out wherever it had room. It ran like a broad green ribbon across rolling flatlands, and they believed they would find a hospitable place for the winter somewhere along it. But Kyra, searching the undulating expanse from a rocky outcrop, felt a sinking of the heart. On a site that in Norway would have supported several manors and countless farms, there was not a shed or fence, no sign of mortals.

The wind howled across the plateau. Though they camped in a hollow thick with small oaklike trees, the night was cold, and everyone rummaged for warmer garments. It was decided to stay there long enough to tan the hides of deer and other quarry they had carried rolled up after greasing them to prevent their drying stiff as boards. While some men helped Kyra with the tanning, others hunted and fished and dried what couldn't be eaten immediately.

Kyra enjoyed the feeling of making a temporary home in the pretty little hollow, cutting grass to heap beneath their sleeping cloths, arranging a windbreak of stone and boughs so that their fire warmed them better, protected as it was on two other sides by the slope.

The hastily cleaned hides had to be thoroughly scraped of bits of flesh and smeared with tallow and brains of fresh-killed game. It was tedious, stinking work, but there was talk and jesting and song.

Flossi was composing the saga of this very journey. Kyra wondered if any but them would ever hear it.

"Daughter and son of noble Ragnar,
   Onward they sailed, sea-stallion champing
   Onward they bore the Heaven Blade . . ."

When Kyra thought Ogier would not notice, she watched him. Her heart swelled with love and sadness. What did she care for sagas? She would rather be his and live in a *seter* than be sung about till the end of time.

The fifth night of their encampment in the hollow, they had an especially good supper, venison stewed with wild onions and grass seeds that were almost as large as grain. Kyra had gathered small acorns, roasted and ground them into meal, making flat cakes that baked on the long-handled iron pan that was among the few utensils they had carried.

"Well, lass," chuckled Flossi, putting down his wooden bowl after four helpings, "if we can just find enough wild grapes like those I brought in today, we can make wine, and what else could we desire?"

"I should like butter," said Baard. "Some nice curds and sour milk . . ."

"That needs only that you sail back to Greenland and fetch hither cows and goats," Gunnar teased.

Halfdan leaned back against a tree. "I would rather behold the sun at Yuletide than sit in a dark sooty hall and eat the best *skyr* and oldest butter in Iceland," he said. "Those winters! Only mead and music made them bearable."

They rested, content after labor and good food. The fire lit and shadowed their faces. Holding Mork in her lap, Kyra looked fondly around at all of them, Ogier and the Halogaland lads bright and young, the others scarred and grizzled, all true and tested comrades. A wave of affection and well-being made her happier than she had been since that terrible revelation about Ogier. She smiled at him across the fire, feeling for once no stab of hurt, no pang of anger.

Like shadows, figures rose out of the darkness. Flames gilded human shapes mantled with spotted hides or feathers and plumed helmets of beasts' and birds' heads atop red-brown faces. Most of the men—if they were men— had ears heavily weighted with ornaments so that the lobes swayed grotesquely, and each wore a green plug in his nose. They carried lances, beautifully decorated feathered shields, clubs ridged with what looked like big fish teeth, and swords of wood with glistening black stone or glass embedded along the edges.

One man stepped forward, spoke and then knelt, touching a middle finger to the earth before laying it on his mouth. The others sank down and did the same.

Arne was the first to recover. "It seems they do us reverence," he said, "and it won't hurt to keep them in that mood."

He took his sword. Then he collected three of the beautiful wooden weapons and shattered them one by one, grinding them beneath his heel. The men cried out imploringly and crouched even closer to the ground. Then Kyra understood Arne's gesture. Gold and silver glinted from ankles, wrists and chests, but of the sterner metals, they had none. To them, the Heaven Sword would be as much a mystery as it had been centuries ago when it slashed into bronze ones. These were humans and their attire was barbarically splendid, but they were truly of an alien world.

VII

The Toltecs were almost as in awe of Mork as of the steel blades, but even without these, they would have marveled at the blue or gray eyes of most of the strangers, the fair skin of the younger people and especially at Ogier's tawny golden hair.

Upon being conducted to Tula, the Northerners were lodged in a long, low palace near two steep-staired pyramids with temples on top, their roofs supported by giant stone warriors. It was evident that the natives took these sky-eyed, pale-skinned folk for supernatural beings and Ogier for chief amongst them.

Tula rose on steep banks above the plain and river. The pyramids and ceremonial buildings were of massive stone fitted so exactly that they required no mortar. There was a great paved court with a crouched beast called a jaguar, and broad streets lined with thatched dwellings that spread all along the ridge.

Canals ran through Tula and irrigated fields stretched for miles below. Kyra was surprised to see under cultivation a plant with saw-toothed, long dagger-shaped leaves that she'd seen often on their journey, and the even more unpleasant clumps of dull green pads studded with thousands of tiny spines, but Xia, a graceful pretty girl with big dark eyes and black hair cut straight across the forehead while the rest fell below her waist, smiled at Kyra's puzzled signing and indicated the woven fiber mats that were used for sleeping and sitting, the sandals they both were wearing, and a basket holding delicious fruits.

"Maguey," she said, and poured Kyra a silver cup of the whey-looking fluid in a graceful red pottery jar. "*Pulque.*"

Everyone drank pulque, even babies, though it could be intoxicating. It would take lots of the plants to supply the whole city. As for the prickly nopal, Xia indicated that it provided fruit and that the leaves, when new and tiny, were also edible.

The food was strange, but Kyra soon came to relish tortillas, thin flat cakes made of maize dough. Beans were about the size of peas, but much tastier, and she savored the piquant fieriness of the chilies that were cooked with them. Squash was insipid, but she liked small, juicy red tomatoes. There were a number of seeds and turniplike *jicama*. Fish was served often, luckily for Mork, but there were no domestic creatures except for small dogs, ducks and turkeys, and the only meat was occasional game or fowl.

Pulque did much to resign the men to the lack of ale, but what Kyra liked most of all was chocolate, whipped frothy and fragrant with vanilla; she sipped several cups of it a day. It seemed fitting that cacao pods were used for money.

These Toltecs did not have iron or steel, but their artisans made beautiful jewelry and images in gold, silver and copper, some set with jade and a green-blue stone, turquoise.

The glorious plumage of birds was woven into mantles, worked into intricate patterns on shields or hangings and used otherwise for adornment. The stonemasons and carvers were as skillful as those of Europe, though Kyra shrank from the motif repeated throughout the frieze on the long wall north of the pyramids, serpents devouring human hearts. One of the pyramids was patterned on all sides with bas-reliefs of coyotes, jaguars and eagles, which Xia mimed to represent various orders of warriors.

Instead of wool and flax, these folk had cotton, which they dyed red, yellow, blue and green, and methods of spinning and weaving not much different from those Kyra knew. When she asked for a spindle and loom, and baskets of the fluffy white stuff, Xia and the other servants treated her with even more deference and began to call her Tlazolteotl, whom they explained was the goddess of the moon as well as of weaving and childbirth. Kyra denied this idolatrous fancy, but Xia only smiled and bowed lower, touching her finger to the floor and then to her lips, "eating dirt," as the sign of respect was called.

Though they were in the same building, perfumed with incense and abounding with enclosed gardens where fountains splashed, fish swam in small pools, and brilliant-hued birds came to feed, Kyra was in a separate wing and saw her companions only at the evening meal and later, when noblemen and priests came to drink pulque with their supposedly divine guests. Kyra was glad when Tezcla, the high priest, did not come. Obsequious to the strangers, he was harsh with servants. He looked like a turtle, bold and wide-mouthed with flat nostrils.

Tumblers performed sometimes, and there were skilled wrestlers. The musicians brought thin, plaintive melodies from flutes and whistles accompanied by tortoise-shell drums, but the Toltecs always requested that Flossi play his harp.

Dining itself was a ceremony. The Northerners sat on low cushioned stools, and handsomely carved tables were placed before them and spread with fine white cotton. Women brought basins of water and poured this over their hands to be caught in shallow bowls. Each was handed a soft towel, and only then was food brought on plates of gold and silver.

"All this washing and a bath in the river each day besides!" grumbled Arne. "These folk are so clean it's unhealthy!"

Kyra liked the well-swept streets, not missing at all the dung and garbage that littered the streets of Oslo, but she found it most wonderful to see the sun when, in the North, it would barely appear for the long months of winter.

Except for the Toltecs' disturbing art, she could almost believe Tula a sort of Eden. And then one day Xia brought her sandals set with turquoise, a long, sleeveless gown of red, a feather mantle, and a headdress of gold and jade with blue-green feathers of the bird they called *quetzal,* "precious."

Halfdan was picking up the language faster than anyone, perhaps because he was a poet, but they all were learning, and Kyra understood without much difficulty that the high priest requested her presence at some awesome ceremony.

Old stories flashed through Kyra's mind. It hadn't been long ago when Vikings offered men to the gods. From what Xia and the nobles said, she gathered that primitive hordes from the northwest had challenged the power of the Toltecs, attacking their vassals and even overrunning several of their cities. Tezcla apparently hoped that the Fair God, as they called Ogier, would confound these enemies and restore Tula's supremacy.

Could he think this best done by sacrificing these strange divinities to Toltec gods who apparently delighted in devouring human hearts? Kyra's scalp prickled at the thought.

She told Xia she was thirsty and, while the girl was gone, arranged Heaven's Gift on a sling under her shoulder, hidden by the splendid mantle. Taut with anxiety but forcing the remote sort of smile she thought a goddess might bestow on worshippers, she swept out of the gold- and jade-ornamented chamber, through a garden and down narrow stone steps to the flower-strewn street.

Ogier and the others were already in the square beneath the ball court and pyramids. Like her, Ogier wore red caught with gold brooches and a collar of jade-encrusted gold. The gold serpent's head on his coronet was plumed with quetzal feathers that shimmered more brilliantly than jewels. He had no weapon, not even the eating knife a Northman was never without. Neither did his comrades, decked in blue and green, iridescent capes trailing behind them.

But the warriors, jaguar, eagle and coyote knights, were armed, and the priests carried shining knives of obsidian and copper bells. Kyra's mouth was dry as Tezcla sounded a conch-shell trumpet, whistles shrilled and men carrying large vertical drums began to beat a rhythm as they marched. Rasping bones, rattles and flutes joined in the weird cacophony. Above on the pyramids, drummers boomed on what looked like halved logs.

Beautiful youths and maidens scattered rushes and flowers beneath the feet of the marchers. Surrounded by jeweled and feathered knights, the Northerners proceeded.

"I wish I had my sword," said Arne. Ogier motioned slightly at the chanting multitudes, the phalanxes of warriors. "Weapons will avail nothing if they intend us ill."

Halfdan grinned. "Methinks our good blades could avail slaughter undreamed of by these eagle-serpent-jaguars," he said. "But we are in the broth and must make the best of it."

"Let us keep together." Ogier nodded, eyes touching Kyra so that a dazzling, poignant ray seemed to pierce her. "If there's need, we'll form around Kyra. Perhaps we can seize some of these weapons and make good use of them before we're sent to God."

"I have Heaven's Gift," Kyra told him. She gave him a bittersweet smile. "You would not take if from my hand before, but now I think you will."

"Right gladly, sister."

She both loved that name and hated it. If only they had grown up together, known their shared blood from the start! But now in spite of name, in spite of knowledge, that consumingly sweet but forbidden fire flamed through her at his slightest touch.

It would always be that way. For her there could be no other man. Yet as she tasted this doom, starting up the narrow steps of the pyramid, she breathed in light and air, the scent of flowers and incense, beheld the blue sky and knew she did not want to die that day.

The booming drums seemed the intensified pounding of her heart. Stone warriors, almost three times life-size, held up the thatch that gleamed golden in the sun. On the great pillars guarding the entrance of the temple, plumed serpents opened avid jaws. At the entrance, jaguars supported a slab of black stone. The floor was dyed brownish red and seemed to reek.

Looming above the altar was a polished black image with staring eyes of shell and turquoise and hideous, gaping jaws stained with blood that had run down over the jade and gold breastplate. Something ill-smelling and shriveled lay in the clawed hands.

Kyra fought a wave of nausea and kept close to Ogier as Tezcla motioned them to the back of the temple. And then Kyra saw what she had not been able to before—a dozen smooth-skinned handsome youths, garlanded with flowers, completely naked, mounting the last steps and entering the temple.

Priests seized the first young man, spread-eagled him

on the altar. Tezcla raised his glittering knife, almost before Kyra realized what he intended. Ogier saw at the same instant, turned to her with his hand out. She cleared the sword and gave it to him.

"Stop!" he cried in Nahua, the Toltec language, but the obsidian blade was already plunging toward the victim's breast.

Heaven's Gift swung. It struck the knife, shattering it so that the fragments fell on the captive. Tezcla clasped only a useless hilt. Holding the sword in a guarding stance, Ogier kicked the other priests away from the youth, who continued to lie as if dazed.

Kyra ran forward and drew him to his feet. From the way he seemed benumbed, she thought he had been drugged, for the other waiting captives watched her blankly as if they couldn't grasp what was happening.

Weaponless though they were, the other Northmen surrounded Ogier and Kyra. Ogier said, with a gesture at the altar. "No more! No kill."

Tezcla's voice was a venomous hiss. They could not understand all that he said but the snatches were enough. "Huitzilopotchli—help in war— Need hearts! Now angry!"

Ogier gave Kyra the sword and strode to the image that seemed to leer at him with malevolent eyes. "Huitzilopotchli?" he asked.

"Is the mighty god!"

Ogier strained to lift the idol, staggered under its weight. The priests wailed in dread, cowering. Tezcla seized another knife but Kyra raised Heaven's Gift and stood between Ogier and the Toltec.

Flossi and Arne caught hold of the image and helped Ogier bear it to the edge of the pyramid, the side facing the serpent wall where no people were assembled. They set it on the edge of the platform and shoved it.

Down it crashed, striking the steps along the way,

breaking into chunks as it struck the court. Spectators had rushed around to see. A great moan rose from below. Ogier raised his arms.

"Dead is Huitzilopotchli! No more kill men for him! I will help you in war!"

Shining with gold, he looked the sun's bright child. From the crowds below ascended a joyous, wondering murmur, softly at first, then swelling till it drowned out the throbbing of the drums.

"Quetzalcoatl! Quetzalcoatl! Our Fair God!"

Tezcla came forward and fell on his knees, touching fingers to the floor and raising them to his mouth. His black eyes burned with fear and hatred, but he spoke in humble tones.

"Welcome, Great Lord. Precious Feathered Serpent, Lord of Dawn and Spring and the Morning Star, well come to your people. I am your slave."

Smoking Mirror, Blue Hummingbird, Huitzilopotchli might not be real but the Chichimecas were. Only a few days after Ogier was acclaimed as Tula's ancient beloved god returned, scouts brought word that thousands of barbarians were streaming toward the Toltecs' sacred city.

"Will the Lord Feathered Serpent destroy the savages with lightning?" asked Tezcla, managing to sound hopeful and sneering at once. "Or will he cause the earth to open and swallow them?"

"Neither." Ogier smiled, using gestures when he lacked words. "My friends and I will fight the Chichimecas."

Tezcla's flinty eyes widened. He looked more than ever an aged, giant turtle as he looked from Northman to Northman. "Eight? To meet the Chichimecas, who number as the stars? It must be, Lord, that you cannot die in this body.''

The commanders of the jaguar and eagle knights protested. ''It would shame us not to fight beside our Fair God. Pray, Lord, let us go with you.''

Ogier considered. Arne muttered in his ear and Flossi nodded. ''Bring your men,'' Ogier conceded. ''But keep them back unless I signal. It may be I can convince the enemy to depart from Toltec lands. Meanwhile, prepare your warriors to march. We leave at first light in the morning.''

The jaguar leader ate dirt and said, ''Lord, we have seen your might, but Huitzilopotchli is the god of battle. Should he not have at least one heart to incline him to us?''

''Offer yours if you will,'' Ogier said pleasantly. ''I will have no man with me who prefers to trust in that broken piece of rock.''

They marched at dawning, through the colonnade of warriors, past the pyramid and Serpent Wall where Huitzilopotchli's remains still lay, and across the rolling green plain toward the distant mountains.

The knights wore the cloaks and headdresses of their order and status, back shields of turquoise, shell and black stone and bore similar shields in front. They carried gold-handled *atlatls,* or throwing sticks, for their spears. Ordinary warriors were clad in loincloths, a cotton cloak to sleep in, sandals and headbands showing war honors. Their shields were small and round, of leather, with long fringes hanging from the bottom, and their *atlatls* were plain. All the warriors had wooden throat shields and bore obsidian-edged spears and war clubs.

Ogier carried the Heaven Sword. His bright head was bare and he had no shield, nor did his comrades. To arm one more man with steel he had yielded to Kyra's wishes and loaned his own blade to his squire, Xolo, the youth he had saved from dying on the altar. Each Northman also had a bow and arrows. As the army faded from sight, Kyra sank to her knees and prayed.

VIII

The defeat of the Chichimecas made one more part of Flossi's saga.
Ogier commanded the Toltecs to halt on a slope while he
and his friends went to meet the invading host. This au-
dacity threw the Chichimecas into confusion that was
multiplied when they saw the blond or ruddy hair, fair
skin and uncanny eyes of the confidently approaching
eight.

Still, these hide-clad barbarians were brave. They
shrieked and surged forward. The Northmen made a circle, facing out, and hewed with such fury, chopping in
half wooden spears and clubs as well as heads and arms,
that the attackers fell back, leaving a great heap of dead
and wounded.

After some argument, the war leaders approached with
empty hands. One spoke broken Nahua. He respectfully
asked who the strangers were.

Xolo, flourishing a bloody sword, proclaimed that
these were gods from across the Great Water, the chief
being Quetzalcoatl, who desired peace but was mighty in
war. Which would the Chichimecas have?

If the Lord Quetzalcoatl would be so gracious, the
Chichimecas would like to see him test his sword on a
thick war club. If indeed the sword cleaved it, there was

315

no boot in fighting. Chichimecas were sensible folk who fought for plunder, not for glory or captives to offer to the gods.

A formidable war club was brought and leaned against a rock. Ogier smote it such a blow that it split down the center. He grinned at the leader. "I think your head is not that hard."

The warriors consulted. Then they bowed, as courteously as their uncouth manners allowed, and the speaker said, "Permit us to go, Lord. Grant this and we will stay north of your territory." He hesitated. "May we have our dead and wounded?"

"Take them," said Ogier.

As the Chichimecas bore the bodies away, a derisive shout rose from the throats of the distant Toltecs, rumbling as if the earth itself exulted. The comrades had not even a scratch. When they came home to Tula, the populace met them with dancing and song.

No bodies would roll from the pyramid. Flowers and fruit covered the bloodstains on the altar. Now began the rule of Precious Feathered Serpent, returned Lord of life and love and beauty.

It was a time that in prosperity and peace rivaled the reign of that first sun-haired Quetzalcoatl who had come from the East on a serpent ship. He had ended human sacrifice; instead people gathered snakes and birds and butterflies, which were set free in the temples, and heaped the altars with flowers. Pumpkins swelled so a man's arms couldn't close around them. Ears of maize grew as long as a *metate* grinder, and those that weren't perfect were used to start fires. Cotton didn't need to be dyed; it grew in the most lovely colors of red, blue, green, yellow, purple, pink and jaguar-spotted.

And Tula was filled with birds whose songs were wonderful as their plumage; brilliant turquoise and green and gold with breasts that flamed like the rising sun. The finest cacao grew everywhere. The people had so much gold and so many precious stones that they went ornamented like royalty and ate off jewel-encrusted dishes. All this was because Quetzalcoatl ruled them from his splendid house of jade and gold, his house of turquoise and fine wood, covered with precious feathers. He fasted and prayed for his people to the unknown power that dwells in the Place of Duality with the North Star, above the Nine Heavens.

No one died or grew old. No one was sick. There was no war. The priests of Huitzilopotchli were furious. They plotted to regain their lost power. Quetzalcoatl did not drink pulque so they got him to partake of the mushroom that causes bright-colored visions. When he was intoxicated, they brought to him a beautiful maiden, who was in fact a sorceress.

She enticed Quetzalcoatl, he who had never lain with a woman, who was vowed to abstain. When he knew his shame, he left Tula. He sailed away on his serpent ship. But he said that one day he would come again. That once more there would be joy and plenty in Tula.

"But Huitzilopotchli has ruled since then," Xia explained. "Though each ruler of Tula has used the title of Quetzalcoatl. The last one killed himself after a defeat by the Chichimecas, and Tezcla claimed all power."

Tezcla made Kyra nervous. He fawned on her and Ogier, but malice made his eyes glint like obsidian flakes. He sat in the dining room every night and watched the Northerners as Mork watched birds he couldn't capture—just yet.

Kyra only saw Ogier at the evening meal and afterward when the Toltec nobles also came to watch entertainers or listen to Flossi's harp. No Toltec women were there except for Xia and Kyra's other attendants. Seated on their stools, they demurely spun fine white threads, but that didn't keep them from exchanging glances with handsome knights, though they quickly cast down their eyes.

They looked at Ogier, too, but with worship. Blond Kol and Leif, all the men, except for Isaac, had taken noble maidens as companions. Lovely women attended Ogier. Their adoration tormented Kyra. Any of them would so gladly be his, and they were slim-waisted, honey-skinned, with bared arms and skirts that reached just beneath the knees, sometimes sewn with tiny golden bells that jingled like fairy chimes when they walked. Their hair was smoothly combed and shone with perfumed oil.

"Ah," sighed Flossi as one filled his silver cup and he gazed at her small firm breasts beneath almost transparent cotton. "If the old heroes could have seen these damsels, they would rather have come to Tula than feast in Odin's hall! Who would want a whooping, battle-scarred Valkyrie when he could enjoy one of these sweet, gentle creatures?"

Indeed, Kyra couldn't see how any male could long resist such loveliness, but she was not prepared for the day when Ogier sent for her after he had finished hearing the most pressing matters brought for his judgment. He was not an idle ruler but spent most of each day adjudicating disputes, responding to problems and talking with architects, water experts and other professionals about how to ensure the health and beauty of the city. Only occasionally did he range forth with his comrades and nobles to hunt deer or small wild pigs in the hills.

Kyra found him in the hall where he rendered decisions. Only Flossi and Isaac were with him except for the maidens who wafted feather fans and stood ready to pour pulque.

"My sister," he said, "let us walk in the garden."

He sounded so serious that when they were walking in the enclosed court, shaded by great trees, where flowers and vines made the air sweet and a fountain sounded as purely crystalline as the water, she spoke first. "Are you ill, brother?"

"No." He pushed back hair which curled damply about his forehead. Except for ceremonial events, he didn't wear the plumed golden headdress but only a simple headband. "It is that I cannot sleep."

She slept none so well. Sometimes she dreamed of Ragnar's falling or of Gudrun-spider, but more often she dreamed of Ogier. Trying to touch with a thick, clear invisible wall between them; seeing his lips move but not being able to hear; or making love, all the time filled with unutterable sadness, a sense of guilt and doom.

"You work too hard," she told him. "It is not good to sit on that stool the whole day listening to all Tula's woes and disputes. You must go out oftener with Kol and Leif."

He laughed sourly. "Spearing pigs or deer will not help me." He paused and then said in a rush, "You must take a husband, Kyra."

She felt as if he had driven a blade into her, but his knife was still sheathed at his side. "Must? Wherefore?"

"Because I must have a woman." His voice was desperately brutal.

Shrinking into herself, cut so deeply she dared not, while with him, let herself feel, she said coldly, "That is done easily enough. Any woman in Tula would crawl to you on her belly. Are you not their god?"

He caught her shoulders, swinging her about, then let her go as if her flesh burned him, as the imprint of his touch continued to sear her. "I cannot—while you sleep alone."

"Is that so great a thing?" she scorned. "Who shall I bed with, then, so you can frolic? Xolo?

"Xolo is noble and steadfast as well as handsome."

Ogier refused to be angered. "But if you've no mind to a Toltec lord, Kol and Leif are fine men—"

"Babies! Though they, for sure, are not lonely in their beds."

"Leif is as old as I am," Ogier reasoned, but as she curled her lip, he said, "Halfdan is a notable chieftain."

She stared in shock. "And old enough to be my father!"

Ogier smiled and tears welled in her throat. He wanted to do as he pleased with God knew how many women, so she must needs bed with green lads, heathen or old men! His patient tone made her strangle. "You are scarce seventeen, my Kyra. Not so great an age. Halfdan is less than forty. You know well that even in Norway with the whole country to choose from, more unequal matches are made."

"Will you dare take a guardian's part and wed me whether I will or no?"

He paled but answered stoutly, "Ay, that I will, for your own good. As closest male kin, sister, I would have that power in Christian lands. Here I have *all* power."

They stared at each other, trembling. His face flushed red. The lean features had at last grown to fit that hawk's nose, and his eyes brooded gray as the clouds on the far mountains.

"Know this," she said tightly. "I will not marry. If you compel me, the bridal-ale can serve for grave-ale, too."

"Kyra! 'Tis sin, such wild talk! And self-murder . . . God forgives not that despairing of His grace."

"The grace He has not shown me?"

"What?" He was angry now, turning on her furiously. "Did you not escape Gudrun? Did we not sail beyond any regions ever known and come safe here? Have we not found comfort and honor among these folk when it might have been death? Think shame for such whining!"

"Shame yourself!" she blazed. "If this is so marvelous, why do you lament that you cannot sleep? Nay, whore as you will! Take all the concubines that you can mount and send to vassal states for more! But talk not to me of marriage!"

"Sister—"

"Don't call me that!"

He reached for her hand. She struck him across the face, gasped with pain that stabbed through her at the look in his eyes. Throwing her arms around him, she whispered what she had never quite dared to think. "Ogier! This is another world. We have the power of gods. Why not use it?" She locked her hands behind his neck, straining to reach his lips, driven past seemliness and laws of either God or man.

He unclasped her fingers, put her away from him. "For myself I do not care," he said thickly. "It is you I love, sister or no, you I shall always love. But I swore to our father to protect you. I will not damn your soul."

He left her.

That night in the hall he let the golden-belled maidens constantly fill his cup, caressed their arms and left in the middle of Flossi's playing, drawing the loveliest one with him.

The Toltecs looked amazed and then began to jest. Flossi's hazel eyes met Kyra's. He handed his harp to Xolo, whom he was teaching, and came to sit by Kyra. She felt as if she burned with fire, as if all must guess her outrage and grief.

"How could he?" she choked. "How could he?"

Flossi sighed and gathered her feverishly knotting hands in his. "Lass, how could he not?"

"It is crazy—mad that we should suffer for our father's looseness here at the end of the world!"

"You have still your honor. You have still the Heaven Sword."

She laughed cruelly. "I should like to fall on it. That would teach my brother-lord of honor!"

"Would you destroy him?" Flossi's tone hardened. "Nay then, if you reck so little of what those before you have undergone or what it has cost Ogier not to take you, belike you are not worthy of the sword."

"Or your saga?" she derided.

He was her true friend, and Ogier's. He had rescued her from Gudrun and sung in the fiercest storms. Shaking her head miserably, she said, "Forgive me, Flossi. I am distraught. What should I do? What is best for Ogier?"

"Marry. Knowing you belong to a comrade will seal the matter. He will take his pleasures then without dreading what you may do."

She drooped, imagining Kol or Leif kissing her as Ogier had. "Flossi, I cannot. I cannot lie in another's arms."

He smiled tenderly. "You will not have to. I have talked with Halfdan. He is devoted to you and Ogier both, and though he would fain have you his bride in truth, he will not force you. The wedding would free Ogier. He need never know you are not a wife."

"I . . . will think about it." Kyra glanced at Halfdan. He had been watching her but colored and turned away. His ruddy hair and green eyes reminded her somewhat of Ragnar. She knew him for a staunch comrade and brave chieftain. And yet . . .

She pressed Flossi's hand. "Thank you. You must be right. But oh, Flossi! It is hard."

"Get out the sword. Think of the lives and loves it has guarded, of the honor of your line."

She swallowed a rude answer. Motioning to her women to stay for more music if they wished, she gathered Mork in her arms and went to her apartments.

The Heaven Sword hung on the wall, but she was in no

temper to remember all those women who had given it to a lover or a son when she must have neither.

Nor could she bear to think of Ogier pushing aside the gold-belled skirt, seeking for the sweet breasts beneath soft cotton. Xia had followed her. Kyra asked for pulque. Then she drank cup after cup of the buttermilklike stuff till her vision blurred and her head began to nod. Xia helped her undress, but while she was brushing her hair, Kyra fell asleep.

Next day she went to the audience chamber. Ogier's eyes were hollowed. He reddened as she approached. "Do not kneel, my sister. What would you have?"

Their gazes met. Her breath knotted tightly in her chest. *Oh, my love. My only dearest love.*

"Brother, grant me a husband."

She and Halfdan wed each other with rings, Flossi intoning what he remembered of the service. It was a mockery, but when Halfdan kissed her lips, she was aware of his strength, his maleness. Had she not loved Ogier, she might have lived content with him. Had she not loved Ogier . . .

It was a line that sounded over and over in her head, like part of a ballad that will not be forgotten. Halfdan treated her gently. He moved into her quarters but slept in a room several chambers away from hers. Sometimes she caught him looking at her wistfully, but he made no move to woo her and spent his days, as usual, with his companions. She was sure he still had his concubine, and that relieved her conscience to an extent, though at times she wondered glumly if, even with his consent, any good could come of using him like this.

Thank Mary Virgin that he did not love her!

Though the marriage was a sham, it did change things. Ogier was in good spirits. He did not get drunk again or behave unseemly, but the Toltecs were glad to see that he favored their women, and nobles brought their wives and daughters. It was a blessing to sleep even one time with the god.

As for Kyra, she was busy overseeing the princely household and going to the childbeds of first noble-women and then any who sent for her. It was part of the moon goddess' power, to ease such pangs, though Kyra did nothing but talk to the women and hold their hands. She helped cleanse the babies and sprinkle them with corn meal, giving each a quetzal feather for good fortune.

Her heart yearned as she held the infants, so tiny, so perfect. Never to have one of her own! Already two of Ogier's women began to show the fruit of his loving. Having a baby to love and care for would fill at least some of her empty heart. But she could not bring herself to smile at Halfdan when he watched her in that longing way, or draw him by the hand into her chamber. Her moods changed so often and violently that she thought she really was much like the goddess who Xia said had four aspects.

The first was a maiden, entrancing yet fickle. The next was an eager woman, fond of gambling and avid for lovers. The full moon blessed marriage, brought children and forgave sins, absorbing them and purifying the transgressor. In the last phase, the goddess destroyed her lovers and robbed mankind of good things.

This waning moon brought evil. And always there was Smoking Mirror, the deceiver, He who Is Closest to the Shoulder, who ever perched near each person's ear and tried to incite them to violence and trickery. His single footprint made the Great Bear in the sky—he had lost the other when the Earth Monster snapped it off, that creature from whom was made the world. Because he was evil, Smoking Mirror-Huitzilopotchli could never reach the North Star, the symbol of ultimate divinity. He would forever hop around it on his remaining foot.

As I circle Ogier, Kyra thought. As I circle Ogier.

Impossible to see him every evening, wonder which woman he would love that night, watch two swelling with his seed. Kyra told Halfdan that she wished they could have a house of their own.

Ogier allotted them a spacious stone dwelling that overlooked the river. At her urging, Halfdan visited the palace each night to be with his companions, but Kyra stayed within her walls except when she attended a child-birth or went to bathe in the river. She and her women spun and wove, making garments for the poor, or for diversion, copied patterns from the white-painted deerskin folders on which were recorded history and legends in stylized pictures and symbols.

She thought she would grow old like this, completing one length of cloth, starting another, helping to bring forth other women's children.

"Ogier asks about you," Halfdan said embarrassedly. "He wishes you would come to dinner at least once in a week."

"He has company enough."

Halfdan said roughly, "You know that is not it."

Kyra shrugged and went back to her weaving.

IX

Flossi *visited often and the others came by when they were in the* neighborhood. Ogier did not, but Xolo called each day to see if she needed anything and to bring flowers or fruit. Saving these, her only visitors were women asking her to assist with a lying-in. She was surprised when, several months after her departure from the palace, Xia announced Tezcla.

More wizened than ever, he smiled, showing gaps in his teeth. He ate dirt before she could stop him, commented on the joy of seeing Precious Feathered Serpent so potent, and then unwrapped lengths of yellow cotton from about a shining black disc the size of a small plate.

"I have brought a worthy gift for Lady Moon." He polished it even brighter and set it carefully on a table. "This is the Smoking Mirror. When you gaze into it, it shows what will happen."

"Surely the high priest needs it more than I."

A wrinkling of the turtle face could have been either scowl or smile. "Ah, since the return of Quetzalcoatl, my skills are seldom needed. All is peace. All is prosperity." He gave a rusty chuckle. "Everyone is happy. Are they not, Lady Moon?"

How much did he suspect? Of the companions, only

Flossi, Arne and Isaac knew that she and Ogier had hoped to marry. She said in a flat tone, "The folk I see appear content enough."

"Yes, the Lord Quetzalcoatl expects a child before summer, does he not? Very proud, very happy, is the beautiful Chima. But you, Lady Moon, seem slim as ever. I know certain herbs . . ."

"Thank you. That will be as heaven decrees."

He winked. "I had not thought that heaven had much to do with it. But look in the mirror, Lady Moon, and you will behold the future."

Before she could insist that he keep his gift, he bowed and slipped out of the house in a slithering fashion that reminded her of a snake. They had not touched, yet she felt as if a snail had trailed slime over her.

With a shiver of disgust, she started to call for the gardener and send him after the priest with the mirror, but she picked it up first, marveling at the way the polished obsidian, cut thin enough to be almost translucent, did seem to smoke—did seem to form shadows that grew clearer, began to assume color . . .

There was Ogier, his bright head bent to a woman. Kyra's hands convulsed. Tezcla did not need to taunt her with this! But then the woman's face appeared as Ogier kissed her throat, smoothed her body with adoring fingers, molding her to his delight. The lips that parted were Kyra's. The dark sweep of hair was hers, not Chima's or another's. And those were her starved, lonely breasts, her yearning loins.

Kyra's mouth went dry. She moaned, moving in rhythm with the figures on the dark surface, imagining Ogier doing to her what he did with the image. When her mirror-self arched high, quivering, straining, received from Ogier that final offering that left her drained, cradling him in her arms, Kyra moaned as hot pulsing thrummed between her thighs, the beating of a strange, separate heart.

She sank to the floor, overwhelmed by radiating waves. When at last she returned to reality, her first thought was, If I can feel this way without Ogier beside me, what would it be in truth? And the next was, He does this with Chima. With all the others. Everyone but me. Now I have seen it, how can I bear it?

But she could not now part with the mirror. Most of the time she kept it wrapped in the yellow cotton, hidden under her pallet, but sometimes, as a long-abstemious drunkard might deliberately allow himself a bout of intoxication, balancing release against sickness to follow, she unwrapped the mirror.

Always, always, the figures formed. She did not believe it was the future. It was a tormenting trick of Tezcla's, simply. But she had more relief, more pleasure from the shadows, than from anything in real life.

Then one bright morning Xolo came to beseech her aid for Chima. Chima had been writhing since yesterday, trying to bring forth her babe. Nothing helped. The midwives said she would die. But Chima pleaded for Lady Moon.

Bile filled Kyra's throat. It was too much! To be called on by his mistress! Yet she *was* called on. Asking Xia to attend her, Kyra wrapped a mantle about her to hide her face and went with Xolo to the palace.

At least Ogier wasn't hovering around the women's wing. The small but luxurious chamber was packed with midwives and physicians. Chima was no longer able to pull on the frame erected to help her bear down as she squatted. She lay on a mat, huge belly a malignant parasite on the slender, frail body that was little more than a girl's. She breathed shallowly.

Beside her, trying not to weep, a woman Kyra recognized as Chima's mother held her hand and told her that those who die in the struggle to bring forth a child ascend to a heaven as blissful as that of warriors slain in battle and those sacrificed for the good of the people.

Gazing down at the woman who had been her unwitting rival, Kyra was suddenly gripped with furious anger. Ogier had enjoyed this girl. Now she was like to die while he strode about light and strong as ever. Chima might love Ogier. Surely she worshipped him. But Kyra knew all too well, deep in her heart, that the young woman suffered in her place. Ogier would never have turned to another save to slake his need for the one forbidden.

Kyra sank to her knees and gripped Chima's hands. "You are going to live. You will have your child. You will give it suck and see it grow. Chima! My strength is going into you. You are full of it. You are bearing down. The babe wishes to be born. Push. Push."

Chima groaned, thrashing her head back and forth. Her lips were bloody from being bitten. But something in her responded to Kyra. The lax fingers tightened. She screwed up her face and strained.

Her first efforts did not bring it, or the second or third. Kyra made her drink a tea that induced contractions, then had two of the strongest midwives support Chima while she gripped her hands and talked. It seemed to her later that she willed that baby through the birth channel, for Chima was too exhausted to do more than whimper, but at last she cried out as if riven and the child slipped out, covered with blood and mucus, into a midwife's hands.

Experienced attendants brought the afterbirth, cleaned the tiny boy and gave him to Kyra. Sweat-drenched and stained, she felt as if she herself had given birth. She studied the wrinkled crimson face for some look of Ogier, but truth to tell, the mite more resembled Tezcla; most babies did. The eyes were an indeterminate hazy brown and the hair was plentiful, silky and black.

She anointed him with meal and put the quetzal feather
Xia had remembered to bring into his tiny fist, repeating
the ritual blessing with a mixture of wryness and posses-
sive pride in this child she had brought into the light.
"Our Lord Quetzalcoatl, who is the creator, has put into
this dust a precious stone and a precious feather."

She placed the infant on his mother's breast and kissed
her on the forehead. "Rest now, Chima. You have a
beautiful son."

A smile wavered on the girl's face. She weakly took
Kyra's hand and pressed it to her lips. In that moment,
Kyra's heart overflowed with tenderness for the mother
and child. But as she stepped out of the chamber, she almost stumbled into Ogier.

He had no flaccid, painfully emptied belly. He had not
writhed in his own blood and wished to die. "You have a
fine son," she said in a cold voice.

"Chima?" He blushed as he asked. Kyra hated him
for a heartbeat, waited a moment before she eased the
gathering fear in his eyes.

"She is tired but should be all right. However, Lord, if
you once watched a child born, you might call it a high
price for simple rutting."

She spun on her heel and fled.

The baby thrived, and at the end of the month, his
naming feast was held. Xolo came to Kyra with an invitation. When she declined, he said, "Lady Moon, this is
important to Chima. She knows she would be dead without you, and her baby, too. It will grieve her and seem
bad fortune if you are not there. And our Lord Quetzalcoatl, he is also grateful."

"I did nothing for him," Kyra returned shortly. But
she remembered Chima's agony and the miracle of a
baby emerging from that slimy blood. Already he would

have grown. He should look a lot less like Tezcla. And she *had* saved him. "I will come."

It was a great feast. All the nobles of Tula were there, literally in their finest feathers, shining with gold and silver, jade and turquoise. Even in palaces, meat was rare, but tonight there was venison; turkey; duck; peccary, or wild pig; and hairless small dogs that were fattened for the table, though Kyra could not touch the savory flesh. There were tender, thin tortillas; tamales; amaranth cakes; beans and squash simmered with tomatoes and chilies; frothy chocolate; and of course, the pulque jars were constantly emptied.

The Morning Star, Quetzalcoatl's heavenly personification, was shining brightly when the Lord Feathered Serpent, accompanied by his companions and chief nobles, took his son and ascended the pyramid, walking on rushes and flowers strewn by the joyous folk of the city who had also feasted that day from the palace kitchens. Kyra, as Lady Moon and the child's female sponsor, was the only woman outside the torch-lit temple, though Chima and other noblewomen watched from below.

Tezcla, as the priests chanted, sprinkled the boy with corn meal and gave him his names: Piltzintechtli, Princely Lord; Cinteotl, the Young Maize; Ehecatl, Lord of the Winds. Long, difficult names for the little golden boy whose eyes were now warm hazel and who had Chima's dimples when he smiled.

"Lady Moon, will you show him to the Morning Star?" asked Tezcla.

Kyra took him from Ogier. Mary Virgin, if only he were theirs! She would never have a child at all. Tears filled her eyes so that the star blurred into many spangled rays. Then Ogier took the babe and they returned to the palace.

Flossi played, and when he tired, Toltec musicians

made music for wrestlers and tumblers and dancers. Tezcla brought Kyra a golden cup of pulque. "You must
drink the health of the young lord," he said. "And keep
the cup. It is a gift from him on his naming day."

"I shall drink but then I'm going home."

Tezcla smiled. "As you will, Lady Moon."

Chima, bearing her son proudly in her arms, came to
kneel before Kyra, who forbade her to eat dirt and managed to compliment her on the boy. It was harder to accept the young woman's thanks graciously, but Kyra
restrained her bitterness. None of this was Chima's fault.
Not really even Ogier's. But if just once what befell in
the dark mirror could actually happen . . .

She smiled stiffly and bade Chima good night. As she
sipped more pulque she thought it unusually strong. Already she felt light-headed, but the drowsy heaviness
weighting her limbs felt delicious. It was good to sink
into this easeful haze, good not to ache with jealousy and
pain. When Xia anxiously inquired if her mistress wished
to go home, Kyra waved her away. Halfdan was snoring
in a corner. Kol and Leif were laughing with two dancing
girls. Ogier—

Kyra squinted toward him, barely able to focus. He
was drinking, too, gazing at her. For a second, his gray
eyes pierced her dulling senses, stabbed till she clenched
her teeth against the wave of longing.

He has a child. Another coming. Into which hot, eager
womb will his divine seed spill tonight?

Kyra gave a harsh laugh. She raised her cup to him,
nodded mockingly and drank to the dregs.

They were in the mirror. It was through a smoky cloud
that she saw Ogier, but there was nothing between their
bodies, nothing between his mouth and hers, the sweetness of his kisses. Amidst the melting, the cleaving together of parts long and painfully sundered to make a

whole, there was a moment's echo of distant pain, and then dissolving, flowing with him, merging in a oneness that was perfect peace.

Kyra roused as she was jarred roughly from that dreaming embrace. She opened her eyes. Light brought a crashing in her head. She lay quiet till it stilled to a molten throbbing, then carefully let her eyes open again.

Ogier stared down at her. "It was no dream!" he choked. "Oh, God, Mary Virgin! What have I done?"

She felt no horror, nor anger at Tezcla, though she was sure he had drugged her. And he—someone—must have brought her here to Ogier's ascetic chamber. But Ogier's distress was so great that she sat up in spite of the hammering in her skull and took his hand.

He wrenched away. That stung but Kyra tried to comfort him. "Ogier, we didn't know—it wasn't on purpose."

His laugh was terrible. "I think I couldn't have done it, even drugged, if I hadn't so often in my dreams—and sometimes, God forgive me, in my waking thoughts."

"Ogier," she said desperately, "it was bound to happen sometime."

She knew the words were a mistake the moment they were uttered, shrank from the torment in his eyes, the agony of self-reproach. "Yes." When he finally spoke again, his tone was quiet. If dead people spoke, they would sound like that. "Bound to happen. I was a fool to think it could be otherwise."

This while they had been naked. Now he covered her and tossed a mantle around himself, rising as if he were an old, feeble man.

She cried out in dread. "Ogier! What will you do?"

He steadied himself against the doorway but did not look at her. "I don't know." His hopelessness wrung her heart. "I don't know. I must pray. That I have mired you in this awful sin!"

Frightened into anger, she crossed to him and gripped his arm. "Ogier, we were drugged. Tezcla did this. Could we confess to a priest, he would absolve us if we undertook it should not happen again."

He moved his head like a stallion tormented by midges, spoke in a shuddering whisper. "That is the trouble. I cannot promise. Even now—" His arms half closed around her. Kyra shut her eyes, lifted her face.

"Ogier, what does it matter? So far from home, so far from laws? It hurts no one—"

"Already I have corrupted you!" Whirling from her, he fled into the garden.

Better leave him alone. When he thought about it, he wouldn't blame himself so sternly. Kyra could not feel it was wicked. He didn't seem a brother. It was possible that Ragnar had been mistaken, that his Halogaland mistress had passed off another man's child as his. The next time Kyra saw Ogier, she would suggest that.

She had no opportunity. She was in her garden that evening when Flossi came to say that Ogier, with Leif, Xolo, Kol, Baard and Isaac, had set out for the coast. They would take *North Star* and sail for yet another world. She and Halfdan were to reign in Tula. Ogier requested that she see to the bringing up of his son and any other children conceived by his women.

"He is already gone?"

Flossi bowed his head. "He is already gone."

Kyra felt ripped by an invisible blade, as if her inner parts were spilling out. She crossed her arms as if to hold in heart and lungs and entrails. Halfdan caught her as she started to fall, helped her to a bench.

"What's this?" he growled at Flossi. "Ogier never consulted me. Why didn't you warn us?"

"He swore us to silence till tonight," Flossi said help-lessly. "He—he thought that if you and Kyra . . ."

It wasn't necessary to finish. Halfdan went crimson. He didn't know what had happened the night before. Servants had borne him home, and he hadn't emerged till noon, groaning and holding his head. Kyra felt a pang of guilt, though they were not truly married, though he had entered willingly into the sham to spare Ogier.

He said grimly, "Ogier should have taken counsel with Kyra and me. It will take all of us to sail the *North Star*—"

"That it will," said Kyra, suddenly deciding what she must do. "We'll start after him in the morning. We have had great adventures, but it is time we went home. You, Halfdan, your outlawry will be over before we reach Iceland. You can reclaim your chiefdom. Flossi, you and the others can go with Ogier to his mother's estate in Halogaland. I—" She swallowed hard and closed her eyes. Closed them forever against the dark mirror. "I will enter a convent."

Be dead to Ogier. So that he may live.

But first she must see Chima and be sure that she and the small prince would be well cared for. To give her courage to do all she must, Kyra took the Heaven Sword and hung it under her mantle. And she took the Smoking Mirror and broke it into gleaming splinters on the boulders in the garden.

The audience chamber was empty. Kyra asked Flossi and Halfdan to wait and went through a courtyard past Ogier's rooms. She smothered a flash of remembering. She could not be sorry. But it was already like something that had happened in another life.

As she neared Chima's room, she heard the sounds of

struggle, a cry, "My baby—" before the voice was strangled.

What could be amiss? Kyra shrank against the wall and hurried forward, freeing the sword as she peered around the door. Chima was held by two priests, one clamping her mouth shut, while Tezcla lifted the baby, obsidian knife poised above his heart.

Kyra sprang halfway across the room, sweeping Heaven's Gift at the hand that held the knife. It seemed to dart to the floor. Blood pumped from the wrist. Kyra caught the prince in her arms and brought down the blade as hard as she could against the neck of the priest stifling Chima. He gurgled, threw up his arms and fell, neck almost severed. His fellow cringed on his knees.

"Mercy! Mercy, Lady Moon!"

"Drag out this carrion!"

Panting, she turned to confront Tezcla. He sank down, gripping the stump of his hand, but the blood surged through his fingers. She would not have thought he'd have red blood at all, but slime. Green, stinking slime. She wanted to strike off his head but could not. She began to shake.

He smiled as if he read her weakness. "I should have killed you first. But I thought to secure the palace first, get rid of the imposter's spawn." He leaned against the wall, but his eyes might have been shards of the mirror. "You have saved this bastard but at least his father is dead."

"What?"

He chuckled. "We priests know there will be no power or honor for us while you Fair Ones rule. No hearts to gladden Huitzilopotchli. So I caused your brother to sin with you. He didn't kill himself as I hoped he might, but when he left with only five men—I sent two score after him."

He slumped to the floor. The blood from the stump was only a trickle.

Kyra frantically wanted to set out that night, but Flossi, Gunnar and Halfdan restrained her. Ogier had left that morning. His fate was already determined. Perhaps, with their steel weapons, even the six had managed to rout the priestly assassins. There was almost no hope of finding their track in the darkness.

Besides, did she not owe it to Ogier to do what she could to protect his son? That argument prevailed. Summoning the nobles, who were so horrified at the sacrilege that they would have slaughtered the priests had they not fled, she told them that Quetzalcoatl was returning to the East but trusted them to follow the good ways he had shown them and to pay allegiance to his son. Till Princely Lord was old enough to rule, a regency would serve. With her comrades' advice, Kyra appointed Chima's father, a wise and respected man, to this post.

Next morning, as Kyra and her friends set forth, Chima followed to the gate of the city with the prince in her arms. She would have fallen to the ground, but Kyra embraced her, kissed her on both cheeks and blinked back tears as she held the baby.

"Good-bye, little prince," she said, letting Mork inspect him. "May all the powers keep you."

If only they had kept his father!

From its zenith, the sun dazzled on the steel that here pinned a man to the ground, here lay in a nerveless grasp. Baard's hand was severed. Never would he steer *North Star* toward home. Kol and Leif had fallen back to back, overwhelmed by numbers. They would not join Uni and their mother in Ottar's hall. Isaac's wanderings were over. His last journey had been across the bloodstained ground, crawling on stumps of arms and shattered legs to lie across Ogier's feet.

Ogier. His face was peaceful, almost smiling. His eyes reflected the sky. But as Kyra, sobbing, closed the lids, she saw the back of his fair head was a mass of blood. It must have been done by the obsidian-studded club in the hand of a man sprawled behind him.

There were so many dead.

Then someone moved. "Xolo!"

Kyra was beside him in an instant, lifting him against her. Flossi knelt, holding a water skin to the pallid lips. Xolo drank thirstily and sighed. A spear pierced his thigh. Ants were swarming over the mass protruding from his abdomen.

"We'll help you," Kyra said desperately. "Flossi, Arne . . ."

Xolo's dark lashes fluttered. He smiled, very sweetly. "No. I go with my lord." He breathed a little longer but did not speak again.

As they burned the bodies that night on heaps of fragrant wood, Kyra remembered another tale of that first Quetzalcoatl. That instead of sailing away in his serpent craft, he had stripped off his splendid garments and burned himself alive. From these flames came all the brilliant birds. He went into the Underworld, atoning for his sin, but on the fourth day he ascended into heaven to be revered as male and female, end and beginning, both the Evening and the Morning Star.

She gazed at that star through her tears, took Heaven's Gift and advanced to the pyre.

Flossi stopped her. "No, lass. Ogier would not want that. He wanted you to live. Live and have a child to bear that wondrous sword."

I shall have no child, she started to say, but a premonition struck her. Perhaps. Perhaps . . .

She looked from the flames to the Morning Star and knew Ogier was with her. *My love*, she thought. *My love*, and put the sword back in its sheath.

Book VI

The Sword Triumphant

Sweden
1520–1533

I

When Rurik, the big red cock, resoundingly greeted the faintest light, Kristina usually cuddled a bit closer to her little sister Margrete for the few delectable minutes till their mother called, but this morning she came awake immediately.

Saint Lucia's Day. And she was Lucia Bride! She had served thus in their household for five seasons, since she was ten years old, but this was the first time she'd been chosen to visit every home in the village with food and drink and the saint's blessings. Shivering in the chill loft, she hurriedly put the long white robe on over her shift and tied the red sash around her waist.

" 'Lucy light!' " she crooned to Margrete, gathering the plump, sweetly limp little body into her arms. " 'Shortest day and longest night.' "

Shielding them both with her mantle, she carried the four-year-old down the outside stairs and put her on a bearskin rug by the blazing fire to be dressed by Hilde, the oldest servant. On the wall above the fireplace hung the Heaven Sword and on a shelf near it perched the Empress' Nightingale, the family's greatest treasures. Hilde's wrinkled face beamed as she took the child and cackled to Kristina, "Lucy light, my love! But before

343

you can wear a crown, that wild hair of yours needs taming! Fetch the comb and sit you down here.''

Kristina finished dressing Margrete but could scarce bide in patience while Hilde worked snarls out of the wheat-colored hair that fell to her hips, thick and waving. Karl, the wiry, freckled stable lad, and Sophia and Ana, Hilde's buxom, yellow-haired daughters, were thrusting long resinous sticks into the wall between logs and boards, filling the principal room of the house with *levande lhus*, "living light," for this celebration that began the Christmas holy days. The odor of *glögg*—wine mulled with costly spices, cloves, cinnamon and ginger—filled the air. Mother bustled in with a birch tray of *lussekatter*, sweet saffron buns shaped like an X with curling ends. They had been made yesterday, but no one got a nibble until this morning.

"You must have smelled the buns!" Kristina greeted her twin brother, who emerged from his loft rubbing his eyes and yawning. Nikulaus' hair was fairer than hers, and in the past few years he had shot up like a young pine, so that he towered over her though she was tall. Kinship was spoken still in eyes the shade of mellow amber that seemed to have trapped the sunlight. His eyes were framed with golden lashes and brows, hers with soft brown. "Are you going to be a troll this year or a star-boy?"

"Neither," he retorted. "I'm going to tie on a red beard to remind you of old Per Olafsson, who's stupid enough to want to marry you!"

"That's no way to speak of your elders," mother rebuked.

Karin Steynsdotter bore herself in stately wise, but she had dimpled cheeks and a sparkle in her gray eyes. It was a blessing that Saint Brigit's good nuns at the cloister in Vadstena had taught her management as well as housewifely arts and fine lacemaking, for Magnus Haldorsson paid small heed to things of this earth. He probably didn't even remember that the Danes had once again invaded Sweden, trying to put their king on the throne. Magnus' gaze was fixed late each night on the heavens. He often went to bed as the household was rising, and that was doubtless why he was the last one to enter the room, limping from a thigh broken in his youth that had healed crookedly. Though he was not yet forty, the hair falling to the shoulders of his pleated black long-sleeved scholar's robe was gray. The chain of his big gold watch reached across his doublet, but he wore no other finery. His face was surprisingly smooth and fresh, and the hazel eyes behind his spectacles watched the world kindly when they noticed it at all.

"Well, Margrete." He smiled, hoisting the little one to his shoulder. "Are you ready for your Lucy bite, then?"

He led them all in prayer as the household gathered around the long table where the queen's lingonberry wreath was surrounded by platters of food. Kristina dipped *glögg* into beautiful wooden beakers with fantastic horns on either side that wreathed the drinker's head when tilted up. Hurriedly she ate a delicious bun before taking down the *loktnek* from beside the door where it had hung since harvest to bless the house.

This last sheaf, cunningly braided to leave a bushy top, held the power that made grain and all things grow. Bread baked from it would adorn the Christmas table and be saved till spring, when it would be pounded into crumbs shared between family and animals and mixed with seed grain to produce a bountiful crop.

Now the last sheaf would go to the beasts in the manger, both food and blessing. Bearing a torch, careful not to shed sparks, Kristina hurried across the courtyard to the barn. Magnus' fields stretched away from the village and were worked by his tenants. Son of a wealthy iron-mine owner, Magnus had been able to indulge his love of learning. Though he had not earned the degree of doctor because of his unfortunate habit of asking questions his teachers could not answer, he had studied philosophy, law, mathematics, medicine, astronomy and Greek at the famed universities of Padua, Bologna and Leipzig, and he still corresponded with scholars he had met in his student days, especially with Niklas Koppernigk, or Copernicus, a Canon of Frauenberg Cathedral in Prussia.

Rurik, lord of the farmyard and exhorter of the dawn, crowed raucously from a post. Kristina scattered some grain for him before she placed her torch in a chink in the barn logs, lifted the bar of the door and entered stalls warmed by horses and cows, redolent of their moist, hay-sweetened breath.

Speaking to her own cream-colored, silver-maned Flicka, she divided the last sheaf so that each of the eight cows and six horses would have some and then went around to the haymow to fetch an extra-large morning's ration. She stumbled into something. Not wood or stone. Something resilient.

She peered into shadows that flickered grotesquely from the wavering flare of the torch. A dark, huddled shape turned into a man who half-raised himself on an elbow. Dull orange light gave his haggard face a deathly look, but his hair was rich yellow and his eyes very blue.

"Ah," he breathed, "you keep Saint Lucia's Day after the Bath of Blood?" A fit of coughing seized him, wracking his body, and he lay exhausted.

He was sick, hurt or a madman, perhaps all three. Still, word had filtered to this province of Dalarna that Sten Sture the Younger, last of the regents empowered by a party of burghers, miners and peasants who rejected the Scandinavian Union and Danish rule, had died of wounds that summer during the Danish invasion. His brave young widow was holding Stockholm against a siege. Nikulaus had begged to go fight the Danes and their German, French and Swiss mercenaries, but Magnus said he was too young. When Magnus thought of going himself, Karin pointed out that he couldn't sit a saddle without disabling pain. After outfitting and giving horses to several young yeoman who burned to fight, Magnus had returned to his ordered, peaceful, distant stars.

Almost as distant as the stars seemed Stockholm, a fortnight's journey from these highlands, but now, gazing at the stranger, Kristina was gripped with foreboding.

"The . . . the Bath of Blood?" she faltered. "What does it mean?"

"You have not heard?" Tawny eyelashes fluttered upward and those eyes blazed. "Sten Sture's widow surrendered on a Danish guarantee of amnesty, but that traitor Archbishop, Gustav Trolle, had barely set the crown on Christian of Denmark's head when the king summoned Sture's principal supporters—bone, muscle and brain of Sweden's independence—and slaughtered more than seventy. They were beheaded in the Grand Square and their bodies left for several days before they were burned. Christian even had Herr Sten's body dug up and burned, too. Anyone who protested was murdered." His voice died.

"Were you there?" Kristina asked fearfully, bending down. "Are you hurt?"

This time his eyes didn't open. "I wasn't there. My father was—under the headsman's axe. So were my uncles and brother-in-law. My mother, grandmother and two sisters are in Stockholm Castle dungeons with Herr Sten's wife. I've been a hostage in Denmark and escaped. 'Tis no wound makes me infant-weak but some cursed sickness."

He looked pitifully young and defenseless. To lose his family so! And the country's leaders slain! Anger and dread swelled in Kristina but she fought them back. "We must get you into a warm bed and give you proper care."

His head moved slightly. "That you must not. The Danes know I'm in the country. They're hunting me. They would pay well for Gustav Vasa, and punish those who help me."

"We'll hide you. My parents . . ."

He smiled wanly though his eyes were still shut. "Saint Lucia you are indeed! But I would not bring ruin on so fair and kind a maid and her folk."

"But—"

His tone, though thin, held a note of command. "If Danish soldiers come pounding at your door, the fewer who know about me, the better for all. But if you bring me food and drink till I can travel, I swear that someday you can boast you did Sweden a service." She started to argue but he cut in harshly, "Girl, can you not understand? If I am found here, your parents can truly vow they knew naught of it. But if you could make me a burrow in the hay where I'd be out of sight and out of reach of pitchforks, I would be grateful."

She did that, shaping a soft hollow on the far side of the fragrant heaps and, in spite of his protests, helped him reach it. She swiftly fed the animals and sped to the dairy room in the storehouse. Hastily filling a bowl with curds, and slicing off part of a cheese, she ran back to the barn and set the food beside the fugitive.

"I'll bring you coverings later," she promised.

His hand closed faintly on hers. "Hurry with your duties, Saint Lucia. Take blessings to the people, and with God's help, I will bring them freedom."

She folded his cloak over him and spread hay on top to warm and hide him before she got the torch and hurried to the house. Nikulaus waited impatiently, his bushy red beard already fastened over his ears.

"You must have said a paternoster over each of the

beasts," he grumbled. "And there's hay all over you!
What a Lucia Bride!"

Hilde picked wisps off while mother set the lingonberry crown on her head and father lit the seven candles
with a tinderstick. Fondly kissing her on both cheeks, he
said, "Carry light and blessings through the village,
child. Our forefathers believed Freya brought them holy
mead and prosperity—"

"Husband!" remonstrated Karin. " 'Tis heathen
talk!"

He chuckled. "Now who's to say the lady in white
who gladdened their hearts on the longest day of winter
was not the same that we call Lucia?" She crossed herself in distress and he took her hand in gentle teasing.
"Nay, wife, we were pagan here centuries after the rest
of Europe was Christian. Surely last night when I poured
your fresh-brewed ale over the roots of our family tree I
did what my ancestors have for countless generations.
The house has changed or burned down many times but
the tree stands and grows."

She sighed with exasperation. "All the same, husband, it will be best if the priest never hears you talking
thus. Children! Be off before folk wonder what's become
of their Lucy bites."

Karl, bewigged and stuffed to troll size, helped Nikulaus carry great wooden jugs of ale. Sophia and Ana bore
torches and *lussekatter* while Kristina carried a birch
basket of the aromatic buns. As they went out past the
huge oak tree that had quaffed family ale from times
unremembered and shaded generations of playing children, they heard the sound of a horse on the frozen earth
outside the wall surrounding the old timbered manor.
Then there was the shuffle of many feet, laughter and
voices. Relieved that they hadn't kept the procession
waiting, Kristina passed through the gate Karl swung
open.

"Lucy light!" shouted the weird assembly of masked trolls and demons who represented winter, starboys and white-clad maidens carrying torches, and a monstrous shaggy goat who capered up to her on two men's legs and louted low, Lucifer captured by Lucia's guards.

Knut Jonsson reined his chestnut horse to the front. When Kristina was little, he had brought her a kitten and used to take her up before him in the saddle, teasing that someday he'd carry her off. She had adored her distant cousin, but she thought he had grown over-proud since returning from the university. There was no denying that he made a comely Saint Stephen, though. Lapp blood showed in dark hair and skin, broad cheekbones and sharp-angled chin, but his eyes were a clear, deep gray. By choice, he spent summers with Lapp kinsmen in high, far mountain meadows, but he was the real manager of his family's iron mines and a member of the reformed parliament, or Riksraad, set up when Swedish patriots declared Swedish independence in 1512. Knut was twenty-five, and in the last few years his reserved, slightly mocking manner had inclined her to avoid him.

He did not mock now but stared as if he'd never seen her before. Sweeping off his plumed velvet cap, he spoke softly. "Indeed, cousin, you shine with Lucia light."

With him in the lead, the procession started off, Kristina followed by her prankishly gleeful retinue. It was only a few minutes' walk to the village, inhabited mostly by miners, that had grown up near the manor. At each dwelling she bestowed *lussekatter* and ale and wished the household good fortune for the coming year. She also visited byres and stables to bless the animals. But all the time, as she smiled and served and kissed the children, she thought of the stranger, sick and desperate, hid in the manor barn. It seemed wrong not to tell her parents, but she knew Gustav Vasa was right in saying ignorance was safer for them.

Safest of all would be for him to go away. But he was in no condition to travel. The responsibility weighed neavily on her. As soon as they had regaled the folk of the last house, she thanked her escort and set off so swiftly for the manor that she outpaced Nikulaus and the servants.

"Methinks the ground too icy for your slippers, cousin." Knut, riding up beside her, slid from the saddle. "Best we have those candles out before they set your hair aflame with real fire." He snuffed the tapers and set his big hands around her waist, lifting her up so that her legs dangled from one side of the saddle.

Mary Virgin! Of all times for him to decide to visit! She could think of no way to put him off. And doubtless her parents would ask him to spend the night though his home was less than five miles away.

When they entered the gate, Karl took Knut's horse and led him toward the farmyard. Knut lifted Kristina down. She thanked him breathlessly and hurried inside. Her parents greeted Knut and urged him to warm himself by the fire. Kristina had to pour *glögg* for him and bring barley porridge; but as soon as she had served him, she left, saying she had to change her dress and shoes.

This done, she took a warm wool sledge robe from a chest, folded it under her mantle and went downstairs to the kitchen, where, claiming hunger, she got porridge, bread and a cup. She went to the dairy and filled the cup with milk.

Rurik strutted amongst his hens, who rushed around pecking and scratching at the frozen earth.

Knut's horse was in a stall next to Flicka's. Karl had rubbed him well and given him hay. Kristina patted his red-brown flank and passed into the haymow. It was so dark that she had to pause till she could make out solid forms from shadows. She held her breath as she saw how still the young man lay, only his face dimly visible.

"Sir?" she whispered. "Gustav Vasa?"

His eyelashes lifted slowly. " 'The soot-red cock of Hel,' " he muttered. " 'A sword age, a wolf age—no mercy among men—' "

Merciful heaven! Those words were from the *Elder Edda*. He must be delirious. If he took to raving, how could she hide him? He had eaten some of the curds but none of the cheese. Dropping beside him, she said urgently, "Drink, sir! It will help you."

She supported his head and shoulders, but when he tried to swallow, he was seized with wrenching coughs and began vomiting. Swallowing bile, she held his burning forehead. When he was through, she wiped his face and mouth with the edge of her mantle and tried to think. He was fevered. A brew of willow might help.

Throwing the fouled hay outside, she rinsed the tip of her mantle in the water trough and went back to the kitchen. Dried plants hung from the rafters in the corner where Karin's medicine shelves held jars of herbs, roots and bark. Kristina put willow leaves in a small pot and poured boiling water over them. With this, a jug of water and old cloths, she hurried to the barn.

Vasa grimaced at the willow tea, but she persuaded him to drink it and bathed his face and hands. She thought him younger than Knut, and with a stir of pity wondered what would happen to him with his father and kinsmen dead.

First, he must get over this illness, grow strong enough to travel. She coaxed him into eating some of the porridge, left bread and water where he could reach them, covered him with the sledge robe she had brought him and went to the house, making sure this time that no bits of hay stuck to her skirts. Knut, father said, had falcon's eyes, noting much that others did not, and ought to have been an astronomer.

As always when he had an educated visitor, Magnus

was expounding Copernicus' theories and lamenting that his *Commentariolus* had only been circulated in manuscript and never published. Magnus' copy was his most treasured personal possession, valued even above the astronomical instruments he had devised from Ptolemy's descriptions. He kept the instruments in his observatory tower—a sextant he had crafted from walnut, a brass quadrant, triquetrums, an astrolabe and an armillary sphere.

"No educated man now believes that the earth is flat," Magnus was saying earnestly. "Someday it will be as evident that Copernicus' axioms are correct. The sun, not earth, is the center of the planetary system, and the apparent daily revolution of the firmament is due to the earth's rotation. The supposed yearly motion of the sun is caused by the earth's circling with the other planets around the sun."

Knut grinned, teeth flashing white. Though he spoke to Magnus, his gaze rested quizzically on Kristina, making her so uneasy that she concentrated fiercely on her embroidery. "Since the voyages of Columbus and Vasco da Gama," Knut said, "no one believes you can sail off the edge of the world, kinsman. And if that bold Portuguese, Magellan, brings his ships around the world, any dolt must admit the earth is a sphere. But it will not be so easy to prove the workings of the universe. Heresy aside—"

"Heresy is falseness and lies. Truth cannot be heresy," Magnus said.

"Let us hope that comforts those who are burned," Knut said dryly. "These ideas are intriguing, Magnus, but what real difference do they make? I'm more interested in the revolutions taking place on earth."

"Peasant uprisings?"

"Those are a sign. Feudal society has broken down, though we've never really had it in Sweden. Free peasants own half the land here. Cannon and firearms have changed warfare. Merchants are more powerful now than nobles. Thousands of books come off the presses, spreading knowledge once hoarded by priests and scholars, full of radical notions.'' He leaned forward. ''I tell you, the theses Martin Luther nailed to the church door in Wittenberg three years ago will turn the world upside down no matter what the planets do!''

''Luther!'' scoffed Magnus. ''He's been excommunicated. Of course the Church is corrupt. But—''

''Besides its tenth of all income or produce, the Church exacts a fee for every building raised, every child born, every couple wedded, every inheritance probated. It even collects for burying the dead. It pays no taxes though its holdings are immense. It has supported the Scandinavian Union which made Sweden a fief of Denmark, and when Sweden rejected the Union, Pope Leo interdicted church services here and sent Christian of Denmark to reinstate Traitor Trolle.'' Knut's voice shook with anger. ''As you know, I helped defeat that first invasion and went blithely into the mountains this summer, thinking Sweden safe. By the time I returned, Sture's widow was besieged in Stockholm. It would do no good for me to ride there, but I have thought on it.''

When he learned of the Bath of Blood . . . ! Kristina's hand wavered and the needle stabbed a finger. She wiped away the blood as Nikulaus sprang up, eyes glowing.

''If you take arms against the Danes, cousin, let me go with you!''

''Nikulaus!'' cried his mother. ''What do you know of war?''

''I've helped track and spear wolverines and lynxes,'' he argued. ''My arrows killed the elk that hangs in the smokehouse!''

His mother said with fear and stern sadness, " 'Tis not the same, God wot, to slay a fellow Christian."

Nikulaus laughed loudly at that. "Christian of Denmark would I fainer slay than some poor beast!" He turned to Knut. "If you go, I'll follow, cousin!"

"Fret not your gentle mother, whelp," advised Knut and, at an imploring look from Karin, smiled at Kristina. "Last time I was here you complained when you had to practice on the virginal, but no doubt your efforts have been rewarded. Would you favor me?"

"*I will!*" squealed Margrete, scrambling for the box-like instrument. Everyone laughed but Karin gave her elder daughter a commanding glance.

There was nothing for it but to sit down and plink the keys, but all the time she played, her thoughts were with the hunted man in the barn. As soon as Magnus said, "Prettily done, child. Now let me ask Knut his opinion of Copernicus' statement that the calendar cannot be reformed until the motions of heavenly bodies are more precisely known," she gratefully rose and excused herself, avoiding Knut's searching eyes.

If only she could ask for help! Mother, a skilled herb-woman and nurse, was sent for when anyone fell sick beyond the ordinary. But Vasa was right about the danger he could bring the household. She would have to do the best she could. If he were tracked down, she could truthfully claim that she alone had known about him.

Tracked? With a frightened start, she decided she had better go out at once and make sure no telltale signs could lead anyone to the manor.

II

Nothing looked suspicious. The farmyard muck had frozen the night before, covering the stranger's footprints, and snow in the fields had shrunken to small patches. If he'd had a horse, he must have turned it loose before sheltering in the barn.

The willow drink had helped, for he was resting quietly. She propped him up and he drank water thirstily. To her question, he muttered that he had set his weary horse free when he realized he was getting too ill to ride. Then he had stored his saddle and gear in a wood-cutter's deserted hut and made for the manor below.

He coughed so violently that she thought someone was bound to hear him sooner or later, and then she remembered her mother saying angelica was the best thing for a hacking cough. Telling him she'd be back, she gave him another drink and covered him well.

"You're kind," he said faintly.

"I wish I could do more. I'm so ignorant!"

The corner of his mouth curved. "There can be no one with gentler hands or sweeter voice." He nestled into the burrow, and she thought hopefully that sleep alone might cure whatever had gone wrong with that strong body.

She moved through the stalls—and froze at the figure

looming in the door. "Knut!" she gasped, shrinking back.

"Who's there?" he spoke furiously beneath his breath. "Cry shame on you, cousin! From Lucia Bride to sneaking to a fellow!"

He started past her, but she grasped his arm. "Don't!"

"Is your gallant fit only for luring maidens?"

"It's not what you think!"

He gave a short hard laugh. "Then what is it?"

She clung to Knut and would not be shaken off. "Cousin, come out!" she pleaded softly. "A man lies yonder, but I swear by Mary Virgin there is naught between us. He is sick."

Knut allowed her to tug him outside, but his aspect was frightening and his eyes pierced her like blades. "Sick? Then why is he not in your mother's care?"

Kristina swallowed hard. "She—she doesn't know he's here."

"What troll-tale is this?" Knut demanded. He turned on his heel, cloak swirling. "I'll wager I can quickly cure that jackdaw and your mother won't know about that, either! 'Twould serve your good parents cruelly to learn their daughter trips through the muck to meet some dallier!"

There was nothing for it but to tell him. "Do you know Gustav Vasa?"

Knut's eyes narrowed. "Of course. One of our mines is hard by Vasa holdings, and he came to the university at Uppsala the year before I finished my studies."

" 'Tis Herr Gustav I have hid," she said, and she told him the fearsome news from Stockholm.

When she had finished, Knut's face was stony. "So Christian and Trolle between them have slaughtered the leaders of free Sweden! Thank God they missed young Gustav."

Faint with relief, she said, "You will help keep him hidden?"

"To be sure." Knut frowned. "I'd like to take him to my home, but Danish officials are forever stopping in to give me trouble over the mines. So long as he's helpless, he's best where he is. But when he's hale again . . ."

Fear gripped her. She thought of her twin, burning to fight for his country. There must be hundreds of ardent but untrained lads like him scattered through the provinces. But what could they do against hardened soldiers, many of them professionals who hired themselves to any cause that paid money?

"You've said it yourself," she warned. "Christian has killed our leaders."

"In striking off their heads, he thought to leave Sweden without a head," Knut said with a grim smile, entering the barn. "But Sweden's body is left—and it may even grow another head."

Vasa was sleeping. Knut didn't disturb him but knelt beside him for a few minutes, studying the gaunt young face. When they were outside again, Knut told Kristina to send for him at once if Vasa was discovered. He had already taken leave of her parents. Instead of calling Karl to saddle his horse, he did so himself. But he did not mount. Taking Kristina's hands in his, he pleaded, "Cousin, forgive my wild words. When I heard a man's voice with yours, I was like to kill him."

Indignation welled up in her and she withdrew her hands. "Indeed, kinsman, you do me little honor with your hot fancies! But even had they been true, we are not so close in blood that 'twould be your task to cleanse my honor."

She had the satisfaction of seeing the aloof Knut hang his head. "You are wroth." He grasped her hands, this time so tightly she couldn't pull away. "Put penance on me as you will, but think not to shut me off with icy looks and words, Kristina. I have not forgot, if you have, how when you were Margrete's age I took you up on my horse and fed you wild strawberries and brought you a kitten.''

Her cheeks burned. Did he remember, too, how she had wanted to hug and kiss a tall cousin who seemed to her so wonderful that she was overwhelmed when he noticed her?

''Methinks,'' she said in her coldest, most dignified tone, ''you showed more courtesy as a boy than you do now. After you came home from the university, it seemed you could scarce waste breath on country folk.''

To her chagrin, that withering blast brought only a chuckle. ''I cannot be the first youngling to puff up with the hot air I inhaled at lectures. But if you liked me best, Kristina, when I was a lad . . .''

He turned up her face and kissed her, lightly, fleetingly, just brushing her lips. But it was not a kinsman's kiss. Before she could speak, he let her go and vaulted into the saddle.

A syrup of honey and angelica eased Vasa's cough, and willow kept his fever below the heat of delirium. After a week he could stand shakily with Kristina's support. He grew stronger each day, moving around the barn to build endurance, eating everything she brought him. Knut had come once and they talked a long time. Kristina's heart misgave her as she listened to them. She, too, wanted Sweden free, but not at the price of slaughtered young men.

Meanwhile, the house was cleaned top to bottom, the copper ware polished, festive hangings draped from lofts and walls, and the great red-painted welcome bowl placed on the table and filled with ale or *glögg* for visitors. Brewing and baking never ceased. Besides the special bread baked from the last sheaf, there were sweet breads and sour breads, some wreathed, some round, some baked in the shape of oxen or goats or pigs. Baskets were heaped for the poor, and each member of the household had a trove composed of each kind of bread which could be munched on at will. The air was filled with tantalizing smells of ginger and almond cakes and tarts filled with dried fruit stewed to delectability with honey. When Kristina took most of her fresh baked share to Vasa, he savored the crusty goodness, enhanced with fresh butter, and grinned in a way that made him seem no older or more life-buffeted than Nikulaus.

"Someday, if God grants me time, I must come back to meet your parents and thank them for this succor."

"I pray it may be so."

Her worry must have showed in her face, for he said cheeringly, "I'll soon be gone. Knut is loaning me a horse. I must be about my business."

Her bones turned to water. "You will try to raise the province against the Danes?"

His jaw hardened visibly beneath the yellow mat of beard. "Dalarna first. Then all of Sweden."

She trembled. He said gently, "If you did not want me to do that, Kristina, you should have let me die—or turned me over to the Danes."

Shaking her head, she spoke through hot tightness in her throat. "God knows I want Swedish liberty. But Gustav Ericsson"—she called him by the name of that father beheaded in the Great Square—"do you call men to arms with any hope of winning? Or is it that you must avenge what happened in Stockholm?"

His eyes flashed blue flame, but he did not answer till he seemed to have examined his mind strictly. "I must avenge my father, yes, and have my womenfolk out of prison. But I would not drag others into it unless I believed we could drive out the invaders, lift Sweden's neck from under Denmark's heel."

"But our army was crushed."

"There are stout men in farms and villages throughout the country, who will fight if shown the way. I will do that."

"God help you, Gustav Vasa. You take on you a heavy burden—men's lives, their families . . ."

"I know it well."

He bowed his head. Her heart was wrung for him. Taking one of his chapped hands between hers, she pressed it strongly. "I will pray for you, Gustav. Were I a man, I would ride with you."

He laughed, bending to kiss her fingers. "Nay, grateful I am you are a maid. When I saw you that first time, methought you Saint Lucia herself come with kindly blessings. But I will be right gladsome for your prayers."

Tending him in his weakness had made her forget he was a man. Now, something different in his manner brought that sharp realization. Freeing her hands, she hastily took her leave. She had become most fond of Gustav Vasa, but it was Knut whose voice and eyes had haunted her since Saint Lucia's Day. That made her angry. He thought her a child, but all the same, it was so.

Two mornings later, Vasa was gone. There was no sign he had ever been there except the neatly folded sledge robe. When she picked it up, something fell out, rolled glittering on the hay-strewn earth.

It was a golden ring engraved deeply with the Vasa crest, too big even for her thumb. In any case, she could not wear it. Clasping it tightly, she breathed a prayer for the owner and started to the house. It would seem strange without him, but she was vastly relieved that he was gone.

On the morning of the day before Christmas, the smell of *dopp i gryta* contended with that of boiling *lutfisk* as ham and sausages simmered in the biggest kettle. This "dip in the pot" went back to Viking days, when those ferocious folk fasted at the solstice except for bread and broth. That night the family ate the traditional barley porridge and *lutfisk,* dried cod that had been soaking in lye since Saint Anna's Day, two weeks ago.

Gathered around the long table, family and servants shared the simple fare in the soft glow of the Yule candles which Margrete had lit before the blessing. Kristina savored each bite of the fish with its dilled cream sauce and looked slowly about the table.

Mother had been wearied with making ready for the holy days but her face was serene now beneath the white lace coif. With a shock, Kristina realized that Karin was beautiful, saw her as a woman of gracious slender body which childbearing had only sculpted more softly. Magnus had spilled sauce on his wine velvet doublet and watch chain, but for once his mind was with his family rather than the stars, and a great wave of protective love rose in Kristina as her eyes met his smiling hazel ones. Margrete, raised high on pillows on the chair beside her mother's, shunned *lutfisk* but scooped up several bowls of porridge and whooped with glee when she bit into the single almond cooked in each pot.

Nikulaus tousled her hair. "You'll be rich and prosperous all year, 'Grete! Will you give your poor brother a gold piece?"

"If I get one," she agreed sunnily. "But then you have to pull me on the sled—won't he, mama?"

"I'll pull you," Nikulaus promised solemnly though his eyes sparkled like dark honey with the sun shining through. "On Twelfth Night, we'll race werewolves through the forest and run over the feet of trolls in the mountains. But if the Wild Hunt's out looking for a little gold-haired maid . . ."

Her shriek was a mixture of dread and delight, "No! No, Nik! 'Grete likes to sled in daytime!"

"Then that's when we'll go," he promised before his

mother could chide, and shot a laughing glance at Kristina.

As children, they had played all over the manor and been into countless scrapes. It seemed strange these last years to watch him go hunting or fishing while she worked at the spinning wheel, hackled flax or helped her mother. Still, no matter how long they lived, there would be that special bond. The sharing of their mother's womb and breast.

Sweet Lord, she prayed silently! *Grant us Thy grace. Let us be together on the next eve of Thy birth.*

The sledge carried them over the fresh snow to mass in the darkness of early Christmas morning. The rest of the day was spent at home. Father had translated the gospel into Swedish and read it to them. Kristina played airs on the virginal, including the *Song of Freedom*, written to honor Engelbrecht, the mine owner who had in 1434 led the men of this province to battle for their ancient liberties.

Nikulaus sang and Karin and Magnus joined in.

"Freedom is the fairest thing,
  That man can seek the
      whole world round . . .
  Will you to yourself be true,
  Then love freedom more than gold,
  For honor follows freedom."

Kristina's thoughts went to Gustav Vasa. When Knut came in the morning, leading Stephen's men, perhaps she could snatch a word with him and learn how the young nobleman fared.

The morning after Christmas, young men raced horses from village to village and farm to farm in honor of the saint who had loved horses and had ridden his five—two white, two red, one dappled—on missionary journeys through Sweden almost five hundred years ago. He was slain by heathen men who bound his body on a colt that fetched him home where his grave became a shrine to which ailing horses were led for healing. Magnus said he had become confused with the other Stephen, the Stephen stoned to death with the help of Saul of Tarsus, who later became the great apostle Paul. However that was, Saint Stephen was much beloved and his dawn cavalcade was merrily welcomed and treated to ale or even imported beer.

Knut came early indeed with his shouting, singing horsemen. They roused Kristina, who, shivering, wrapped her hooded mantle around her and ran down to help serve ale and beer from wooden *stanka* three feet high. Nikulaus hastened to join the band. Kristina carried an ale-filled beaker to Knut. He kissed the horn where her hand had held it, raised it and drank her health. When they were out of earshot of the other revelers, he said softly, "Our friend is going to try to raise Rattvik and Mora. He intended to wait outside the churches and tell the folk what happened in Stockholm."

"Think you they will take up arms?" she whispered, between fear and hope.

"If they do, my smiths will forge them."

In a moment, the riders were off again, singing in the faint dawn.

The Yule candle was lit each evening through Twelfth Night. Father said there was nothing to tales of demons and evil creatures prowling the darkness at that time, but Kristina was glad she didn't need to slip down to the barn in the early-falling dusk.

It would have taken a bold werewolf to snatch one of the dancers circling the fiddlers each night in front of the village church. Though the manor contributed food and drink to these merrymakings, there was still plenty for the final feast on Knut's Day, twenty days after Christmas.

Folk came from miles around to drink Karin's famous ale and partake heartily of sausages, hams, venison, cheeses and mounds of various breads. This feast was lit by torches. Magnus had snuffed the Yule candle on Twelfth Night and set it on the shelf till time for spring planting, when it would be rubbed on the plough to bring a good crop.

Knut Jonsson came to the feast on his name day. As soon as they could talk without being overheard, he told her that Vasa hadn't been believed in Rattvik or Mora and had despairingly set off for the Norwegian frontier; but the day after Christmas, a townsman came to Mora and confirmed the hideous butchery. Men from Mora had skied after Vasa and vowed to put themselves under his command. He was now Captain of Dalarna and training volunteers.

"Meanwhile," said Knut, "I'm having javelins forged and plenty of iron heads for pikes. Those work well against cavalry and will serve better than the axes and bows and arrows our yeoman know."

"Is that not dangerous for you with Danish soldiers near?"

"My smiths, Bengt and Nils Martinsson, served in the reformed parliament and hate Danish rule. A guard is posted. If any stranger approaches, he starts whistling and the smiths hide the weapons and work on a plough-share or horseshoe." There was a zestful glint in Knut's eyes. " 'Tis a good time to own iron mines."

A fatal time, more likely. She feared for him, this tall cousin she had worshipped since childhood, but she thrilled with admiration. If men all over Sweden were willing to risk as much, wouldn't they prevail? Christian was at odds with the nobles in his own country. He couldn't forever cross into Sweden to put down revolts.

But while she hoped for her country's liberty, Kristina shrank from devastation and slaughter. Nikulaus would certainly want to join the rebels, and there must be many a lad like him, just coming into man's growth.

She wanted to beg Knut to be careful of himself and not to take Nikulaus, but shame sealed her lips. Every sister, mother and wife felt so. Were she a man, she would go with Vasa.

That night, the table set to the wall and lit by flickering brands, the company performed the archaic Sword Dance. As Kristina passed beneath the flashing blades she felt a wave of eerie premonition and remembered Vasa's words: *"A sword age . . . a wolf age . . ."*

She glanced at the Heaven Sword above the fireplace. Its blade looked red with blood. She muffled a cry, almost ran into Knut's sword.

He steadied her. "What's wrong?"

" 'Twas only torchlight," she whispered.

But she dared not look at the Heaven Sword again.

III

Candlemas passed with the blessing of candles to be taken home and lit for protection in time of storm, but folk feared the news of Christian more than ever they had worried about lightning bolts. He was traveling about Sweden, the rumor spread, having gallows set up in each sizable town. And he was levying new taxes on people already crushed by them. He meant for Swedes to pay for their own subjugation. Knut came in early February that year of 1521. After talking a decent time with Magnus, he suggested to Kristina that they walk in the woods. From the time of Knut's arrival, she had sensed his excitement and burned to question him. As soon as they were alone, she asked what he knew of Vasa.

"I've already sent pikes and javelins to him at Mora, and I go myself tomorrow. We're going to try to take the copper mountain at Falun. Half of my miners will go with me. My smiths will make weapons as long as they can and send them to us." He laughed. "Will you give me a favor, Kristina, to carry along for luck?"

Surprised but touched, she started to undo her necklace, but he stopped her and bent down. "I would sooner have this heather bud, cousin, if you would bear it a while in your bosom and fold it into some bit of ribbon or cloth from an old gown.''

" 'Twill crumble,'' she said doubtfully.

"The memory will not.''

She stared at him and his smile faded. "Do you not know?'' he asked softly. "Can it be you have not guessed?'' He kissed the bud and dropped it down the neck of her bodice. She felt the prickle of the tiny leaflets between her breasts and sweet fire pulsed through her. He towered above her. Feeling swayed by a strong wind, she closed her eyes and waited for his kiss.

"No!'' Knut's cry was anguished. "You're but a child. We'll speak of this if I come back.''

If? He had always been part of her life. She had missed him woefully when he first went off to Uppsala and was crushed when he'd returned so changed, so superior. For him not to come back at *all*—?

"Oh, Knut, you must!'' she cried.

He stroked her hair. "For certain, I must,'' he agreed, "since you say it. Come now. Those thin shoes must be soaked and your parents will think the Wild Hunt's carried us off.''

He kissed her lightly, but put her aside when she clung to him.

Since the day he had futilely appealed to the Dalesmen at Mora between snow-covered Lake Siljan and the dark forests, Gustav Vasa had taken Falun with a few hundred men, and at Dalaborger his men withstood the Danish cavalry and routed the infantry. Miners, peasants and villagers joined him daily to be drilled in the use of pikes and javelins. The crossbow and regular bow they already knew. Nikulaus begged to go, but Magnus, called down from his stars, shook his head.

"You're not yet sixteen, my boy. Next summer, if the struggle is still on, then we will talk of your going.''

Nikulaus' eyes glittered with vexed tears and his voice shook. "Next year! Father, Vasa needs men now!"

"*Men*," Magnus agreed.

Clenching his hands, Nikulaus quelled an outburst by clamping his teeth and whirling away. Next morning he was gone, and Karl with him. For the first time in Kristina's memory, Magnus went into a rage. "He's scarce dry of mother's milk! I shall send a messenger straight to Gustav Vasa and order him to make the young fool come home!"

Tears ran down Karin's cheeks, but she said in a calm voice, "No, husband. Younger men than he from your line and my own have fought for what they believed." She looked at the Heaven Sword on the wall. "Had I known he was going, he would have carried that blade."

Magnus said no more, but he hid his face as he got clumsily to his feet and limped off to his observatory. Karin's gaze turned blind and helpless. She was making a shirt for Nikulaus. It fell from her hands. Kristina ran to her, sinking to her knees. They wept together but Karin's face was buried in her daughter's shoulder, and, in amazement, Kristina found she was comforting her mother.

The earth had thawed enough for ploughing. On the day his men were ready to start, Magnus took the Yule candle stub, warmed it and went to the fields. Kristina went with him. She had always enjoyed this ritual, watching her father rub the candle over the ploughs while the horses, decked in their handsomely carved wooden collars, snuffed the fragrant morning air, jingling their harness. The ploughmen looked gratified that their master, usually up in the clouds, still troubled to remember this.

Magnus rubbed his eyes as they walked toward the house, and his limp was heavier. He must be thinking, as

Kristina was, that this was the first time Nikulaus had not been with them for the benison.

Five days he had been gone, five nights when Kristina believed her parents had scarcely slept, for they looked wearier each morning than they had the night before. Margrete cried for her adored big brother, but Kristina thought no one could feel bereaved in quite the way she did, as if part of herself had vanished, the twin who'd entered the world with her and shared it ever since. His empty place at table made her lose her appetite and wonder with sick fear if she would ever again smile into those dancing eyes.

"At least Knut will look out for Nikulaus as much as he can," she said reassuringly as they passed through the barnyard.

Magnus snuffled gloomily. "I'm sure he'll try. But Nikulaus is so young and rash! I never meant he shouldn't serve his country, but if he had waited . . ." He sighed explosively and slammed his hand on the gate. "No! I hoped he wouldn't have to go! I wanted *my* son to be spared, wanted other men's lives to buy our rights! All I can do now is pray that God will punish me for this selfishness, but protect Nikulaus!"

His gray head pressed against the gate and he began to weep. Kristina was appalled. Before she could think what to do, the sound of horses startled them. A number, trotting smartly.

Magnus got out his handkerchief, wiped his eyes and thunderously blew his nose. "Well," he said, "if we're to have company, I must change out of these muddy boots." His voice was firm, steadying Kristina. As they crossed swiftly to the house neither of them said what they knew, that this was an unusual time for a party of riders to stop at the manor.

The captain, a German mercenary, was a short, plump man with an immense curling moustache that almost hid his thin red lips. Pale blue eyes wandered over Kristina before leaping back to Magnus, who stood near the fireplace with his wife. Three troopers stood behind their leader and five more guarded the doors. All wore swords and carried halberds. Kristina was shocked to see that at least one was Swedish, a red-haired young man from the village who had ridden at Christmas as one of Stephen's men.

"Will you answer, Magnus Haldorsson?" rapped the captain. "Did you shelter and aid the rebellious traitor, Gustav Vasa?"

Magnus swallowed but his tone was even. "I have told you. I do not know the man."

The German jerked his head toward the villager. "This soldier says that near Christmas word ran through the village that someone who looked like Vasa was seen riding away from here."

"I know nothing of it."

The captain grinned unpleasantly. " 'Tis well said that Swedes are stupid, but could even a Swede not know if he had such a rascal beneath his roof?"

Magnus stiffened and did not answer. Spots of red blazed in Karin's white cheeks. Her gray eyes fixed on the informer in a way that made him quail, broad and burly though he was.

"I took food to a sick man who sheltered in our farm," Kristina said, voice faint. "My parents never knew of it." She sent them a glance pleading forgiveness.

Magnus drew himself up. "If our daughter aided one in distress, especially in the season of Our Lord's birthday, then we are glad of it."

The captain puffed out his chest and glowered at Magnus. "Glad to hide a traitor?"

Magnus was silent. The commander took a long step forward. "Will you acknowledge Christian II as King of Sweden and pledge him fealty?"

"He is not rightful king."

"Change your mind or the headsman will change your height."

Magnus sighed. He looked fuddled and old. For a heart-stopped moment, Kristina feared—and hoped—that he would waver. Then his voice rang out clearly.

"Christian is not our king. God save Swedish freedom!"

He seized the Heaven Sword from the wall, lunged at the captain. The blade entered the mercenary's throat as he raised his own weapon. He staggered backward, grasping at Heaven's Gift as halberds and swords hewed Magnus down.

Karin tried to shield him. A halberd cleaved her head. Blood stained her white coif as she collapsed across her husband's hacked and battered corpse.

Screaming, Kristina ran forward but the troopers dragged her back. The red-haired Swede hauled her to a corner. There were other screams besides her own, bruising hands, tearing pain. She bit deep into a wrist, her head was banged on the floor while fingers dug into her throat. She drowned in black and crimson.

When she came slowly, reluctantly, back to consciousness, Hilde was trying to lift her up. "Hurry, child! Hurry! The troopers fired the house."

They had taken the captain's body, though her parents lay where they had fallen and flames were licking at them. Stumbling up in spite of blinding pain in her head, Kristina saw Sophia run through the door with Margrete. Ana was tugging at Karin.

Kristina seized her mother's shoulders. They got her outside, and when they returned, old Hilde had managed somehow to pull Magnus away from the blaze. When he was laid beside his wife, Kristina started back inside, numbly, not thinking, driven to try to save what was already lost—her family—the years of happiness—her life.

Hilde caught her. "Don't, child! The roof's afire! The troopers stole the money chest and the silver cups and your parents' jewelry—everything valuable they could snatch."

But they hadn't gotten the Heaven Sword. Kristina had seen it on the bloody floor. Wrenching away from Hilde, she ran through the flaming portal, bent low at the blast of searing heat, bringing her skirts up to cover her face and hair as she dropped to the floor and crawled toward the sword.

Blood had baked to it. She used her skirts to protect her hand from the hilt and backed away, straightened at the door and sprang out.

Margrete was shrieking. Oh, God, the little one, to see her parents so! Though at least she hadn't seen the slaughter. Kristina sank to the earth and gathered her small sister close, rocking her, murmuring. They were still like that, the terrified serving women huddled near, when the ploughmen came from the fields and, from the village, a few of the braver folk.

The priest gave Magnus and Karin a hasty burial without any lying in state. It was clear he feared the Danes though the troops had gone back to their main command at Västeras. Seeing her beloved parents hastened into the earth, Kristina thought of placing the sword between them. Magnus, the man of peace, the lover of the distant, perfect traversing stars, had used the sword right worthily.

The thought of Nikulaus stayed her. Heaven's Gift was all that was left of their family's past. She must take it to her brother.

Magnus had been kind to his tenants and generous to the village folk. Now they tried to repay him, offering to take in his two daughters and the serving women. Bitterly shamed, the parents of the red-haired soldier begged Kristina's forgiveness.

She looked at them in dull wonder. They hadn't killed her parents, done to her body what she couldn't think of without a wave of maddened terror. She forgave them and did not tell them what else their son had on his soul besides accusing Magnus.

It was her fault. She kept coming back to that, shuddering violently. If she hadn't hid Vasa, he wouldn't have been seen leaving the manor. This weighed on her till she was almost glad she had suffered. But Ana and Sophia had suffered, too.

They sheltered with the blacksmith, who, though a bachelor, had the largest house in the village. A shrewd, massive-chested, black-haired man, Olav Stensson forbore a day while Kristina sat in a daze except for when Margrete crept to her for comfort. Then he gave her a beaker of ale.

"Drink, Kristina Magnusdotter. You need strength. With your brother gone and no close kinsmen, you must save what you can for the little maid and yourself." When she looked at him in dull surprise, he said bracingly, "Come now, young mistress, the house is gone, and the manor sure to be confiscated, but the storehouses bulge and there are good horses and cows in the barnyard, not to speak of pigs and chickens, ploughs, wagons and gear."

"The Danes—"

"Of course! They will take all if you leave it waiting!" As Kristina blinked he explained patiently. Let her give the word and he'd dispose of the supplies, beasts, implements, everything that could be carried away, a cow here, a horse there, scattering the manor's possessions in a way that couldn't be traced. "To aid you and make a good bargain for themselves, folk will dig out a silver or gold piece, some old bracelet or ring or brooch." He hesitated. Cool green eyes softened. "You are most welcome to stay here, mistress. I've been planning to join my cousins with Gustav Vasa as soon as I've sharpened all the scythes and ploughshares. My old mother would be happy of your company."

Forced to think, Kristina did so as if she were considering another person's problems. "You are good, Olav Stensson. I think even the Danes would not imprison a four-year-old, so I would be thankful if my women and the child could dwell in your house till—till I have another place for them. Any money you raise could be saved for Margrete except for enough to pay their keep and the women's wage."

"Ana is going to marry," Olav said. "Her sweetheart wants to help her forget what happened."

The smith went red and Kristina wondered if he knew that the same thing had befallen her. The strange part was that it seemed unreal, a horror blurred and merged with the killing of her parents.

"Then Ana must have her pick from the storehouse for her wedding gift," Kristina said. The decision working at the back of her mind took immutable form. "Save my mare and her gear for me, Olav. I must seek my brother."

"He's gone to Vasa?"

Overwhelmed at what the tidings would do to Nikulaus, she could only nod. " 'Tis no time for maidens to travel about the country," Olav remonstrated with her. "I will go and tell your brother what has happened."

"I must do it myself."

Olav's dark brows drew together, but after a moment he said, "Then I will take you. But give me three days to sell your property and ready the ploughs and scythes."

On the fourth morning, Kristina kissed Margrete and gave her into Sophia's strong arms. The small maid would not inherit the hangings and carved furniture that had graced the manor, or the feast-day garments and jewelry in the chests but Magnus' treasured brass quadrant had been burnished bright as new and the empress's blue sapphire bird from Byzantium had been rescued from the ashes. It perched now in the loft window by Margrete's bed, and in a chest reposed the small fortune in jewelry and coin that Olav had raised. It would keep Margrete and give her a respectable dowry.

Before dawn, Kristina visited her parents' graves. She had already planted roses there. The stone-cutter was working on their markers. Karin's would have a cross and dove encircled by a bridal wreath. On Magnus' would be a representation of God as architect-engineer, measuring the universe with calipers.

Dove or architect, Kristina could not pray to the God who had let her parents die thus. She had paid for candles. Let others pray. All she could do was weep and there was no boot in that. To keep from breaking down as she and Olav rode past the churchyard, she didn't glance toward the new mounds.

Flicka paced briskly, arching her neck as if to flaunt her spun-silver mane. The air was sweet with the first unfolding of new leaves and the sun dazzled off the snowy peaks and tranquil lake, but beyond Margrete's safety, the only comfort Kristina had was that she would see her twin and put in his hands the sword from heaven, scabbarded now from her saddle horn. Further than that, she had not tried to plan.

IV

They met no soldiers. Cattle were being driven up to the mountain pastures, and fresh ploughed fields stretched between forested slopes and shimmering lakes. Miry roads slowed the horses. Stopping at small inns or farmsteads, Olav managed to learn that Gustav Vasa was encamped in a mountain meadow near Västerås, training men who were rallying daily to his three-tongued blue flag with the yellow cross.

The cathedral town with its castle, where in Engelbrecht's time the Danish bailiff had hung peasants up to smoke in the great hall and harnessed their pregnant wives to ploughs and wagons, was the commercial center of the iron- and copper-mining country. Here these metals were traded for goods all too often funneled through the Hansa merchants, beer, cloth, spices and, above all, salt. If Vasa captured the city, he controlled Dalarna.

"I hope I'll be in time for the battle," Olav said eagerly as they turned off down a valley leading into the mountains.

Looking at her companion, Kristina realized that in spite of his serious practicality, he was younger than Knut. He had fulfilled his duty to ready the neighborhood's farming equipment. Now he could soldier. But

Kristina suspected that should the strife last till next spring, he would beg time to return to his anvil long enough to tend to the ploughshares.

She had to smile at that. Olav's quick glance of relief touched her. Courteous and gentle he had been, speaking of this and that thing as they traveled, trying to divert her though he had not seemed put out at her somberness and brief answers. Lighthearted she could not be but she would try to be an easier journey-mate.

So they talked of Engelbrecht as they rode down the valley. After expelling the Danish bailiffs from Sweden, he had called a general parliament in 1435 that included burghers and yeomen as well as lords spiritual and secular.

"A pity Engelbrecht had only a year as regent before he was murdered," Olav mused. "But his ideas lived. Sten Sture the Elder revived them and reigned thirty years. He abolished the law that each town council must be half German, proving Sweden's independence from the Hansa League, masters of the Danish kings, who owed them money." He spat. "We've sent Danes scampering before. With God's grace, we will again, this time forever!"

The Scandinavian unity forged by Margaret in 1397 had profited Denmark but exploited Norway and Sweden, and the unpopular Union had crumbled in the inept hands of her heir. If Sweden and Norway had suffered since the glorious Viking years, Greenland had been abandoned after the Black Death followed famine through Europe and Scandinavia in 1349 and 1350, and Margaret had paid no heed at all to Iceland save to wring from it all possible taxes. That once-proud, independent little republic, long dominated by a greedy Church and Danish officials, had only its wonderful sagas to keep its heritage alive.

"Vasa's story *is* like a saga," Kristina said, glancing at the sword which had its own.

Was that shining history to end with her and Nikulaus, Kristina wondered, or would Nikulaus, in this present struggle, bring a new sheen to the sword?

Olav had not asked before but finally he did. "Is it true? Did Vasa hide at the manor?"

"It's true but my parents didn't know." Almost strangled with guilt, Kristina explained. "And so," she finished, "my parents died for what was my blame only." Olav rode in close. His green eyes smoldered.

"Blame? Had you told Magnus and your gentle mother, would they not have sheltered Vasa?"

"Yes, but—"

"You were trying to protect them."

Her only answer was a smothered sob. Would there ever come a time when she'd see them as they used to be, Magnus rapt with some new discovery in the universe while he spilled gravy on his doublet, mother at the spinning wheel or measuring yeast into the brew? She could keep those images only an instant before that last horrible scene blotted them out. Thank heaven, Margrete had not seen; bad enough that she had heard. But she was so young that surely in the care of doting women those memories would fade to a dim nightmare.

"Kristina," said Olav sternly. "Your father died for our country sure as if he'd fallen in battle. Think of him like that."

"And my mother?" choked Kristina through an aching throat. "Am I to see her as some Valkyrie or *fylgya,* she who never hurt anyone in her life? Nay, Olav! You mean well, but my father delighted in the stars and philosophy. He never wished to be a hero."

"Ay, but he was."

With startled wonder, she knew it was so. Hiding her face, she wept into her mantle, but for the first time, tears

cleansed some of the poison from her soul, and she
reached out to touch the sword.

Magnus, who knew nothing of weapons, had wielded
it as bravely as any who had ever gripped it. He had not
fallen a meek victim. That was what she must show
Nikulaus.

Sentries stopped them at the pass into the meadow but
greeted them warmly when Olav said he had come to join
them and that Kristina was looking for her brother.

"Young Nikulaus Magnusson?" asked one of the
blond giants. "He be over beyond the tents casting javelins." Grinning at Kristina, he added, "Lucky lad, to
have so fair a sister!"

They thanked him and rode on. Vasa's blue-and-
yellow flag whipped above the largest tent. Around it,
leaving room for cookfires where a few women busied
themselves, were more tents, huts and wagons with
sailcloth-covered frames. Men drilled in one part of the
broad field, planting their wickedly pointed eighteen-
foot-long pikes solidly against the ground as if awaiting
an invisible charge. Archers winged arrows toward slender wands. Halberdiers swung their heavy long-handled
axelike weapons into tall tree stumps or warily confront-
ed each other, feinting but not striking home.

A little way off, officers shouted insults and praise at
men feinting with swords. One of the instructors was
Gustav Vasa, unmistakably the commander though most
of his Swedes were half-a-head taller. Kristina wanted to
talk with him, but first she longed to see her brother,
throw herself into his arms, though she dreaded what she
must tell him.

She knew him for his golden hair before she could see
his face. He was hurling javelins at a straw target with a
dozen other men while Knut Jonsson went from one to
another giving quiet advice, showing how to grasp the

shaft, draw back the shoulder. Knut saw her before
Nikulaus did but Kristina ignored his eager cry. Slipping
down from Flicka, she ran to her brother and put Heaven's Gift into his suddenly nerveless hands.

Knut led them off to his own tent and left them alone.
Perhaps he, too, needed time to master his shock, but
when he joined them, he poured ale for them both.
Nikulaus still sat shuddering, head buried in his arms. He
seemed not to hear any of Kristina's words about heroism
or liberty. Knut sat down by him on the straw pallet and
made him drink.

At last Nikulaus spoke, moving his head in anguish,
"If I had been there—"

"You would have died, too," Knut said harshly.
"Much that would cheer them!"

Nikulaus' face looked as haggard as when, two years
before, he was stricken by a grave illness. Father had
worn a hair shirt and mother fasted, praying, till he began
to mend. "I stole off without their blessing—angry I was
with them both!" A sob wracked him. "Now I will never
see them again!"

"In heaven, they know your heart. And even on earth,
I think you were forgiven." Knut looked at Kristina. The
pity in his eyes was more than she could bear.

Faltering, then taking Nikulaus' hand she said, "Indeed, brother, they were not angry. Only sad and fearful."

"That's better?" he demanded.

Knut said coldly, "Is that all you can think of? Your
boy's trick of running off? Have you no care for your sister, what she has endured? Or for little Margrete?"

Nikulaus flinched. He turned to Kristina, his eyes widening in horror as he gazed at her. Shamed blood rose to
her face. He seized her hands in a crushing grip. "Kristina! Did those soldiers—?"

She did not answer. He shook her and she broke loose
in a fit of wild rage. "Would you rather I were dead?"
she flamed. "Would that be more—*honorable?*"

"Sister!"

"Ask me no questions! You were not there! I had to
bury our parents alone, hold Margrete and try to tell her
they are happy now, safe in heaven—that they still look
down and love her! While Danes fired our house, *you*
were playing soldier!"

Quivering, she clamped her jaws shut, fighting for
control. Her fury ebbed. She flung her arms around him,
sobbed against his neck. "Forgive me, brother! I, more
than you, have guilt. I hid Gustav Vasa."

Once again, Knut left them.

Vasa came to them in the long blue twilight, sat with
them silently, his fair head bowed. At last he said,
"Rather would I have been taken, Kristina, Nikulaus,
than have this happen. But I swear it will not be in vain.
We will free Sweden."

"I will give no quarter." Nikulaus stared at Heaven's
Gift, which lay on the pallet beside him. "Not to Danes
or even to Swedes if they fight for Christian."

"God grant you be the one in a position to give quarter," Knut said gruffly, coming in with bowls and bread.
He had moved out of the tent so Kristina could use it.
"Now, cousin, camp fare is not tasty, but you must have
some."

Kristina took a sip of stew and put the birch bowl
down, but Knut picked it up. "A regular bone-bag you
are, lass. Eat, or I'll feed you like a babe."

She had taken only sops, curds or milk since the disas-
ter, but her queasiness gradually subsided as the soup,
thick with barley, warmed her. With that easing, her taut
muscles relaxed. The effort of holding up her head was

too much. It began to droop. This week she had slept only in exhausted snatches haunted by nightmares.

Now she was with Nikulaus; there was nothing more she had to do. Now she could rest. She roused as Knut took off her shoes and she kissed Nikulaus as he bent down to her.

From the entrance, Vasa said, "God rest you, dear friend." She thought Knut covered her; her eyes were already closed.

Physically renewed next morning, though it would be long before her heart ceased to weigh like an icy stone, Kristina cooked porridge for Nikulaus, Olav, Knut and his skillful blacksmiths, Olav's cousins, who had forged many of the pike heads and javelins in use here before they joined the camp.

These Martinssons, Nils and Bengt, had clear blue eyes, red cheeks and hair so fair it was almost white. With curling moustaches and thick beards, they looked proper Vikings. They were glad to see Olav. Now, they said, he could help shoe horses and repair weapons. These five men shared the tent next to Kristina's. The smiths treated her with rough reverence, and she quickly lost her shyness of their bluster and bigness, deciding that, for all their strength, they were overgrown boys.

Already Nikulaus had ripped his doublet, torn his cloak, raveled his hose. After breakfast, she got thread and needle from her pack and settled down to mend his mistreated attire. Nikulaus' eyes were red that morning but he went to drill. Olav had promised to put an edge on the Heaven Sword but Nikulaus was loath to mar the heirloom in practice bouts. He planned to use it in battle.

As Kristina stitched and watched the men training, Knut left his group in charge of a fellow officer and came to sit beside her on the log that served as a seat by the cookfire. Sun had turned him darker, making his gray eyes even more startling. He was thinner, hollows beneath those broad cheekbones almost like gashes. For camp, his black hair was cut short, and there was a bit of curl in it that made him look younger.

"You are skillful with your needle."

"My mother taught me well." She tried to answer naturally but her voice broke.

"I am sorry, cousin."

"Nay." She fought for control. "I have no wish to forget my parents." She scowled at a slatternly patch on his shirt-sleeve. "Who put that blue patch on a white garment with stitches an inch long?"

"I did," he admitted. " 'Twas better than having my elbow tear it wider."

"It cannot long prevent further tearing. Put on another shirt and let me tend to this one."

Sheepishly obeying, he put the despised garment beside her and gazed off toward the lake, as magical a blue as if the sky had dropped to earth there among the pale-trunked birches. "Kristina, Olav says Margrete is well cared for and that you're welcome in his house. But if it is painful for you there, I have a kinswoman who is an abbess. She would welcome you and the little maid till the Danes are driven out. I have spoken to Vasa. He has given Nikulaus and me leave to collect Margrete and escort the two of you to the convent."

Kristina had not yet thought much of what to do. Now she considered Knut's offer, pondered returning to the village, and hesitated. She longed to cuddle Margrete, brush her hair, tell her stories. But at this time, craven as it might be, she could not bear the thought of living where every day she must see her parents' graves, be haunted by the ruins of her beloved home.

"Thank you for your kindness," she told Knut. "I would rather stay here for a while if I may. I can cook and Saint Brigit knows there's no lack of mending."

"A camp is no fit place for a gently reared maiden."

"There are women."

"Yes. Some few are wives. The others . . ." He reddened. "You don't belong here."

"If you want your tent back—"

"You know it is not that. Apart from anything else, we might be attacked."

"So was my home."

"Margrete—"

"Sophia is her nurse. Hilde's brews have brought her through croup and fever and childish ills. Olav's mother gives her ginger pigs and honey cakes."

"She will still miss you."

"Not too sorely nor too long, I trow." Kristina stopped sewing and looked desperately at her kinsman. "Knut, canst not understand? Just now, so near to where it happened, I think I would run mad!" She blinked back tears. "I—I want to be with Nikulaus."

"Ay," Knut said after a moment. "No doubt your twin and you are best together for a time, though I could wish you in a seemlier place." He inclined his head and went back to his men.

Kristina finished Nikulaus' doublet and picked up Knut's shirt, unable to keep from smiling as she undid the huge, sprawling stitches. Knut was a master with the sword and a splendid archer, but a needle did not fit his hand.

She mended, cooked, made Nikulaus and Knut new shirts and was called to anyone who fell ill beyond common camp diarrhea, for word spread that she had nursed the commander himself through an illness that had been near the death of him. In spite of what those other soldiers had done to her, she walked through the camp after a few days without the slightest fear of being rudely addressed or even watched too intently. Vasa's army had gathered reluctantly and only when convinced that Christian's tyranny would be insupportable. They were Dalesmen, lovers of their province with only a dim notion of Sweden, the country; but once determined, they drilled with fervor equal to Vasa's.

Let Christian come hither with his gallows! They'd give him a warm welcome.

The young peasant wives who had accompanied their husbands were shy of Kristina and stopped their laughing chatter when she approached. The other women had their tents at the far end of the camp and kept to themselves. Kristina didn't mind. When she wasn't busy, she wandered in the woods gathering wild greens and herbs, delighting in the larks and swallows that sang and flashed through the trees. Where boots or horses had not trampled, this meadow between lake and mountain was full of flowers. The world was beautiful. That would remain, whatever people managed to do to themselves.

This life, so different from the one she had led, soon seemed natural. Adoringly protected by her camp circle who vied to make her smile or bring her some gift—a carved staff, a shining rock, a bright feather or blossom—she felt both sister and mother to them, except to Knut. The way his gray eyes dwelled on her made her uncomfortable. Did he still think she should be with Margrete?

Vasa often shared their evening meal. He placed great store by Knut's military experience and sound judgment and treated Nikulaus like a younger brother. "You do not wear my ring," he said once to Kristina.

She touched the chain at her neck. "I do, sir, though 'tis too big for any finger."

"Keep it safe." He was only half teasing. "I wish to redeem it almost as much as I hope to see the heels of the last Dane."

"When that happens, my boon will be granted," she said.

Next day, Knut found her wandering among the birches and said. "How is it, cousin, that you have Vasa's ring?"

"He gave it to me before he left the manor." Knut's searching gaze fuddled her.

"He only wished to thank you?"

"Small wonder if he did," she retorted. "He promised to do whatever I asked of him."

Knut's voice was strange. "What will that be, Kristina, if he should wear a crown?"

"I have not thought on it." She shrugged. "He has already vowed to rebuild the manor and restore our lands. He will knight Nikulaus—"

"And perhaps you, too, will have a title?"

Kristina stared. " 'Tis nothing I would seek. But if Vasa is king and offers, what harm?"

"You must surely know 'tis a custom kings have with mistresses."

It took her a moment to understand. Flushing, she sprang to her feet. "Fine talk, cousin! Think shame for such notions!"

Knut blushed, too, but plunged doggedly on. "He is handsome and noble and you saved his life. Women oft love for less. God knows he has told us often enough how he thought you Saint Lucia herself when you found him in his fever."

"Never has he said one word to me that the whole camp might not hear!"

"And probably he will not—till he's in bed with you."

"You have no right—"

"I am your kinsman. Better I anger you than let things

take such a turn that young Nikulaus might have to fight
his lord for your honor.''

Quivering with furious hurt, she said, "Trouble not
yourself about my honor! Methinks I can take care of
what the soldiers left!''

His lips went pallid. "Then they did—''

"They did!'' Tormented by his shocked face, she felt
driven to make him regret his prying. "Vasa has not put a
lustful finger on me, cousin, but if he did, it might help
take away the smell and feel of those others!''

Knut groaned. He caught her in his arms and began
to kiss her. Powerless against his strength, she went
cold and lifeless, the horror of that day at the manor
paralyzing her as it came rushing back. Then Knut was
sitting down with her on his knee, chafing her hands,
pleading.

"Kristina! Sweeting, I am sorry. Don't be afraid . . .''

She pushed away from him, regained her trembling
legs. "Indeed, you teach me to have care.''

Knut rose. His head drooped but he looked straight at
her. "It drove me wild—to think of those men—to think
of Vasa . . . But Kristina, trust this. I would rather die
than hurt you.''

"Except with suspicions and pious warnings?''

He winced, then threw back his shoulders and sighed.
"This is not the way I've dreamed of telling you. But I
love you, Kristina. When the war is over, I pray to
wed you.'' When she gazed at him in astonishment, he
gave a sheepish laugh. "Had you no inkling? When I
asked you to warm the heather in your bodice? I have it
still.''

He would have bespoke her further, courted her and
wooed in honorable, accepted fashion. And she would
have been glad, for it struck her cruelly now that she
had ever thought him all that a man might be. But their
lives had been turned upside down. The manor was

burned; she could be no virgin bride. War lay before them.

Glancing through the birches to the men in the valley whose weapons glinted in the sun, she said painfully, "Would you had told me that day, cousin. This is no time to talk of love."

She left him standing still and silent among the trees.

V

Nikulaus fell in the battle for Västeras, a bolt from a crossbow through his neck. He had been in the forefront of the charge that broke the Danish garrison and won the castle. Vasa fastened his own gold spurs on the dying man's feet and knighted him on the field. The spurs glittered as Knut brought the body to Kristina. When Knut unwrapped the mantle, revealing Nikulaus with Heaven's Gift, Kristina cried out and fainted. As she roused, she did not at first remember, but as she straightened in Knut's arms, she saw her brother.

It could not be! Not Nikulaus. Not in his first battle! She crept to him on her knees, shaking him, calling his name, imploring him to open his eyes. The covering about his throat slipped and she saw the jagged wounds, the source of the blood matting his hair, staining his doublet brown and stiff.

She could not bear it. He had come into the world with her. How could he leave before her? *Mother! Father! He is with you now. You are together. But I am alone.* She could not weep but crouched over the body, fought hands that tried to raise her. Later, she knew dimly that Knut was holding her, carrying her away someplace.

"Kristina. He was so brave." It was Gustav Vasa, triumph damped with grief. "Kristina! He knew we had won!"

She could not speak. Her throat, her body, felt clogged with chilled blood. Knut was making her swallow spirits that made her cough but trickled warmth through her. Sputtering, she tried to evade the cup, but he made her drink, cradling her so that her trembling eased. Thick darkness shrouded her. She was sinking in it and was glad, for beyond the heaviness, Nikulaus was dead.

Nikulaus!

When her fever sank low, she knew she was cared for by strangers, an old woman who reminded her of Hilde and one of middle years with a plump, kind face beneath her coif. She lay in a proper bed near a small glassed window with roses outside. Sometimes she thought her mother tended her and called her name. Sometimes she thought she and Nikulaus were sick again with children's illnesses. When her mind cleared, the truth was more than she could sustain; she slipped again into the haze.

One day that didn't happen. She lay watching the roses and blue sky and slowly faced what she must accept unless she would choose madness. Her brother was dead. He must have been buried already. The army had surely moved on. She sat up, weak and trembling, and set her feet on the floor. When she tried to stand, she fell back and her head swam, but she gripped the bedpost and dragged herself up.

"Bless us, it's time!" The kind-faced buxom woman slipped an arm around her. "Come sit on the balcony and get some fresh air! I'll bring you porridge."

As Kristina ate, Sara Svensdotter explained that Vasa had sought out this place for Kristina, in the home of a prosperous merchant, a member of the town council, who, like most of the citizens, had been glad to have the

Danish garrison defeated. After quartering his severely wounded with trustworthy folk, Vasa was advancing toward Uppsala, seat of the hated Archbishop Trolle, his army swelled with recruits from Västeras and the countryside.

Anticipating Kristina's question, Sara told her that Olav had carried Nikulaus back to be buried by his parents. Stopping off at Västeras on his way to join Vasa, the young smith had tried to tell Kristina that little Margrete was thriving, but the fever had been high that day and Kristina had not heard him.

"Now," said the housewife briskly, handing Kristina a flagon of milk to replace the emptied bowl, "you are welcome to bide with us, my dear, till your good cousin Knut Jonsson can take you under his protection. Or Olav said his mother would be fain to have you with her, and my husband would escort you thither." She patted Kristina's knee. "No need to make up your mind at once. You need time to grow strong."

Kristina did indeed feel boneless. Tears welled from beneath her eyelids. With a soft murmuring of consolation, Sara helped her to bed. "Your brother's spurs and sword, they're wrapped in that mantle on the chest," she said.

Kristina's mouth twisted. Those golden spurs that he died in winning! But the sword— It gleamed in the darkness of her mind as she sank into sleep.

When she woke she knew what she must do. She would take the Heaven Sword and fight in Nikulaus' place. Vasa could not refuse her. With this resolve, she recovered quickly, eating and exercising with grim purpose. Vasa had left money for her and Flicka was in the merchant's stable. She began to take short rides, and one day, after leaving a grateful note on her pillow, with

Heaven's Gift and the spurs hidden beneath her mantle, she simply kept on riding.

At the village where she spent the night, she was able to buy the innkeeper's son's feast-day garments from the innkeeper. These fitted loosely and made riding much easier. With her hair fastened up beneath a slouchy velvet cap, she looked a thin, handsome lad. When she told folk in the farms or villages where she slept that she was joining Gustav Vasa, they blessed her and usually refused money for her lodging.

She found him encamped on the river upon which the ancient city was located, his army multiplied.

When Kristina identified herself to a sentry who remembered her and was taken to Vasa's tent, he looked up from a pile of maps. "Nikulaus!"

She swept off her hat and shook back the tawny mass of hair. Knut said behind her, "By all the saints!" Vasa leaped up and came to embrace her.

"Kristina! Why come you here and in a lad's garb?"

"I brought back your spurs." She handed them to him. "And I have come to fight."

"Fight?" Knut roared. Then his voice dropped. He said fearfully to Vasa, "Her brain is turned. You must let me take her home, Gustav."

"I have no home, nor want one, till all the Danes are gone."

Vasa shook his head. "You are wondrous brave but sure you know it cannot be. You have used a needle, not a sword. You have nursed men, not killed them."

She pulled the chain with ring from beneath her doublet. "I will ask my boon, Gustav Vasa. By this ring and the deaths of my brother and parents, grant that I ride with you."

"You must not!" Knut cried.

Vasa gazed at the spurs in his hands, glanced at the sword belted from her waist. A sudden light flared in his eyes. "Jeanne d'Arc led the French," he said. "We are a people who not so long ago saw battle maids and *fylgyas*. In bright armor, hair flowing, carrying this sword and our banner—would that not be a sight to confound our enemies and hearten our men?"

"If she is slain—" Knut burst out, but Vasa cut in.

"She will not be. The men will rally around her. All she need do is be there and hold the flag high. As soon as men and horses are rested, we start for Uppsala."

With his own hands, Vasa fastened the gold spurs to Kristina's boots. She wore dress armor, patterned in gold with arabesques designed by the great German artist, Albrecht Dürer, of a slight young nóbleman who had joined the rebels. Her hair flowed from beneath a gold-encrusted helm with a white plume, and Flicka was outfitted with gold-studded armoring and silken caparisons.

Knut still detested the idea, but Vasa had quieted him a little by promising that after the first charge, she would keep to the rear. When the trumpets sounded, Kristina steadied the flag which rested in a socket fixed to her pommel and whispered beneath the stirring music to the sword: *"Help us this day. I cannot wield you as Nikulaus would, but lead us with your spirit."*

The two hundred cavalry, armed with axes and maces as well as couched lances, were spread in a line four riders deep. As they moved forward, slowly at first, then at increasing speed, the crescent of alternating pikemen, archers and halberdiers waited behind. Vasa's command to his cavalry was to keep close ranks till they met the Danish horsemen, but after the charge to regroup behind the infantry while archers rained arrows into the confused enemy and pikemen braced against the cavalry. Then Vasa's horse would divide to harry the flanks and drive the enemy toward the pikes.

"After the first charge," he reminded Kristina, "you are to stay behind the halberdiers."

He and Knut were in front of her. The horses moved now at a fast trot. "Liberty!" shouted Vasa, crouching over his lance and spurring forward.

"Liberty!" a thousand voices echoed.

A splintering shock, the ringing smash of maces on armor. Flicka reared, Kristina had all she could do to control her without losing the banner. Then Knut rode against her, turning the mare, and they were racing toward the crescent, veering wide around it.

Danish cavalry thundered into the pikemen. Horses screamed. Javelins found some of them. Halberdiers waded in to finish downed riders. In the milling, shrieking tangle of men and horses, any plan seemed lost, but Vasa's small cavalry, even thinner now, had reformed in two squads and fanned to either side. They did not charge the enemy pikemen directly but swept along the lines, swinging axes and maces, ploughing a line of death down either flank of the densely packed main force.

The Danish vanguard marched forward, but the rebel horse wheeled and meted death as they made for the rear. This time, as panting men and lathered horses rested for a few minutes, Vasa lifted his visor.

"We've done bravely, men, but we're too few for splitting. This time, all follow me! We'll circle around and hit the main body from behind—cut right through their middle. At the same time, our infantry will advance." He grinned. "Be sure you don't hack into any of our brave fellows!"

An audacious plan, but one that made the most of the dwindling horsemen. When it came to foot soldiers, Vasa had as many as the Danes. Kristina urged Flicka toward the commander and begged, "Let me ride with you! The flag should lead the attack!"

"It shows well enough here," he said. Knut rode close and frowned from beneath his raised visor.

"Keep out of the way," he growled. "You could wreck things by making us defend you instead of concentrating on the foe."

Her cheeks burned but she held her tongue. She was no fighter, true enough. But the flag! And Heaven's Gift! She longed to flourish it high for a beacon, unsheathe its virtue. She thought she could hear it singing in the scabbard, awakening amidst the sounds of battle.

Rising in her stirrups, she strained to see, but the melee raged too fiercely. Waves of attackers struck the crescent, which wavered but held, men closing ranks when a comrade fell, contracting the lines but keeping solid. Kristina and the flag were the center beyond which they would not retreat, and she shouted above the tumult, "Liberty! Vasa! God and Sweden!" But the cry in her heart was *Nikulaus!*

Her visor was raised and her hair streamed like another banner. A Danish officer spurred for her, shouting, "Vasa has brought his fetch! Slay her!"

His horse impaled itself on a pike. A halberd knocked the rider to the ground. Kristina saw no more, except the Danes who kept coming and the fury with which they were brought down. She had become, with the flag, what Danes must defeat, what Swedes must defend. Heaven's Gift sang louder. She held her reins in the hand that gripped the socketed banner, and drew the sword.

Most of Vasa's men knew its story, for the saga had been repeated around the campfires after she brought it to her brother. The ancient blade caught the fire of the sun and the burnished hilt gleamed brightly.

"The sword from heaven!" Olav cried, swinging his halberd. "The Heaven Sword fights with us!"

"The Heaven Sword!" roared Nils and Bengt. They hewed like berserkers of old.

The Danes fell back. Bursting through their center rode Vasa and Knut. "Close on their sides!" Vasa shouted to the foot soldiers.

A crossbow bolt dented his horse's armor, and a Danish pike thrust under and drove into the stallion's entrails. They spilled out as he reared, striking up with his hoofs before he fell. A mace knocked Vasa from the saddle. Knut spurred in front of him but Danes swarmed from all directions. If they could kill Vasa . . .

Kristina shouted and rode forward. "Vasa! Sweden!"

Halberdiers surged after her, cleaving away Vasa's attackers as harvesters scythe grain. She held the flag above the fallen commander. The battle formed around them. Vasa was on his feet again. Olav had captured a riderless horse and led it up. Once more in the saddle, Vasa gave his war cry. Kristina stayed just behind him as he cut through the Danes like one immortal.

"The fetch!" cried a Dane. "She guards him! He cannot die!"

Retreat was sounding. Vasa's army pursued the fleeing Danes to the gates of Uppsala. The battle was won.

So was the city. That night Archbishop Trolle fled. The garrison surrendered, the Swedes joining Vasa, the Danes allowed to withdraw. Vasa was joyful he had not been forced to damage this lovely old city with the university he had attended and twin-spired Gothic cathedral boasting splendid paintings and carvings and the remains of Saint Eric, Sweden's patron saint, entombed in a silver shrine.

This was a great triumph. Though power had been shifting to thriving Stockholm, Uppsala was the ancient heart of Sweden, and to send running the hated Archbishop gave the men such a taste of the sweetness of victory that though they mourned their comrades, they were eager to follow Vasa even to Stockholm.

He was not ready. Ensconced in a mansion where Kristina was helping minister to the wounded, he called a meeting of his officers and invited Kristina to attend. ''For,'' he said with a rueful laugh, ''had you not raised flag and sword above me, none of us would be here.''

Except to growl that God must sure look out for fools or she'd have been killed, Knut had said nothing to her since the battle, and he ignored her now, listening with a frown as most of the leaders urged an immediate march on Stockholm.

''The men are jubilant,'' cried Jan of Berga, the young count who had loaned his armor to Kristina. ''They feel we cannot lose while this maiden holds the banner and the Heaven Sword.''

''And we want them to go on feeling that way,'' Vasa retorted. He had let his beard grow and no longer looked a fresh-faced boy. Command had etched lines in his brow, and he wore his arm in a sling; it had been injured in his fall. ''We have not cannon to breach Stockholm's walls and a long siege would drain our energy and supplies. We'll push eastward and gain a port through which we can be supplied, then take the other fortresses. Stockholm will be left like a severed head without a body.''

He unrolled maps, showed where the Governor of Värmland was raising forces against the Danes, and where a friend who'd escaped from the Bath of Blood was leading attacks from the forest of Smaland. Finnish privateers were already harassing Danish supply ships, and Finland was sure to join the rebellion if there was a chance of success.

"The commoners of Västergötland are pressing their governor to declare against Christian," Vasa concluded. "It's an easy matter to set timber castles afire inside their log palisades by lobbing red-hot iron balls on them or fireballs made of willow, saltpeter, oil and brandy. But Stockholm, Kalmar and Alvsborg castles are all stone. They will not fall to men armed with pitchforks and bows."

"Then what do you propose?" asked Knut.

Without looking up from the map, Vasa said, "I've friends in Lübeck."

"Hansa merchants who already grind us and control our trade?" Knut cried. "Ask their help and you'll be their vassal."

There was an echoing chorus. Vasa reddened but said no more on that head, going on with plans for his thrust toward the Baltic. Kristina braced herself to oppose a command that she stay in Uppsala, but Vasa did not even suggest it. That was left for Knut, who, after the other men were gone, lingered to help Vasa roll the maps.

Kristina started out but Knut said, "Wait." His gray eyes inspected the gown she wore. "May I hope that you have resumed your right mind along with proper dress? There's enough for you to do here, God knows, tending the wounded."

"You do not command!" she flashed.

"Indeed not, or you would be safe in Västerås or with Margrete!"

She whirled toward Vasa, who stood watching with a quizzical smile. "Gustav! Let me stay with you until the Danes are gone!"

"I think it would be hard to march without you now." He crossed to her and took her hand, kissing it. "Thank you for my life. In truth, I begin to believe you are my angel, first on Lucia's Day, then in battle. But you are free to stay in this mansion or go under escort wheresoever you will.''

She lifted her head. ''Nikulaus would go with you.''

''So be it.''

Knut stared furiously at them both, then swung about and strode out, boots resounding on the polished floor.

''He behaves like more than a kinsman,'' Vasa mused, studying her. She suddenly felt he was too close and stepped back a pace. ''Forgive the question, but are there vows between you?''

''Till what my father and Nikulaus died for has come to pass, there can be naught between me and any man.''

Vasa laughed at that. ''Said like a true Valkyrie.''

He bowed and let her pass, but something in his gaze, a deepening of his voice, filled her with certainty that he would not sleep alone this night—and that, had she but smiled or cast down her eyes, he would have tried to win her to his bed.

This did not long dismay her. Vasa would never roughly woo her, and when he considered, he was sure to know that one who shared a commander's couch could not later carry his flag. Vasa would prefer the standard-bearer to a mistress. And to her he had become not really a man, but Sweden's soul.

She had a mind to visit the old church built on the ruins of the great temple once sacred to Frey and Thor and Odin, walk the same paths that Kati, Frey's priestess, had traced so long ago and take Heaven's Gift there. Next day, after making the rounds of the wounded, who seemed heartened by her presence, she asked Olav if he would go with her the short journey to Old Uppsala. He brought their horses, and they were soon gazing at the three huge grave mounds of buried kings descended from Frey himself.

The church, though of stone, was built like a stave church, with slanting gables at several levels. Before Uppsala Cathedral was raised, Swedish rulers had been crowned here. Kristina and Olav went inside. She placed the Heaven Sword on the altar and prayed in that age-hallowed place that Sweden would be free.

VI

Christian, *believing he had executed all the Swedes who could cause* him trouble, had gone to the Netherlands that summer to plot policy with his Habsburg relations while the clergy and nobles of his own country intrigued against him. Meanwhile, in Sweden, province after province joined with Vasa, but there was little his peasant army could do against the few remaining sea-supplied stone fortresses, especially the principal city of Stockholm.

His forces held virtually the rest of the country, though, and late in August representatives of the Sten Sture party joined with burghers, yeomen and miners in electing him regent in Vadstena. Kristina stayed in the cloister where her mother had once learned all the womanly skills from Saint Brigit's good nuns.

Since there was nothing more to be done against the coastal fortresses, most of the yeomen went home to their fields and families, hoping to bring in a good harvest, and Kristina asked leave to visit Margrete.

This was gladly given, and Vasa detailed Olav and his cousins, Bengt and Nils, to accompany her. "For I can't lose my luck," the regent said. "Do you mind, Kristina, that 'tis not a year since you found me in the barn?"

Lucy light. And she had come back from him to the *lussebiten,* all the gathered family, before setting off for the village with her torch-bearers. Nikulaus had worn that red beard and croaked like a very troll. Only eight months ago!

She had to turn to hide her tears. Vasa came to put his arm around her, caress her cheek as she hid her face on his shoulder. "I'm sorry—I didn't think," he muttered. She drew away and smiled proudly.

"My parents and brother must be right joyful to see what you have done. A year from now, who knows? The Danes may well be gone entirely."

"God send it," Vasa said. "Wait, I have something for you to give your little sister." He rummaged in his gear and produced a brightly painted carved wooden horse with stiff straight legs. "A Dala horse for a Dala lass! And give her my kiss."

Olav's mother was delighted to see her son and glowed when he told her of Vasa's triumphs. She was happy to see Kristina, too, once she understood the other had not come to take Margrete away.

Cosseted by the mistress, Sophia and old Hilde, it was a wonder Margrete was not in need of the switch, but indeed she was the light of the house. Sophia told Kristina that she seldom had nightmares since she had been given a kitten who was now a majestic golden-eyed beast with the softest dark-gray coat.

Margrete loved the wooden horse and promptly named it Vasa. She had grown inches since Kristina saw her last and was no longer chubby and cuddly, though she had a most sweet way of going around the room of an evening to kiss everyone good night. When Kristina went to her family's graves, she found anemone and hepatica scattered on the grassy mounds beneath the young rose bushes.

"Oh, yes," Hilde said later. " 'Grete goes there often and sings and talks to the master and mistress and her

brother. She's sure they hear her. And who's to say they
don't?''

Kristina was thankful that the child had made peace
with what had happened, but she could not. Being back
in the village, close to the graves, brought everything
flooding back. She had not dared go to the ruins of the
manor. In these last months she had seen burned houses
enough, and many dead.

Tormented by memories, after a week she asked Olav
and his cousins if they would mind returning with her to
Vasa. They were back in camp before the leaves fell.

Vasa greeted her warmly. Knut watched with narrowed eyes. The first time they spoke in private, he said,
''I had hoped the sight of the little maid would call you to
your senses, but it must be you are drunk with playing
Vasa's *fylgja*.''

She saw those graves, those three graves. What did he
know about lying alone in the night, seeing it all happen,
knowing she had caused it by shielding Vasa? What
could he know of feeling that with Nikulaus, one half of
her had died, the half with her heart?

Unable to speak, she turned to go. He stood in her
way. ''Kristina! By all the saints, you are like a *gast,* one
of the cursed dead who cannot rest.'' He seized her
hands. ''Where is our Lucia Bride? Where is the maiden
who gave me a heather bud in the spring?''

''As dead as my mother and father and brother.''
Didn't he know that if she didn't wall herself in ice, she
would shatter to bits? ''I have the sword. That is all I
have.''

''Margrete . . .''

''Margrete does very well. She has a sunny heart.'' As
he stared at her, she began to tremble. ''I should not be
with her,'' she said painfully. ''I am a *gast,* you have
said truly.''

She went from him and then she wept, but it did not release her.

Early in the new year of 1522, the fortress of Stegeborg fell to Vasa. The commander, a German mercenary named Berend von Melen, immediately offered to fight on Vasa's side. The friendship that developed between the regent and the swaggering, boldly handsome professional soldier increasingly troubled Kristina. Though he never said so, von Melen's insolent smile made it clear that he believed her a trollop. Vasa still insisted that she come to his councils, but the easy camaraderie between him and his old supporters had vanished.

Regent he was in name, but he must capture Stockholm before he could rule and begin the almost impossible task of restoring order to the war-ravaged country. With so many of Sweden's leaders killed in the Bath of Blood, it would be a formidable undertaking to constitute a parliament and find capable governors and sheriffs. In his desperation to end the chaos, Vasa began to speak once more of asking for help from the Hansa merchants of Lübeck.

" 'Tis the only way to take Stockholm,'' he argued stonily over the protests of Knut and his old officers. Von Melen supported him in this.

Overriding the warnings of Dalesmen who had formed his first army, Vasa began negotiations with Lübeck. In April, he called a council to declare triumphantly that he had a firm promise from Lübeck of 750 seasoned men-at-arms with weapons and supplies, to be transported on ten men-of-war which would thereafter undertake to cut off supplies and troops bound for Stockholm, Kalmar or Alvsborg.

Kristina gazed at von Melen and withered inwardly at the thought of foreign mercenaries, like those who had killed her parents, following Vasa's banner.

When the council was ended, she went to Vasa. "Gustav, I am going home."

He stared at her. "Why? Or is it too much for the regent to ask?"

"I will not carry a banner followed by foreign troops."

Vasa crimsoned and gnawed his lip. Von Melen laughed softly and got lazily to his feet. With an exaggerated bow to Kristina he said to Vasa, "I know, sire, how you value this maiden and her sword. She is a legend to your men. Since I stick in her throat, I will gladly take myself out of the country if that is your wish."

"Nay. My peasants have fought well, but they have ever their hearts and minds on their families and farms. I must have those men-at-arms, those warships and you for my general, to crack these last hard nuts." He looked sorrowfully at Kristina. "Can you not see that, my fair friend? I must take Stockholm before peace can come to Sweden, and I cannot be over-nice about how I do it."

Relief and sadness showed in Knut's eyes. Kristina inclined her head. "I cannot judge what you should do, Gustav. I only know what I cannot."

"Then go!" he shouted, but before she reached the entrance, he came after her, and shook her hand. "I will not try to persuade you. But, oh, Kristina! Beyond all others, I had hoped to have you carry my banner into Stockholm."

Tears filled her eyes. "God be with you. I—I will always pray for you."

He let her go. "Remember," he said a bit coldly, "that you still have a boon of my ring, though it will be some time before I have gold to spare."

"You have confirmed my possession of the manor," she said. "That is all I need."

He gave her a man's look, direct, reaching depths she

had kept buried this whole long year. "We shall see."
He stepped aside and let her depart.

He would not take back the golden spurs. "Save them
for your son," he told her. "I hope to knight him myself
and fix them on his heels."

Jan of Berga, to whom she had returned his splendid
armor, Knut, Olav, the Martinssons and many others escorted her beyond the fortress and bade her farewell with
husky voices and moist eyes. Then they all turned back
except Knut, who rode along beside her. She noticed for
the first time that he carried a pack behind his saddle.

Hesitating gladness warmed her. Could it be . . . She
was so tired of war, of campaigns and marches. Still not
daring to hope, she made an effort to keep her voice
even. "Cousin, whither are you riding?"

He gave a rueful laugh. "Canst not see? Do you think
however vexed he is that Gustav would let you journey
alone halfway across Sweden?"

Her pleasure shriveled. "Oh. He sent you."

"Nay. I asked to take you home and he consented."

"Then—you are not staying in Dalarna?"

Knut said heavily, "I like these mercenaries no better
than you do. Von Melen is a rascal who changes masters
at a nod, and I doubt not Gustav will repent trusting him.
But, Kristina, 'tis true what Gustav says. He cannot take
Stockholm without aid from Lübeck. He is doing what he
must—and I must fight beside him till the Danes are van-
quished."

Feeling that a reproach, she said, "That may be what
you must do, but it is nothing for the Heaven Sword."

He grinned crookedly. "I should be overjoyed that
you have come to your senses. There has not been a
charge in this whole year when I have not been near out
of my wits with fear for you. But sorry I am, sweeting,

that you will not share the triumph you have earned when we ride into Stockholm.''

''Will you come home after that?'' she asked in a small voice.

He rode close and the glow in his gray eyes melted the hard crust around her heart. She breathed more deeply, freely, than she had since that wretched day at the manor when her beloved, safe world had ended.

''Do you want me to?''

She nodded.

He laughed and leaned over for a swift kiss that sent a warm flow of delight surging through her. ''I will come, then. The day that Gustav has Stockholm's surrender.''

Their journey northward through meadows golden with coltsfoot and brilliant with anemones was filled with birdsong. She could not have contained her happiness had he been going to stay with her. Even knowing he must go back to battle, they laughed like children, glorying in love that had grown silently, strongly all the time she was denying it to carry Vasa's banner. When they rested in the forest, he cradled her in his arms and kissed her till they were both breathless and dizzy with the sweet pain of desire, but he would not possess her.

''You will have your bridal wreath,'' he said.

''Knut! Who knows what may chance—''

''Who, indeed?'' He kissed her and tightened Flicka's saddle before he helped her mount. ''I have waited for you to grow up, waited for you to change from battle maid to woman. Now we must wait till we can wed in honor and I can be there to father our children.''

It was not maidenly to argue, yet she did, clinging to his sinewy brown hands. ''Knut! Could we not marry before you go back to the army?''

''What if we had a child and I did not come home?''

''Then I would have something of you to love.''

"It may be years before this war is over. What if I come back crippled?"

"I would rather have you like that than any other whole man."

He pressed her hands to his face, covered the palms with kisses. "I should not let you take such risks. But to know you're mine—to cheer my heart with that . . ." He swallowed. "Let me think."

Laughing, she leaned down to kiss him. "Yes, think! Of how much I love you!" His dark eyebrows drew together but she knew that she had won.

Margrete, nearly six, was growing thin as she shot up. She was shy of Kristina for a little while. This stung, but by the time Kristina and Knut had given their news while devouring curds and bread, Margrete had pulled a bench close to her. At first opportunity, she asked, "Are you staying home, Kristina?"

At Kristina's nod, the little girl gave her a breathless hug. "I'm glad!"

Holding her sister, Kristina understood that in spite of the love surrounding her, Margrete had missed her family. Smoothing the gold braids, Kristina laughed. "I'm glad you're glad. And someday we'll have a house again."

"A house?" Margrete frowned.

" 'Grete," bade Hilde, "get your embroidery to show your sister."

When the hanging with the boyish Saint Stephen and his foals had been thoroughly admired, Knut proposed that they walk to the manor.

Kristina flinched. But she was going to live here now. She had to see the ruins before she could start thinking about how to rebuild. For the time being, one of the storehouses might be furbished into living quarters.

Walking between Knut and Margrete, Kristina was

amazed that her sister tugged impatiently as her own feet
dragged and strength drained from her knees.

Just beyond this bend— She stopped and gasped.

A house! Not the manor, but a timbered two-story
dwelling of ample size. Before it stood the family tree,
the mighty oak that Magnus and generations before him
had nourished with ale on feast days.

"See!" cried Margrete, dancing up and down. "We
have a house! Hurry and look inside!" She ran ahead
while Kristina looked at Knut. He was smiling.

"You knew!"

"Olav told me what was afoot. Folk hereabout loved
your parents and have been mightily proud of you for
bearing Vasa's colors. The men raised the building and
the women have . . . well, you'll see."

She scarcely could, for tears that filled her eyes as he
opened the door ornamented with wrought-iron mount-
ings and looked into a main room decked for a feast with
linen wall hangings, bench cushions and covers brilliantly embroidered with flowers, birds, trees and animals.

Shelves covered one wall. On them ranged horned
wood beakers, a few goblets of Venetian crystal, gleaming copper bowls and platters and many beautifully
carved and painted wooden bowls, tankards and jugs.

Every inch of a sewing chair was swirled with leaves
and flowers, and so were the sides of the benches and
table supports. A wrought iron candlestick stood in the
center of the table beside the huge welcome bowl. On a
shelf above the fireplace was Magnus' polished brass
quadrant. Someone had lit a fire in the hearth to take
dampness from the air, and an iron kettle hung there,
ready for use. A large flat stone, where hot pans could be
placed, was by the hearth. Carved stairs led to a half-loft
and Margrete ran up them. "This is my place!" she
called. "They carved horses on my bed just the way I

wanted, and the mattresses smell sweet—there are rose leaves in the straw!"

A shuttered bed was built against one wall. Besides two block chairs carved from logs and brightly cushioned there was an armed, high-backed master's chair. A spinning wheel stood by the diamond-paned window, and on a bench beside it, handsomely carved as if made for a sweetheart, were a skutching knife to prepare flax for hackling, the comb with which it was done, several distaffs and a mangle. The chest built into the sewing chair was outfitted with brass needles, shears, skeins of yarn and thread wound on carved spools, and a loom stood near the fireplace.

Knut grinned at Kristina. "The good folk seem to hope you haven't forgotten women's arts."

"If you have," said Margrete seriously, "I can teach you." She tugged at Kristina. "Come see the chamber!"

This room had a large shuttered bed made up with wool coverlets and feather pillows. Three beautiful chests were each painted and carved by a master hand and embellished with wrought-iron hinges and clasps. "Look inside!" Margrete pleaded, dancing up and down in eagerness.

As Kristina raised the lid of the largest chest, decorated by a tree full of birds, a sweet odor of roses drifted out of the neatly folded layers of sheets, towels and pillow casings, dozens and dozens of finest linen, some worked with embroidery. Since washing was only done in spring and autumn, an ample supply was a necessity. Each article represented the growing of flax, the tedious preparation before it could even be spun into thread, the weaving and hemming. All the linens Kristina had prepared for her dower chest had been destroyed in the fire, but this supply rivaled Karin's. Staggered by the amount of work and caring that had gone into the gift, Kristina held back from opening the other chests, but Margrete urged her on.

The red one was full of coverlets, patterned and plain, and two sledge robes worked with birds and deer. The claw-legged chest carved with Gustav Vasa's sceptered lilies, Kristina's name and the year, opened to reveal carefully folded garments, some for Margrete, others for Kristina, many trimmed with lace as exquisite as that Karin had learned to make at Vadstena.

Kristina would not have gone through the whole trove, but Margrete burrowed down, almost toppling into the chest, and tugged at a sheet-wrapped bundle. "You have to see this!"

Bridal finery of the treasured kind passed on from mother to daughter! A red satin belt with silver panels showing the wedding at Cana, a velvet bodice with silver "eyes" for the lacings, a lace blouse and full red skirt. Margrete produced a copper box and opened it to Kristina's cry of wonder.

The parish bridal crown! Of silver gilt, with points set with precious stones, it was worked with doves and roses. Wealthy families had their own crowns—Karin's had been stolen by the looters—but each parish had one that all brides could use. For this to be here, the people must have agreed to give up this splendid treasure.

"I can't keep it," Kristina whispered. "But, Knut, I would fainer wear it than even my mother's!"

There was other wedding jewelry in the copper box, treasures given by every family of any means—silver brooches, chain, rings and neck ornaments. When Knut wed Kristina at the church door, there was not a villager or one of Knut's miners who did not laugh and cry, and none who did not contribute to the great feast held in Olav's house. When Knut led Kristina in the dancing before the church, she believed her parents saw and blessed them—and Nikulaus.

Eyes brimming, she whispered to her bridegroom, "We must not dance too long!"

"So eager?" He smiled.

She nodded. It was true. His loving was like balm after this year of war, of nerving herself to what was not her nature.

Already she dreamed of a lad named Nikulaus who would wear the golden spurs and a daughter who would look at her with Karin's eyes and smile. She hoped that neither would ever have to use the Heaven Sword, that it could stay above the fireplace generation to generation, taken down only for burnishing.

After the bridal pair had danced with everyone able to move to the fiddlers, they were escorted home with flaring torches. Hilde, Sophia and Olav's mother took off Kristina's festive attire, helped her into a pure white lace-trimmed gown and left her seated against the pillows. Knut's groomsmen saw him to the door. Then laughter and voices moved toward the village, and the lovers were alone in the house that would be their home, together in the great bed where their children would be shaped in the fruiting of their love.

VII

Kristina and Knut had a single brief but gloriously happy week before he left. She missed him sorely and prayed often for his safety but did not mope. After a year of hardening her heart to death and suffering, it was blessed to love little Margrete and dream of Knut as she went about her tasks in the house built by her neighbors and filled with their affection. Knut had worn a borrowed wedding shirt. Now she made him one, working her love into every stitch of the embroidery that would adorn collar, cuff and front.

She had not progressed far before she found that indeed she would have his child, and put aside the shirt to work on small garments. Hilde and Sophia joined her in this, and Margrete, excited to near ecstasy, said she would give her doll to the baby and began fashioning tiny clothes from scraps.

Knut had bought several good cows, so there was butter and cheese to be made. Rurik once again strutted in the barnyard. Knut had bought Margrete a pony, and the two sisters went riding until Hilde warned Kristina that she had better stop until after the child was born. People from the village or farms stopped by frequently and bespoke the household kindly when they came to church. Though Magnus and Karin had been kindly and generous, there had been some reserve between manor and village, but the people now looked on Kristina and Margrete as their own.

In spite of this peace, dread gripped Kristina each time a bit of news trickled in from outside. In June, Vasa had gotten his warships from Lübeck, loaded with German mercenaries, weapons and supplies. While these ships engaged the Danish and harassed the embattled fortresses, von Melen, under Vasa, was besieging Stockholm. In October, the warships captured a convoy of soldiers and supplies bound for the city. Kristina began to hope Knut would be home before their child was born, but that was not to be.

The women and Margrete had just returned from Candlemas service, crude tallow dips blessed instead of the tapers that could no longer be obtained because of the war, when Kristina felt as if a vise tightened within her before it let go. When the cramps continued, she told Hilde. Sophia took Margrete to stay with Olav's mother at the same time that she summoned the best midwives of the village.

It was a long ordeal. Between the pains, women walked with Kristina. They bathed her face and gave her brews. All were kind and encouraging, but Kristina longed for her mother even more than she wanted Knut. Karin would know what to do, or even if she didn't, it would help so much to feel her embracing arms, be able to trust those gentle, skillful hands.

The night was black with pain. "Is something wrong?" Kristina panted to Hilde. "Am I going to die?"

"No, lamb," Hilde soothed, bathing her face and giving her a pungent tea. " 'Tis only that this is your first babe. The wee one will come when you're ready.' "

It was twins that came at dawn, a bright-haired boy and a dark little lass. When they were placed in her arms, Kristina could scarce believe it. Pressing her lips to the fragile skulls, with their soft fuzz of hair, Kristina thought this must be how Karin had felt with her twins and smiled tearfully, to imagine how amazed Magnus must have been. If only they could see these perfect tiny beings, so fresh, so fair, with eyes that still dreamed of heaven! And Knut, when he returned, wouldn't he say she had done well in their time apart?

In spite of poignantly missing her parents and brother, and yearning for her husband, Kristina overflowed with joyful pride and a tenderness that swept away the last hard shell that had encased her after Nikulaus' death. Her beloved dead lived in these children. Already she could see Knut in small Nikulaus' features.

She wished she could consult with Knut about names but was sure he wouldn't mind if she named them for her family and worked in the names of his father and mother. Hilde and Olav's uncle acted as godparents. When they returned from the church, the boy was Magnus Jon Nikulaus and the maid Karin Birgitta. By the time for her churching forty days after the birth, Kristina could walk without aching, and her milk, insufficient at first, was now abundant enough to nourish both little ones.

The twin's godfather had one cradle ready, and by the time they grew too large to share it, he had carved one for Karin showing unicorns feeding among lilies. Margrete rocked the babies for hours, crooning, and did not shrink from changing their clouts. Apart from the impossible wish that her mother could have helped with their nurturing, Kristina's pleasure in her children was marred only by regret that Knut was missing this time of their milky-breathed innocence. How much longer could the siege go on?

Harvest was beginning, and the twins were six months old when Knut himself brought the first tidings of great events. As he held the twins in one arm and Kristina in the other, and Margrete on his knee, he told how Vasa had been elected king at a council in Strängnäs, June 6, and how Stockholm had surrendered June 17 that summer of 1523.

"Then Sweden is free of Danes!" Kristina exulted.

Knut shook his head. Though he was only twenty-eight, war had taken a toll. Deep lines were graved from nose to mouth. There was white in the black hair at his temples. "Kalmar still holds out. The king has sent Berend von Melen and his mercenaries to capture it. But I will not serve under that faithless man. I kept my vow to see Gustav ride into Stockholm. Then, swift as I could, I've hurried home to you." He laughed, marveling at the twins. "For sure, sweeting, you've wasted no time in making me a man of family!"

"The better to keep you home," she whispered.

After he had steamed himself clean in the bathhouse and eaten, Hilde tactfully suggested that Margrete help her take the twins out to play in the grass. Knut gazed at Kristina in a way that sent sweet wildness building in her. He took the coif from her hair and ran his fingers roughly, cherishingly through the strands before his mouth found hers. Catching her up as if she weighed nothing, he carried her to the great bed where for so many nights she had missed him. As he caressed and held her, swearing her body even fairer and sweeter for bearing the children, she could not believe her happiness, that he was truly home. Truly in her arms.

An aged relative had done his best to run the mines while Knut was away. Now, in order not to be constantly riding over, Knut put Bengt Martinsson in charge. His brother, Nils, had stayed with Vasa's army, as had Olav, till Kalmar should be taken.

Once the mines were running in proper fashion, Knut set about replenishing the manor cattle and goats. He put new heart into the tenants, swinging a strong scythe in the reaping. Magnus had been loved but some took advantage of his otherworldliness. It was soon clear that Knut was fair and generous but no one to trifle with. Because he had been in the king's councils, and now directed the manor, he was soon the man to whom folk came for advice and help.

He also spent considerable time in defending Vasa. The Dalesmen had expected that once the crown was on the young leader's head, peace would bring prosperity. Instead, Vasa had raised taxes higher than they had ever been to repay his staggering debt to Lübeck.

"These German traders are worse than the Danes!" Bengt complained. "They buy our butter, hides, copper and iron dirt-cheap but charge so dear for English and Netherlands' cloth and Danzig beer that only the rich can afford them."

"We can brew ale," Knut said. "We can weave our own linen and wool."

"But what about salt?" Bengt growled. "That we must buy and the Lübeckers squeeze us hard for it!"

" 'Tis difficult," Knut admitted. "But I think we can trust Gustav to send the Lübeck merchants packing once his debt is paid. He means to unite Sweden—make it strong enough to discourage invaders."

Bengt snorted. His big hands, blackened from the forge, tightened on the beaker of ale Kristina had fetched him. "Who wants to be united? We Dalesmen have made and unmade kings! We brook no nobles here. The king may not travel through this province without our safe-conduct."

Knut was silent for a long time. Clearly, he was torn between loyalty to his province with its ancient liberties and hope in the king. "Vasa will not ask for safe-conduct. But given time, he will make Sweden strong."

"Devil take Sweden and its kings!" Bengt flashed. "I be a Dale man!"

Such murmuring increased through the next year as taxes grew heavier and salt scarcer. Nor was the mood of the Dalesmen improved by learning that the king had rewarded Berend von Melen's capture of Kalmar with that castle, the hand of Vasa's cousin and a seat in the State Council.

Crops were poor that summer and imported grain too costly for most to buy. Salt was still exorbitantly priced. Heavy rains soaked the fields so that no dry hay could be got in. It rotted and molded in the barns, sickening the cattle, which died in vast numbers. Their meat was so tainted it could not even be fed to dogs and pigs, and of course, these deaths meant there was little milk. As always, in famine times, people ate nettles, buds, roots and hazel leaves and ground up bones for flour. Most of all, they resorted to bark bread.

The thin membrane beneath the bark had to be collected in summer. If the iron scrapers were used later, the trees might die. Whole families went to the woods and flayed the trees, scaling off the thin edible inside layer. This was dried, beaten with a flail and ground into flour. Many trees had to sacrifice their coverings before a kneading-trough could be filled.

The manor's harvest was as poor as any, and most of the cows, gifts of the villagers and painstakingly acquired by Knut, died from poison fodder, but there was grain from the year before, wheels of cheese, tubs of butter and fish and hams. Kristina and Knut shared what they had and ate bark bread themselves.

"Elm tastes the best," Kristina decided. "Aspen and silver birch are all right, but pine tastes sour. And it takes a mouthful of water to each of bread to swallow it down."

"I've been telling you for years that reindeer moss

makes a filling dish.'' Knut grinned. ''Our Lapp cousins live well enough without crops.''

''Not if their reindeer should die as our cattle have,'' Kristina retorted. She cuddled little Jon to her breast. At least he had her milk and had been born last April before the hunger time, while she was still well fed. The twins, Margrete and old Hilde got their usual barley porridge and the small supply of milk. There was dried fish and a little pork to flavor stews. But oh, how Kristina wept when it was clear that Rurik and his hens could not be fed through the winter! He went to make broth for Olav's ailing mother. Kristina missed his familiar greeting to the dawn more than she could have imagined.

Early in December, when the lakes were frozen and no fresh snow had fallen for a time so that the ice was slick, Knut organized a hunting party. The men pursued a dozen elk onto the ice where the animals could not keep their footing. There they were slain with spears and arrows. The meat was divided among the folk and the hides traded for a bit of salt, for elkhide jackets were tough enough to be used in place of armor and moreover were believed to have magical protective powers.

This good meat put strength into people, and throughout the winter, Knut and his huntsmen ranged the forest for game, dividing what they got with those too feeble or young to fare into the woods. For all that, many aged and young died that winter, prey to illnesses that would not have carried them off had they been well nourished.

With spring, hazel and heather buds could be gathered, dried and ground for meal. There were wild greens, the harvest promised reasonably well, and there was plenty of grass for the remaining goats and cows. Ironically, there should be plenty of hay now that there were few beasts to eat it. But there were two new calves in the meadow and several frisking kids. In three or four years, the stalls could be filled again.

Then Vasa's bailiff came collecting taxes. He would have carried off all the beasts of the village and farms had Knut not bargained to pay the levies in iron. He could not pay the tax for all Dalarna, though, and anger against the king waxed hotter. It might have broken into open rebellion except that in July 1925, Gustav Vasa took possession of Kalmar to the confusion of conspirators against him.

Olav, returning in August, came to see Kristina and Knut. The once-jaunty young blacksmith looked middle-aged, and his hand shook as he drank Kristina's ale. "A sad sight it was, dear friends! Von Melen, may God damn him, fled the country but had first sworn the garrison to defend the fortress to the last man. They were mostly Germans and some Swedes of the Sture party who had never vowed fealty to Vasa." He gritted his teeth. "Now, von Melen I would chop up myself, and with right good will, but those poor soldiers. . . ."

He bowed his head and began to weep. "What do you mean?" Kristina whispered, fearing to hear yet compelled to know.

"Vasa promised them liberty to return to their own land," Olav said brokenly, "but they refused to surrender. The slaughter of king's men was terrible! Fifteen hundred of us, Vasa's best soldiers, and half dead in the first assaults—arms and thighs chopped off, heads lopped—so fearful was it that the king wept. And you wot well this he has never done. But the defenders were heavily outnumbered and gave their surrender on Saint Margaret's Day. And then—"

"Then?" demanded Knut as Olav's voice choked off.

"The king had the garrison seized and brought to a court-martial. He condemned them to death on the wheel as traitors but changed it to beheading. Seventy brave men were cut off. When the axe grew so dull it would not hew, the executioner smashed skulls with a mace.''

"Seventy?'' Knut echoed in disbelief. "Men under safe-conduct?''

Olav nodded. "I have loved Gustav Vasa but that was too much. Nils and I came home straight from Kalmar. Nor will I lift weapon again for Vasa should Christian himself come back!''

Knut tried to comfort him, but after their old comrade was gone, Kristina had to open her arms to her distraught husband. They both wept, for the crushing of a dream, for the man they had believed in as Sweden's fairest hope.

At last, Knut said, "The Kalmar men were in the main hired foreigners. It is good that von Melen is gone. And now that Kalmar is no longer a bed of sedition, perhaps the king can govern instead of battling intrigues.''

"Let us pray so,'' said Kristina, but she was sickened. That night she took off the king's signet.

VIII

In October, Gustav Vasa called Dalesmen to an assembly at Tuna Mead, a big open spot in southern Dalarna that had long been a place of historic gatherings. Leaving the children in Hilde's and Sophia's charge, Kristina and Knut in their best clothes—Knut wore the beautifully embroidered wedding shirt—rode to the gathering in company with Olav, Bengt, Nils and other villagers and miners.

The king welcomed them heartily, vowed that Kristina was fairer than ever and that he would fain have them in the capital—that he would give them a manor near Stockholm. But when they tried to speak of the province's woes, he imperiously said he would deal with such matters in open council.

There he proved a master persuader. "Am I God?" he asked the Dalesmen. "Can I govern the weather? My friends, I am grieved at your sufferings, but now that there is peace in the realm, salt and supplies can be sent to you. I will do what I can to reduce the tax, though you understand I must pay my debt to Lübeck or they'll bring the Danes in on us again. But have patience and I swear all will be well."

Exhorting, promising, joking in rough language they understood, he won the Dalesmen with sheer personal force and charm, though they were aware of the well-

423

armed knights and men-at-arms he had with him. As he parted from Kristina, he glanced at the chains about her neck.

"I think you do not wear my ring."

She flushed but looked him in the eyes. "No, sire. I took it off after I heard of Kalmar."

He reddened. His eyes glittered wildly for a moment. "What can a countrywoman know of a king's necessities?"

She answered with a look.

"I must bide your reproach, Kristina," he said after a moment. "I cannot forget you saved my life and bore my banner. And I still owe you a boon."

"All I desire, my lord, is that you reign according to our ancient liberties and laws—those you vowed to uphold!"

"Kristina, this is not the old world. Sweden cannot exist as a mass of sovereign provinces, accepting or denying kings as they see fit. The kingdom must be strong and united or it will be rent apart."

"Can we not be strong—and free?"

"First we must be strong."

She gazed at this man who would not be king save for her and wondered painfully if she had served her country well or ill. "Good-bye, my lord. God guide you."

He made to follow her and Knut, but one of his nobles called him and they slipped away. As they journeyed homeward, Knut said, "If he keeps his word, he may yet prove Sweden's greatest king."

"Great kings oft do great wrongs." Kristina plucked up heart and smiled at her husband. "Still, he heard complaints today with good grace and didn't threaten anyone or seize prisoners. We must hope things will run smoother now."

The bailiffs were a shade more lenient and there was

salt—for those who could afford it—but it was their own crops that saved Dalarna.

There was much bitterness against the king and now a new grievance was added. In 1526, a young Swede, Olaus Petri, who had studied with Martin Luther, translated the New Testament into Swedish and he and other Lutherans went about attacking the Church. Vasa protected them. It was no secret that he expected the Church, which had generally supported Christian, to help pay his debts to Lübeck. The Church owned a fifth of the country's scarce farming land, the crown a twentieth. The taxes so hated by the commoners could not begin to appease the Hansa merchants. Rumors flew that the king had turned Lutheran and meant to despoil the Church. By early 1527, many Dalesmen were joyful at the appearance of a comely young man who claimed he was Sten Sture's son, Nils.

"That he cannot be," said Knut, scowling. "Young Nils is with Vasa. But this *Daljunker*, this Young Gentleman of the Dale, can move a crowd to tears by weeping for Herr Sten and falling on his knees, asking them all to join in an Ave Maria and paternoster for his father's soul. The good folk weep with him—and I fear they are like to weep in earnest should this foolishness grow. The *Daljunker* claims Vasa is dead but I think that part of the whole cloth his tale is cut from."

"Can you not warn people?"

"Olav I persuaded, but Bengt and Nils . . ." Knut shook his head. "They are ready to march off if this false Sture gives the word."

It was only a little later that Knut was summoned to a meeting of the *riksdag*, or Council of the Estates, in Västerås. Little Jon was sick so Kristina didn't accompany her husband. He returned with momentous news.

"Gustav was never more eloquent," he said dryly. "He told the Estates that he must have their advice and help with his difficulties or he would give up the crown. Since the *riksdag* doesn't want Christian back, or Fredrik of Holstein, either, they wound up voting him everything he asked for—support against rebels, especially the *Daljunker;* the confiscation of bishops' castles and excess property; and a decision clearing his Lutheran protégés of heresy. It came down to a struggle between Vasa and the Church. He won.''

Kristina cared little for bishops, but she drew much comfort from her faith and parish church where she prayed for her beloved dead. "What will it mean?"

"For one thing, bishops and the archbishop will no longer have their own small armies or so much luxury. But the *riksdag* was strong that the Gospel should be purely preached and the good old Christian ways safeguarded. Gustav gives not a whistle for theology, but it fits his purse to incite people against what he calls lazy rascals and hypocrites."

"But the Pope—"

"If he protests, Gustav will ignore him and appoint bishops himself." At her horrified look, Knut drew her onto his knee. "Look, my sweetheart, scripture says naught of a pope. So long as a Roman prelate dictates, it is like having a foreign prince to whom we send much revenue. No, in this I agree with Gustav. The Pope's power should be spiritual, not worldly."

Kristina did not know how to answer this, but she was disturbed. Would life never be simple again, right and wrong easy to discern?

The *Daljunker* fled to Norway. The humiliated papal archbishop took himself off to Denmark, and Vasa seized the episcopal tithes for the Crown. In January of 1528, he was at last formally crowned. His oath left out the promise to safeguard the rights and property of the Church, and the vow taken by the *råd* omitted their obligation to see that king and people kept their pledges to one another. For the first time, the *råd*'s allegiance was to the king only.

" 'Tis as if Vasa put off being crowned until the *riksdag* gave him all the powers he wanted," Kristina said uneasily. "Are you going to the assembly at Tuna?" For the king had called the Dalesmen to meet him there and answer for their support of the *Daljunker*.

"Yes, I will go. But it will be no place for women."

"Have you forgot—" Kristina began with temper, but he laughed and took her in his arms.

"Nay, I remember well you were our standard-bearer. But—" He punctuated each name with a kiss. "You are my wife now—and a mother—and my love."

The king came to Tuna Mead that March with armored knights, heavily armed soldiers and artillery. "We were herded like cattle into a packed mass," said Knut in a numbed, still disbelieving tone. "He called us traitors and haughty rogues who thought we had the Crown in our gift. The headsman's block was brought and a score of those hottest for the *Daljunker* were plucked from the throng and axed on the spot."

Kristina swallowed twice before she could speak. "Bengt? Nils?"

"Both lost their heads."

She cried out. Knut held her. Hot tears dropped from his eyes to her cheek. "I tried to get loose of the throng and plead for them, but by the time I broke free, it was too late." He laughed mirthlessly. "Gustav begged pardon for my having been treated like the rest; he had not thought that I would come, he said, for he knew I was no traitor. But I think he counted it a useful lesson."

Gustav I was not yet to wear his crown in peace. In 1529, the Småland peasants rose, and later the clergy and

nobles of Västergötland, but they were quickly sup-
pressed. After a comparatively quiet time, early in 1531,
the king demanded that each church give up a bell to the
treasury along with one year's land tithe except what was
needed for candles and sacramental wine.

"This is too much," Knut said.

Kristina gazed at him in fear. "Husband, I pray
you—"

"Some things are not to be borne. Next he will take the
holy vessels and bridal crowns—all the things the common people have sacrificed to buy for their churches. I
care not what he takes from bishops, but this is impious
robbery of ordinary folk—the ones who helped him from
the beginning."

Kristina thought aloud. "I could send him the ring and
ask for our parish bell."

"And what of other parishes?" Knut got to his feet.
"Nay, sweeting! This time the king has overstepped all
reason. I will meet his bailiffs at the church door. If they
get the bell, 'twill be over my corpse."

Olav and other villagers stood with Knut. The bailiffs
retreated without a fight but in some parishes they were
beaten well nigh to death. In the end, Knut and other
leading Dalesmen negotiated with the king. They could
keep their bells if they gave instead two thousand marks,
the value of two hundred good cows.

"I am surprised the king would bargain," said Kristina with misgiving.

"He sees he went too far." Knut shrugged. "He pardoned 'one and all' as the agreement reads and has taken
us back into his friendship."

"He has made promises before."

"He can scarce quarrel with his people," Knut pointed
out. "Christian is trying to invade through Sweden to

win back the throne. That will keep Vasa busy for a while."

It did, but when the king had for the last time defeated his persistent enemy, he came again to Dalarna. This time he accused the leaders of the church-bell revolt of having conspired with Christian. Knut would not let Kristina go with him when he was summoned to the inquisition.

A week later, Olav, trembling and weeping, told her of the horrid accounting.

"Again, the king had us packed together with the cannons trained on us. Some leaders were beheaded. Others he took to Stockholm. Knut was one of them."

Kristina lips would scarce move. "Will—will he be executed?"

"I know not. The king said he had forgiven the Dalesmen too many treasons. Two of the men cut off at Kopparberget were old friends. He had their heads placed on a plank set on a high stake. Nils of Söderby's wore a high crown of birch bark." Olav's voice broke. "After manacling the seven he's taking to Stockholm, the king pardoned the rest of us. But our best and bravest men are dead, or condemned."

Kristina fetched him food and drink, moving in a trance. Horrible visions rose before her, Knut at the block. Knut's head staring from a stake, parts of the body she knew and loved sundered and nailed to city gates.

Margrete, a sweet, capable maid of sixteen, recently betrothed to a prosperous farmer's son, had much of Karin's gentle nature and tried to comfort the children, but ten-year-old Nikulaus ran to his mother.

"Let me take the Heaven Sword and go help Father!" he cried. "I—I won't let the king hurt him!"

"I won't, either!" Jon, dark-haired like Knut, tried to do everything his elder brother did and often succeeded.

Kristina gathered them in her arms, including Karin, who had her grandmother's eyes. "Nikulaus, Jon, you must stay here and look after Margrete and Karin. The king has long owed me a boon. I shall go and ask it."

Both to comfort her and in hope that sight of it would recall powerfully to the king those days when she and Knut had been his comrades, Kristina took the Heaven Sword with her when she sought audience with Gustav Vasa. Guards would have taken it from her, but the king himself, hurrying to the antechamber, sent out his attendants and kissed Kristina on both cheeks before he led her to a chair and made her sit down.

"I know why you have come." His tone was sorrowful. "Kristina, I cannot grant Knut's life. There must be an end to rebellions. Better a few die now so that others will heed."

Her fingers trembled as she drew his ring from beneath her gown. "My lord, I beg you—for all that has been between us."

"Fair friend, it cannot be. Ask anything but that. I will knight your sons, give them fiefs—"

"And slay their father?"

He straightened. The cold mask of power hardened his face. "Will you deny that your husband drove off my bailiffs?"

"Will you say you have a right to plunder parish churches?"

"I have a right to raise money to defend this realm where and as I can! The Lübeckers are paid. Priests attend to their preaching and meddle not in policy. Christian is defeated. Now this country can become a great power. *That* is worth whatever I must do."

She unclasped the ring chain and put it in his hand.

"Kristina! Gladly will I give you any other thing."

She showed him the scabbarded sword. "Very well. If Knut must die, use this sword to kill him—and me, at the same time."

Vasa recoiled, paling. "Kill *you?* Nay, that I cannot!"

"What matters how you do it? I swear to you, if Knut goes to the block, that day, I follow him." She smiled bitterly. "I am not like you, Gustav Vasa. I keep my word."

His face contorted. It seemed he would fall into one of those rages that were becoming notorious, but he controlled himself with obvious effort. Turning from her, he went to stare out the window.

Kristina scarcely breathed. Her heart thudded as if a small frightened animal were trapped inside it. It was an age, an eternity, before the king swung about.

"Think well, Kristina. Let justice take its course and your sons will be ennobled and fiefed; you may dwell at court as my dearest friend. Your sister and daughter will make splendid matches."

When she said nothing, he went on harshly. "I know you are mad enough to do what you vow. Much I have taken on my soul, but you were my standard-bearer—you were—more than I can tell you." Their eyes held. He sighed. "You may have your husband on this condition: that you go into the woods and dwell there to the end of your days. The other Dalesmen will die on the block. It will be given out that Knut died in prison."

Kristina's knees dissolved. Light filled her, like that when the torches blazed for Lucia Brides. Knut would live! Nothing else mattered.

But the king was saying, "I will not confiscate your manor, though Knut's mines I will claim." He added a bit dourly, "And I will keep this promise, Kristina Magnusdotter. When your eldest son is grown, let him bring me those golden spurs I gave your brother, and I will my-self knight him.''

"That will be young Nikulaus' choice," Kristina said. "But it may be well for Dalarna, if we have no nobles there.''

"A stiff-necked people," Vasa said. But he smiled faintly. "Well, Kristina, I will send for your husband. You must sup with me, like old times, before you go your ways. And before I become wholly a king who cannot have a comrade.''

Back at the manor, Kristina hung the sword above the fireplace. The joy everyone felt at Knut's return dimmed as the cost was explained, but Knut embraced his children and said hardily, "I am not the first of our line and doubtless not the last to shelter in the woods. Olav will bring you to visit us sometimes, and your mother can be sent for if anyone falls ill. You must do what your Aunt Margrete bids you and build up the manor.''

He gazed at Kristina, asking a silent question. For she did not have to go; the king had said only Knut must dwell in the deep forests. She moved her head slightly.

Margrete and her betrothed would foster the children in this familiar home. All would be well with them. It was Knut who needed her most—they would be comrades again, as they had been in the campaigns, but this time they were lovers, truly one flesh.

And the forest was free.

What of a sword?
What of years it hangs unused
Or covered, blinded?
Does it dream iron dreams?
Hands that held it?

Hearts it drank from?
Arms it strengthened?
Does it remember?
Does it murmur?

Sword dreams . . .

Book VII

The Sword Bartered

Sweden
1868

In 1810 at Leipzig, Napoleon was defeated for the first time by Russian, Swedish and English armies serving under Napoleon's former marshal, Count Bernadotte, who only that year had accepted a desperate offer of the Swedish crown. The result in the great world was that Napoleon lost Pomerania and the third generation of Bernadottes now sat on the Swedish throne; the result for a twenty-year-old Dalarna lad was that he lost a good strong leg and made his way home on a crutch.

Karl Vane wasn't one to quit. He made himself a wooden leg, carved it with roses, and got up when he fell down. By harvest, he led the scythes, and that night led the dancing. Ulrika Tessin, the prettiest girl in the village, lay in his arms that sweet, warm night of St. Olaf's Feast. When she told him something more than pleasure had come of it, he was glad enough to have so fair and skilled a bride, and after the wedding feast, she came to be mistress of the old house that had been in his family for generations.

Several homes had burned down since the original manor, but a lofty spreading oak had sprung up near the stump of the ancient one beside the door and the great log barn had been kept in good repair from the time Gustav Vasa had hidden there.

Karl knew more about Kristina and Knut than he did about his great-grandparents. He always played a special tune for them when he visited the family graves on Christmas Eve and stayed there with his fiddle long after everyone else had gone home, and his music blended with the candles reflecting on the snow from each mound and throwing soft shadows from wrought-iron crosses fashioned in every ornamental shape.

There were stones, like those of Magnus and Karin and Nikulaus, but in the main the graveyard showed the artistry of craftsmen who had worked in iron time out of mind. It saddened Karl to see the newfangled plain markers used now that the local ironworks had disappeared. During these last years, the old smelters and smithies with small forges and slow hammers had been closed, unable to compete with the great foundries.

A grim century this was for Sweden. She had lost her steel trade to Switzerland and her people—well, they were going, and who could blame them, to the United States, where a poor man could have rich virgin land for little more than the asking. There were few freeholders anymore; they toiled for the big landowners, many of whom lived far away in Stockholm.

But once, Karl sang as he walked among the graves, *once miners owned the mines they worked. Once the king himself could not enter the province without the people's consent. Once most men owned their land, ploughed and harvested for themselves. Once the church, now so plain, glittered with silver and was bright with hangings and altarcloths. But Gustav Vasa took those away and gave them to his queen to make clothing for the royal children. Once Dalesmen helped that same king gain his kingdom. They followed a bright-armed maid who bore a banner and the Heaven Sword. . . .*

And the sword still hung above the mantel, the last of the old glories. Karl knew what treasures had once been in the big chest carved with Vasa's sceptered lilies and the name of Kristina Magnusdotter, 1522. The Empress' Nightingale had gone during one famine, the golden spurs had been sold by Karl's father in a vain

effort to keep the land. Bridal and feast-day finery
was gone.

But there were still things to dream over, things to tell
his granddaughter Analiese about—Magnus' old brass
quadrant, a battered Dala horse rumored to be Gustav
Vasa's gift to a child of the family, a bit of embroidered
ruffled cuff from Knut's wedding shirt, and the only
thing of value to strangers, Kristina's wedding belt of red
velvet and silver.

"You will be married in that," Karl told his granddaughter. He was determined it should be so, that she
should have one thing from the days of the family's
pride. And there was the sword.

Karl sighed heavily this autumn of 1868 as he helped
Analiese grind the dried inner layer of elm bark into
meal. He had eaten bark bread before, in the starving
winters of 1812 and 1813, when the twin boys had died
and Ulrika near went mad with grief. She had always
been a little strange after that, insisting that Frida, the
next and last child, was really a boy.

Poor Ulrika! Well, she was with God now, and her
sons—Frida, too, for the child who'd had to become too
soon a woman had married a miner and moved with him
to a foundry town. Her lungs were weak. She died when
Analiese was eight years old. When the father remarried,
Karl had asked and been granted the rearing of his granddaughter.

No use asking Lars for help. He had all he could do
to feed his brood from his second wife. No, Karl
didn't mind bark bread. He had come to know it for a
gift of the forest, which was sometimes a poor man's
only friend and comforted him from the time he rocked
in a cradle to the day he was carried in a coffin. Shelter
for man and beast came from the forest: beds and
chairs and chests, wagons, wheels, boats, harrows and
ploughs, spinning wheels and looms, tools and uten-

sils, clogs of alder, even Karl's fiddle. From the forest came bark for tanning leather, charcoal, tar, fuel, and there wandered game that made a difference, often, in eating or not.

So Karl revered the forest, all the more because it had been a refuge for Knut and Kristina till the day they were brought to the churchyard. Both had been dead, peacefully, when their children found them. Karl liked to believe that the hearts that had beat together for half a century had failed at the same moment.

He was eighty now, probably older than they had been. He needed little food. But Analiese— It hurt him to see her great blue eyes more sunken in the transparent fair face with each day, the dwindling of smoothly rounded arms, the gauntness of her cheeks and throat.

Karl's heart ached for the child who had been the light of his house these lonely years. Why hadn't he been able to do better for her? She was the best pupil Sexton Johan had ever taught, she could make something of herself in the world beyond the dale had she been given any sort of chance. Many girls took service with city families, but that wasn't the thing for her. She should have had a fine big farm to manage, a busy household to run.

But it seemed she might not even marry. Her sweetheart, Nils Lange, had gone to the United States a year ago, hoping to send her passage money to join him, but the wonder tales of American prosperity were exaggerated. It was true that in time Nils could take up what they called a homestead—160 acres of almost free land! But he must first prove his intention of becoming a citizen and save money to get started. He was working for another Swedish emigrant in Minnesota, a place he said was so full of lakes and forests that he felt nearly at home. He earned little above his keep, though he was sure in a few years . . .

Analiese might not live that long. Or if she did, she might be permanently weakened by starvation. Karl would miss her sorely, but it would be better for her to go than rest in the churchyard.

He was too old himself to start anew. Such time as God left him he wanted to spend fiddling for these people he had known all his life, playing at the feasts that marked the end of haymaking, the construction of a new house, completion of the spring and autumn laundry when hundreds of sheets and garments dried in the bushes, or for Midsummer Night, which, short as it was, set many cradles rocking.

Most of all he liked to play for christenings and weddings, but he also honored his old friends by fiddling their favorite tunes at their grave-ales. His melodies, merry or solemn, wove through everything that happened, celebrated each season from the cuckoo's spring song to the owl's winter hoot. He wouldn't know how to play in America.

But Analiese must go where there was a future, where her babies could thrive, where there was land for them, a chance to be more than ill-paid hirelings.

So long as there was food, it was fine to be patient and wait for Nils; but this was a time of starving. Karl went hunting, but elk and deer had been almost wiped out by the huge slaughters organized by noblemen who shot for the lust of it, not to eat. He did bring fish from the lake, but when the water froze as it soon must, that help would be gone.

The only things of value left in the house were the wedding belt and the Heaven Sword. Karl had set his heart on Analiese's having Kristina's belt and passing it to her daughters. But the sword . . .

Wouldn't it be lonesome in America? There was nothing for it now anyhow but to hang on a wall and dream. Sometimes Karl heard those dreams and made tunes of them, playing for the sword as for a loved one. No, the wedding belt could go anywhere with a bride, but the sword, surely, belonged where it had lived.

That October, without telling Analiese, he wrapped the sword and took it to the big fair in the market town ten miles away. It was cruel to see the burned crops. Turnips and potatoes hadn't even sprouted, and the slopes were black where forest fires had raged unchecked. It was a dead and blasted land.

He found no buyer for the sword. People were trading for food, getting rid of animals for which they had no hay. There was little for sale at the booths, and rope-dancers and organ-grinders got so few coins that they went off hoping for better luck at other places. Many men asked to hold the sword; it was famous in the dale. But no one had money for dreams or glory.

The stump of Karl's lost leg pained him as he gave up on the third useless day and traveled home. As he passed the churchyard, he was so weary and despairing that he went to sit among the family graves and let his fiddle tell the dead about the living's troubles. He played of flailing bark—which many of them had done in their times—and of the desolated countryside, and he played a dirge for those who would die before this winter passed. But then he closed his eyes.

He imagined a vast country—plains and lakes and mountains and forests—he played of freedom, of hope. He could not leave his forests and mountains and glimmering lakes, but in that other country, Analiese's children would be at home among *their* lakes and *their* forests and *their* mountains.

But only if she could reach that land before she was

withered and blighted as the fields. Rising from the mounds where rosebushes and flowers had died, he wished for the first time in all his life that he, too, was in the grave, released from this terrible hopeless need to help Analiese.

She scolded him for trying to sell the sword, but he said, harshly, because of his impotence, "We can't eat it. And if the Good God will, your children will be Americans—they won't care much about a rusty old sword."

"Grandfather!"

"It's true." He tried to straighten his slumping shoulders. "At the fair, even in this province, people marveled at it but bought food instead."

"Well, of course. What else would you expect?"

He gave a sheepish chuckle. "Oh, I suppose it seemed to me that when I finally got up the courage to sell it, eager buyers would be rushing after me from all directions, offering me everything they had."

She put her arms around him and kissed him soundly. "I'm glad you couldn't sell it! I want you to have it all your life."

They ate their supper of boiled roots and moss and bark bread and went to bed soon after. But an idea had started to fill Karl's head.

Hungry people bought food instead of swords, but somewhere there must be rich folk—those of the kind who hunted elk and lived in mansions, who owned big foundries or banks or railroads.

One of *those* gentlemen must be found—one who would pay enough for the Heaven Sword to send Analiese to America. As soon as he had rested from the journey to the fair, he'd see if the pastor could give him some rich men's names, and he wouldn't give up till someone had bought the sword.

As it turned out, Karl didn't need to go roving about the countryside. Two days after his return, he was chopping firewood when he heard the rumbling of wheels, and a polished black gig drew up in front. Karl's eyes widened.

Such horses! Matched bays that would have gladdened the heart of Saint Stephen himself. They must have been eating oats and grain to be so sleek and shiny. The thought of oat porridge came irresistibly into Karl's mind, and his mouth watered before, put out at the rumbling of his stomach, he went to meet his visitor.

The stranger wore a tall silk hat, just like the one God wore in the church mural, but his coat was shaggy wolfskin and his gloves were of the same fur, trimmed with sharp horny claws. He gave the reins to his servant and got down from the vehicle. He had a long, thin face, blond hair and the coldest gray eyes Karl had ever seen.

"You are Karl Vane?"

"Yes."

"You have a sword?"

Karl's neck prickled as he looked at the elegant but oddly dressed man. Could he be the Dangerous One, come to buy a man's soul?

Well, thought Karl, if he is, and will pay enough to send Analiese to America, he's welcome to whatever soul I have. If God wanted it in heaven, He should have given us food on earth.

"I have a sword, sir. Very old. Long in the family—"

"No doubt," said the man brusquely. "I suppose we are related—very distantly—for from what I know, that sword could hang with equal right in my own home."

Karl stared.

"No, no, I'm not accusing you!" said the man impatiently. "But my family goes back to a Danish chieftain named Harald who stole away an English girl, and with her, the sword. I collect weapons. I have one of Canute's and one used by Harald Fair-Hair. But this is the one I desire above all. I'm sure it's been neglected but—"

"It's been used, sir." Karl couldn't resist adding, "The last time was when it helped drive the Danes out of the country in the time of Gustav Vasa."

The visitor looked down his long, straight nose. "Are you prepared to sell it?"

Karl couldn't speak but he gave his head a quick nod.

"Very well. Let me see it."

It pained Karl to take down Heaven's Gift and place it in the stranger's hands. But at least it would stay in the Northern lands—even with folk who had a certain claim. God had heard his prayers. Then why were his eyes blurred? His hands trembling? It was a piece of luck that Analiese had gone to tend a sick old neighbor. She'd make a to-do and this would be harder than it already was.

Karl blinked as he watched the Dane caress the hilt, run his fingers along the nicked blade. A kind of sigh came from him. "The same blade through all these centuries! The hilt and pommel were added long after the forging, of course. I haven't traced it past Kyra and Ogier, so I'll want you to tell me what you know. First though, what do you want for it?"

Karl's heart pounded. Seeing Heaven's Gift in the stranger's grasp must be, he thought, like seeing one's wife embraced by another man. Only the thought of Analiese, those dreams of America's boundless land, gave him the strength to say, "What will you offer?"

The Dane considered. He named a sum in *talers* that dizzied Karl though any price for the Heaven Sword was sacrilegious. "Is that enough, sir, to buy passage for my granddaughter to America? To pay her train fare to Minnesota?"

The stranger glanced about the bare, clean room. His eyes changed. For the first time, he sounded human. "So that's why— But after all, it's better off with me. Not much use for swords in Minnesota, eh?" He pulled out a purse that clinked. "Yes, Karl Vane, the *talers* will get your granddaughter to Minnesota and leave enough for a start there and to keep you. Is it agreed?"

Karl's chest tightened. For hundreds of years the sword had been his family's pride. He felt as if he were betraying his dead in the churchyard and the sword itself. But what else could he do?

The silver burned his hands, but he put it in a bowl and asked the stranger to have the old high seat while he told him the sword's later story.

Baltzar von Fersen had been generous. On the eve of Analiese's departure, they held a feast with food plentiful enough for folk to carry home. There had been money to buy passage for Nils' sister as well, and the two young women would travel together. But Analiese wouldn't take extra money.

She would work. She and Nils would save. What Karl didn't need should go to buy food for the poorest of the village. Because he had to visit his parishioners, the pastor had kept a sledge and team. He agreed to drive them to the market town, which had a railway station.

Karl put his granddaughter's chest—the one with Vasa's lilies and Kristina's name—aboard the train. Analiese kissed him and sobbed. "How can I leave you, grandfather? I hate to think of you alone! Can't you come, too?''

He looked over her head to the mountains. "No, child. This old tree would wither if its roots were pulled out. You'll plant yourself deep in the new soil. But don't forget your country. Don't forget your people.''

One last time he kissed her before he broke away, stumbling as he hurried to the sledge. He stood and waved as the train chugged out. Then he could put his face in his arms and weep.

As the pastor reached the churchyard, Karl asked to be let out. He must tell the family that the sword was gone, ask them if they could, to watch over Analiese.

Night fell softly. He brushed snow off a stump and began to fiddle. He played selling Heaven's Gift and his hopes for Analiese, and then, since, strangely, he wasn't cold, he began playing the story of the sword, all that he knew, its lives with his kindred.

It shone before him. Then he saw a young woman in armor with golden spurs. Beside her was a tall, dark man who put his arm around her as they yielded place to a golden-haired warrior and a girl whose Lapp clothing faded into a gown of heaven blue. She trilled with the notes of Karl's fiddle and danced back to let a couple garbed in white, adorned with gold and brilliant feathers, advance to smile at him. A priestess glittered beside her black-haired lover, and last of all came a beautiful woman with sea-colored eyes who took the sword and gave it to the man who had forged it so many centuries ago. They welcomed him into a great hall filled with warmth and light. They weren't angry with him. They understood.

Tears froze to his cheeks but he didn't feel them. He

played for the bright assembly, played till his hands and arms were numb.

And then, when he could play no longer, a young woman came smiling toward him, bright as a Lucia Bride, shining as Freya, but her face was Analiese's.

She held out a beaker of foaming ale and he drank deep.

THE CAVE DREAMERS

A NATIONAL BESTSELLER BY
JEANNE WILLIAMS

THE CAVE DREAMERS is a vivid, passionate
novel of the lives and loves of the women
across centuries who share the secret of
"The Cave of Always Summer." From the dawn
of time to the present, the treasured mystery
of the cave is passed and guarded, joining
generation to generation through
their dreams and desires.

86488-6/$3.95 U.S.
86496-7/$4.75 Canada

An AVON Paperback

Available wherever paperbacks are sold or order directly
from the publisher. Include $1.00 per copy for postage
and handling: allow 6-8 weeks for delivery. Avon Books,
Dept. BP, Box 767, Rte 2, Dresden, TN 38225

This is the special design logo
that will call your attention
to Avon authors who
show exceptional
promise in

THE AVON ROMANCE

the romance
area. Each
month a new novel
will be featured

SURRENDER THE HEART Jean Nash   89622-2/$2.95 US/$3.75 Can
Set in New York and Paris at the beginning of the twentieth century, beautiful
fashion designer Adrian Marlowe is threatened by bankruptcy and must turn
to the darkly handsome "Prince of Wall Street" for help.

Other Avon Romances by Jean Nash:
  FOREVER, MY LOVE   84780-9/$2.95

RIBBONS OF SILVER Katherine Myers   89602-8/$2.95 US/$3.75 Can
Kenna, a defiant young Scottish beauty, is married by proxy to a wealthy
American and is drawn into a plot of danger, jealousy and passion when the
stranger she married captures her heart.

Other Avon Romances by Katherine Myers:
  DARK SOLDIER   82214-8/$2.95
  WINTER FLAME   87148-3/$2.95

PASSION'S TORMENT Virginia Pade   89681-8/$2.95 US/$3.75 Can
In order to escape prosecution for a crime she didn't commit, a young English
beauty deceives an American sea captain into marriage—only to find his
tormented past has made him vow never to love again.

Other Avon Romances by Virginia Pade:
  WHEN LOVE REMAINS   82610-0/$2.95

Catherine Lanigan
writing as

Joan Wilder

Romancing *The* STONE

87262-5/$2.95
Based on the Screenplay Written by
Diane Thomas

LOVING THE FANTASY

Lost in the steaming Colombian jungle with brutal killers closing in, she felt like the heroine of one of her romance novels. Except that romance was the last thing on her mind...especially with Jack Colton, the bold American adventurer on whom her life now depended.

But there are certain times, certain places, and nights that may be the last, when a man and a woman can only be meant for each other. And suddenly she knew that he was the right man for her.